My phone beeps as I'm leaving: Jules. I'm sure you'll agree that it's best we don't live together anymore. You obviously liked living with Catherine, so I think that is what you should do. So much of the stuff there is mine anyway, and I know you've always been worried you can't afford it. I've asked Lola to move in, and she's agreed, so no need for you to worry about the rent.

THE
LAST
TIME
I SAW
YOU

THE LAST TIME I SAW YOU

ELEANOR MORAN

Quercus

Quercus

New York • London

© 2013 by Eleanor Moran
First published in the United States by Quercus in 2014

ISBN 978-1-62365-133-6

Library of Congress Control Number: 2013913392

Distributed in the United States and Canada by
Random House Publisher Services
c/o Random House, 1745 Broadway
New York, NY 10019

This book is a work of fiction. Names, characters, institutions, places, and events are either the product of the author's imagination or are used fictitiously. Any resemblance to actual persons—living or dead—events, or locales is entirely coincidental.

Manufactured in the United States

2 4 6 8 10 9 7 5 3 1

www.quercus.com

For my grandmother, Rosemary,
with much love

June 18, 2012

Speed. I've always been fast—a low boredom threshold will do that to a person. How fast is too fast? I think I've just taken myself to the edge.

Can't count the junctions anymore, they're nothing but blurry smudges in the farthest corners of my eyes. I can't see much at all, not with the acid tears that are biting into my face, the sobs cresting up inside me and smashing me against something hard and cold and unforgiving.

I'm swerving now, cutting across lanes, speeding up to make it past gas-belching monsters so much bigger and fiercer than my stupid little shell of a car. Horns blare, lights flash, and I'm speeding up.

Speeding away from everything, as if it doesn't matter.

It does matter. Another sob reaches up from deep inside me, grabbing hold.

Sirens are starting up now. They're howling like animals, chasing me down. They're distant, but they're getting closer with every passing second. They'll trap me. You can't run away, that's the God's honest truth, but my foot grinds down on the accelerator without me asking.

Once you start running you can't stop.

You can't stop.

PART ONE

. . . I would not wish
Any companion in the world but you.

—William Shakespeare, *The Tempest*

CHAPTER ONE

Tuesday's not the kind of day you expect your life to change forever. That feels like a job for Friday or Saturday—a flashier, shinier day that has surprise sprinkled over its surface.

This particular Tuesday I'm doing the end of the day soft-shoe shuffle, glancing between the clock, my computer screen, and my batshit scary boss Mary, trying to work out which will give way first. It's a huge, retro-looking wall clock, with thick black hands that are currently crawling sluggishly toward six thirty. The wall behind it is papered with pastel pink roses, and the room is peppered with big velvet sofas that are designed to encourage the kind of impromptu brainstorms and shared confidences that never quite seem to happen. Mary presides over the room from her huge glass desk at the top, mistress of all she surveys. It's like a twisted sort of nursery—soft on the outside, with an underlying air of menace.

I'm working on a campaign for supermarket organics, but even if my computer hasn't turned off yet, my brain certainly has. I want to get home—I'm cooking dinner for James before I have to go out again—but I don't want Mary to think I'm a slacker. Better to sit here playing with the same sentence for half an hour than appear halfhearted.

Mungo, my optimistically titled "assistant," has no such compunction. He came in on work experience, bestowed by Mary, his godmother, and never left. Right now he's already standing up, shoving a musty old hardback into his leather satchel and snapping off his monitor without so much as a backward glance in my direction. I take an unattractively loud slurp of water, but he fails to notice, just as he fails to notice every command or plea I throw his way: good cop doesn't work, bad cop doesn't work, the only authority this boy might possibly deign to respect is Martin Amis or Salman Rushdie, fellow Oxford graduates all. He styles himself as some kind of literary giant in waiting, all long scarves and corduroy jackets, with lustrous auburn hair that falls around his face like plush velvet drapes.

"Mungo," I call out. "Before you go, how are you getting on with that research on the level of consumer spending?"

A fleeting look of panic crosses his face, like he's spotted a herd of elephants stampeding toward him through the long grass, but then he remembers it's only me.

"It's all in hand," he says glibly.

"I need an ETA," I snap, before losing heart. "Or at least a rough idea of when I might expect it," I add, lamely.

"Tomorrow, latest," he says, already halfway out of the door, "you have my solemn word."

I suppose it's not surprising he's indifferent. He's stayed on as an intern, unpaid by anyone but the relentlessly generous bank of Mom and Dad, which is pretty much the only way to get into a job like this these days. It's lucky for me that I started more than a decade ago, as my dad's ingrained frugality and sense of right and wrong would have afforded me about three days max. I came in as a bright-eyed graduate trainee, as relentlessly keen as Maria taking up residence with the von Trapps, and, much like her, soon got the corners knocked off me. Up until then, hard work and diligence had gotten me through. I'd smugly collected my degree with honors, then barely broken a sweat when I got my prestigious traineeship. This side of life—the ticking of boxes, the academic achievements— was easy for me; it was the other side, the messy business of other people, that I found so difficult to wrangle.

I soon discovered that achievement in the big wide world was a complicated two-step between the two: 30 percent inspiration, 70 percent the ability to sell that inspiration as genius, and pull your genius out of exactly the right make and model of handbag. Luckily Mary saw something in me, didn't dismiss me as the gauche goody two-shoes I was, and allowed me to carve out a niche for myself. It's not a comfy nook, it's more a thin, precarious shelf, but I know how to keep my balance and, when it's going well, I love my work. Well, sort of—I definitely like it. I'm incredibly lucky that I get paid to make things up, it's just that I'm not sure that this is what I'd choose to make up given the choice. My imposter's handbag currently contains the scratchy beginnings of a short story I'd like to enter for a magazine competition. I don't know if I'll ever manage to finish it—I've rewritten the opening lines so many times that it's started to read like Greek.

It's nearly an hour later, and Mary's still showing abso- lutely no sign of leaving, despite the two young children she's got stowed at home with the nanny. Her perfect nails are tip-tapping a tattoo on her keyboard, her eyes scanning the room at regular intervals. She's midforties at least but you'd never guess it: time hung up his arrows and admitted defeat long ago. Any grays are disguised by discreet, expensive blond highlights and her outfits are so outrageously high fashion that the term "age appropriate" seems laughable.

I look at the picture of a sad-looking pig on my computer screen, oinking out a plea to harassed shoppers to save him from a life lived in a tiny pen, and just for a second he feels like my brother. Mary's engrossed in a phone call, which seems like the perfect moment to make a run for it. The only other person left is Amy, a junior copywriter a few years younger than me who sits at the desk behind. She's wearing a T-shirt for some obscure indie band, her wild torrent of blond hair caught up in something that looks suspiciously like a bulldog clip, her bitten-down nails painted with tiny Union Jacks. It all gives her the kind of effortless Hoxton cool that should make her desperately annoying, but she's too sweet to dislike. She's poring over a folder of notes, but she looks up when she spots me shaking the ironic Reykjavik snow globe that sits on her desk.

"You off? I was going to ask you if you fancied a glass of wine across the street when Mary's gone."

At roughly midnight, I think, looking at the expression of grim determination on Mary's face as she stares down her screen, but I don't depress Amy by pointing it out.

"I'd love to, but I've got to go home and then go out."

It sounds stupid when I say it: I should just go straight out, but I need my fix of James to propel me into the night.

"We've got to go and have a proper boozy one soon."

"Soon," I promise emphatically, even though neither of us really believes me. I feel a stab of guilt—I like Amy, I really do, but I'm not very good at this stuff. What's that phrase? Women beware women. I know in my head that it's not true, but in my heart there's still a skulking fear that it is.

"Livvy," calls Mary, as I push open the door.

"Yes?" I say, swiveling around. She's off the phone now, her eyes fixed on me, her expression cold and blank. She pauses for what feels like an eternity: it's stupid, but my heart starts to race, the handle suddenly clammy to my touch.

"See you tomorrow," she says, bestowing a smile.

Our apartment—located to the left of Kennington tube, perched above an electronics store—is most definitely shabby. Not shabby chic, just shabby, but it's homey, and to me that's more important. I also think it's hard to make a home out of one person, so, while it means that I'm fighting my way past James's squash racket and piles of my dog-eared paperbacks to get to the stove, I don't really mind.

The grease-spattered kitchen clock is edging toward 7:55, and there's still no sign of him. The thing is, while he might burst through the door at any second, he might just as well have forgotten what we arranged—got distracted by work, or worse. I try to pretend that I'm cool and unconcerned, stirring the Thai chicken curry that I've rustled up and singing along, loudly and tunelessly to the Carpenters, who are blasting out of the tinny transistor radio on the kitchen counter. I don't even hear him come in.

"*Close to you-oo*," he harmonizes, coming up behind me and switching it off.

"I was listening to that!"

"I know. I'm saving you from yourself."

He's towering over me, ruddy and damp from the gym, smelling not of sweat or of aftershave, but of a smell peculiar to him. He's gingery-blond, with a boyish lankiness that suits the irrepressibility of his personality. He's bendy and springy and unstoppable, constantly in motion, and yes, before you ask, I'm more than a little bit in love with him. I always have been, ever since he walked into my high school politics class, his timing impeccable: my parents were in the middle of their gruesome separation and I was ripe for distraction.

James was an army brat, the youngest of three boys, and the family had recently been transported to Northwood, the boring north London suburb we lived in, which was dominated by the naval base. A life spent being uprooted from place after place could go two ways. For James, rather than making him shy and mistrustful, it had given him the cast iron certainty that he could walk into any situation and charm his way to the very heart of it. It wasn't oiliness or manipulation, it was pure self-belief combined with an innate knowledge that he was attractive.

It was that age and stage where boys and girls first peek over the barricades and try out being "friends"—a funny old version of friendship in which you can snog furiously at a party one night and go back to being mates the very next day. Or at least other people could do that. James and I had one such night at school, an hour spent kissing in the boys' cloakroom during the first-year Christmas prom—it was brief and clumsy and awkward, and yet I did nothing but daydream about it for months, staring wistfully through my clumsily applied eye makeup and playing "Wuthering Heights" on a loop, while he remained utterly oblivious.

I hoped with every fiber of my being that he'd come back to me, that I'd be able to prove myself the second time around, but he'd already moved on, climbed back aboard the romantic merry-go-round and recast me as his long-lost sister. That's not strictly true, there was one more time but now— now is not the time to think about it. Sally whispers across my consciousness but I push her away. Perhaps it's the ferocity with which I suppress her that makes her continue to surge up, like those schlocky horror films where the hero tries more and more elaborate methods to destroy the invincible slasher.

James leans across me, digging the wooden spoon into the pan and taking a greedy mouthful.

"Perfect," he says, grabbing a bottle of wine from the fridge and plunking down plates on the table.

"It needs another ten minutes," I protest.

"Yeah but you've got a date."

It's yet another soul-destroying Internet date born out of necessity—I'm thirty-five, and most of my contemporaries are coupled up, though not necessarily happily. Even so, I don't think many of those discontented partners are looking to roll the dice again, and even if they were, I never envisioned being someone's difficult second album. I want to be the answer to a question they've never been able to phrase, for me to feel the same way about them, rather than a compromise born out of a disappointment.

It's not like I haven't tried the compromise route. My last proper boyfriend was a perfectly nice man called Marco whom I met at a Christmas party a few months after my sister Jules had got married. I was secretly, silently panicking, and I managed to convince myself that I'd alighted on my one true love, rather than admitting that it was the romantic equivalent of a game of pin the tail on the donkey, the two of us flailing around in the dark, desperate to believe we'd somehow found the sweet spot. We moved in together far too quickly, and immediately started arguing about the kind of piffling, trifling things, like whether the pepper should live on the table or in the "condiment cupboard," that made it clear that when we had to make decisions about things that really mattered, we wouldn't survive. As I wept fat, salty tears of disappointment on James's shoulder he came up with the brilliant suggestion we should live together and here we are, eighteen months on. He's an employment lawyer—unlike me, he easily earns enough to live alone—but I think that he values having someone to come home to just as much as I do.

By now he's shoveling the curry into his mouth like he's rescuing a very, very small casualty who is trapped under the rice.

"Let me have a look at him then."

"Who?"

I know perfectly well who.

"I'll get your laptop."

As he goes off to find it, I try not to brood about the unfairness of the fact that he doesn't have to submit himself to this kind of indignity. Women just seem to appear in his life, like fruit flies around a mango, and, while he's not exactly a bastard, he's not exactly not. Take last month's victim (Anita? Angela . . . something beginning with an A). I met her shaking the last of my granola into a bowl. When I futilely rattled the empty box she fashioned her mouth into a theatrical "oh!" and promised to replace it. She was as good as her word, leaving a replacement on my bed the very next day with a sweet, flowery postcard saying how much she was looking forward to getting to know me better. No time: before I'd got so much as halfway through it James had finished with her, spooked by the seven individually wrapped presents she'd lovingly bestowed for his birthday. "How did she take it?" I asked, knowing from even those brief fragments of contact how gutted she'd be. "It was like shooting a fawn," he said, shoving his gym bag into a backpack, and I thanked my lucky stars for how it had played out between us.

It's not like I'm one of those weird masochists who marries serial killers and gaily drowns out the sound of their victim's screams with the vacuum cleaner: James as a friend is a million miles away from James as a boyfriend. He truly is my best friend—the only person in the world that I'm as close to is Jules—and until I meet someone I feel a real heart connection to I'm truly grateful to have him there to shield me from the chill.

"Do you really want to go out?" he says, coming back in, with my ancient laptop whirring into life between his hands.

Of course I don't, what I want to do is slob out on the sofa watching *The Apprentice* and getting drunk with the person I like being with most in the world, but 365 more days like that equals another whole year consigned to a loveless wasteland.

"Yes," I say, slightly unconvincingly, "sort of." I'm fighting to stop myself from melting in the face of his obvious glee that I might nix my plans and stay in with him. "Anyway, I have to."

"We haven't hung out for days," he says, turning the machine toward me so I can log on, while he gives me puppy-dog eyes from over the top of it.

"And whose fault is that?"

"I miss you," he says. "It's been a mad week. But here I am, your willing slave, ready to go out and buy more wine and watch Siralan kick some corporate butt."

"You know perfectly well he's Lord Sugar," I say, swiveling the computer back toward him so he can check out Luke, a quantity surveyor with kind eyes, who at this very moment is probably sitting in his office mentally rehearsing a few witty opening gambits in his head. I hate Internet dating.

"Why are you meeting him so late?"

"I told him I'd probably get stuck in the office."

"Or is it because he looks like the spawn of Mr. Baxter?"

"He does not!"

Mr. Baxter was our chubby, well-meaning history teacher, whose sweaty hands invariably left a damp imprint on your essay when he handed it back.

"Look at those cheeks. He's definitely got a bulimic hamster vibe going on."

"Don't be mean!" I say, peering critically at his picture. He's not madly good looking, it's true, but there's something honest about his gaze, and I liked the way his profile didn't read like a psycho's shopping list of nonnegotiable attributes—he sounded like a proper human being. Sounds.

"Just saying, Livvy, I don't think we've found the one."

It was half an hour later when I stepped out of the house, having guiltily and inevitably canceled my date, and somehow ended up volunteering to be the person to go to the liquor store. James called me as I got to the end of the road.

"I know, I know. I won't get anything rank just because it's on special."

"Livvy, you need to come home."

"I'll only be five minutes."

"Seriously. Turn around now," he said, his voice shaking. James never sounded like that.

"What is it?" Slivers of dread crawled down my back like icy raindrops down a window pane. "Tell me."

"I'm just going to say it," he said, steeling himself. "Sally's dead."

OCTOBER 1995

My first day at Leeds was one of those rare, lethal occasions I couldn't keep Mom and Dad apart—both of them were determined to propel me into adult life, and it would have been too cruel to play favorites and condemn one of them to the parental scrap heap. We squashed my stuff into the trunk of Dad's brown Volvo (a vehicle that I knew embodied why Mom left him: by then she was tearing it up in a zippy Japanese candy kiss of a car) then squashed ourselves in after it, all set for four hours of sticky, congealed tension.

"Would you mind if I opened the window a crack, Jeremy?"

"I'd prefer you didn't, if you don't mind, it negates the air conditioning." Translation: you're irresponsible and flighty, same as it ever was.

"I do so love to be able to breathe."

Translation: you stifled my womanly magnificence for quarter of a century.

I sat in the back feeling nauseous, for so many reasons I couldn't have identified the root cause—polishing off a family pack of malt balls solo, the irony too great to risk offering them around, probably clinched it. As the junctions crawled past, fear knotted my intestines and compressed itself in my chest, the reality of being hundreds of miles from all that was familiar starting to hit home. It wasn't just the prospect of losing the prickly, scratchy comfort blanket of my family, it was also the idea of being severed from James. He and I had done everything together the last couple of years—everything other than the thing I most wanted to do—and now he would be at the University of East Anglia, right at the other end of the country, girls vying for his attentions. The thought was almost too much to bear.

But it was me who had chosen to go so far north: I knew very little about myself at that age, but one thing I did know was that I was clever, and that had given me options. I was denying something that another part of me had intuitively sensed, that I needed to find my own place in the world, far away from everything that currently defined me.

Many moons later we finally parked, Dad efficiently hauling my suitcases out of the recesses of the trunk, Mom critically surveying the shabby façade of my halls through her gigantic sunglasses. Dad dragged my luggage up the stairs, refusing any help as if to do so would emasculate him even more, Mom and me clattering behind him. Sally was the very first person I saw, hanging out of the kitchen with an oversized cartoon mug in her hand saying "WORLD'S BEST DAUGHTER. The sight of Dad's red, sweaty face made a spontaneous grin break out across her own.

"D'you want a hand with them?" she said, taking in the bizarre tableau we made. Her voice was a little nasal,

infused with a merriness that felt a million miles away from our dreary middle-class repression. There was an instant confidence about her, like she could read it all in a heartbeat and know exactly where to put herself. She wore a stretchy, red Lycra minidress, offset by a pair of black woolly tights that rescued her from looking like she'd just come from a night out clubbing. Her black hair—dyed? Couldn't quite tell—was cut into a complicated layered bob, held fast by a thick coating of hairspray, the volume speaking of hours spent with her head upside down blasting it with a dryer. She was skinny—the way the Lycra hugged her jutting hip bones advertised the fact—but there was a soft padding around her bottom, the final frontier that she was yet to overcome. Her eyes were a bright blue, constantly roving around, intelligence-gathering. They'd alighted on me, and I gathered my parka closer around me, embarrassed by my ill-fitting jeans and warm green sweater: I'd just thought north equals cold, whereas Sally, she'd constructed a look, each component part balanced on top of the last, like an elaborate game of Jenga.

You couldn't keep your eyes off the ultimate effect—she was magnetic, compelling—but it was more attractive than pretty: prettiness suggests a softness that Sally rarely surrendered to. I was probably prettier, in a quiet way that I was yet to even really notice; my blondy-brown hair was thick and long, but I had no idea how to style it, so it simply hung there like a rug on a washing line, my makeup collection consisted of a few cheap bits and bobs from Boots, so my hazel eyes never got emphasized, and I was scared of lipstick because it always ended up painting my teeth. As for my perfectly decent body—permanently encased by baggy knitwear, it never got a look-in. No wonder Sally was mapping me so carefully with

her eyes: she always knew when someone was ripe for trans-
formation. Transformation or corruption? Sometimes it's
hard to tell the difference.

"Very kind, but I've got it under control," said Dad, drop-
ping the cases a little too heavily to convince. He was trans-
fixed, his eyes locked on her. "Jeremy Berrington," he added,
sticking out his hand.

"Sally Atkins," she said, leaning forward to kiss him on the
cheek at the exact same moment. She was mocking him, but
so very subtly that he couldn't quite catch it.

She unsettled me, the way she exposed us with a few light
brushstrokes. "I'm Olivia, and I think that's my room," I said,
pointing to the door.

"I'll come find you later, yeah? Few of us were gonna head
down to the bar. Tryouts," she added, with a naughty laugh.

"Absolutely. I think we might head out for supper, but if
I'm here then count me in." I hated the way I sounded, like a
pastiche of the geeky grammar school girl that I was, more
me than me.

"Come on, Mom and Dad, you know it makes sense," she
said, voice a lilting tease.

I looked at them, imagined the awkwardness of dinner,
our glasses chinking in a celebratory toast with too much
undertow to ever ring true. Mom was smiling at her, taken
by her cheek.

"I'll see how it goes," I conceded.

"You do that," she said, tenacious. She held my gaze,
grinned at me, and suddenly it felt imperative that I
grabbed the opportunity with both hands, that I didn't miss
my moment. A girl like that wouldn't hang around—my
friendship window would slam shut and I'd be left shiver-
ing in the cold.

Dad deposited my suitcases in my bare matchbox of a room, and we all stood there for a second.

"Nice girl," he said, and I waited for the inevitable post-script. "Quite a strong flavor."

"I like her," I said, defensive.

"She's a live wire, but she's quite right. Livvy needs to dive right in, like an otter heading upstream."

Mom's ridiculous analogy clinched it. Soon I was hugging them goodbye, unable to look as the Volvo made a heavy left turn around the corner. I looked up at my unprepossessing new home to see Sally watching it all from the window, blue eyes darting around so she wouldn't miss a thing.

It wasn't that I'd stopped being scared, if anything I was more scared, but at least now I knew I was in the right place. Or at least I thought I was.

She was as good as her word. An hour later she gave a cursory knock, and then came crashing through my door, quickly taking in the room. There wasn't much to see—so far my illustrious university career had consisted of hanging my backpack of clothes in the utility closet and arranging my toothbrush and toiletries on the narrow shelf above the gray, speckled sink, all to the soundtrack of Carole King's Tapestry. It was my favorite album back then, probably because I overidentified with the soulful girl on the cover, wistfully looking out with only a cat and a guitar for company.

"What's this shit?" said Sally, laughing, and bobbing her head along to the music. It was "You've Got a Friend" that was playing, at least until I'd scrambled across the room to my stereo and turned it off. "Tapestry," I said, slightly pomp-ously. "It was one of the best-selling albums of the seventies."

"That's great and everything, but there's a vodka and tonic with your name on it going begging." She paused. "I know this'll sound stupid, but what is your name again?"

"Olivia. Livvy."

"Which is it? No, scrub that, I can't call you Olivia. O-livia," she repeated, in a faux posh voice. "No, definitely Livvy."

I bristled a little: surely it was my prerogative to give her permission to use my nickname, but I let it pass.

"What course are you doing?" I asked.

"English."

"Me too!"

"Great minds . . ." she said. "I heard we only get about three tutorials a week and there's study guides for the rest."

"Quite."

Not quite. I loved English, loved the books but also loved the writing. I'd had a tiny article published in a newspaper the year before, and I'd nearly died of pride.

"Come on then," she said, impatiently shaking my parka at me and setting off down the stairs.

A few of our new housemates were waiting on the doorstep for us; there was Phil, a pimply engineer, a girl called Catherine, and Lola, a chubby, smiley history student who reminded me of the kind of friends I had at home. A couple more people arrived, and I tried to remember everyone's names, but it was only Sally I could really hold onto. We set off in a gang, but she firmly interlocked her arm in mine, declared us a huddle.

When we hit the dingy, neon-lit student bar she looked around with wide-eyed disdain and I suddenly saw the world through her eyes, even though our worlds had collided less than two hours before. Everyone looked so young and green, their nerves palpable, their bodies straining forward like coat hooks *as they fought to work out who they were going to be, what territory they should colonize.*

"Dunno about you, but I reckon this is a double-shot scenario," she said. "Back in a flash, don't move."

I didn't even really like vodka—I'd only been drinking for a couple of years, and I tended to go for gin and orange because it disguised the taste—but there was no time to tell her that, and even if there had been, I'd never have done it. We'd already laid down some silent laws, and I was following them to the letter. I turned back to our housemates, by now engaged in an earnest pissing contest about their relative A-level grades, then turned away. My learning had already begun, but it wasn't about renaissance poetry: thanks to Sally I knew that it wasn't cool, that it was faintly tragic, and I was invisibly spiriting myself away. I wish I could go back in time and swivel myself back around—let myself be naive and young and full of pride at my hard-won two A's and a B—but instead I shifted from foot to foot and counted the minutes until Sally reappeared. She was mercifully fast, having inveigled her way to the front of the scrum without even breaking a sweat.

"Chin chin," she said, chinking glasses with me, oblivious to the drinkless ignominy of the wider group. I took a swig, returned her wide, cheeky grin, and reveled in the sensation of the vodka hitting my bloodstream. I could feel it in every cell, every particle, like it was something far stronger. And in a way it was.

I loved that Sally had chosen me, but I had no idea what had swung her vote. There were trendier people, sexier people, richer people; in my more paranoid moments I worried that it came down to nothing more than proximity. To be fair to her, she never made me feel that way. She'd come watch TV with me at night, the two of us at opposite ends of my bed in our pajama bottoms, swilling red wine and munching on a doorstep of Galaxy. Sometimes Lola would join us, but often, as the bed began to sag in the middle, so would the atmosphere. It was funny, because other times we could make quite a happy three: we would have lunch in the basement of the library or go for an "emergency vodka" at the pub at the end of our road before racing back for EastEnders. I couldn't quite put my finger on what it was that made it feel so different—it must be Lola, I reasoned, she couldn't always keep up with Sally's quick-fire wit. I didn't want to look at who was really pulling the strings.

Sally would take me shopping, make me try on clothes I never would have dreamed of wearing, and convince me I looked like a million dollars. It wasn't like I didn't have a group of friends at home, but this felt different, there was a visceral intensity to it that I couldn't quite articulate. Part of it stemmed from the fact that we were living in next-door rooms, but Jules and I had never been close like this: at that stage I was still more of an irritant than a confidante. I loved the feeling of having a person who was more mine than anyone else's—I hadn't had a serious boyfriend yet, and I suppose I was getting some of the intimacy without any of the scary stuff. Surprise, surprise I was a virgin.

Surprise, surprise Sally wasn't. Unlike me she had taken a year off, horrifying her parents by moving in with an older man she met in Barcelona. The relationship sounded passionate and real and scary, their sex life unimaginable to a suburban innocent like me. She would be jokily explicit, and I would try to laugh along like a woman of the world, hoping

she wouldn't question me too closely about the boys I men-
tioned in return, none of whom had merited more than a top-
half grope, most likely through a turtleneck.

Of course I'd been secretly saving myself for James, lost in
my impossible fantasies about him rapping on the door and
begging my forgiveness for taking so long to realize we were
destined. I didn't want to tell Sally how much of my energy
it had taken up—still took up: she was funny, but her jokes
could be spiky, could wound in a way I was sure she didn't
intend.

I was still trying to get the measure of her, our friendship
a new instrument that I'd not yet mastered. She, however,
had worked out exactly how to play me, enjoyed finding out
what notes would squeak out if she suddenly changed her
technique. We sat in the corridor one day, hungover, waiting
for our English tutorial to start, watching a pregnant mature
student huffing and puffing toward us.

"Have you ever been pregnant?" asked Sally innocently.

I tried not to look aghast.

"N- no," I stammered.

"It's so weird," she said, staring into the middle distance.
"Like all your senses have been turned up to the max. Even
the colors look brighter."

I sat there, panic gripping me, trying to come up with an
appropriate response, horribly conscious that we were sur-
rounded by people in easy eavesdropping distance. Our TA
emerged just in the nick of time, and Sally swept toward his
study, barely looking back. I scuttled after her, hoping she
didn't think my muteness was down to indifference, deter-
mined to work out how to ask her all about it as soon as
we were alone. But when I tried she was coldly dismissive
and I backed away, feeling like I'd failed a test. I wanted

to apologize, but, ironically for someone who loved words as much as I did, I couldn't think of a combination that wouldn't make it worse. She was in pain, and I was too inadequate to help her. I vowed to myself that I'd try harder next time.

Sally would despair of the men on offer. "They're all boys, you know what I mean?" she said later in our first term, casting a disparaging glance around the first-year common room, adorned with tattered posters for the mountaineering club and the like. "Totally," I agreed, even though I was harboring a secret flutter for a fresh-faced boy in our English tutorial, the first non-James-related response I'd experienced since I didn't know when. He was friendly with Lola, and he'd told me he'd be at her birthday drinks in a couple of weeks' time. I never assumed boys fancied me, but I knew my nascent prettiness was starting to peep through, and so I held onto the idea that there was a motive behind him casually dropping it into conversation in the queue for the brackish brown water that passed for coffee. When he paid for mine along with his, I was almost sure.

Sally busted me in the next class, spotting the geeky blush that spread up my face when he asked me what I thought of the sonnets our handsomely grizzled tutor Dr. Roberts had sent us off to read. She teased it out of me, then cocked her head to look at him.

"I s'pose I can see it," she said, in a voice that suggested the polar opposite, "if you've got a Bagpuss fetish."

"What do you mean?" I said, laughing despite myself. I tried to imagine what a cat from a children's television show had to do with it.

"Oh, you know," she said, making her hand into a paw, rubbing her sleepy face with it as she gave a slow yawn. She was brilliant at that kind of thing, as sharp as glass, and I saw immediately what she meant. There was something slow and soft about him, a gentleness that could be something to mock or something to treasure. I watched him as he laid out his books and folders with studious deliberation, his pens arranged in a neat line. I liked the care he took, it added to the sense I had that he would want to look after me if I let him.

"I reckon I could be his Professor Yaffle," I said.

"Just ask him out then!" said Sally, digging me so hard in the ribs that she almost winded me. "Or I'll do it."

"No way!"

I was far too shy to do something so brazen, quite happy to watch from afar—it was a vantage point I knew all too well.

I felt like our nighttime gossips were a bit less frequent over the next week or so, but I hoped I was imagining it. I distracted myself with thoughts of Matt, both cheered and horrified to find my habit of building a whole fantasy relationship on the flimsiest of pretexts extended beyond James. By our next tutorial I felt almost too embarrassed to speak to him, worried his X-ray vision would turn out the contents of my addled brain.

"It's an odd choice," he said, referring to the semi-erotic e. e. cummings poem that Dr. Roberts had passed around a week after a raft of Shakespearian sonnets.

"It certainly is," I said pompously, then backed away to my seat next to Sally, cursing myself for squandering his opening gambit.

Sally had heard it all. She smirked at me as I eased my way into my chair.

"Smoothly done, don't you think?" I said.

"You're a goddess, what can I say?" said Sally, and we tried to stifle our giggles, my humiliation evaporating. I loved the way any kind of pain or embarrassment or wrongness I felt could be fed through the machine of our friendship and transformed into something good—it would become ours, another shared experience, the newest piece in the warm patchwork of our friendship. Of course I didn't like to think of the moments when the threat came from within our little bubble.

"Do you really think it's an odd choice?" she asked, a few seconds later.

"Yes, a bit."

She giggled, looked over at Dr. Roberts.

"My fault. Chose it last night when we were in bed."

I gasped, then tried to conceal it, aware how closely she was studying me. It was like a talent show, like I had a single moment to prove to her that I was worth putting through to the next round.

"You go, girl," I said, like I was in an American high school movie.

She didn't say a word, didn't react, simply turned her kohl-ringed eyes back down to her open book. She knew I was a fraud. Even worse, so did I.

CHAPTER TWO

IT'S THE DAY OF SALLY'S FUNERAL, A LITTLE MORE than three weeks on from James breaking the news. I remember I took the phone away from my ear and vomited violently by a tree. Then I stumbled home, keeping him on the phone all the way. When he met me at the door I almost collapsed on him.

Lola had called on the landline, knowing it wasn't a bombshell to drop without warning. Sally had been in a car crash in New York, killed outright on impact. I've always hated the humiliation of hearing Sally's news second-hand—I remember when I heard she'd had her daughter, having never even known she was pregnant. I couldn't quite bear it. "Oh, she had a girl!" I said, as if I'd just been waiting for this final revelation. Now I'd never have to worry about this kind of petty blow to my pride, not now the biggest life event of all had taken place. And it was only now, knowing she was gone, I realized how big a part of me had always wondered if there was a secret trapdoor I'd one day stumble upon that would lead us back together. It was a fantasy in the purest sense; I hadn't done much about it, hadn't even wanted to after all the ways in which she'd twisted the knife, but I also hadn't been able to truly say goodbye to the possibility. However sturdy I was, a part of me knew that Sally could always find a way to wriggle around my defenses if she'd shone her headlights full beam.

She had married a man that I'd only seen in the wedding photos that I'd pored over for clues. He was less handsome than I expected, square and slightly balding, with a look of pure delight on his face in every shot. He was a little older than us, but then, he looked like one of those people who was born forty. She was perfectly made up, smile never slipping, but I could have sworn that it didn't have the unadulterated liquid joy that his contained.

He was English, very English, but they'd moved to the US for his work. The fact that she'd emigrated made it easier—everyone saw less of her, so I could convince myself that our estrangement was no different. Life carried on, acquired new aspects that postdated her, and her absence became a fact of life rather than a weeping sore. I never forgot her though, never stopped feeling the lack of her, despite my enduring anger. In fact its furnace-like intensity was what told me it still mattered—I know for sure that the opposite of love is not hate but indifference.

Do the people we love always remain part of us, even when they've absented themselves from our lives? I like to think that they do—that anyone we truly love changes some part of us forever, like waves pounding against a cliff until its shape is indelibly altered. Or is that no more than wishful thinking, a futile attempt to dodge the reality that however much you love a person, you can never guarantee they won't get ripped away from you? There are only two letters separating love from loss—the first always contains the threat of the second.

James knocks on my door just as I'm deliberating about shoes. My least scuffed black pair are some suede skyscraper heels, which seems faintly inappropriate. It's so much easier to focus on the trivialities than to really engage with the reality of today.

"We should get going," says James, gently.

I slip my left foot in, threading the strap through the fiddly silver buckle. It seems utterly beyond me. I sit down heavily on the bed.

"Remind me why we're doing this."

"Because you said you needed to say goodbye."

I look up at him. He's pale and anxious, and I wonder whether I've got any right to put him through it. I search his face, like it'll somehow answer the questions that are swarming around my brain.

"I just feel like if I don't, I'll never really believe that she's gone. It'll still feel unfinished and horrible and . . ." I look up at him. "You don't have to come if you don't want to. It's not like you . . ."

"It's not about whether I liked her or not, Livvy. Anyway, you're not going on your own. Put your shoes on. I'll find your coat."

I smile at him, grateful, love welling up inside me unbidden. My feelings are so close to the surface right now, constantly erupting, like a shoal of tropical fish breaking cover and flashing up out of the water.

"Are these too tarty?" I ask, looking down at my shod foot, not wanting him to see my face. "Not that it matters."

It does though, weirdly: I feel deeply self-conscious about all the people whom I haven't seen properly in years. When I lost Sally I lost a whole chunk of friends who quietly snuck into her camp and took up residence. They're all Facebook friends, eagerly swapping news and commenting on each other's photos, while I lurk on the sidelines, hating the fact that I'm somehow compelled to watch. There shouldn't have been camps, it didn't need to feel like a divorce, but somehow with Sally everything always took place in Technicolor.

"They're not too tarty, but . . . they might not be a good idea for the graveside, not when it's been so wet."

My hand flies up to my mouth, another wave of shock washing over me. I've been to two of my grandparents' funerals, have grieved them and then passed through to a wistful kind of acceptance, but this . . . this is outside my remit. Just for a second I think about taking the shoes off, curling up in bed and pretending that none of it ever happened. But I know in my heart it's not an option.

Sally is being buried in a church near the family home in Kent, the same church in which she posed for those high-gloss wedding pictures. James drives us there, through relentless gray drizzle. We try out a few other well-worn topics of conversation—why our landlady always wears a sun visor, even in winter, how to persuade my dad to try online dating—but nothing really takes.

"When did you last see her?" asks James eventually.

"The last proper time was just before she got married. I told you about it."

We'd seen each other at the odd social event, stalked around each other like cats, my pride too hurt to risk moving any closer. I'd seen her at someone's twenty-fifth, obediently admired the rock that shimmered and sparkled like a strobe light, and felt silently crushed by her brittle, impersonal breeziness. I'd probably been jealous too, truth be told, even though midtwenties felt incredibly young to be tying the knot, especially for someone as free-spirited and mercurial as Sally.

But then she called me. I remember my body told me what my brain was trying so hard to deny: just hearing her voice triggered a fizzy sort of excitement, a chain of memories like a snatch of bubbles, taking me back to a time when she was the person whose company I craved above all other. I wasn't a total amnesiac—I still remembered all the hurt she'd caused me—but some stubborn, optimistic part of me wanted to believe that the diseased part of our friendship could be sliced out, like a malignant tumor that's caught before it's spread, leaving the part that I'd loved to thrive and grow. Good sense dictated that I play hard to get, but she knew me too well to let me wriggle off the hook, and three phone calls later I was ensconced in a private members' bar that I could never have dreamed of getting into myself, clinking a wide-rimmed martini glass and hoping, with an unhealthy desperation, for the best. It was the height of summer, and the windows were all flung open, the warm air thick with tipsy, nonsensical chatter that spilled from the mouths of the beautiful people who treated it like a second home.

It was like a diva coming out of retirement for one, single Oscar-winning performance. "It's soooo good to see you," she kept saying, squeezed right up close to me on a velvet banquette as if she couldn't bear to endure the cold expanse of a table. I started out trying to remain aloof, but she wouldn't allow it. "I'm so sorry about all that shit," she'd say, clinking glasses for the hundredth time, "what are we like?!" I made a feeble attempt to dig into what had happened between us, but she swept it away in a tsunami of love and warmth and something peculiarly Sally-ish that still had the power to hypnotize me. Besides, there wasn't much in it for me: I wanted to believe her, for order to be restored and to be finally liberated from the feeling that my judgment was fatally flawed—it had made the world feel like a very unsafe place.

I asked her about the wedding, glowing internally at the thought of my thick, cream invitation and my reestablished status at the hen night, but she rolled her eyes and made a funny face. She was still a brilliant mimic, Sally, a great physical comedienne, but I knew it was more than a joke.

"Tell me!" I said.

"Nothing to tell. In two months' time I'm going to be Mrs. Sally Claire Harrington," she said, each word over-enunciated, rolling heavily from her mouth like a cannonball.

"Are you not sure?" I said, shocked and also not shocked. The innocent in me couldn't believe that someone would walk into that kind of commitment with any kind of doubt, but the wise one knew that nothing was beyond Sally's reach.

"He'll be good to me, Livvy," she said, suddenly intense.

"Yes, but that's not a good enough reason," I said, earnestly. "You could just live together . . ."

She flung up her hands and summoned the waiter, ordering yet another round. Of course she didn't want to live with him: it was a half measure, and Sally never lived her life by half measures. She wanted my opinion, in fact I felt sure it was what had brought her out of hibernation, but she was determined not to listen to me, which made me increasingly evangelical.

"You need someone you're crazy about," I told her, "even if it means you have to wait." Sally hated being single, whereas me, I was a bit of a terminal case.

"The One," she said, theatrical.

"Yes!" I insisted. "He's definitely out there." I remember as I said it, I tried to imagine Sally's "One," but it was hard to get a fix on him, this hypothetical man who could love her so skillfully that he'd trick her into a relationship instead of a duel. As for William, I didn't get much sense of him either, only of her in relation to him. When we parted she hugged me for an age. "You're the best, Livvy, you know that?" she said, swaying off on her vertiginous heels in the direction of a cab. I meanwhile took myself to the night-bus stop, pregnant with the sense of a job well done, of a friendship restored.

It was the last time she ever contacted me. There was no heavy white envelope plopping on to the mat, far from it. There wasn't so much as a text message, despite the increasingly pathetic messages I sent her, unable to believe that the guillotine had come whistling down all over again. I insisted that Lola show me the wedding photos, even though I knew that doing so made her deeply uncomfortable. I ripped each one from the packet, rejection reverberating off me. I tried to tell her what had happened, but I sounded petty and bitter, a suburban single girl with an ax to grind.

"I think that's why," said Lola sharply, two high discs of color throbbing on her plump cheeks.

"What do you mean?"

"She said you were unbelievably negative. You really hurt her feelings, Livvy."

Was she hurt? I suppose it was possible, but it seemed more like an inexplicable counter-move. I didn't understand her, and even more painfully, I didn't understand myself. Why had I been stupid enough to go back for more? It's a question I've never really been able to answer, a question that's lingered and festered ever since.

"You know what she was like," says James, momentarily taking his gaze away from the driving rain. "She had to be the one calling the shots. It doesn't mean she stopped caring."

"Oh I think she did."

"But that was Sally, wasn't it? She was a good actress."

The atmosphere thickens and congeals, both of us rendered silent. Not in our comfortable, easy way: it's a lid we've slammed down so we don't have to go back to a time that we move heaven and earth to avoid. Maybe it was a mistake to invite him, I think, but as soon as I've thought it I feel how grateful I am to have the solidity of his presence.

"There are special oldie sites my dad could try, aren't there?"

"Yeah, totally. My Single Tooth?"

I laugh, laugh too much in fact. I'm actually starting to feel slightly hysterical the closer we get to our turnoff, my heart pumping like a piston, my palms clammy and cold.

We drive into the nondescript commuter-belt town Sally grew up in. I remember coming here one Easter for a visit, the ordinariness of it in total contrast to Sally. I was so fascinated by her then, transfixed; it almost felt to me that she must've been found in a Moses basket, transported from somewhere more fitting. "Manhattan," she cried, gleeful at the compliment, too cool to say New York.

The streets around the church are packed with cars, and I can't help thinking how gratified she'd be. She thrived on attention, on popularity; it was a drug for her. James narrowly avoids scraping a BMW, his hands shaking on the steering wheel.

"Shit," he mutters.

"It's fine, you missed."

The churchyard is thronged, Sally's gray, wan parents surrounded by family, her younger brother at their side. The sight of them makes a lump rise up in my throat, the enormity of what it is that they're facing horribly vivid. I stand there for a second, but before I can get myself together I'm ambushed by Sinead, a girl from college who was much more Sally's friend than mine. She gives me a long hug, eyes full.

"It's awful, isn't it?" she says.

"It's horrible," I agree, wondering what else there is to say—absolutely nothing, judging by the long pause. It seems crass to swap news, but I feel so awkward talking about Sally when we'd been so long estranged. Why did I come? I can't order my thoughts enough to recap on my reasons, and yet I know in my gut that it was right. "This is James," I say eventually.

"Hi!" says Sinead, unable to avoid looking impressed. James does look particularly handsome in his dark suit. "How long . . ."

"Oh no, we're not a couple," I say, swiftly. "James is my roommate . . . he, he knew Sally."

We're spared further social embarrassment by the sheer volume of mourners. I have the same exchange about the tragedy of it with person after person, some of them people I'd almost forgotten existed. It's such a terrible way to glean an instant snapshot of how time's moved on. "It's a shocker, isn't it?" says Max, a pothead chancer who we shared our first year halls with. He's plumped out now, got a kind of toadiness about him that makes total sense. "Can't believe she's actually dead." I feel myself recoiling—I believe he's shocked, but there's something about him that's tangibly enjoying the drama of it all. "What you up to anyway?" he adds, already more cheerful. "Married? Babied up?" I mutter a halfhearted response, looking around at the throng. How many of these people are moved by the loss of Sally herself rather than by the ghoulish, faintly thrilling reminder of our mortality?

Now the hearse draws up. The undertakers open it, the dark-suited pallbearers step forward: Sally's father is there, as well as a cousin I met once and her brother. Last to take his place is William, her husband. He's kneeling on the ground, eye level with a dark-haired little girl clad in a blue velvet frock. He's holding her small hands in his, urging her toward Sally's mother, the tableau almost too painful to watch. He gives her a hug, a gentle little push, then helps heave the coffin aloft, shouldering the weight. He doesn't stumble or break down, he just keeps his eyes fixed on the black mouth of the church doorway.

We file in behind them, the coffin now resting at the front of the church. I can't tear my eyes from it, it's only now it really seems real, if you know what I mean; the idea that Sally's body is held by that wooden box feels chilling to me, absurd and horrific. I stare at it, keep thinking that this is the closest I will ever be to her. I lean into James, sucking in the warmth and solidity of him, my jaw clenched tight.

The energy in the church feels physical in its intensity, taut and stretched. I can hear Sally's mother sobbing from the front of the church, a heart-wrenching sound that makes me want to go to her, even though it would be totally inappropriate. But then, nothing about this is appropriate.

It's a Catholic funeral, full of pomp and circumstance, which should be comforting but is somehow the absolute opposite. I don't remember Sally ever talking about religion, let alone Catholicism. The priest tries his best to instill some kind of sense of spiritual order to things, talking about how we can't always know why, how tragic it is to preside over a funeral of this kind, and as he speaks I can't help but grow more and more frustrated. Surely there is no order to this, divine or otherwise—parents burying their children can never be right. I wish I knew for sure what I believed—I wouldn't want to be a spooky happy-clappy type, thumping a tambourine and urging people to repent, but I would love a little more certainty. Even the certainty of real atheism would be better than my wistful half belief: I want there to be something—for Sally to be playing whist with my grandmother, wise enough to have consigned our feud to the fires of hell—but wanting and believing are very different things. I try to engage with his description of her, to feel her presence conjured up by his words, but the blushing bride and obedient schoolgirl he describes don't resonate.

We sing a hymn, voices breaking, then listen to a reading her cousin gives. Now William crosses to the pulpit, slow and dignified. There's a longish pause before he begins to speak, emotion pulsing and surging in the heavy silence.

"I'm sorry," he says, clearing his throat. "It feels so extraordinary to be stood here that it's hard for me to find my words. The last time I took my place here was for my wedding, and I would never have envisioned that this would be how I would return." He speaks so beautifully, despite his distress. He's incredibly posh, but it's not the grating version, instead his words weave and dart, taking you on the path he's carving out with them. "When I first met Sally I couldn't believe that someone as vital and lovely as her would look twice at a dull old fart like me." What a relief to have a moment's levity, a tiny lifting of the smog of tension. "But incredibly she did. All I had to do now was convince her I was more than a flash in the pan, and so began my relentless courtship. She was far too clever to let me know I'd made an impression, she kept me guessing right up until she finally accepted my proposal. Colin will remember me rushing here to ask for her hand, only for her to miss the Eurostar I was patiently waiting on with a ring box." Now she's starting to appear for me, flighty and infuriating, but always somehow forgivable. I couldn't believe how tenaciously her university boyfriends would hang on—it would be a game for her, like chicken, seeing how far she could push them. "I finally proposed at the top of the Eiffel Tower, seriously worried she'd turn me down for being such a cliché. And she could have, being Sally—but happily she didn't, a fact many of you could attest to because you were . . . here." Not me, I think, narcissistically. Not me. William looks into the middle distance, steadying himself, then looks at his daughter and gives her a pained smile. "And before long we were bound for New York, Sally unselfishly putting her own blossoming career in PR on hold to follow my latest posting. I don't think she ever regretted it though, because the result was our daughter, Madeline." He looks to her as he says it. I can only see her profile from here, her face set as if she's repelling the weight of us all looking at her—what poise she has for one so small. "Madeline was a great joy to us both, and I know the proudest achievement of Sally's all too short life." He pauses, too emotional to continue. "My wife was a unique creature, a person of great beauty both inside and out. I will remember her wit, her vivacity, her sharp intelligence. She never missed a trick, never let me get away with anything, and I hope she will continue to watch over us from wherever she is now. I believe she will, because it is unthinkable to me that a spirit as vivid as hers could simply cease to be. And all I can do, all I can promise, is that I will ensure that that spirit lives on via Madeline and me, that our lives going forward are a testament to her. She will never be forgotten. My beloved . . . beloved wife."

He looks to the coffin, puts the pads of his fingers to his lips, and strides back to take his place next to his daughter. Just for a single, self-centered second I wonder if anyone will ever love me the way he loves Sally, will mourn me the way that he mourns her. Even so, I haven't seen him shed a single tear.

The same cannot be said of me. Sally's well and truly here for me now and I do nothing but sob for the rest of the funeral, my face red raw and my handbag stuffed with sodden Kleenex. Her father's eulogy is equally heartbreaking, memories of childhood taking their place alongside William's picture of her as a wife and mother. Finally it's over, and we file out to the strains of Mozart's Requiem. The burial is family only, and the cowardly part of me is

relieved—I don't think I could bear the finality of watching
the ground swallow her up.

The wake takes place at Sally's large, well-appointed
and slightly tasteless parental home. I don't want to be a
snob, I always liked them, but there's a definite leaning
toward brass horseshoes and slogan-ridden doormats.
It's thronged with people, and I feel a bit disoriented. William is standing next to Sally's parents, fielding a barrage
of people who are determined to offer their condolences.
Somehow I can't tear my eyes away. What was he to Sally?
Did he become the answer that she'd been looking for, or
was he another question—a puzzle that she rattled and
shook to try and get it to settle into the shape she wanted?
I watch his face, the reflexive way he molds it for each person, as they clumsily try to express the inexpressible. Each
one of them thinks it's a moment of connection, but I can
see the switch flicking on and off like a light. He's retreated
to a place far away from here—perhaps it's the only way to
endure it.

"Livvy!" says Lola, appearing at my elbow, her eyes
brimming over. "I still can't believe it."

"Me neither," I say, awkwardly hugging her. We haven't
exactly lost touch, but nor are we bosom buddies. Partly
it's cowardice: I've never quite forgiven myself for how
Sally and I dumped her as a roommate in our second year,
but I've never had the guts to properly have it out with her
either. While she and Sally made a full recovery, we never
quite managed to repair our friendship. She's moved out
of London and had a clutch of kids, our lives so different
it's been all too easy to let it slide. The other reason makes
me feel ashamed: I don't think I could stand the sense that

I'd ended up being the one on the outside, she and Sally signed up to a club that I was blackballed from.

"It was beautiful though, wasn't it?" says Lola. I want to agree, but it feels like the wrong word.

"Yes. Was she Catholic? I don't remember her ever . . ."

"William is," she says, looking over to him. "I only saw her a couple of months ago." She looks at me, helpless, like she's hoping I'll have some kind of blinding observation that will make sense of it all.

"Where?" I ask. "Was she in London?" It still hurts, that she could be so close and never call.

"New York." There's an awkward pause. "She invited me out for my birthday."

"Was she . . . did she seem well?"

"She was great. You know—Sally!"

I wonder what that means. Lola was always such a foot soldier, running to keep up with Sally: I can't imagine her ever promoting her to an equal. I look over at William, still trying to imagine the two of them together. He's moved across the room, flanked by a stern-looking man with a beakish nose who must be his father. I don't see it so much in their faces, as in the way they inhabit their suits, their ramrod posture—years of breeding translated into a million tiny signifiers. I smile at Lola, too proud to ask for details, to admit that I don't know if her Sally—the polished married lady—was the same as mine.

"And they still don't know what happened," adds Lola, her voice low.

"What do you mean?" I ask, the hairs on my arms prickling to attention.

"She was meant to be picking Madeline up from school, but she never turned up. She was somewhere out in the depths of New Jersey in the middle of the day. No one knows why. It was pouring with rain. She just lost control of the car, spun into the median strip."

Is that why it's taken weeks for the funeral to happen? I've thought of her, lying there, cold in some morgue, waiting to come home. I haven't even voiced the thought, ashamed of how ghoulish it seems, but it wasn't that—I was worried about her, in a childish sort of a way. It seemed so long, but perhaps they wouldn't release her back to her family until they had some answers.

"It would've been instant, wouldn't it?" I demand, bile rising in my throat.

"Yeah, I'm sure it was," says Lola, tearing up. "She wouldn't have suffered." She reaches out and grabs my hand, her fingers tight around mine, their grip anchoring me in the living present. She always had that easy, instinctive warmth about her. My neurotic, competitive, younger self never valued it enough; it was easier to protect my position with Sally by joining in her sly, semi-affectionate mockery. Lola was an easy target—earnest, her heart worn proudly on her sleeve—but we were the ones who got it wrong.

"Let's not be so crap at keeping in touch," I plead, and she nods, mute, overcome by emotion.

"Lola?" interrupts a glamorous-looking American woman, around our age but far better groomed. She looks both younger and older all at the same time, her figure-hugging, beige wool tube dress reeking of money, the gold hoops at her ears setting off her caramel highlights. She reminds me of one of those gated communities so beloved of Americans, all pristine façades and manicured lawns, sinister in their refusal to let anything be less than perfect.

"Mara, hi! This is Livvy, she lived with me and Sally at uni. Sally and Mara were . . . you did everything together, didn't you?"

Mara turns her green-gray eyes on me, her smile reaching her face a fraction later. She's wondering why I'm here if she never met me—a question I'm still asking myself.

"Our daughters met on day one of kindergarten, and that was it: done," she says, with that rapid fire pace that New York women often have. It's a little too much for me right now. "So it sure was lucky we felt the same way. Richie and William too," she adds, gesturing toward what I assume is her husband, a grizzled bear of a man who's standing near the buffet. He's handsome in a rough-hewn kind of a way, his dishevelment artfully designer labeled. He's wearing black, but it's not a suit. It's a collarless shirt, worn over a pair of dark chinos, a jacket flung over the top. He's gazing into space, a sense of disconnection about him, but he starts toward us when he sees she's looking over. I'm finding it incredibly hard to engage, Lola's words pinballing around my brain. It opens up a million new questions, but it answers one: Sally was still Sally.

Richie introduces himself, his manners impeccable. Despite that, I sense he's struggling every bit as much as me, and it makes me like him more than his wife, who I somehow imagine could mix a perfect martini in a fallout shelter.

"How long are you here for?" I ask, unsure what the social etiquette is at an occasion as awful as this. Is it disrespectful to digress from the subject of Sally? I'm not sure I'll be able to keep it together if we keep talking about her, and I dread anyone probing too much into where I was in the intervening years.

"We're heading out on the red-eye," says Richie. He's one of those men who gives you his complete and utter attention when he talks to you, as if the rest of the world has receded into nothing. His dark hair is flecked with gray, but it only adds to his rough-hewn good looks. "We left the kids with my sister. We've gotta get back."

There's something about the way he says it that speaks of more than practicalities.

"We'll be there to support those guys when they get home," says Mara, looking over at Madeline, standing at William's side like a small, dogged guard. "That's our job, right?" she adds, looking to Richie.

"Yeah," he agrees, but then sinks back into numb silence.

I stare at Madeline—I can't help myself—this little sprig of Sally, the part of her that she's left behind. There's something about the cast of her face, her self-determination, that is so evocative of Sally that I can no longer trust myself to stay here.

I clumsily excuse myself and head for the bathroom, but the door is locked. I cast around for somewhere to go; there's Sally's childhood bedroom, the door firmly shut. Tears prickle at the back of my eyes as I remember the two of us holed up in there, talking so late, so obsessively, that her mom had to bodily haul us out of bed the next day. It takes all my self-control not to open the door, check inside in case our student incarnations are still there, babbling in giggly whispers, trapped in some kind of suspended animation. It's insane, but as William said, standing up there in front of a church packed with mourners, it seems more insane that a spirit as sharp and bright as hers would simply evaporate.

I push my palms against the wall, needing to feel the solidity of bricks and mortar, of the world that holds me.

How fragile that holding is, however much we delude ourselves that we're safe. I miss you, I think. Or is it that I miss the feeling state—a friendship for which friendship is far too flimsy a word? A friendship that creeps into all the hidden spaces inside yourself and turns them inside out, exposing them to the light. But with you—every single shard of sunlight was equaled by the shadow that lay behind it, ready to blot it out at a moment's notice.

I head for the garden, suddenly struggling to get enough air into my lungs. There are a few people milling around on the lawn, and I back away, unable to endure any more constipated conversation. I inch my way around the side of the house, hoping to find somewhere to hide.

There is William. He's holding his phone, just looking at the screen, a lit cigarette in his other hand. He takes a deep drag on it, then spots me.

"I'm sorry I—"

"No, please don't apologize," he says, guiltily dropping it and grinding it into the ground before picking it up and neatly secreting in the packet. "So sorry, disgusting habit. I don't think we've met."

It is a horrible habit, and oddly nihilistic at a funeral. Sally always loved her Marlboro Lights, but even she, I would have thought, would have given them up by now. I chide myself for being so judgmental: surely he's entitled to whatever props he needs to get him through today?

"I'm Olivia."

I don't know whether it's my imagination, but I feel like it shakes him.

"You're Olivia?"

"Yes," I say, self-conscious. What did she say? If she told him that I pleaded with her not to marry him, he'll surely want me seen off the premises.

"You're Olivia!" he says again, smiling. I can't quite work out if this one reaches his eyes. "The card you sent when Madeline was born had pride of place on our mantelpiece."

"Really?" I say, trying to keep the shock from my voice. It was the last time I tried to breach the gap—stupidly, naively hopeful that giving birth would have transformed Sally into some kind of beatific madonna, her hard edges planed off and replaced by something yielding and soft. In a moment of madness I decided to write a poem, something I used to love doing at university, then felt doubly humiliated when the only response was stony silence.

"Oh yes. It was never a case of out of sight, out of mind. She was terribly cast down when you couldn't come to the wedding."

Is it remotely possible that my invitation got lost in the post? Of course not: I hate that Sally's still making me question my own knowing, even in death. I consider William, my heart thumping inside my chest, trying to work out how to pick my way through the marshy ground of our conversation. It's funny—looking at him now I realize I was both right and wrong when I made my sharp, bruised little assumptions on the basis of those wedding pictures. I spotted that honesty in the joy that he exuded, but I'd assumed it was puppyish, that Sally had picked up yet another acolyte. There's a strength about him I couldn't have divined, a surety about his presence that's far more fundamental than that horrible sense of entitlement that's drummed into public schoolboys as their birthright. He's even taller than he looked—of course, now I think about it, Sally would inevitably have worn the kind of heels that made walking up the aisle as treacherous as an ice rink—with a comforting kind of solidity to his body. I can't imagine he's packing a six pack under the charcoal suit that he wears like a second skin, but his bulkiness adds to that sense of presence. It's his eyes that I like most. They're soft and dark—deep set, with a kindness about them that isn't extinguished by the pain that they radiate.

"So you know who I am?" I ask, hesitant.

"Know who you are? Madeline's middle name is Olivia." I can feel the blood draining from my face. I remember her, that very first night. "O-liv-ia," she said, like she'd never heard anything more ridiculous. "She very much regretted you drifting apart."

Drifting: it sounds so gentle, so dreamy, so unlike the Sally I knew. I'm falling, losing my footing in the chasm between the girl I knew and the woman he describes.

"Yes, me too," I say, the words as dry as sawdust in my mouth. I should go: I should go before my anger starts to spit and bubble and show itself against my will. I feel like I'm in that children's party game, the one I always hated, where they blindfold you and spin you around and around, your friends transformed into unidentifiable enemies who will only stop once you're too sick and dizzy to do anything but beg for mercy. William shoots a quick, surreptitious glance at his phone when he thinks I'm not looking. Why am I even here? It must be torture for him to have to endure more small talk. "I ought to go back," I say, expecting him to sag with relief, but instead he looks almost disappointed. I grope for the right words. "I'm so, so sorry. Please know if there's anything I can do—"

"There is," he says, jumping in. "Just sharing your memories of Sally at a time when I didn't know her will help Madeline and me immeasurably. I know that you were the best of friends at Leeds—I want her to have the fullest possible sense of who her mother was."

Anxiety races up and down inside me like a child playing a scale with the gleeful swipe of a single finger. Why is he asking me, of all people? If he knows what close friends we were, he must also know that I didn't simply disappear in a puff of smoke. I've got that acute sense again that we're talking about a different person, and yet, if what Lola says is true, he must be wrestling with his own sense of the world spinning dizzyingly fast.

"I could try . . ." I say, hating myself for my own reluctance. I don't know how to do this, I want to tell him; I don't know how to lay my version of Sally next to yours and not taint it. A coldness crosses his face, like he's snapped up the drawbridge and retreated into the gray depths of the castle. Who can blame him? I must seem to him like nothing more than a grief tourist, taking a day trip into his pain and gawking at it before blithely returning to normal life. "No, please do call me," I say, reaching out instinctively to touch his arm, to breach the gap between us, but it's stiff and rigid under my fingers. "I'll write down my number for you," I add, embarrassed, yanking my hand away and searching my handbag for a pen.

"Thank you," he says, and I look up, struck by the cadence of his voice. It seems to contain a depth of feeling, his thank you, and I hold his gaze for a second, trying to convey to him that my reluctance wasn't born out of indifference or laziness. It was fear, pure and simple. His phone erupts in his hand, breaking the moment. "I need to take this," he says, his face suddenly grim, all vulnerability gone.

"Goodbye," I mouth, backing away, but I don't think he even sees me. I can hear him as I round the corner.

"I can only congratulate you on your impeccable timing," he says, his voice full of cold, controlled fury. "To ask this of me at any time would be extraordinary, but to ask it today absolutely beggars belief."

CHAPTER THREE

SHOCK IS A STRANGE THING; TIME SEEMS TO HAVE developed a mind of its own, galloping ahead and wheeling backward like an angry animal. It's the day after the funeral and I'm feeling more discombobulated than ever. Now it's happened, now I've had to accept the extraordinary truth that Sally really was confined within that wooden box, was committed to the ground, I've lost the option of denial. I feel different: I feel like a person who knows something that the Livvy of last month, or even last week, had no idea about. The outside of my life is a carbon copy—the hot water and lemon I always have first thing, the eight-fifteen exit for the tube—but I've been switched off autopilot. The world feels fragile and sharp, its colors and noises assailing me like burning fat spitting up from a pan.

James has left at his normal time too, six-thirty, early enough to swim halfway across the virtual Channel before his first meeting. He's left a note propped up against the granola: *Chin up mate*, it says, with an *x*: I slip it into my handbag before I go.

The tube feels like an assault course. I stand back, quietly observing the frantic commuters contorting themselves into a section of space that could only accommodate a No. 2 pencil, faces mashed up against the glass like a Munch painting. All that effort feels pointless, energy that's being poured into the wrong place. I watch four trains going past before I realize that I haven't metamorphosed into an existentialist philosopher, and that I too must subject myself to the indignity of the Victoria line. It's horrible in there, airless and close, my heart beating out a tattoo in my chest. Must not cry, must not cry. It spits me out at Warren Street, shaky and distressed. I get myself above ground, gulping in air as I search for emotional equilibrium. I can't help but think of William, how it must have felt to wake up to today, how wrong it must seem that life has viciously kick-started itself again, the funeral nothing more than a memory. Would he even want to carry on if it wasn't for Madeline? I think he would—despite his love for Sally, I sensed a stoicism in him that was about more than being a father. Was that what she saw in him, that he made her feel safe? The Sally that I knew was too fearless to fall for any knights in shining armor. I can't stop myself from trying to fill in the blanks, even though I know that it's pointless. Who was it that he was arguing so fiercely with when I crept away from him?

I decide that a double-shot macchiato might help pull me back to the real world, particularly if it's delivered by the sexy Aussie barista at the trendy coffee place around the corner from work.

"You okay?" he asks. "You know there's nothing in the world that a brownie can't fix."

"You're right," I say, promptly bursting into tears at the fact that it's patently untrue.

"Hey," he says, handing me a wad of paper napkins, "you're having a shocker, aren't you?"

"I am," I reply, gratefully mopping my face. "Thank you." I'm smiling at him a little too intensely, my gratitude for his kindness almost overwhelming. If our grip on life is as tenuous as I now know it is, then maybe this is all we've got: the minute-to-minute choice to be the best versions of ourselves we can muster up.

"Good morning," says Mungo brightly, surreptitiously shoving a copy of the *New Yorker* under a pile of folders.

I'm actually relieved that I'm irritated. I obviously haven't had a complete spiritual epiphany.

"Hi. Did you write up the notes from that directors' meeting?"

"You'll have them before you know it," he says, then swivels his chair back toward his screen like I'm harassing him.

I roll my eyes at Rosie, my kindly, motherly colleague who sits on the next station.

"Cup of tea?" she signals, and I hold up my coffee in response. "Go on," she mouths, and I slip out to the kitchen, keeping an eye on Mary's vacant desk. Hopefully she's gone to make a long personal phone call, rather than for a ruthlessly efficient fifteen-second pee.

"Poor you, it must've been terrible," she says, giving me a hug. I've been trying so hard to switch back into work mode, and just for a second I allow myself to collapse into it.

"I can't even tell you . . ." I say.

"At least you've got it out of the way," she says quickly. "I know how much you were dreading it." She gives me a big, open smile, hands tucked in the pocket of her roomy floral pinafore dress, and I feel a bit like her three-year-old son Alfie must when he's fallen off the slide and she's trying to persuade him to be brave.

"It doesn't feel out of the way . . ." It doesn't, it feels accordion-like, stretching and contracting, as I try to make sense of things that refuse to submit to small-minded logic.

"It's the shock," she says, rubbing my arm. "Now do you want black tea or herbal?"

I think about trying to explain, but it feels too hard to marshal everything that's churning around inside me, the unanswered questions that yesterday threw up. Besides, she doesn't know about me and Sally's murky history—she thinks she's no more than an old pal I lost touch with—I can't face peeling back the flesh of it and revealing the bone and sinew that lie beneath.

"Black, definitely." She smiles kindly, relieved I've submitted to the most British form of comfort, splashing boiling water into our cups. I can feel the crackle of it, loud and scalding. "How's Alfie?" I ask, determinedly steering a path back toward normality.

"He's furious the babysitter's got a new little girl coming. He tried to ram an ochre Crayola up her bottom yesterday."

Just then Honey, Mary's rail-thin, Alexa Chung–like assistant, arrives.

"There you are!" she says admonishingly, casting a disapproving look at the spare layer of flesh that Rosie carelessly failed to shed post Alfie. "Mary's called a flash meeting. You need to be in the board room ASAP."

We grab our mugs and run like the wind, schoolgirls summoned by the headmistress. Mary's at the top of the boardroom table, entirely focused on her iPhone despite the six servants who are sitting around her, poised and ready to do her bidding. She's wearing a loud, pink jump-suit with ostentatious silver snaps running up her toned tummy. It's garish, particularly combined with the cascading gold hoop earrings she's wearing, but it's a statement of intent, and a very expensive one at that—it reminds us that she's forceful enough to carry an ensemble like that off and somehow make it work.

Charlotte, a viperous senior creative who's recently been parachuted in from another firm, has positioned herself at Mary's right-hand side. She's as groomed and glossy as a show pony, utterly focused on the pursuit of success. I'm not sure that she's the artistic genius she's been painted, but that level of self-belief ensures results. I admire it, in a way, but it doesn't stop Rosie and me calling her Robot Girl behind her back. I think Mary knows how ruthless she is, but she's a firm believer in healthy competition: my worry is that there is no such thing.

Eventually Mary deigns to look up.

"All present and correct," she says, then looks to me. "Hello, Livvy, I hope yesterday went as well as something so awful *can* go."

"Thank you," I reply, smiling gratefully, but she's already moved her attention. That's the thing about Mary, she can be incredibly human when she wants to be. Shortly after I broke up with Marco she found me crying in the loos midmorning—I braced myself for a reprimanding, but instead she canceled her meeting and marched me around the corner for a cup of tea. "There's a saying," she told me, pushing a calorific treat in my direction. "Make sure when the clock goes off you're not sitting next to a St. Bernard. And you're just too savvy for that." I loved her for it—loved her for caring, loved her for perceiving something that I knew to be true of myself. My loyalty to her is pretty unshakeable, despite the fact that work often feels like an assault course.

"Today is a very exciting day for this firm," she's saying, "and let me tell you why. It's not because new business is down fifteen percent." Oh God, maybe this is a Mary-style segue into a downsizing announcement. Everyone looks stricken, even though the downturn is across the board, and she takes a moment to savor our discomfort. "No one could blame the people around this table for that," she concedes eventually. "No, we need to think differently in a climate like this. We will survive on our excellence, and one of the best ways to demonstrate it is with pro bono work. Last night I had dinner with Flynn Gerrard." Gerrard's a gorgeous Irish actor who made it big in Hollywood, but, truth be told, hasn't had a box office smash in a good five years. He veers between obtuse indie flicks and big budget action films, none of which reproduce his massive early success. "I know, it's a tough life," adds Mary with a self-deprecating giggle.

"Was he inthanely handsome?" lisps Charlotte, emboldened by Mary's good cheer. Charlotte has patented a nauseating strain of girlishness that she uses to try and cloak her scheming.

"If you like that kind of thing," says Mary without much warmth. "Flynn spent his early life in Africa, and is planning to take the next year out to devote himself to putting something back." Translation: Flynn can't net a good script for love or money, and is desperately searching for another way to raise his dwindling profile. Actors, you've gotta love them. "He's actually a wonderful man," adds Mary, and I chide myself. Since when did I become so cynical? If he has realized that life is short, that we've got only a limited time to do what it is that we're here to do, then I couldn't agree with him more. Stupid, disobedient tears spring up behind my eyes, Sally's presence almost tangible. Fragments of the times we spent together keep whirling up in my mind's eye, like the spin of a kaleidoscope. I think about excusing myself and running to the loos, but I force the feeling down, and ask a question instead: if I act normal, perhaps I'll start to feel normal.

"Is he setting up a charity?"

"It's a trust," says Mary, "which is going to give out grants to give deprived young women life-changing educational opportunities. He wants to raise money in Hollywood, and also here."

Surely if he just donated his take-home pay from playing a loose-boweled rock star in *Sh*t Happens 2*, an ill-judged, multimillion-pound gross-out movie from last year, he'd be able to educate a whole university's worth.

"How inthpiring," says Charlotte, sweeping her perfectly blow-dried flaxen locks up into a ponytail like she's readying herself for action.

"So here's my thinking. Two teams: a couple of weeks to come up with a pitch for a print campaign that will cut across all those bleeding heart liberal pleas for cash and make an impact. Now who wants to lead?"

I can feel myself physically shrinking, every part of me recoiling from the idea. There's no lack of candidates; Charlotte's straining forward like a slice of thin white bread popping from a toaster, and Chris Minky, a copywriter at my level, is apparently foolhardy enough to want to take her on. Mary looks straight through him, her gaze—oh God—her gaze alighting on me.

"Livvy..."

"Thank you, Mary, but . . . I don't think I'm in the right head space this week . . . Chris would be great. Or Amy . . ."

I trail off, her stony silence the only cue I need. I know nonnegotiable when I see it.

"So there we have it, Livvy versus Charlotte. I'm expecting great things."

"May the betht woman win," says Charlotte, extending a bony hand over the table, a fat lozenge of a diamond hovering on her ring finger. "In all seriouthness, Olivia, good luck." She cocks her head prettily and smiles without any discernible cheer.

"Ditto," I say, my hand trapped in hers a second or two longer than I would like—despite its bloodless appearance, she has a surprisingly vise-like grip.

Mary swiftly divvies up the teams, leaving me with a crowd of doleful-looking colleagues, all sensing inevitable defeat. Before my team can slip out, I take them into an adjoining meeting room. I've got to push through.

"We can do this. We just need to make a plan."

"No offense, Livvy," says Chris, "but she's a force of nature. She's got a cabinet full of awards."

I look at him, exasperated by his casual assumption that he would have done such a vastly superior job. I sort of like Chris, but he's a bit of a moaner. He should be attractive, but he's too vain, the kind of man who'd use up all your moisturizer and then whine that it had run out. I need to get him on my side: there's so much that's pulling me away, and I don't want to fail. I saw the complicated look that Mary gave me when she pushed the task on me against my will—despite her flash of sympathy, she needs to see that I know how to let professional take precedence over personal.

"We'll do research, we'll look at campaigns for completely unrelated products that have worked, we'll look at his films and see if there's a pattern to his taste. It's totally winnable."

Rosie gives me an encouraging smile that doesn't quite reach her eyes, while Chris continues to exude his poisonous combination of resentment and disbelief. When my phone starts to ring I could almost cry with relief. Of course I should ignore it, but today is asking too much of me and it feels like a parachute.

It's an unfamiliar number, so I duck out of the office to take the call. I know Mary likes to keep her beady eye on us, but open-plan working is madly inefficient—there's always hordes of people congregated like pigeons in the corridor, furtively squawking into their cell phones.

"Olivia?" says an unfamiliar cut-glass voice. Hardly anyone calls me that.

"Yes?"

"It's William Harrington, Sally's husband."

"William, hi." I want to ask him how he is, but it feels too crass. "I've . . . I've been thinking about you."

"Thank you," he says, stiffly. "I hope you won't think it presumptuous to follow up on our conversation at . . . yesterday but I would very much like to talk to you about Sally."

"Oh," I say, my voice no more than a squeak.

"Please say if this is too soon, but I wondered about tomorrow evening? I'm not sure how long we'll be here and I don't want to let the opportunity slip through my fingers."

Something in his voice, in the way it catches, reminds me of me, the way my thoughts are catching on the jagged edges of impossible questions. Fear begins to thrum through my body, a fear that I can't put a name to but I know could engulf me if I let it. I feel rooted to the spot, words frozen in my throat. I can see the page in my diary, see its blankness, but something in me can't say yes.

"I'm really sorry, but tomorrow's . . . I can't do tomorrow," I say, hating how alien my voice sounds. It's the voice of a liar, a bad one at that, high-pitched and tinny.

"Of course," he says, "I knew it would be a big ask at such short notice."

I'm a horrible person. A hypocrite. I made him a promise, after all. Perhaps in a couple of days I'll feel less fragmented, more capable of giving him what it is that he needs. Although my truth surely cannot be what that is.

"Will you be here later in the week?"

"Perhaps." He pauses, his voice dropping to something more gruff. "Everything's very much in flux."

As he says it, I feel a stab of deep, illogical empathy. Flux, chaos, confusion—they're all words that could add up to a dictionary definition of Sally.

"Please try me again once you know," I say, emphatic. Surely I can do this if I put my mind to it?

"I will. Goodbye, Olivia and . . . thank you."

Thank you—like yesterday, I can hear something in that one little word that speaks to something bigger. Something that's just as overwhelming as the fear that stalks me every time I teeter on the verge of opening the door back to the past.

January 1996

There was distance between us, I knew that, but it was shadowy and insubstantial, hard to name. Sally still offered me lifts to campus, afforded me the odd Friday night out, but we didn't have that Galaxy-munching intimacy of term one. I tried to reassure myself it was nothing more than the fact that we'd met people—my romance with Matt was spluttering into life, and I knew that her fling with Dr. Roberts was still happening, even though she was hazy about the details every time I fired a clumsy question at her. I'd find her and Lola sloshing back wine in the kitchen, snorting it down their noses as they creased up about the "Nutty Professor," and I'd somehow feel like the fun police. "What?" I'd say, and they'd try to fill me in, but the joke always fell pancake flat once they tried to translate it.

The fact that they didn't try very hard made me guiltily aware how blasé I'd been when it was Lola making the bed sag in the middle. Insights crept up on me unbidden, like an evening tide making its slow progress up the beach. The truth was that when you were cosseted inside Sally's warm, seductive inner sanctum there was no advantage to looking at the shadow that it cast, but now, condemned to stand outside in the cold, my nose pressed against the glass like a Victorian urchin, I could see how she kept the furnace burning so fiercely. It needed someone to be wrong, to be the stooge: it was the intense, silent conflict that kept the energy fizzing and spitting. What frightens me is that the realization didn't make me run for my life like a cat with a burned tail. Instead I resisted applying my brain too closely to the problem, trusted my instincts, which told me that before too long the merry-go-round would come full circle and deliver me back to my rightful place. I was like an addict, only capable of thinking about the next fix, not where that fix would ultimately leave me.

The wilderness had its own charms; it was far enough away from Sally's all-seeing eye to give my new relationship a fighting chance of survival. I'd never had a proper boyfriend before, only a crippling crush on James, and I had no idea what it was supposed to feel like. Most of my ideas about love came from books—Nancy Mitford and Jane Austen—so poor old Matt was subjected to quite a few dates that lacked much action. Obviously none of the Bennetts got taken out for crispy potato wedges with a ten percent student discount, but the sentiment was the same: I wanted to be wooed. We'd kiss on my bed, almost fully clothed, but if Matt tried to take it any further a bolt of fear would strike me and I'd roll away. Was it really fear? When I track back to those emotions now, they feel more like misplaced loyalty—something far more destructive and complicated, much harder to decode. Eventually his patience started to wear thin.

"Are you just not that into it?" he asked, trying to mask his wounded pride. "You can just say it if you're not. I'd prefer it if you did, to be honest."

"No I am . . ." I said, clutching his arm, suddenly frightened I would lose him. Here was fear, real fear, and it told me what we had was worth fighting for. His face automatically melted and softened, transformed by his relief, and I saw in that moment what he felt for me. I'd felt my own face do that in the past, had hidden it behind my A-level textbooks so it wouldn't give me away. I really liked Matt, really liked having a boyfriend, but I knew my heart had some catching up to do in this particular race.

"Then . . ."

"I just, it's just I haven't actually . . ."

"That's okay," he said, smiling down at me, and I knew that with him it would be. There was never an agenda with Matt, never a complicated subtext lying beneath what he told me. It was something I should have held dearer for longer, but I was too young to know how rare and special it was.

I lost my virginity to the strains of Tapestry, worried that otherwise someone might hear. I don't know what I expected—perhaps I thought he'd howl like Heathcliff on the wilds of the moors—but it was totally unnecessary. I lay there afterward, my head on his pigeon chest, wondering what the fuss was about (does everyone think that the first time?) and yet deeply relieved that the deed had finally been done. I wasn't a virgin anymore! He hadn't run screaming from my clumsy attempts at foreplay! He hadn't screamed at all, and maybe that was a bad thing, but the way he was stroking my hair told me that he was happy to be here with me.

I spent the whole of the next day reveling in the idea of how womanly and sophisticated I now was—I bought *my fair-trade common room coffee with a flirtatious smile, I pulled out my library card with a Gallic flourish— the world had a different complexion now I was part of its secret conversation. I couldn't help wondering if Sally would sense the change in me, even if she couldn't put her finger on what it was.*

My newfound confidence made me risk finding out. Matt had practice for swimming team, so I had a night to myself, and I gingerly approached her door, tapping on it lightly with the neck of the bottle of wine I held trapped between two glasses. I could hear noises from inside, but she didn't invite me in.

"Sally?"

"I can't deal with you now," she shouted, voice shrill, and I felt like she'd hit me.

"Okay, I'll just be next door if—"

At that moment she flung the door open, her face a mess of mascara, her hair a tangled mop. I'd never seen her like this; there was something genuinely frightening about the rawness of her, the lack of veneer.

"Livvy," she sobbed, flinging her arms around me so hard she almost winded me. I dropped the bottle, hugged her close, following her into her chaotic room. She was clad in a ratty old sweatshirt, far removed from the polished kind of outfits I was used to seeing her in. I rubbed her back through the fabric, waiting for her gulping sobs to subside.

"Sally, what's wrong? What's happened?"

"He doesn't love me," she wailed.

"The Nutty Professor?"

"Don't call him that! Gabriel. He doesn't love me."

I hadn't really thought about it as a love affair. Sally seemed so blithe and knowing when she talked about men,

*and I guess I thought she was living out a rite of passage—
the passionate affair with an older man—rather than risk-
ing her heart.*

"Did he actually say that?"

"Yes, I wouldn't be saying it if he hadn't! He said that I was
very beguiling"—*she put this in angry quotation marks that
she drew in the air—*"but he can't leave Monica."

"What, he's married?"

"No. He lives with her, but they sleep in separate rooms."

*Even I, a virgin twenty-four hours earlier, could smell the
whiff of bullshit. How could someone as worldly as Sally have
fallen for it?*

"Did you know? I mean, that he was living with someone
when it started."

"He told me like, the second time, but he cried." *She turned
to look at me, big eyes as wide and vulnerable as Bambi's.* "He
cried in my arms." *In that moment my heart went out to her,
my bruised heart that knew all too well what it felt like to love
someone who felt for you, but not in the way that would make
sense of everything, that would turn a jumble of notes into a
symphony. I put my arm around her shoulder, poured a glass
of wine with my free hand.*

"He's a bastard, Sally. He's got no right . . ." *I felt myself
puffing up with outrage at the thought of this smug manipu-
lator taking advantage of my amazing friend.* "You're better
off without him." *Unfortunately my lack of life experience
meant that most of my advice sounded like a direct steal from
the* Just Seventeen *agony column.*

"But I love him," *she said, a fresh sob erupting from the
depths.*

"I know you love him now, but it'll change," *I said, painfully aware of my own feelings for James. I forced myself to*

think of Matt, his mottled arms slicing determinedly through
the water, his belief in the importance of committing to everything he signed up to. "It's got to."

"It won't," she said, a bleakness about her that made me
feel helpless. I could sense she'd gone into terrain that I didn't
recognize, a place where my upbeat appeals to the essential
rightness of the world would fall on stony ground.

"When did you fall in love with him?" I thought of her giggling in the kitchen, her salacious stories about him. It must
be recent, easy to unpick.

"That night he cried. That's when I knew."

She must have been hiding it all along, trying her best to
fight it off because she knew it was wrong. How lonely she
must have been: I berated myself for not barging into her
room weeks ago and grabbing our closeness back with both
hands. Perhaps it was me who had abandoned her.

"You poor thing. I'm so sorry."

She collapsed on me, put her head in my lap and sobbed
for what felt like hours. It was unnerving but also oddly exciting; there was something so unbridled about her. I felt like the
scales had balanced, like I had become vital, and it made me
brave. I stroked her arm and tentatively spoke.

"I do get it. At least a bit." I always felt a tinge of shame
back then, a slight sense of wrongness, for reasons so hazy
and nonspecific that I could never grab hold of them and beat
them into submission.

"How come?" she said, rolling onto her back and looking
up at me through those mascara-laden lashes. Sally always
wore layer upon layer of the stuff, the blackest she could find.

"He's called James," I started, gaining confidence as I took
in her rapt expression. I told her all of it; how long I'd loved
him, how I'd waited for him, and now, how I'd finally given

up the wait. Tears came as I described it, and now it was her turn to comfort me. It was the closest I'd ever felt to anyone, that sense of wrongness vanquished by the fact that I could pour out all my secrets and she could simply hear them without flinching. They were schoolgirl secrets, I see that now, but back then they were the map of me, and I guarded them fiercely. She must have known how it made me feel, because she transformed herself, her teasing insouciance replaced by a quiet intensity that banished all the questions and doubts of the weeks just passed. I was hers now, my trust and devotion absolute.

If only I'd known then what a precious commodity trust really is—that once it's broken the scars can take more than a lifetime to heal.

CHAPTER FOUR

Maybe it's guilt that propels me over to Jules's house the next night, a desire to make my claim I was busy retrospectively true. I've been worrying about the lie all day, trying to make myself pick up the phone, but a force as strong as gravity seems to pull me back.

I stand on the doorstep for a full seven minutes stomping from foot to foot, too scared to give the doorbell another push in case I wake four-month-old Nathaniel from his hard-won sleep. Eventually she appears, a glob of pureed carrot stuck in her bangs.

"Sorry, sorry, sorry," she cries, enveloping me in a hug. "You haven't been here long, have you?"

"No," I lie, a white lie this time, trying to prevent my teeth from chattering in her ear like a pair of maracas. "Here, I brought this," I say, handing her a bottle of wine.

"Ooh, thank you!" she says, leading me downstairs to the kitchen. "But don't let me have more than a glass."

The thing is, even with the carrot and the sleep deprivation, my sister looks lovely. There's an infectious warmth about Jules, an aliveness, that means she's always seemed prettier than the sum of her parts. Not that her parts aren't pretty, but she's got an extra sparkle that comes from somewhere else. She's four years older than me, and we seem to have sectioned off our parents, with me looking more like Dad's side and her more like Mom's. She's got dirty blond hair with a bit of a curl to it, a small, curvy body and the kind of gappy teeth that look cute rather than like a dental emergency. Boys always fancied her, and in the best possible way—not because they thought she was a femme fatale, but because they couldn't find a reason not to. She took it in her stride, didn't let it go to her head, then took herself off the market pretty early, marrying her university boyfriend soon after they'd graduated. When she's not on maternity leave she's an architect, a partner in a small local practice.

"Where's Phil?"

"Parents' Night," she says, pouring the wine. "He's been practicing different analogies for 'your son's a psychopath' all weekend."

Much as I love my brother-in-law, I love it even more when I get Jules to myself. I look around her married-lady kitchen, which always seems so much more grown up than mine. It's tidy, for starters, with carefully selected fixtures and fittings, as opposed to the dingy MDF that our landlady installed sometime last century. The four years that separates Jules and me sometimes seems more like four decades. Maybe older-sister years are a bit like dog years.

"Cheers," I say. There's a cozy sitting area that Jules designed to open off from the kitchen, and I tuck my feet under my bottom and sink into the soft squidge of the sofa.

She clinks my glass, then crosses the room to peer inside the stove.

"I'm afraid everything comes out of a carton and the only vegetable is mash. If you get scurvy, don't tell Mom. Oh, and she's popping around at some point. She says she's forgotten what you look like. And she left her Kindle behind when she was babysitting."

It has been nearly a month, it's true. My visiting rotation somehow always tilts toward Dad, and as I went to an interminable Czech art-house movie with him last Wednesday, I felt I'd done my duty for a couple of weeks.

Jules sits down next to me, and rubs my arm with long, comforting strokes.

"So tell me about it properly," she says.

"It was . . ."

And I try and describe it, but it's so hard to translate the feeling of it into words, the sense of collective fear that permeated it. We're so unconscious, we humans, until we can't be anymore: what is global warming if not a cheerful collective middle finger to the truth of our own mortality? I almost don't want to tell Jules how it felt. She's an optimist, my sister, and I don't see why she should have to do battle with this one.

"He sounds like a lovely bloke," she says, after I describe William delivering his eulogy.

I think of him pacing up and down around the back of the house, pulling sharply on that cigarette. He probably is, but "tortured" is the word that shouts the loudest. I tell her about what Lola said, the fragment of his call that I overheard.

"Can't stop thinking about it," I say, dipping my fingers distractedly into the hot wax of the scented candle that is burning. "Though it's not really even my business."

"Well he's kind of making it your business," she says. "At least if you see him you might find out what the truth is." The weird thing is, I feel the opposite—like the closer I get to him, the more elusive it will become. "Christ, I wonder how he . . ." Jules trails off. "Sorry, I shouldn't speak ill of the dead."

"No you shouldn't," I say, sounding sharper than I feel: why is it that even now there's a part of me that surges up in her defense? "If you saw her little girl . . ."

"Calm down, Livvy, I'm not saying I'm glad she's dead. I just—she must've been hard to be married to."

"Yeah, maybe," I say, suddenly desperate to change the subject. It's not just the bare facts of Sally's death that are obsessing me, it's also that gap. The gap between the loving, vivacious woman he described, and the woman who seemed to haunt him as he paced obsessively up and down that strip of concrete like a man held prisoner. "Don't hate me, but I think the chicken kievs might be burning."

When we've finished them, Jules reaches into a stack of recipe books, and extracts a brown envelope that she's hidden there.

"Look at these," she pulls out a couple of black and white photos, slapping them down on the table, "and tell me, honestly, who my celebrity doppelganger is."

They're professional four by eights, of her and a wriggly-looking Nathaniel. Jules is wearing a gray shift dress that has been her go-to outfit for years, and is admittedly looking a little too snug post-pregnancy. She's smiling, but the smile's gotten lost in translation—it's gone crooked and toothy—and her hair is welded against her head in an odd pudding-bowl. For a very attractive woman she does look—I don't know, but she doesn't look like Jules.

"Um . . . Angelina Jolie on the way back from a smash and grab?"

"Martin Clunes, that's who I look like, Martin bloody Clunes."

"Oh Jules, you don't!" I say, snorting with laughter, despite myself.

"I bloody do! This is what Phil asked for for his birthday: a professional photo of the two of us. I can't give him this."

"Have it done again! I'll come with you, do your makeup, hold Nathaniel between shots."

"Maybe," she says, ruminative. "I dunno, I just blew it really out of proportion, like it was symbolic of everything."

Jules doesn't normally go in for things like symbolism.

"Everything?"

"Like I'll never be me again."

"You are you!"

"I'm not though, Livvy. You're not ever quite the same after you've had a baby." She looks at me, searching for the right translation for what it is she wants to tell me—I don't know if it's because she doesn't think I'll understand, or because she doesn't want to hurt me, but it makes her feel very far away for a second. "I swear to you I'll never be one of those smug freaks who elevate motherhood to some kind of religious experience, but it does move the pieces around inside."

Maybe I'm a bit in denial about this fact, about the part of Jules that's gone to a country I don't have a visa for yet, that I might never get a visa for. Don't get me wrong, I adore being an aunt—the rush of love I felt when I first set eyes on Nathaniel almost frightened me with its ferocity—but it doesn't mean I don't miss the way it used to be. The way we could dip casually in and out of each other's lives without needing to make a plan, every piece of them a titbit in an ongoing conversation.

"You'll be back at work in two months, that'll be a massive dose of normality."

"I know, but . . . Livvy, it takes me ninety minutes to get to the shop and buy a packet of butter. I've timed it. It doesn't really seem possible at the moment."

"It's only been four months, of course you're still adjusting."

"It's not just stuff. I feel like I'm still working out who my people are, you know? They're not those awful ubermommies going on about Boden discount codes on Facebook, but I'm not going to be in the office until eight o'clock anymore either." She waves a dismissive hand, tops up my glass. "I'm being ridiculous, ignore me."

But it doesn't sound ridiculous to me. That was one of the reasons I treasured Sally's friendship for so long—when I was with her I felt like I'd found my tribe, it was a small tribe admittedly, but it didn't matter, because it was small and perfectly formed. To me it felt a bit like we were cymbals, like we struck against each other and all of the parts of myself that I'd never let reverberate suddenly became colorful and noisy and worthy of notice. We all need someone who holds up a mirror, we just need to make damn sure it's not the distorting kind.

"You're not being ridiculous."

"I am, I'm just tired. The most important headline is that it's amazing." Her eyes dart to me quickly, guilt crossing her face. "Not that you couldn't . . . they're not compulsory."

I don't want to think about that. I want to hold onto my childish certainty that eventually, if you listen hard enough and long enough, fate whispers in your ear who you should be with.

"Besides, Phil's your person."

"Hopefully. He might have a rethink when he sees these," she says, shoving the photos deep in the envelope, and wiping down the table.

He is, he most definitely is, but I don't think it's ever been a grand passion, more a comfortable pair of slipper socks. Maybe that's what she needs, after the simmering, silent resentment of our parents' marriage, but I know for me it would never be enough—although life would probably be simpler if it was. I think fleetingly of William, his face when he talked about Sally. Is there really a person for everyone? I hope so. But what happens if your person is your person, but you don't happen to be theirs? Now it's James I think of, even though I was trying with all my might not to.

Once it gets to nine thirty I can see Jules swallowing down the yawns of a person who hasn't had more than three hours' sleep on the trot for four months. I'm making my excuses, shrugging my coat on, when the doorbell goes.

Mom comes sweeping into the kitchen, a red velvet shawl flung around her shoulders, lips painted a similar shade, white-blond hair blown about by the windy night. She's not glamorous per se, but she's got enormous presence.

"All the girls together! What a treat. I'll have a glass of red please, Julia."

Jules waggles the bottle at me and I shrug my assent. She puts on the kettle for a peppermint tea, politely stifling another gigantic yawn.

"I'm sorry to be so late. I was at my Zumba class, and it ran on. It's so freeing! I really think it would do you good, Livvy, get you out of your head and into your body."

"I'm quite happy with yoga, Mom."

"But darling it's so controlled. The liberation of Zumba, I can hardly put it into words . . ."

"So you were Zumba-ing until nine?" I say.

"No, no. I went for a bite to eat afterward, the most delicious *tor-tel-loni*," she says, adopting a ridiculous Italian accent, "smothered in the most exquisite *pes-to*. Meals like that make you glad to be alive."

Jules and I roll our eyes, very very slightly. We're good like that; we can communicate, at least about our parents, with a mere tremor.

"Who'd you go with, Mom?" she asks. "Was it a class thing?"

"In a sense. Kevin is in the class." Oh God, here we go. "Don't give me that owlish look, Livvy, Kevin's just a friend. How's your electronic dating going anyway? You haven't told me anything for weeks."

"Yeah, what's going on?" asks Jules. "And also, have you sent your story in?"

Mom looks at her questioningly. "She's been working on this short story for a competition. It's brilliant, of course, but she's too much of a bloody perfectionist—"

I stop her midflow.

"It's only okay, and anyway it's not finished. To be honest, I haven't been able to think about anything very much the last couple of weeks."

"Oh darling," says Mom, coming over and enveloping me in a hug. The smell of her—Pears soap with an underlying hint of garlic—is familiar and comforting. "I was just waiting for the right moment to ask."

So I try and describe it, all over again, finding it even harder than I did with Jules. "It was just so sad," I say, leaning back into her, grateful to stop searching for words that won't come to me. She holds me close, and I sink into that familiar breast.

"We just can't know . . ." she says, rocking me a little.

"Can't know?"

"The mysteries of the universe. When our time is."

I pull away.

"How can it possibly have been her time? She's got—she had"—I correct myself, anger increasing exponentially—"a seven-year-old child. She was only thirty-five!"

Mom gives me the sage nod of a wise elder in a remote African village.

"Precisely. There's no logic to it, and yet in some cosmic sense there must be."

I stand up, glowering at her.

"So here's your Kindle!" says Jules, brightly.

I treat myself to a cab home, still fuming. How could she be so insensitive? As I get nearer home the guilt starts: is my resistance to seeing William any better? Mom, in her infuriating Mom way, is refusing to engage with the bleak horror of what's happened, trying to make it somehow justifiable. And me, I'm burying my head in the sand, waiting for time to restore a sense of internal order and allow life to pick up where it left off. I dig my phone out of my cavernous leather handbag and dial quickly, cheating the devil inside me that's urging me to hang up. He picks up on the third ring, classical music playing in the background.

"Hello, it's Olivia." My voice is shaking. "I hope I'm not calling too late."

"No, not at all. Wait a second, let me turn this down."

There's a warmth to his tone that instantly makes my heart, which is beating like the wings of a trapped bird, slow to a pace close to normal. The music is oddly soothing too—it's something slow and melancholic, played on a cello. He comes back to the phone and I find myself gabbling, trying to get my words out before I overthink them.

"William, if you're here at all this week I'm around. Just tell me when and where."

"Gosh, that's wonderful news. Madeline and I are staying at the Berkeley." He pauses. "I hope this suggestion won't fill you with horror, but I wonder if you might like to have dinner in our suite? Monday perhaps?"

I freeze for a second as the reality of his proposition hits home; his suite, his daughter, none of the distracting hubbub of a restaurant to carry us through.

"Of course. What time?"

"Eight p.m.? That should give me time to get her safely tucked in."

I bet nothing feels safe to that little girl.

"I'll see you then."

I hang up and stare out of the cab window into the encroaching darkness. It stretches out forever.

CHAPTER FIVE

I ARRIVE OUTSIDE THE BERKELEY JUST BEFORE THE appointed hour, and take a couple of minutes standing outside its impressive façade, steeling myself for what's to come. It's right in the heart of Knightsbridge, a stone's throw from Harrods, a tall, imposing building that I've only ever walked past—there's never been a reason to go in before. I enter the hushed warmth of the lobby, which is all soft lighting and liveried doormen. I can hear the siren call of cocktail glasses chinking in the bar, the steady hum of conversation underneath; how many bars did I prop up with you, Sally? How many nights did we set the world to rights, ordering round after round as if we could somehow stretch out time and stay floating in our haze of sentiment and certainty? The slightest tremor brings her back to me right now, the smallest tweak on the chords of my memories, but tonight is not about my feelings. I take the padded elevator up to the sixth floor, trying to calm my nerves, trying to remember the fleeting ease that I felt last night on the phone.

It's Madeline who answers the door to me, slowly swinging it open. She's clad in a long, white Victorian-style nightdress, almost ghostly.

"Hello" she says, turning her unwavering gaze upward to meet mine.

"Hi, Madeline!" I say, hating the patronizing, syrupy undertow in my voice—it's not that I don't like children, it's that I don't quite know how to pitch it. "I'm Olivia. It's lovely to meet you."

William appears beside her, plucked from somewhere deep in the recesses of the cavernous suite. He's wearing a striped shirt, the sleeves rolled up in some kind of half-hearted nod to casualness, tucked into a pair of rigidly belted dark pants. His smile of welcome momentarily illuminates his pale face, but the light drops out of his hooded eyes as fast as it appears.

"Come in, come in. I'm afraid bedtime's still something of a work in progress."

"Please don't apologize," I say hurriedly. "It's nice to meet Madeline properly." I look down at her, trying to identify what parts of her are Sally—that dark, chestnut hair a smudge against her white nightie, her pert little nose—but William's receding hair is also dark, and surely most children have snub noses: am I imposing a resemblance that's not really there?

"Do you like being called that or do you go by Maddy? Lots of people call me Livvy."

"My name is Madeline," she says.

"And it's a gorgeous name too," I say, feeling a true whisper of Sally, of that sense of wrongness I so often experienced. It's not that I'm egotistical enough to think a grieving child is trying to psych me out, but there's something about that certainty, that innate self-possession, that conjures up Sally more than a mere arrangement of features ever could. "I brought you a present," I say.

I did an emergency lunchtime dash to Hamleys for it, panic exacerbated by the fact that nonworking lunches invariably elicit a raise of Mary's perfectly threaded eyebrows. I settled on a plush brown teddy bear—something soft and yielding that she can cuddle—which is wrapped up in my handbag.

"How kind, you really shouldn't have," says William. "Besides, before we get to that, we need to take your coat and organize you a drink. Would a gin and tonic hit the spot?"

"Sure," I say—I don't know why, Sally long ago turned me from gin to vodka—and then let him help me out of my coat. I can't remember the last time anyone but a waiter did that for me. "I'll just pop this next door," he says, leaving the room, but as he does so the phone that never seems to leave his hand starts to ring.

Now it's just Madeline and me, marooned in the vast living room. It's desperately plush—littered with plump cushions and elegant table lights—but it still has that impersonal feeling of a big hotel. Madeline eyeballs me from her vantage point on the sofa, her small feet dangling above the thick cream carpet, waiting for me, the so-called grown-up, to make the next move. Is the set of her face—that jutting chin, those burning eyes—fury that I haven't acknowledged the terrible thing that's happened, or is it an electric fence designed to stop me intruding into their makeshift version of peace?

"I . . ." I want to say Sally's name out loud, her absence and her presence both so tangible, but at the last minute

I bottle it. "Let me find your present," I say, pulling out the parcel, and thrusting it in her direction.

"Thank you," she says, slipping her fingers under the paper and painstakingly peeling back the Scotch tape. "Oh, it's a teddy." A polite upward inflection is injected into her tone.

"Do you . . . do you like teddies?"

"I used to, when I was five. Now I prefer dinosaurs."

"Dinosaurs?"

"Yes, I want to be a paleontologist when I grow up. The dinosaurs lived thousands of years ago. They were very, very big. Now they're extinct, which means that all of them are dead."

Her words hang in the air, a challenge: I search desperately for the perfect, sympathetic return serve, but nothing seems remotely adequate. I'm incredibly relieved to see William coming back through, but his expression immediately makes the relief evaporate. He's even paler than before, his face tense.

"What a fine bear," he says, picking the teddy up and smiling fixedly. "Has he got a name?" I feel for him, I really do, and yet the falsity of it makes everything feel even more wrong.

"No, not yet," says Madeline, barely giving it a backward glance.

"Madeline was telling me how much she likes dinosaurs," I interject, desperate to avoid any kind of standoff about her lack of enthusiasm: I sense that William treats manners with an almost religious reverence. "Have you been to the Natural History Museum?"

"No," she says.

"It's near here and it's packed with dinosaurs."

"But they're all dead, I told you that."

"I know that, I meant models of dinosaurs." Madeline looks dubious, but I blunder on. "Maybe Daddy can take you before you . . . before you go home." I feel a lurch in my stomach as I say "home," starkly aware of the difference between bricks and mortar and a true home: maybe this impersonal space feels more true to their state of being than the prospect of returning to what was "home" with the heart ripped clean out of it. Madeline doesn't even dignify my comment with a response.

"Daddy, it's past my bedtime, please will you tuck me in?"

"I most certainly will!" says William, giving me an apologetic smile. "Back shortly."

"Really, take your time," I say, sinking, relieved, into a squashy beige sofa.

William's still gone ten minutes later, which gives me ample time to get over my antipathy to the gin. There's no question he's poured me a double, and I can't help but feel a certain relief at the warm muzziness that starts to fizz and bubble its way through my consciousness. Is this how alcoholism starts—the seductive softening of life's sharper edges, the picture pleasantly skewed? I don't think life's ever been tough enough for me to realize how easy it might be.

My eyes catch on a silver-framed photograph displayed on the mantelpiece above the fireplace and I cross to it, a little unsteady from the heady cocktail of anxiety and alcohol. Madeline stands in front of a well-appointed New York brownstone, in the kind of gray flannel school uniform that screams exclusive prep school, with Sally standing behind her, hands on her narrow shoulders, smiling into the camera. It's recent: I can see that just by looking at Madeline, but also from the almost imperceptible network of fine lines that thread their way around those familiar deep blue eyes. I stare at myself in the mirror above the mantelpiece, comparing battle scars; how strange it is to think that the way we remembered each other was so out of date, that we changed in parallel, but apart. And now she'll be frozen in time as her thirty-five-year-old self, spared the indignity of gray hair, of arm flab, of all the things that I know that Sally would have hated and fought even more fiercely than the rest of us—but in escaping them she's paid a price that even she would have balked at.

"Can I top you off?" says William, appearing suddenly behind me in the mirror, our eyes meeting in the reflection.

"Oh! I'm sorry, I . . ."

"First day of term, hence the shiny shoes and pristine lunch box."

God, does he ever loosen up? My eyes unconsciously flick back to Sally's photo: how did she find that kind of equilibrium with him that any successful marriage needs—that silent, subconscious agreement about how to seamlessly turn two into one? I hand him my glass.

"Just a dribble, I'm a bit of a lightweight."

"They'll be bringing supper up in fifteen minutes or so. I ordered the lamb, I hope that meets with your approval."

"I'm sure it'll be delicious."

We move to the sofa, and I perch, awkwardly, my fingers wrapped around the slippery coolness of the glass.

"Did you come from work?" asks William. He's smiling as he says it, but I can see a nerve throbbing on the left side of his forehead, a pale worm of stress that refuses to be held in check.

"No, I went home first. I live with James, I don't think you met him. He was with me."

"So sorry, I should have asked if you wanted to bring your partner. Are you married?"

"Oh no, we're . . . we're just roommates. He knew Sally too." Color creeps into my cheeks, a blinding sense of how much hangs here, unsaid: the truth, the real history of our friendship, left to languish in a dark basement like unclaimed lost luggage. I try and pull the conversation back into safer waters. "Have you found out how long you'll be here?"

"A week, maybe two. I can't be away from work indefinitely, and Madeline's got to get back to school."

He enunciates perfectly, words clipped, emotion drained out of them, like flat, gray pebbles skimming the sea. I look at him, shocked by his brutal practicality. Is it coldness or self-preservation? My eyes flick to Sally's picture on the mantelpiece, that misplaced protectiveness rearing up inside me.

"Surely no one will expect you to be straight back into normal life?" His jaw tightens, his eyes suddenly cold. He must have detected that sharpness in my tone that I didn't intend to allow. "What is it that you do?" I add quickly.

"I put words in other people's mouths." I look blank. "Sorry, too obtuse. I'm a diplomat, a speech writer. I work between New York and Washington."

We're interrupted by the arrival of dinner, the liveried room service man making a great show of setting the dining table with a proper cloth and laying out the heavy silver cutlery. "Thank you very much indeed," says William, palming him a ten-pound tip and pulling out one of the ornate dining chairs for me to sit on. "Shall we move on to red?"

"Yes, let's," I say, my chest tight and heavy with the sheer effort of holding so much in: I need to try and make some kind of real human contact, break through that rigid carapace of good breeding. This is probably the last time we'll ever set eyes on one another and, while I don't want to do any damage to his memory of Sally, it suddenly feels vital that we show something of ourselves. "William, I hardly know what to say—anything I think of sounds trite, or trivial . . ."

The words are benign, but I think he hears something different in my voice, almost a cry for help. He seems to uncurl a little, although he's twisting his napkin around his hand as tight as a tourniquet, his knuckles blanched by the pressure.

"I just can't seem to make it past disbelief," he says. "I travel so much anyway—I keep expecting Sally and me to be reunited, like she'll walk through the door any minute and tell me how gruesome my shirt is." He looks away as he says it, almost like he's hearing her. A shiver goes through me, a sense I'm walking on her grave, inveigling myself into the nucleus of her life when she'd so summarily rejected me from it. But William invited me, and maybe in one sense, so did she: why else would she have given Madeline my name? I glance back at the photo, at Sally's smiling face: is it me, or does that wide, confident grin not quite convince?

"You must still be in shock." He looks me full in the face, a nakedness in his expression that I haven't seen before. It impels me forward. "I don't mean to pry . . ." I say, searching his face to try and judge if I've inched my way too far, "but Lola told me that there are some questions . . ."

"There are," he says, his tone a full stop. We sit there, subsumed by the leaden silence—I take a sip of my wine to give myself a valid distraction. It's extraordinary, rich and complex—it tastes of money. William unexpectedly tips his glass toward me.

"Olivia, I wanted to thank you for venturing out tonight, and for not shying away. Sally often used to talk about all the fun you had, and I appreciate that this is the utter antithesis."

"Thank you," I say, suddenly feeling tears flooding my eyes. His distress is so palpable, and yet so teeth-grindingly controlled. It's like a heat haze filling the room, static and oppressive. "I'm sorry . . ." I say, "I'm really sorry." I can't hold the tears in any longer, the buildup of pressure too much to bear. William swiftly walks round the table, kneeling in front of me.

"Please don't apologize," he says, imploring, handing me my discarded napkin. "I'm the one who should be apologizing. The last thing I wanted to do was cause you more distress." I try and get hold of myself, but the more I try to regain control, the more it runs away from me.

"I'm such an asshole," mutters William vehemently, handing me another napkin.

"You're not."

"I am, I'm so bloody useless at this stuff."

He looks stricken, like some Dickensian headmaster is issuing directives from somewhere deep in his psyche. What "stuff" does he mean? I sense there's a story there for him too, his own left luggage.

"No, I'm glad. Truly, I'm glad to be here," I say, tears subsiding, realizing as I say it that it is at least partly true. If there had only been the funeral and the brutal return to normal life I wouldn't have been able to rest, I'd have worried away at all my unanswered questions like a fox in a trap, gnawing its leg off in desperation. I give him a half smile, moved by the sight of him kneeling on the ground. He doesn't seem nearly as unreachable now he's crumpled on the carpet, shirt spilling out from those stiff pants.

"You don't have to stay down there you know."

"I made you cry. The least I can do is grovel."

He gives me a sheepish smile as he says it, and I can see as he does so that all the others have been nothing but well-drilled facial reflexes—he's like an empty house suddenly flooded with light, darkness chased away by something more powerful. It melts away the stiffness, brings his vulnerability to the surface. For a moment I can sense exactly what it is that Sally would have seen in him, but then I realize that it's what I would see, not her.

He stands up, awkwardly brushing the lint from his pants, and retreats to his side of the table, pausing for a fraction of a second to reassure himself that I really have collected myself. He reaches to fill my glass, and holds my gaze.

"I'm sorry, you asked me a question."

"Please don't feel like you have to—"

"No, it's actually . . ." He looks at me. "There aren't actually that many people I can talk to at this precise moment in time." Again, that sense of Sally: her presence and her absence like two electric currents running through the room. How terrible it must be to lose your closest confidante, and in losing them, lose the very person who you would go to for comfort. "The police obviously released the . . . the body . . ." He grinds to a halt, looks away, and yet again I grope in the dark for the best way to reach across the breach. I think about moving my chair around the table and sitting beside him, but it feels like a bridge too far. He collects himself, straightens his shoulders. "For burial, but now the insurance company is asking questions."

"Insurance company?"

"Life insurance. They're trying to get the investigation reopened."

That lizard of dread starts to crawl and slither across me, my gaze unconsciously pulled back to the photo. What did you do, Sally? She smiles out at me—those whitened teeth, that perfect hair—she's giving nothing away.

"But why?"

"They're saying that it could be suicide." He looks at me, his dark eyes full of pain, "Which is patently absurd."

"Of course. Of course it is." I'm talking too fast, thoughts careering around my mind like moths wheeling around a light. Surely not? Surely not that? She had so much, and yet . . . some part of me won't throw the idea away like it's trash.

"They've discovered points on her English license that I didn't know about, and they're saying that the fact she had a few sessions of therapy indicates a history of depression. They want to talk to us all, get more *background*."

His tone is one of outrage, but I detect a bleakness that sweeps across him like a wall of sleet. How awful it must be to have to focus on these spots of darkness at a time when all you want to do is focus on the good. And what if the darkness was more than mere spots? It certainly was when I knew her. I think of him delivering that eulogy, the sheer force of will it must have taken. He wants to believe in that version of Sally—the white queen, not the wicked witch—even more than I did. Protecting it is his very survival.

"It doesn't sound like much," I say, trying to ape his certainty. "Loads of people have had counseling, I know I have." Again, that pull to the past. My twentysomething self, sobbing about the kind of girl politics that sounded petty, but had cut me to the bone. "And a few points for speeding..."

"They don't see it like that. They called me—the day of the funeral." He looks at me, almost ashamed. How much does he think I overheard? "They want to exhume the body." I take a gulp of air, suddenly light-headed as the blood drains from me unbidden. He looks at my chalky white face, concern in his eyes. "I'm sorry, I shouldn't be burdening you with this."

"No, please . . ." I say, looking at him, trying to regain some composure. "They can't ask you to do that!" My voice is high-pitched, shrill, like it's coming from somewhere outside me. I don't feel fully resident in my body; I look down at my hands lying on the heavy oak wood of the dining table, trying to coax myself back inside my shell. What is Sally now; is she the body that's lying in the cold ground? Is she the energy that's pulsating in this room? Or is she nothing more than a collection of our conflicting, overlapping memories?

"I've point-blank refused, but they're trying to mount a case. They want to do a toxicology report. They're trying to suggest she might have been driving under the influence. These awful suits who don't know her—it's ludicrous to suggest she'd do such a thing."

A memory hits me like a camera flash—Sally: not just drunk, high, willing her nippy little Peugeot to take the corners faster as we drove back from a Manchester club, me singing along at the top of my lungs while my white fingers gripped onto the seat for dear life. It doesn't sound so ludicrous to me.

"Oh God, William, I'm so sorry," I say, too shocked to even cry. "Is there anything, anything at all that I can do?" I mean it this time. I couldn't mean it more.

"There is in fact," he says. "I have to go and speak to the investigators. They need me to make some kind of deposition this coming Saturday. I couldn't help but notice your kindness with Madeline, and she talked nonstop about you when I tucked her in." How can she have done, when I was so clumsy and hopeless? I don't say that, I just smile my assent. "I'm sure she'd relish that trip to the Natural History Museum you suggested, but perhaps with you?"

"I can give it a go."

"Thank you."

It's as though, at least for a little while, we allow ourselves to breathe out. He asks me about my work, I ask him about his, and although it's a false sort of normality, it feels like a tonic, a cold compress on a scalding burn. Still, when the carriage clock on the mantelpiece hits ten-thirty I can't help my streak of relief at being able to make a polite escape. I want to get home to see James: in time to bitch about Charlotte and talk about whatever rubbish is on TV—in time to pretend that those kinds of things really matter.

William helps me on with my coat, waiting patiently as I try to thread my arms into the sleeves.

"Thank you again," he says, his gaze direct. There's something very grown up about him, that's about more than his young-fogey outfits. He's a man, not a boy, and witnessing it makes me realize how few men can really lay claim to the title.

"No, thank you," I say. "And I'm glad I'll get the chance to see more of you and Madeline before you go."

"Olivia," he says, suddenly intense, "will you do something for me? Can you tell me something about Sally that you think that I mightn't know?"

Here it is, the million-dollar question, the reason he asked me to come. How interesting that it's only now, when I'm standing in the doorway, he feels safe enough to ask it. I take a breath, try to think just enough, but not too much.

"She always lit up the room, made everyone else in it seem about twenty degrees less bright. She could be kind—I mean, she was kind. When she was caring about me, I'd have this toasty sort of feeling inside." I hope the truth of that feeling will counter the equal truth of my hesitation. I can't read much in his expression, he's watching my mouth, like he wants to catch the words the very second they spill out of me. "She could make me laugh like no one else could, she always had the best nicknames for people. She always seemed to win on the Grand National even though she knew nothing about horses; one year she spent it all on a pair of boots I wanted that I couldn't afford. She cried when Miles didn't marry Anna in *This Life* but she didn't cry at *Schindler's List*." I pause, look at his drawn face, his eyes pools of sadness. "Is that enough?"

"I'm not sure 'enough' is quite the right word," he says, his voice soft.

We stand there for a moment, submerged in a complicated sort of silence.

"I should go."

"Of course. And thank you again. You reminded me about some bits of Sally I'd maybe . . ." He pauses. "It's good to remember."

It is good to remember. At least I think it is.

CHAPTER SIX

IT'S EIGHT P.M. ON FRIDAY NIGHT, AND WHILE WHAT I *should* be doing is drinking wine in a noisy bar, what I'm actually doing is trying to make up for lost time, specifically the lost time of the last few weeks, in which I've gone home at six and sleepwalked my way through my working hours. The pitch is less than a week away, and we're yet to have a eureka moment; I'm hoping that if I sit here long enough, in an empty office looking at clips of Flynn Gerrard and Googling stray news stories, inspiration will strike. When Amy taps me on the shoulder I nearly jump out of my skin. I pull off my headphones.

"Where did you spring from?"

"I've been in the conference room. Charlotte's asked me . . ." She stops, remembering we're on rival teams.

"On a Friday night?"

"Yeah, on a Friday sodding night. To be fair, she didn't ask me to do it tonight, but it's so much work that I thought I'd get a head start so I'm not doing it all Sunday."

"Couldn't she help you?"

"She's going away with Peter."

"The boyfriend?"

"Have you met him?"

I shake my head, secretly enjoying where this is going.

"I met him once at some BBH Christmas drinks. He's like a postbox." I try not to look baffled: Amy has a peculiarly off-center way of looking at the world. "You know, square and red and solid with a big mouth. Kept going on about his investments and lumbering up to the bar like he was going to fight it."

We snort with laughter.

"Why don't we call it quits?" I say, a bit tentative. "Have that drink we were going to have?"

"Aah, I'd love to, but I'm meeting Evan for dinner."

"Oh, okay," I say, feeling knocked back, even though I know it's not a slight. "Maybe next week?"

"Behind enemy lines? Exciting!" She grins. "I'll let you get on." She glances at my screen as she gets up. "What's that then?"

It's another side-effect of my blinding realization that life is frighteningly short. Frustrating though it is, I've gone back to peering at those tiny website photos trying to find men worthy of "favorite" status. What Amy has spotted is a profile for Pete the Pilot, a good-looking forty-something who I've been exchanging e-mails with for the last couple of days.

"Check him out!" she says, having a good look at his photo. He's wearing his uniform, which is possibly a little over the top, but he looks so handsome in it that it's hard to hold it against him. "He's hot, no question."

"He e-mailed me at lunchtime checking there was nothing in his profile that worried me, but, you know, no one's perfect. He's got a couple of kids, but they're teenagers so they probably do their own thing."

I can hear myself jumping ahead in the way that always proves fatal, but I can't help myself. I just want life to throw up some answers, some certainties. "That's when I knew," I'll say, as a fleet of Red Arrows fly in formation over our wedding, "that I couldn't live life like a dress rehearsal."

"Definitely dateworthy," says Amy. "Besides, they've all got kids by now and if they haven't, they're probably weird."

I think of William, of his pale, harassed expression as he juggled yet another piece of bad news with Madeline's bed-time. I'm glad that I'm going to be able to help out tomor-row, even if it's only a tiny drop in the ocean of what he's going through.

"Does Evan have kids?"

"No, but we've been together for . . ." She trails off, not wanting to sound patronizing. "Pete sounds great, you should go for it."

"Thanks."

I end up staying until after ten, scribbling down random ideas that don't really hold up and scattering grains of couscous from my M&S takeout supper across my messy desk. I call James a couple of times, but there's no reply. The house is dark and silent when I get back, and I drag my computer onto the kitchen table and pour myself a glass of wine, logging on one final time. A new message from Pete! *Great!* he's written. *If you really are not worried at all, let's make a plan without further ado.* Sweet, *no further ado,* how lovely and old-fashioned. He's given me his number, which I'm trying to transcribe into my phone, when there's a piercing shriek behind me. I whip round, to find a skinny blond clad only in one of James's work shirts framed in the doorway. James comes bolting out of his room, a towel wrapped around his waist.

"Oh man, sorry," he says, "should have told you . . ."

"It would've been nice . . ." I start.

"This is Livvy, my roommate."

Beanpole Girl's face floods with relief at the news that I'm not his vengeful wife, lying in wait with a bread knife and a Google search on the temporary insanity defense.

"Silly me," she says coquettishly, "it was just a shock."

Maybe if you bothered to—I dunno spend more than two hours with a woman before dragging her back to your lair—there wouldn't be any nasty surprises, I think, trying to convey it through my narrowed eyes. James is oblivious.

"This is Matilda," he says, peering nosily at the screen. I try to slam it shut, but he whips out a hand and flips it back open.

"Pete the Pilot," he says, scanning it in double-quick time.

"James!" I say, glancing toward the Beanpole. I almost feel sorry for her, shifting from foot to foot, futilely attempting to pull the shirt down to a modest length.

"Oh come on, Livvy, even if he is handy with his joystick, it's not gonna be worth it. You'd never be able to handle it."

"Do you know what, most people have kids by our age. It's a fact of life." My eyes swivel toward BG, whose perfect twentysomething tummy looks like it's never accommodated as much as a croissant, let alone a baby. It's so bloody unfair that he can date down as well as up. Suddenly I'm feeling properly furious. "I didn't ask for your opinion. Take Martha . . ." James looks around with me, leaving me deeply suspicious he doesn't know either.

"Matilda," she clarifies.

"Take . . . Matilda back to your room and leave me alone."

"Fine," says James snappishly, "but I didn't mean the bloody kids and if you think I did, there's something seriously up with your priorities. How can you want to go out with a naturist? It's so fucking obvious it's internet code for a swinger."

I stop in my tracks. "What are you talking about?"

Matilda gives the shirt a final tug. "I think I might just go back next door."

"I'm really sorry about all this," I say, with an embarrassed laugh.

"I'll be there in five," says James, giving her the kind of crumpled, sexy smile that will ensure she won't do the sensible thing and run for the last tube as fast as those skyscraper legs will carry her. "Here," he says, jabbing at the screen. "I have a wide variety of interests, including naturism."

I slump back on the kitchen chair, the fight having left me. "Oh," I say, in a small voice. It feels momentarily disastrous, symbolic of the wrongness of everything: Pete the Pilot and his naked member has made the world seem a dark and unforgiving place. Suddenly I'm dreading tomorrow, wishing I could fake an illness. My moods are so fragile right now, like I'm holding a brimming cup of scalding water and trying not to stumble, but the more I try not to, the more inevitable it becomes.

"You thought it was nature?"

I nod.

"I didn't read it properly. Maybe I should go on one of those adult literacy courses," I say, feeling myself choke up.

"That's not the only sign he's a perv. *'You look like you're having loads of fun in the pic in your red dress.'*"

"I was, it's from Jenny's wedding when we went to Scotland."

"Translation: I'm wanking over you."

"Don't be so disgusting!"

"Trust me. There's a million ways men say it. 'I was thinking about you last night.' Translation: I'm wanking over you. 'It's been ages since we spoke.' Translation: I'm wanking over you."

I look at him, doleful. Sometimes I really, really wish I was a lesbian.

"Come here, you muppet," he says, putting his arm around me. "It's easily done. You just read it too quickly. That's why you need me."

"I just wanted . . . I just want something to make sense," I say, leaning into his familiar bulk. I'm probably covered in a light dusting of Timotei Girl hair, but I don't pull away.

"I know," he says, voice low, words muttered into my hair. "Don't we all?"

I stay there a second longer, then force myself to pull back. "You ought to get back to Martha."

"Matilda."

"Yes, Matilda. You ought to get back to Matilda."

"You're right," he says, making no attempt to leave. Eventually I force myself to get up. "Thanks, James," I say, my voice soft.

Sleep just isn't one of my talents. Sometimes I lie rigidly in bed listening to CDs of creepy mid-Atlantic men telling me how relaxed I am, but tonight I know it's pointless. I'm thinking about James, wondering why it is that, although we speak the same language, we speak a different language:

even now, there are these moments where we seem perfect for each other, the Marthas of this world nothing more than an amuse-bouche that brings out the very worst aspects of his character. Surely someone as intelligent as him must be able to see that he needs a more sustaining meal? He was attracted to me once, twice even, so there must be some kind of physical spark on his side. It hurts tonight in a way that I never let it anymore, particularly when I hear a little mewling giggle coming from down the hall.

The morning sees me hitting snooze repeatedly, finally forced awake by the sound of Beanpole Girl calling through my door. "Lovely to meet you, Livvy," she sings, and I look, horrified, at the time. William will be fully decked out in a casual weekend tank top by now, dipping toast points in his egg with geometric precision. James, by contrast, is munching on a bowl of Crunchy Nut cornflakes, the debris sprayed out around him like a hurricane's blown through.

"Morning," he says. "How'd you sleep?"

"The question is," I ask archly, "how did you sleep?" Why do I pretend that his sexual antics are some kind of shared source of hilarity?

"Yeah, very funny," he says.

"Where's she gone?"

"I told her I had to work. I'm playing squash with Adam, but I thought it'd sound a bit harsh." He munches away, unconcerned, half an eye on the *Guardian*.

Tension bubbles out of me as my equilibrium returns. This, this is why I have the perfect version of James. My toast pops up at me, and I hastily butter it so I can eat it en route to the tube.

"Wish me luck," I say.

"You'll be a natural," says James. "Mary Poppins eat your heart out."

Let's hope he's right.

Sorry, domestic meltdown. Meet you at the museum at 11? Save me a stegosaurus.

I so wanted her to come meet William and Madeline with me, break up the cloying intensity, but it's not to be.

They're waiting in the lobby of the hotel, holding delicate china cups, facing outward on a low couch as though they're posing for a portrait.

"Olivia!" says William, reflexively standing to attention. I misjudged him on the tank top, he's wearing a starched green shirt that brings out the hazel flecks in his deep-set eyes. Another memory hits me, Sally talking about the first time she met him—at a dinner party that she'd been taken to by another date. I asked her all about it on that night we had. "He wasn't fit exactly," she'd said, "but he had a look about him. Hidden depths, you know what I mean?" I hadn't, of course, not then, but I think I might be beginning to.

"Hello," I say, forcing myself to focus on the moment at hand. "Hi, Madeline!"

"Hello, Olivia," she says, giving me a long stare. Did she ever even want this—"play date" is so not the right phrase—scientific outing?

"Are we waiting for your sister?" asks William. "Shall we organize you a cup of coffee while she's en route?"

"No and yes," I say. "I mean, yes to the coffee, and Jules is meeting us there." Soon I'm dropping sugar lumps into my steaming coffee with a pair of tiny silver tongs, imperiously holding it out so an obsequious waiter can dribble milk into it. I keep enjoying little pieces of this life, and then feeling guilty as I'm slammed by the terrible context. I bet Sally took to it like she was to the manor born.

"Would you like me to bring Madeline back here afterward?" I ask him, trying to silently convey my sympathy to him. He doesn't flinch, doesn't communicate anything back, and I wonder if he's willing me to back off.

"My cunning plan was to meet you on the front steps at one and take you all out for a slap-up lunch."

"That sounds like a great plan. What do you think, Madeline?"

"Thank you, Daddy." She turns to me. "But I don't eat certain things. I don't like sushi because it's a bit like slime and I don't like sausages because of the pigs."

"Got you," I say. "I don't like sushi much either. It's too fishy."

"And I don't like green beans, even though Mommy says they are very good for me."

William's eyes flit away for a second, and I feel him wince.

"And she's right," he says, voice steady. "Green beans are very good for you."

There's another gaping pause, and I cling onto my bone china cup like it's a life raft. I soldier on.

"Your mommy didn't always eat things that were good for her." A flash of memory, the two of us munching on our beloved family-sized Galaxy, the concept of a real family not even a blip on the horizon, cheap red wine sluicing its acidic path down our throats. I look at her, this little piece of Sally's future. "We both hated beetroot," I tell her, trying not to choke on the words, trying to make myself strong and safe for her.

Madeline turns those big eyes up to meet me, pale face set.

"Let's go and see the dinosaurs," she says in a high voice. "And I want to see if they have any rulers in the gift shop."

To my profound relief, Jules is already out front at the museum, a sleeping Nathaniel strapped to her chest. I tried my very best with Madeline on the walk over; I asked open-ended questions in the hope she'd feel able to talk more about Sally, I inquired about school, about pets, even about her pencil case—nothing elicited more than the briefest and coldest of answers. It gives me that deep feeling of help-lessness, the mountain too big to scale, even though there's an arrogance to ever thinking that I could. I introduce the two of them, and Jules offers her hand. "It's lovely to meet you," she tells her, as Madeline gravely shakes back. What a genius move, such formality is obviously written through every frond of her DNA.

"Do you like dinosaurs?" she asks, with great seriousness.

"I adore them," replies Jules firmly and I try not to look incredulous.

Madeline casually slips her hand into hers. "Let's see the Tyrannosaurus rex," she says, pulling Jules ahead as though she's known her forever: she must be giving off some kind of motherly musk that intoxicates anyone who's less than four feet tall.

"Let's wait for Livvy," she says, shrugging apologetically.

"Come along, Olivia," says Madeline sternly.

"Yes, wait for me, I love the tyrannosaurus rex!" I cry, scuttling across the grand entrance hall after them.

We make our way around the museum in painstaking detail, learning about every spit and cough that came out of the dinosaurs' enormous bodies. Jules oohs and aahs in all the right places, while I try and fail to look sufficiently fascinated. One of the fatal flaws to my character is that I either absolutely love things (Kate Bush's back catalog, schnauzers) or hate them (beetroot, Justin Bieber). And also, maybe, I'm a tiny bit jealous that it's Jules that she's taken to with such enthusiasm. I couldn't help but be flattered by the enthusiastic picture that William painted—I liked the sense of symmetry, the idea that some part of her might know that I had meant something to her mom when she was no more than a star in the sky. I feel idiotic now, like I've fallen prey to another attempt to try and make sense of something that is beyond the reach of sense. Right now Jules is perfecting her listening face as Madeline takes us in minute detail through the daily diet of the stegosaurus.

"So how do they know all that?" I ask.

"From their *droppings*," says Madeline, with a despairing look at my utter stupidity. "Their droppings make fossils and the . . . and the sky-entists look inside them and then they know."

There's something very sweet about her mispronunciation, a rare moment of childishness, bringing into sharp relief how unnaturally poised she seems the rest of the time.

"Scientists," I say, smiling down at her.

"I know, scientists," she snaps, spinning back to the sign at the base of its enormous foot.

I look to Jules, out of my depth, and she gives me an encouraging smile, subtly stepping backward to give me space. "So tell us about how long they lived for," I say, trying to sound like I haven't even noticed how cross she is, but she turns her body squarely toward Jules, and directs her answer to her. Definitely Sally's daughter, I think, yet again, quietly admitting defeat. Madeline's fit of pique lasts until the point when we get to the tyrannosaurus rex rulers, where she stops to make a thorough inspection. I grab Jules, who is soothing a grizzly Nathaniel.

"I think I need to go and feed him."

"Yeah do, but Jules, I literally don't know what I would have done without you."

"Oh you'd have been fine," she says. "She's just playing us off. There's no way she'd have been so tricky if you'd been on your own."

We look down at her, sitting cross-legged on the floor, rulers and erasers fanned out around her like a garish fence. She looks so incredibly alone, and yet I can't bring myself to kneel down beside her and break into the bubble.

"Dunno, maybe I'm just rubbish. Nathaniel wailed his head off when I picked him up last week."

"It's just his age," says Jules. "And don't you go making out I've turned into some hellish earth-mother-baby-whisperer type. I'm a ball-breaking career woman. I've got a BlackBerry and I'm not afraid to use it, I'm . . ." She trails off. "Do you think we can have wine at lunch, or is that completely inappropriate?"

When Jules goes to find somewhere to feed the baby, I look over to Madeline, holding an eraser in each small hand, peering at them like it's the hardest decision of her life, and my heart squeezes up in my chest. I walk over quickly before I can overthink it, gingerly kneeling down on the periphery of the stationery wall.

"Can I help you choose?"

"No thank you. I have chosen the velociraptor. They lived in the Jurassic age, but then there was a big explosion that made them all die."

She's holding on very tight to the velociraptor ruler, like she's keeping it safe from any unexpected meteor catastrophes that might be about to strike.

"Tell you what, why don't we get two? Maybe we could get an elephant or something, they're not extinct."

"No, they're in the zoo," she points out. "Mommy took me to see them. We went to our secret place and then we went to see the elephants."

"What was your secret place?"

"Our secret place!" she says. "It was secret so I can't tell you. Then it wouldn't be a secret anymore."

"Was it Daddy's secret place too?" I say, looking at her a little too intensely. There's something about the way she says it that makes it feel like a real secret, not a child's fantasy.

"No, Olivia. That is how a secret is made. You don't tell anyone else. It's me and Mommy's secret. You don't understand and you don't know my mommy. I'd like the velociraptor, please. Thank you."

Madeline runs off, without a backward glance, making sure I can't pry anymore. William's given her some spending money, and she stands on tiptoes at the desk, carefully laying down a five pound note while I hover behind, not wanting to force myself on her any more than I already have, pushing down the questions I'm desperate to ask.

With half an hour left to kill before William arrives and my anxiety levels reaching new heights, I'm incredibly relieved to see a sign advertising a special filmed exhibit. SEE THE DINOSAURS LIVE AND 3D, it says. WATCH THEM IN THEIR NATURAL HABITAT. We settle down into the comfy seats, and I immediately start thinking about work. I'm fretting about my presentation, wondering what the hell it is I'm missing, when one of those accursed stegosauruses jumps out of the darkness in all its 3D glory and looms toward me. From that point on I'm gripped: seeing those lumbering beasts moving around, thundering through their habitat, predatory and magnificent, suddenly stops the whole experience seeming dry and irrelevant and brings it to life. I turn to Madeline when the lights come up.

"That was great," I say, then notice how sad and pensive she looks.

"I'd like my daddy now," she says. "I'd like to see him."

"He's probably waiting for us outside."

She nods, bottom lip quivering.

"Madeline, darling, what's wrong?" I say, my heart going out to her.

"It was like the dinosaurs were alive," she says.

"Was it too scary?" asks Jules.

"No, I'm not scared," she says stoutly. "I don't get scared."

And I see it then, the unfairness of the fact that the dinosaurs could seem alive, even though they're extinct, while her mom has disappeared without trace. It's yet another reminder that Sally's gone, that there are no miracles to be had. "They're not really alive," I say, trying to convey with my face what I can't seem to convey in words—that I get it, that it seems unjustifiable and unimaginable to me too, even though I'm supposed to be a grown-up. "It's like a film, like *Finding Nemo* or something. Nemo's not real."

"I know that," she says wearily, sliding out of her seat. "I'm not a baby." She stomps off down the aisle without a word, and I trail uselessly in her wake, watching her thin little frame cutting its way through the space in search of her father.

Jules links her arm through mine and I squeeze it hard, the steady rhythm of her blood pulsing through her veins feeling like the most precious of gifts.

CHAPTER SEVEN

WILLIAM STANDS ON THE STEPS, TALL AND ERECT, gazing out into the middle distance. We're following Madeline from a few paces behind—I hope he won't think that we've simply abandoned her to her grief. "Daddy?" she says, and as he turns I see that proper smile again, that smile that makes him feel like he's thinking only of you.

"Hello, darling, did you have a nice time?"

My body clenches in preparation for her telling him how useless I am, but she does nothing of the kind.

"Yes, in fact I did. The stegosaurus ate mostly like he was a vegetarian."

"I see," says William, smiling at me over her head. "And have you said thank you to Olivia and Julia?" he asks.

"There's really no need," I say hurriedly, "we enjoyed it, didn't we, Jules?"

"Yes we did!" agrees Jules heartily, while she struggles with the folded up pram. William steps forward without being asked and pulls it out for her. "I didn't know anything about stegosauruses before today."

"They are very interesting," says Madeline solemnly, and I'm suddenly overcome by a desire to hug her, even though I know how unwelcome it would most likely be.

"Dinosaur investigation is hungry work, I'm sure," says William. "You must be famished. Will the little one's nap schedule allow for some lunch?"

"It's his favorite meal of the day," says Jules, and we set off.

We follow William through the wide streets of Kensington—the tall, gray houses looming over us like elderly dowager duchesses—until we finally reach a corner restaurant with big picture windows. Jules and I exchange an almost imperceptible glance, and I know exactly what she's thinking. Our dad would never have taken us somewhere like this, not in a million years; on the rare occasions we went out to eat it was a pub lunch or perhaps a Pizza Express if he was feeling particularly ritzy and Continental. Madeline sails in, utterly unfazed by our surroundings, casually allowing a waiter to pull out a chair for her.

"I want you to sit next to me, please," she says to Jules, and yet again I try not to feel crushed. I sneak a look at William, wondering whether he'll think I've failed in some way, but even if he does, he doesn't show so much as a flicker.

"Are you terribly Presbyterian about lunchtime drinking?" he asks.

"No, she definitely isn't," says Jules, ears pricking up, bat-like.

"Well that's a relief," laughs William, and just for a moment the whole situation feels normal—no, more than

normal, rather lovely—but then I remember what surrounds it and feel a sting of shame at my callousness.

"Wine would be fine," I say, stiffness descending over
me. It's so hard to know how to be.

"Righto, I'll order some white," says William, effortlessly summoning a waiter. I study his profile as he efficiently scans the list: at times like this it feels like those
unimpeachable manners cover every peak and trough of
emotion like a heavy blanket of snow, giving everything a
perfect, icy uniformity.

When the wine arrives we all cling on to our glasses,
awkward, before Madeline thrusts her juice glass forward.
"You're meant to say cheers," she says reproachfully and we
do, the spell broken. Jules turns out to be my secret weapon.
She acknowledges what's happened, respects the context
of why we're here, but the fact she's bonded with Madeline
let's some lightness in. She asks her questions and elicits
more than monosyllables, even extracting a few giggles. It
seems to allow William to drop his guard a bit, the table
comfortably splitting down the middle.

"How's the fight to the death with your arch nemesis
going?" he asks, a smile playing around his lips. I'd forgotten that I'd even told him about Charlotte.

"Robot Girl? Disastrously," I say, and his brow furrows.
"Everything I come up with feels so ordinary. Flynn Gerrard's a star. He's going to want something that twinkles."

Charlotte's a star in her own tiny firmament too, twinkling out a harsh, artificial kind of light. Sally streaks across
my consciousness, the biggest, shiniest star I knew at one
time in my life. I sneak a look at William, wondering if he
feels a tremor of her here between us. I should tell him what
Madeline said, but I can't do it here, in front of her. Perhaps I

should e-mail him, but the thought of delivering that ambig-
uous information in such an impersonal way feels somehow
cruel. Maybe this is all my stuff, me arrogantly assuming
that I know more than I do about his feelings, projecting my
own complicated relationship with Sally onto his.

"Apologies if this sounds hideously patronizing, but do
you care about it? The issue, I mean, as opposed to beating
the princess of darkness?"

"What princess?" asks Madeline, ears pricking up. "Do
you know a real princess?"

"Far from it," says William. "Now eat up a bit more of
your salad so you can have pudding." He turns back, dark
eyes burning into me.

"Of course. I feel like these women's lives are defined
by an accident of birth. They don't know what they can
achieve, because the world never shows them. There's . . ."
I try and find what it is I'm trying to express. "There's no
room for fate. It's all preordained."

"Or rather it's all down to fate, but it's a terrible one."

"Yes. I suppose I think of fate as heralding something
good."

Sometimes I worry I put too much faith in fate, that it's
a cop-out.

"When you talk about it, I can feel your passion, and I
don't believe for a single second that Charlotte's got that in
her armory. It's yours for the taking, I'm sure of it." He looks
at me, such belief in his face that it feels infectious. "When
I'm writing a speech and it's not coming, that's what I do.
Go back to the emotion of it, and then sprinkle the facts and
figures over it right at the end."

"But what if you don't believe it?"

"Sorry?"

"If you don't believe what you're writing. If it's not the truth."

"It might not be my truth, but it's someone's truth," he says, fiddling with the stem of his glass. "That's what I'm looking for."

Is truth really that fluid and unquantifiable? Surely our own truth has to remain our personal gold standard, even if we choose to ignore it or hide it in the moments where it's too much to bear? Or maybe the very fact that we can do that proves the veracity of what he's saying.

I look away, to Madeline—determinedly wrestling an untamable plume of spaghetti around her adult-sized fork—and think about her passion for those dinosaurs. She couldn't convey it to me until I saw them moving, engaged with them as living beasts—that was when I realized that her seven-year-old self knew more than me about whether they were worth my notice.

"A print campaign is a waste of time," I say. "There's no way of making it stand out. You just end up with those awful, generic pictures of sad-looking Africans."

"So?"

"A viral film that tells a story about how well it can go if someone gets the right support."

"And the reverse too," he says. "How disastrous your life can be if you make the wrong choices."

I can see that sadness hovering there, ready to break over him if he were to let it. I give him a tentative smile, suddenly seized by an illogical, overwhelming desire to protect him—to keep him on the side of the light.

"How was it today?" I ask, keeping my voice low.

"It was . . ." He looks at me, almost helpless. "It had to be done," he adds, facing it down.

He must have to keep finding that hardness, that grit, to get through everything that life is throwing at him, but at what cost? Is it not the softness, the moment of surrender, that allows you to heal? I remember what he said, about not having anyone to talk to. Will it be better or worse when he's back in New York? I think of Mara and her elusive-feeling husband, his name escaping me, her promise that they would look after them when they returned. I truly hope that they're up to the job. I need to step away for a moment.

"Will you excuse me? I'm just going to pop to the toilet."

"So, what's for pudding?" I ask Madeline, smiling brightly as I sit back down.

"Jules is having meringue islands and she says I can have some and I am having chocolate pudding, though Daddy says I might not like it because it's hot, and if I don't he'll eat it all up."

"So you can imagine what I'm hoping the verdict will be," he says, looking at her fondly. "How about you? I'm thinking about jam roly-poly."

"Are you getting in a bit of British stodge before you leave us?" I say.

It gives me a twinge, the idea that they're going, although I'm not entirely sure why considering how briefly I've known them. I suppose there was a strange, complicated kind of intimacy to that evening we spent together at the Berkeley. The fortress around him feels so hard to penetrate: the fact that he let me pass, chose me to share his vulnerability, feels more precious than it would if he was the kind of person who emoted all over the place.

"I might come back," pipes up Madeline.

"For holidays and things?" I say.

"No, to school."

"What, like university?" says Jules. "That won't be until you're much bigger."

"No, *school*," repeats Madeline, frustrated. "Like in Malory Towers."

"Boarding school," I say, my eyes flicking to William. "It'd still be when you're much bigger."

"Daddy went when he was eight."

My eyes flick round to William, appalled.

"But Daddy's parents were probably just a drive away. Not a plane ride."

William flicks a look back at me, his jaw set. There's an awkward silence before Madeline speaks.

"I'm going to go and help Jules change Nathaniel's diaper now."

Once they've gone, William and I lock eyes.

"I take it you don't approve," he says.

"You can't possibly think that's a good idea," I say. It's none of my business, I know that, but in this precise moment it feels like it's got everything to do with me. Life keeps reminding me that I never truly let Sally go—surely she would never have wanted this?

"She wants to go," he says, his tone icy. "She's talked of nothing else since she started reading those books."

I imagine her there—that reserve solidifying and calcifying until it's become her personality, a shell that's as tough and intrinsic as a tortoise's. Her beauty and her poise will assure her fear and admiration, but will they allow in real love? Of course William will love her, adore her even, but that love will prevent him from seeing how alone she is, out there in the world, her wound buried too deep for her to even make the connection.

"Every little girl reads those books and thinks that's what they want," I snap. "They think it'll be midnight feasts and jolly japes, but the reality is very different."

"Did you board?"

"Of course I didn't."

"Then what on earth qualifies you to judge?" he snaps back, angrily signaling for the bill. I feel an illogical surge of fury as I watch him yanking his black Amex out of his pigskin wallet. There's a sense of surety that his kind of upbringing gives you, when all the time it's robbing you blind, denying you any perspective beyond the gold-plated blinkers that you're not even conscious you're wearing.

"Um, I don't know, being a sentient being?"

I see him crumple, his righteous anger burning itself out.

"Trust me, it's not much of a life for a little girl, me working the hours I do, no mother to come home to. It's an easy flight, grandparents and cousins on tap. At least she'll have a sense of her heritage."

"You're everything to her," I say. "You mean far more than some abstract sense of Englishness."

"I think you'll find that was Sally," he says softly.

Before I've got time to apologize for being so presumptuous we're silenced by Madeline appearing at his elbow.

"Has my pudding arrived?" she asks.

"No my darling," he says, stroking her face. "But I'm sure it will."

We plow through our puddings, Jules's easy banter with Madeline keeping the conversation afloat. I will time to slow itself, to give me time to rebuild a bridge between us, but Nathaniel needs to go home, and the moment of goodbye comes all too soon. I risk a hug with Madeline, gratified to feel her small body press back against mine.

"Thank you for the dinosaurs," she says.

"No, thank *you*. I enjoyed it. I never knew that stegosauruses were vegetarians."

"You could go again on your own if you wanted to."

"I'm going to wait until you come back," I tell her. "It won't be the same without you." I look to William, but his face is implacable. "Do you think you will come back soonish?" I say, awkward.

"Right now it's hard to predict," he says, his tone neutral.

"I really hope you'll be in touch when you are," I say, trying to silently communicate how sorry I am that I overstepped the mark.

"I will," he says, stepping forward for a hug that takes me completely off guard. "I'm very glad to have met you," he adds, his words pitched low, lost somewhere in the mess of my hair. Again that strange sense of intimacy, an intimacy I can't quite find a way to quantify—maybe that's because it's located in the silence, in the shadows that gather around what we're prepared to express, an absence so loaded with meaning that it becomes a presence.

"We should go," I say, suddenly needing to swim away from it. I grab Jules's arm and we say our final goodbyes, pushing out into the blustery day and setting off for the tube.

I don't speak for a couple of streets, glad to leave Jules to fuss over Nathaniel. That said, she only lasts five minutes.

"I really like him, Livvy."

I can hear something in her voice that I'm not ready to hear. I wriggle my shoulders, aware how heavy the energy felt between us, but also how disconcertingly weightless I feel now he's gone.

"Yeah, he's lovely."

She pauses, weighing up her words.

"Don't hate me for saying this, but men move quickly. They can't handle the quiet."

"Don't! Just don't," I say, pulling ahead. The fact she's even saying it feels scalding to me. She locks her arm through mine, pulls me into step with her as if we're still little girls and she's that tiny bit bigger. I put my hand on the pram's handle next to hers, and look down at Nathaniel's open, innocent face. "She's barely cold in her grave."

"I know, I know it's too soon, but . . . I've seen the way he looks at you. He might not even know it yet, but there's something about you that he's fascinated by."

"Yeah, Sally." She rolls her eyes, but I plow on. "He wants to know about me and Sally, that's all it is. I think you're right, I don't think it was easy and he can't say it out loud. If he guesses it was hard with me too, then perhaps I'm the nearest thing."

"It's not just that. They're rare, the good ones, and you'll turn around and find he's plugged the gap with some primped up little Park Avenue Princess who didn't have your morals."

"I don't want to plug a gap!" I say, hotly. "He's walking wounded, I think I'm worth a bit more than living my life as someone's emotional aspirin."

"I'm not saying right now, of course not, but . . . when you're talking it's like he's got tunnel vision."

"Rubbish," I say, my cheeks flaring red and hot. "He's just fraight-fully well brought up." I hate myself for mocking him. It feels like a tiny act of betrayal.

"OK, fine—forget it. I never said a word."

"The only thing he can think about is Sally. And I bet he doesn't know the half of it."

The certainty of that statement reverberates through me as I release it into the ether. What did you do, Sally? Just what was it that took you away from here?

February 1996

The next few weeks were some of the happiest I had at university. I felt there was a new mutuality in Sally's and my friendship, like I was less of a lapdog and more of an equal. Sally always raised the tempo of everything; when I was sad, she hugged me like she'd never let go and when I was happy she would make me laugh so hard my ribs would ache. She would sneer at the student bars, scarred by that inauspicious first night—instead she'd insist we dress up to the nines and sink cocktails at fancy hotels. I couldn't remotely afford it, but somehow with Sally rules only existed to be broken. Me and Matt were going well too and, while I didn't feel like I was rewriting the Kama Sutra *with my devilish moves, I was enjoying the new sensation of confidence and womanliness that came from having a real relationship.*

Looking back now, I can see how selfish I was being. Matt got the scraps in one way, the two-for-one cinema night or the

*all-you-can-eat curry on a Tuesday. And it wasn't just mate-
rial, I think I saved my secrets for Sally too, the real exposure
of my heart.*

*I loved her vividness; her descriptions of the passionate
relationships she'd had, the blazing rows she'd had with her
parents in her quest to be exactly who she was destined to be.
I was ripe for transformation, my certainties already shaken
to the core by my family fragmenting: I wonder if a friendship felt like a safer place than a romantic relationship in
which to emerge from the chrysalis? How wrong I was, Matt
and I were never going to be the love of each other's lives, but
he was as safe as an oak, whereas Sally . . . not so much.*

*She needed a special one—a taut, vivid kinship that
brooked no ambiguities or surprises, unless they were sprung
by her. So yes, while I was selfish, I think I subconsciously
knew that I could only keep her burning focus by signing up
to her unspoken code of honor.*

*I chose not to see what tunnel vision I had, just as I chose
not to see what was happening in our little household. Lola
had a boyfriend now, Justin. I'm not sure which came first,
the chicken or the egg, but as Sally's searchlight swung back
toward me, she had begun to retreat into the relationship. I
didn't risk thinking too hard about it.*

*One of those Friday night cocktail quests sticks in my
mind. We were drinking in a rooftop bar, Sally insisting we
had to have a fruit martini in every color, me controlling a
nagging anxiety that my card would get thrown back in my
face. It was low-lit and glamorous and the two of us were
perched on high stools at the long zinc bar, the city spread out
before us like we owned it.*

*"Just get one from the kitchen and stick it in the blender,"
she laughed, insisting to the dubious barman that a kiwi
martini was a real drink.*

"Ignore her," I said, "we can just have raspberry, it's fine."

"We've already had pink," said Sally, waving a hand and giving the barman her most persuasive smile. "Anyway, raspberries are for plebs."

She got her way of course, but when she called for the next two I tried to intervene.

"Seriously, my card's going to bounce out of the window. Let's just have a glass of white." I was so wobbly on my high stool that all I really needed was water.

"Ignore her," she said, an edge to her voice.

But paying for them never became an issue, because two sharp-suited businessmen had slimed their way into the seats next to us and offered to pick up the round.

"Thank you but we're fine," I told them primly, just as Sally accepted.

"On one condition," she added coquettishly. "You have to drink the same." She signaled to the barman to make it four blackcurrant daiquiris.

Of course after that there was no getting rid of them. My guilty conscience went into overdrive thinking about how Matt would feel if he could see us, the pudgier, sweatier specimen weighing up whether or not he'd be making a move. It was Matt's swimming night, a commitment he reverentially honored, giving me and Sally a guaranteed weekend pass. He was so trusting of me, pleased I had a friend good enough to spare him earache about his weekly absence: it never would have occurred to him that I would abuse that trust.

"So what is it you do, girls?" asked the better-looking one, his eyes skimming Sally appraisingly.

"We're students," admitted Sally, though I half expected her to lie.

"So I guess tonight's on us then," said the fox, a carnivorous grin spreading across his chops.

"Well actually . . ." I started, determined to reassert our independence, to wave the white flag of my coupled-up status. Sally kicked me, actually kicked me, and I winced.

"I guess you will!" she agreed, smiling that hundred-watt smile at the fox.

They drove the conversation, laughing loudly at each other's jokes and making eyes at each other over the drinks. I couldn't believe for one moment that Sally really desired him, all he did was drone on about the property deals he did, but you'd never have known it from her rapt expression. Eventually I dragged her off to the toilet.

"What are you playing at?" I asked. "Do you actually like him?"

"He's all right," she said, shrugging.

"Can we go? I'm too drunk already, I've got an essay to do and I'm seeing a concert with Matt tomorrow night."

"Ooh, a concert," said Sally, mocking. Matt loved classical music, which she thought was the ultimate square affectation.

"Look, I can just get the bus. I'm sure his mate will take the hint and you can stay out with Rob."

"No way," she said, her fingers digging into the flesh of my upper arm with unexpected force. "You're my wingman." She turned her gaze on me. "We can't all be loved-up like you."

"But you don't even really like him! Seriously, let's just go . . ." I said, trailing off as I took in her hard look.

"We're having a laugh. We're just having a few drinks, with a couple of randoms. Honestly, Livvy, why do you have to get so uptight all the time?"

I felt stung by that, sensed she was rolling out one of her tests.

"But Matt—"

"Fucking Bagpuss," she said, with a laugh that lacked any kind of warmth. "You're not doing anything wrong. He doesn't own you."

With that she turned on her heel and headed back to the bar, strutting across the room like it was her catwalk. The next time she took a toilet break it was with Rob, and it was an extended one. She came back all hyped and giggly, her eyes like saucers. I was too naive to read the signs; all I wanted to do was get out of there. I'd tried telling Graham I had a boyfriend but it had ignited his interest, not dampened it, like I'd laid down the gauntlet.

We were the last left in the bar, she and Rob talking nineteen to the dozen, me removing Graham's paw from my knee with worrying regularity. Even though I hadn't twigged they were all on drugs, I knew that I felt out of my depth, longed for the dull certainties that I'd spent the last few months shrugging off. Of course I should have left, I don't know why I didn't, but that was Sally's thrall. I tried to peel off when we got downstairs, but the boys had invited us back to Rob's, and Sally's expression made it quite clear what I had to do. I remembered what she'd said in the loos, felt guilty that I had the temerity to have something that she didn't, and before I knew it I was in an unfamiliar apartment with butterflies in my stomach. They could do anything to us, and it'd be our word against theirs. There was no room for denial now, with Rob teasing out fat caterpillars of cocaine across his pretentious glass coffee table.

"Ladies first," he said, eying Sally lasciviously. She didn't need telling, expertly inhaling a line before she handed the rolled up note to me.

"I'm fine," I said, determined that I'd get her to leave once its effects had worn off.

"Just try it," she said, giggly and flushed. "Won't last long. It's like a tequila shot."

I felt so far away from Matt right then, so far from Jules, so far away from everything I thought made me me. Maybe there was no me, just a series of experiences. Whatever my feeble justification was, I found myself taking the note and sniffing up the foul-tasting powder.

The rest of the evening passed in a blur, me drinking and smoking like I never could have imagined. I was flying at first, consumed with euphoria—I told Sally I loved her, gabbled away at Graham and Rob who reacted with cool amusement. "Thank you," I whispered to Sally, the world a Technicolor playground with no worries or responsibilities. It didn't last of course, soon I was consumed with anxiety, exacerbated by Sally disappearing off into Rob's bedroom without a backward glance. I managed to peel Graham's octopus arms off me, falling into a feverish sleep on the horrible leather sofa, my clammy cheek sticking to it like Scotch tape, hoping Sally would come deliver me from my racing thoughts. How could I have done this to Matt? I could never tell him; he was so clean living, would have been disgusted by me taking drugs, let alone taking them with a couple of predatory chancers. Now I'd have to lie to him, forever knowing that the comforting innocence of our relationship was polluted by my dirty secret. My guilt was rolling outward now, taking in my parents, my sister, even my tutors. I'd let them down, let myself down, and for what?

Eventually Sally emerged, shaking me awake as the milky dawn poked its way through the cold metallic blinds. My head was throbbing, my mouth was dry, and a crippling flatness had descended, which felt like it would never lift.

"Come on," whispered Sally. "Let's get out of here."

She linked her arm in mine in the elevator, bound us together.

"That was a proper old school night out!" she giggled.

The walls felt like they were closing in on me, the grayness all-consuming. An old school night for me would have involved a couple of gin and oranges in the local pub, hoping that we wouldn't get IDed. I hated Sally for a second, actually hated her, but then I pinballed my way back to love, the speed and velocity as exhilarating as a fairground ride. I'd made my choices, I had free will. I squeezed back.

"Yeah, it was a laugh."

I didn't even sound like me.

PART TWO

"I loved you first: but afterward your love
Outsoaring mine, sang such a loftier song
As drowned the friendly cooings of my dove.
Which owes the other most? my love was long,
And yours one moment seemed to wax more strong;
I loved and guessed at you, you construed me
And loved me for what might or might not be—
Nay, weights and measures do us both a wrong."

Christina G. Rossetti, *Poems*

CHAPTER EIGHT

IT'S AN ODD THING: I LONGED FOR LIFE TO RETURN to normal, for the frightening strangeness of the last few weeks to release its grip, but now William has slipped back into the shadows, I cannot shake that illogical feeling of weightlessness, that something indefinable is missing. For all his polite insistences, I know that I may never lay eyes on him and Madeline again—the very fact that he let me see through the cracks making it more likely, not less. Perhaps, for all my fighting talk, I never will know what happened to Sally. I used to feel our friendship was an unfinished chapter, but now she's scrawled a postscript across the sky that blasts those feeble questions into oblivion.

I've tried my best not to think about it, to focus instead on work and the unexpected clarity that William gave me. It's funny how often while I've been scrambling to make our rebooted campaign make some kind of sense I've thought of him. His quiet attention gave me a faith in myself, made me risk sticking my neck out, and weirdly, once I led the way with confidence, my reluctant team seemed to sense it and pull together behind me. Maybe the next thing to tackle is that bloody short story, still languishing in the bottom of my handbag.

Here comes Honey, clip-clopping across the office in high heels so trendily ugly that they look orthopedic. She looks strangely flushed.

"Come on. I mean, Mary's ready."

I was sure we had another half hour: I've not seen hide nor hair of Mary all day. A gulp of panic spreads through me at the thought of standing in front of her and singing for my supper—for all of our suppers—but I tell myself not to be such a wuss.

"It's do or die, mate, do or die," says Chris, slamming his laptop shut with an air of grim determination.

"We'll be fine," I say, as Charlotte sweeps past me without a backward glance, as tall, elegant and certain as the Eiffel Tower.

It's hard not to simply stand there and stare into those perfect aquamarine eyes, but Mary swiftly breaks the spell. "Surprise!" she says, giving Flynn Gerrard the easy smile of a woman who wouldn't be intimidated by a rampaging silverback gorilla, let alone an international movie star. His presence is immense, as if he's filling more space than his surprisingly compact frame actually occupies. His dirty-blond hair is doing that just-out-of-bed thing that prevents his heart-stopping good looks from rendering him too perfect, too untouchable. He lounges, limbs flung out like a lazy lion, totally in command of the room, grinning at us as though there's nowhere in the world that he'd rather be right now. We're all trying to mix it up like the cool media professionals we're billed to be, but there's a palpable sizzle of nervous excitement that zings around the crowded boardroom.

"I know you don't have long, so let's just say this is everyone," says Mary, clapping her hands. "Charlotte and Livvy are the women of the hour, so I think we should just kick off. We'll start with Charlotte."

Of course we will, I think, my heart sinking: it's so clear where Mary thinks the killer pitch is lurking. She steps forward, producing the first of the boards with a self-conscious flick of her platinum-blond ponytail. There's a picture of a sad little African girl in raggedy clothes, next to a larger shot of a perfectly uniformed white girl, grinning out into her shiny future. She reminds me of Madeline, but for that wide, joyous smile. Charlotte starts to rattle out facts and figures, life expectancies and happiness indicators, all with an expression of heartfelt gravity, blue Lady Di eyes downcast with the sheer tragedy of it all. Flynn gobbles up every second, straining forward in his seat, his rapt face mirroring her artfully contrived pain. I'm toast. It's not the content—polished, but hardly groundbreaking—it's the slickness of the package. She's gone for that slutty secretary look that men are powerless to resist; a black pencil skirt with a tight white blouse, unbuttoned to the optimum level. There's not a single tremor of self-doubt in her presentation, just that steely focus that dares you to resist. She's reaching the final board now, holding eye contact with the helpless Flynn as if he's just some Joe Schmo who's walked in off the street. I can't help but be impressed.

"This inequality has got to thtop," she says, "and we know you are the man to thtop it. Contrasting our Western child with our African child, thtating those figures in all their thtark truth, making it clear how a small donation can change a life forever . . . let's move the public the way my team and I have been moved. I want to perthonally thank you for opening my eyes to how lucky I am. How lucky all of us are. Without you we'd still be living in ignoranth." She holds his gaze, risks a tremulous smile, and then sits down.

Flynn pauses as if he's too emotional to speak. "Wow," he says eventually, emotion making his Irish brogue more noticeable. "I want to thank *you*," he continues, his piercing eyes boring into her. "You've made it even more real to me, even more vital I do this."

They sit there staring at each other like they're having some kind of virtual compassion shag until eventually Mary breaks up the party.

"Lots to think about there," she says, smiling approvingly. "Now let's see what Team Two have got to say for themselves."

I stand up, my legs shaking, trying to replicate that irresistible connection that Charlotte managed to seduce Flynn into. Unfortunately he can't seem to take his eyes off her cleavage; is it me or has she somehow managed to ergonomically burst open another button on her slim-fitting blouse? And how is it that she manages to pull off that unsquarable circle of being both skinny and busty—I hope they're horrible, silicone melons of death that lose all appeal close up.

"Um . . ." I start, utterly thrown by his lack of focus. "We considered a print campaign, but then we decided to mix it up a bit," I say, looking to Chris and the laptop. Charlotte shoots me an almost imperceptible glare. Chris is such a doofus; he fumbles around, too starstruck to find the right file. "Bear in mind this is a rough edit," I add apologetically. "But what we felt was that people needed to see the issues in motion to stop these people feeling like hypothetical victims."

We've had to look for bits of documentary footage on YouTube, and it does all feel a bit DIY and clumsy. "This is Susan," it starts, with images of a girl we found. The images don't entirely work with our voice-over, inexpertly recorded by me, which tells us about her life of extreme hardship and her descent into prostitution. Then we turn the story around, describe what a difference the charity could make, how it might change the course of her destiny. I study Flynn as it plays out, but his reaction is so much harder to gauge than it was when he had Charlotte delivering her message up close and personal. Maybe he's creeped out by Chris's insistence that we put "Every Breath You Take" over the top of it, which is nothing more than an ode to stalking. The film finishes, and I stand up, looking between him and Mary.

"These women deserve to live a life that's more than a foregone conclusion," I say, a surge of energy running through me. I do care about this. It's not just about winning some stupid competition. "We should all be allowed the chance to choose our life, not have it foisted upon us. Thank you," I add, hurriedly sitting down, hoping I haven't sounded too raggedly emotional; Charlotte's version of caring was so expertly designed.

"That was great," says Flynn, much more businesslike than he was with Charlotte. "Wow-ee, this feels like one of the hardest decisions of my life." What, harder than leaving the mother of your two children for your makeup artist? I think meanly, then try and erase all the editions of

Heat I've read in the dentist's waiting room from my mind. "Shall we take five?" he says, running his hand through his tousled hair.

"Sounds like a great idea," says Mary brightly. Soon a big box of pastries has appeared, as well as trays of coffee drinks from across the street.

"I shouldn't," says Flynn, laughing, as he reaches for a brownie. "My trainer will have me up on charges."

"Hard to resist though, isn't it?" says Mary, reaching for one too, flirtatious in a way that doesn't cost her any status. She doesn't mean any of it, least of all the brownie—she subsists entirely on carrot sticks and hummus—but she knows exactly how to make him feel at home. I don't know if it's because he sees me spying on them, but before I know it, Flynn is loping toward me, that lazily sexy smile playing around his perfect mouth.

"Thank you so much," he says, holding my gaze. Don't blush, don't blush, I implore myself, but the crimson tide rolls across my hot cheeks unbidden.

"No, thank you," I say, terrified I'm going to be afflicted with some kind of terrible celebrity Tourette's and end up asking him if he really did shag that married A-list actress in a jacuzzi.

"I'm just so impressed," he continues, too polite to mention that I look like a traffic light. "To pull together something like that at such short notice, fuse all those facts into something coherent . . . I just couldn't do it." He shrugs in mock defeat.

"Of course you could!"

"No-oo, I'm telling you, I couldn't. There's a few things I'm pretty good at"—I try not to think about the jacuzzi—"but plenty more I'm a to-tal dunce at." He looks into my eyes as he says it, almost imploring me to believe him, his Irish brogue drizzled over his words like molten honey. Luckily Mary sails over, brownie subtly discarded by a cheese plant, before I can make even more of a fool of myself.

"The moment of truth," he says. "You'll have to excuse me. Shall we have a huddle?" he asks Mary.

"You read my mind," she says, playfully turning on her heel and leading him toward her office. As soon as they've gone the whole room erupts into a totally uncool frenzy of celebrity jungle fever. Only Charlotte keeps her cool, small white hands clenched around her coffee cup tight enough to cave it in, an expression of grim determination on her face. I look at the glittering jewel on her finger, find myself wondering what it means to her: much as I loathe her I also find her oddly fascinating. She's like some exotic animal nearing extinction; fascinating to observe, but only if you can maintain a safe distance. Does that ring give her a sense of confidence, a feeling that someone is holding her dear, wherever she is or whatever it is she's doing? I hope that's what it would do for me, but maybe that's the kind of rosy fantasy you can only weave out of romantic thin air. It's hard to imagine her in her downtime, slobbing around in front of *Come Dine With Me* in a pair of sweats, arguing over the remote control: it feels like work is her own unique version of oxygen, vital to her very survival. What does her kind of vulnerability look like?

It's ten minutes or so before Mary and Flynn reappear, conspiratorial and giggly. My stomach balls up like a frightened hedgehog, and I cast an anxious look around my team. I led them over the cliff, took a risk on something we didn't have time to hone and polish. I wanted to believe that substance could triumph over style, but I fear it was wishful thinking.

"Gather, people," says Mary. "These are exciting times."

"Certainly are," agrees Flynn.

"Head girls, come to the top of the table," says Mary. "It goes without saying that both presentations were exemplary." I look at her, desperate to believe she really means it, that it's more than spin. She reads it off me, smiles. "They really were," she says, and my insides liquefy with gratitude—I wish her approval didn't mean as much as this. "There was an immediacy and slickness about Charlotte's presentation that was hugely impressive."

James is coming to meet me at home in time to celebrate or commiserate, but we both knew what was more likely. I'm so lost in my own sense of doom that I actually miss the moment of truth.

". . . so despite the more DIY aspects to the presentation—"

"—though let's face it, crafts are so in right now," interjects Flynn.

"—we ultimately felt that Livvy's presentation had the edge."

"We won?" I croak.

"You did," says Mary, beaming, and I dance a little internal jig at her visible pride in me.

"Oh my God," I shriek, grinning like a loon at my jubilant team. "Thanks so much." Flynn's smiles are shot through with a sobriety, reminding me a little too late that too much crowing is inappropriate. I risk a look at Charlotte, expecting her to shoot me daggers, but she's far too clever.

"Well done, Livvy," she says, rosebud mouth perfectly held. "Very imprethive." She looks to Flynn. "The important thing is the charity," she says, smiling prettily. "And if there's anything more I can do to help, please know that you've got me on speed dial."

I grab my team and hug them, stupidly close to tears.

"Thank you so much," I tell them.

Chris smiles distractedly, unable to drag his eyes away from the Oscar nominee in our midst. He's going to be dining out on this for months.

"No, thank you," says Rosie, beaming. "You were amazing up there."

"Really?"

"Yeah, have to say you knocked it out the park," agrees Chris.

"You were different somehow," says Rosie, her head cocked, considering me. "You, but with added value."

After a bit more backslapping everyone starts to disperse. I'm late for James, I realize, but as I'm working out how best to say goodbye to Flynn, Mary grabs me.

"Flynn wants the three of us to go and raise a glass. I assume you can do it?"

How can I not be? Besides, I'm far too uncool not to secretly thrill at the prospect of a drink with a bona fide movie star.

"Course," I say, still flooded with warmth and gratitude. "I just need to make one call."

"Be quick," says Mary sharply. "He's not a man who's used to being kept waiting."

I take my phone out to the corridor, hoping James won't mind me dragging him across town for nothing. I'm about to dial when I see a missed call: William. My heart jumps— what could he possibly be ringing to say? His message is brief, to the point, his tone even as he asks me to call him whenever is convenient. I can't help myself, I know that I'll worry about it until I know why it is that he's rung. I try him once, and get a busy signal. I should just let it go, but instead I go to the toilet to give myself a few more minutes, then try again.

"Olivia. That was prompt."

"Is there anything wrong?" I ask, then curse myself for the stupidity of the question. "I mean, has anything more happened this week?"

"I was calling for two reasons. Firstly to find out how you fared in your presentation."

I can't believe he remembered it was today. That he not only remembered but that he took the time to call— although I don't know what reason two is yet.

"We won!" I say, unable to squash my excitement. "We actually won!"

"Congratulations," he says, pleasure and warmth rippling through his voice. "Richly deserved, I'm sure."

"Thank you."

"And secondly, I wanted to ask if you were free on the eleventh? So four weeks next Tuesday?"

"Um, I don't see why I wouldn't be."

My eye catches Mary, glaring at me through the smoked glass of the conference room as she yanks on her coat, distinctly unamused by how long I've been.

"I have to come over for a few days and there's an official dinner that night. I thought it might give us some more time to talk."

"Of course. I'll keep it free."

We exchange a hurried goodbye and I hang up, oddly disoriented. It's lovely to hear him, to know that he hasn't evaporated from my life, and yet . . . What is it that he's asking me for?

"I'm so sorry," I say, rushing back in, simultaneously texting James an apology.

"No sweat," says Flynn, with an easy smile that leaves Mary with no choice but to pretend that she doesn't mind. She's overreacting, but then, I shouldn't have hit her Achilles' heel, her need to feel that she is in complete control of anything that happens within these four walls. "My driver's downstairs." He gives me that self-deprecating moue. "Don't look at me like that, Livvy, they laid it on—I'd be happy with a cab."

"I wasn't looking—" It's hard to know what's a joke. "It sounds perfect."

"And I need a drink," says Mary, hand whisking through the air to snatch up her handbag.

I'm expecting us to go back to his hotel—after all, I'm becoming quite a dab hand at five-star etiquette—but instead the driver heads for Flynn's penthouse on the corner of Hyde Park. Flynn rides up front, asking the graying cockney about his myriad grandchildren, all of whom he seems to have an encyclopedic knowledge of, while Mary permafrosts me in the back seat. I venture a couple of conversational openers, but they fall on deaf, diamond-laden ears, so that by the end of the journey I'm feeling like the world's worst employee, worse than that rogue trader who bankrupted Barings.

"Thanks, John," says Flynn, racing around to open both doors for us. "See you at six!"

"No rest for the wicked," laughs John.

"You're not wrong," agrees Flynn, tapping a code into the door. A couple of flashbulbs go off, making me jump. "Just ignore them," he says.

"I don't know how you stand it," says Mary, when we're in the elevator. "You must feel like a hunted animal."

"Aah, it's part of the territory," says Flynn dismissively. "This job's got enough perks. I can't be complaining."

I'm warming to him, I can't help it. He's both how I imagined a film star to be, and also not, with the nots in all the right places.

"Let's see what's on ice," he says, leading us into his incredible pad. I try not to gawk even though the floor space of the living room is almost the size of my entire apartment. Big plate-glass windows give a panoramic view over the park, and I have to stop myself pressing my nose against them to see how far I can see. The room is quite bare and minimalist, but every carefully chosen piece of furniture screams of expensive good taste.

"It's gorgeous," I croak. "How long have you lived here?"

"Oh no, sweetheart, it's not mine!" laughs Flynn. "It's just another rental. I'm nothing but a jumped-up gypsy when all's said and done. Now, what we thinking—I'm wondering if we should treat ourselves to some bubbles?"

"Sounds like a marvelous idea," says Mary, all bonhomie. I risk smiling my agreement at her, but she stares blankly back.

"Coming right up," says Flynn, uncorking a bottle of Veuve Clicquot with a satisfying pop. "Cheers," we cry, and as Mary meets my eye she gives me a tiny smile. Finally, finally, the sun comes back out.

"To a fabulous collaboration," she says. "Honestly, this is the kind of project I came into the industry for. We're going to have so much fun."

"And I just want to say thank you again," I add, my voice embarrassingly quavery. "I can't believe you've both given me this incredible opportunity." I look to Mary. "I won't let you down."

"Honestly, Livvy, we're not going to war," she says, giggling.

The next hour is almost fun (note the almost). It's certainly exciting, but there's a knot in my stomach throughout, and it's highly dangerous that I'm infused with all this additional information about Flynn from the patchwork of lurid press stories I've absorbed by trash osmosis. The immaculate apartment shows no sign of the two, or could it be three, children he's meant to have, and I'm not sure whether he's still with the home-wrecking makeup artist. I get a bit more clarity when I ask him how long he's in town for.

"Only another couple of months, thank God. Can't be away from the kids longer than that or they'll forget what I look like! And I can't be flying them around the world now they're in school. Wanna see some pics?"

Soon Mary and I are making the appropriate noises as he scrolls through his iPhone showing us shots of Edith, Stanley, and Zara, an African girl he adopted after a long shoot in Tanzania. Honestly, someone needs to tell Paris Hilton how last year Chihuahuas are. He stares intently at the tiny images, like he can't drag his gaze away.

"Sorry. We're meant to have joint custody, but I'm away so much . . ."

Mary cocks her head sympathetically.

"I've always believed with children it's about quality, not quantity. I'm sure they love having you around when you are there."

I think of her perfect mini-me daughters, catapulted out of her womb long after you'd expect to hit the fertility jackpot; the cakes she brings in, baked with them on a Sunday, their provenance declared a little too loudly, the splotchy mess of paint, with *Mommy* scrawled underneath that's framed, pride of place, in her office. It's hard to know what it translates into behind closed doors.

"I hope so," says Flynn bleakly. "Ach, enough. Do you have kids, Livvy?"

"I don't, no," I say, feeling an unexpected stab of sadness at the fact.

"Any likely contenders in the frame?" asks Mary, giving my arm a friendly squeeze.

They both look at me expectantly, like I'm on stage.

"No, not exactly. I mean, no, no there isn't."

"There's something she's not telling us!" says Flynn. "Who's the lucky fella?"

"There is no lucky fella, there really isn't," I insist, so flustered that I've adopted some kind of dodgy simpatico Irish accent.

"It's life's great challenge, isn't it?" says Flynn, smiling sadly. "Finding someone makes it worth signing up for the long haul."

"But you must have your pick," I say. "I mean, women literally throw themselves at you."

"How so?" he says, sounding suddenly less friendly.

"I mean just generally, women . . ." Flynn and Mary are both staring at me now, unsmiling statues. How is what I've said so wrong? Perhaps he thinks I'm talking about him dumping his wife. "You're like a proper heartthrob."

Oh God, now I've made him sound like a piece of meat rather than a serious actor: I should probably cut my losses and hurl myself through that plate-glass window.

"Very kind of you to say," he says, with a cold smile. "Now I don't wanna be a bad host, but I'm afraid these lines won't learn themselves."

I spend the entire tube journey cursing myself, going over and over what I said until I feel like I'm going mad. The words themselves don't sound that bad, and I know when I tell James he'll think I'm being ridiculous, but they somehow curdled and mutated into something disastrous when they reached the outside air. Mary didn't mention it when we said goodbye, she even gave me a quick, staccato kiss on each cheek, but I could feel the waves of disapproval quivering off her.

When I get through the door the lights are on, but there's pure silence, despite the fact that James can't stand to not have the TV on. He's sitting, mute, on the sofa and I steel myself for a barrage of abuse about my flaky behavior.

"I'm really sorry . . . it was completely crap of me, I know you rushed to get there . . ."

James looks up, an absent look on his face.

"It's fine, Livvy, no sweat."

I perch on the other end of the sofa, baffled by the odd, pregnant silence.

"Have you been here all night?"

"Not exactly, no."

Why is he throwing out these wispy little puffs of conversation? I jab him in the ribs.

"Earth to James, earth to James. Can you believe I won? I actually won? You're two degrees of separation from Scarlett Johannsson. Allegedly."

He shakes himself out of his weird torpor.

"Go, Livvy! I'll get you a glass."

He comes back, pouring my wine with great ceremony. He's looking particularly handsome this evening, a green V-necked T-shirt slung on over his jeans, his skin a lovely caramel color.

"Cheers, Big Ears. What's he like then?"

"Flynn? He seemed really normal, but then . . . I think I might have really fucked up. And I don't want to, it's the first thing in ages that I've felt properly into, like it could actually mean something."

I'm about to launch into the whole story, but I can feel I've got no audience. James has gone back to staring into space, his hand stroking one of the sofa cushions. I might as well be speaking Estonian.

"I dunno, it sounded like you were amazing."

"I haven't even told you—"

He interrupts me.

"This weird thing happened, Livvy, but I don't want you to get all uptight about it."

"Weird how?" I say, trying to keep my voice light.

"I met Charlotte."

"Charlotte?"

"Yeah, this—this girl"—he says it in a way that has "totally hot" in brackets—"came downstairs, and I asked if she knew where you were, and she just—she looked like she was going to cry. And then we ended up going for a drink. Like I said, it was weird."

"You know she's engaged?"

"Yeah, no, yeah it's fine," he says, unconvincing. It's not what he says, it's the way he says it. He's always ironic or laconic when he talks about girls, like they're characters in a film he can walk out of any time he wants. Now he sounds like he's got trapped on the other side of the screen.

"So it can't go anywhere."

"Yeah, course. She's just nice. I liked her."

"Oh really?" I say, irritation mounting. It's perilous, the way we live and it's times like this that I remember that fact. "Because I don't find her that nice. You know that."

"She's probably different outside work. More of a laugh."

"That's definitely different," I say, hating how mealy-mouthed I sound.

"I've gotta go to bed," he says, standing up. He stretches, yawns, relaxed about the way his worked-out stomach unfurls itself from under his T-shirt. "It'll all be fine, you know, it'll blow over. And well done!"

"Thanks," I say, hoping my voice sounds the way I meant it to sound.

I sit there for a while, after he's gone, trying not to give in to paranoia. These days it's hard to know what tomorrow will look like until it arrives.

MARCH 1996

Sally was yanking packets out of a carrier bag, thumping them down triumphantly as if she'd gone out with a quiver of arrows and hunted for them.

"Bread and butter pudding, chicken quesadillas, crispy potato skins, margherita pizza, chocolate chip ice cream, and no salad."

She ground to a halt, face flushed, as me and Lola eyeballed the haul in awe. We were students, Marks and Spencer's was a luxury beyond the dreams of avarice, but Sally seemed to have cleaned it out. It was good to see her eating at least, often she seemed to subsist on little more than Ryvita and Philadelphia, but recently she'd swung the other way, loading up on stodge and snacking on high-calorie treats in the in-between times. She'd even put on some weight—I knew her too well to mention it, even though I thought it suited her. She looked too gaunt sometimes, taut and wired.

"Oh yeah, and three bottles of cava with some orange juice. That should take care of the vitamins."

We'd come to Filey, a Yorkshire seaside town, for a girls' weekend. It sounded like such a grown-up idea, but when Sally had heard about Lola's aunt's cottage she'd become fixated on the trip. We seemed to have become more of a trio again recently, with Sally going out of her way to invite Lola along when we went out. I liked Lola, I really did— there was something solid about her, a trustworthiness that made me feel like I knew where I stood—but what I didn't always like was being one third of a three. I seemed to have turned into a tracker dog, my whole being trained to react to the tiniest movement in the terrain: I was constantly on high alert, watching for the slightest shift in the dynamic between us, or for one of Sally's legendary mood changes.

Sally had already popped the first bottle of cava, even though we were still muffled up in our coats. She was rootling through the kitchen cupboards, slamming the doors like a one-woman tornado.

"You've got to let us pay you back," I said, anxious, imagining the huge receipt. Sally gave an airy wave.

"Forget it."

"If you're looking for glasses, I know where they are," said Lola territorially. "Just wait a minute and I'll find them for you."

I stiffened, but Sally was oblivious. She'd found them now, filled each one to the brim.

"Cheers, girls!" she cried, eyes bright. "This is gonna be great."

"We can go on a proper country walk tomorrow," said Lola. She always had such a heartiness about her, a ruddy good health.

"Didn't bring any proper sneakers," said Sally, quick as a flash.

"I've got to do a couple of hours of work first thing," I said, simultaneously. Sally looked at me, hurt in her eyes. I smiled at her, reminded her with my look that I'd warned her I had an essay to finish. It was for a Renaissance poetry course that I was secretly loving. I reckoned I might get a first for it if I put the work in.

"You do know the first year doesn't even count, don't you?" said Sally. *"Long as you pass."*

I nearly told her the truth; that I wanted to savor and appreciate every last drop, had no interest in scraping through.

"Just give me an hour," I said.

"Say I'm a pathetic geek," she said, raising her glass, and looking at me admonishingly.

"I'm a pathetic geek," I parroted, and Sally smashed her glass into mine, satisfied.

The house was ridiculously cold, even after Lola had fired up the ancient heating system, and we went to look at the bedrooms with our teeth chattering. Sally made hers gnash together like we were walking across the North Pole and we all laughed, the slightly depressing quality instantly dissolved. Lola swung open the first door onto a plain but cozy little room with a bunk bed pushed against the wall.

"Me and my brother used to sleep in here," she said, smiling. *"He'd throw water bombs off the top bunk."*

"It's lovely," I said, but the other two had already gone next door. *"And this is the maa-ster bedroom,"* said Lola, revealing a room that was indeed much more impressive. It had a big

double bed, a cream carpet that squished underfoot, and a bay window that would afford a lovely sea view in the morning. "I mean there's no reason why I should have it," she said, looking at Sally. "You bought all that food . . ."

"Tell you what," said Sally, quick as a flash. "Me and Livvy can double up in here. Then you get a room to yourself still. Your childhood bedroom," she added, smiling.

Lola paused a second, and looked at me. A bit of me would have preferred the safety of a single bunk—I'd never shared beds with my girlfriends at home and it felt almost transgressive, like it could go somewhere I couldn't quite name—but another part of me felt special, like Sally had anointed me. I wondered for a fleeting second if Matt would mind, but then I dismissed the thought as ridiculous. "Whatever you want, Lo."

It was settled. We went back downstairs, loaded the oven with goodies, and ripped open the jiffy bag overflowing with chick-flicks that Sally's mom had sent from home. They hadn't really been my thing growing up—my bookish friends and I had sneered at them as something for the trendies, so I'd always favored Hitchcock films or something with Joan Crawford sweeping about in a glorious gown—but I didn't admit it. In fact, silly girl that I was, even though I'd never even seen Pretty Woman, I pretended I loved it too. Lola was way more practical than us, so while Sally cued up the tape, she set about building a fire, and soon we were glued to the film, supper on our knees, toasty and warm. Now all I had to do was watch Sally out of the corner of my eye, so I could time my whoops of recognition to chime with hers.

"This'll be what it'll be like when we get a place of our own," said Lola happily, her arm shooting out from under a rug to pour herself more wine.

Sally had recently announced that the three of us should share a house next year, and Lola had leaped on the idea. I was more cautious, but I hadn't voiced my worries. They would either sound like a petty dig at Lola, or, infinitely worse, an attack on Sally. Besides, I reasoned, the way Lola and Justin were going, she might end up living with him. There was something destined about them, even then—they had an ease, a synchronicity—Lola wasn't one for grand declarations, but she glowed. When the phone rang during Pretty Woman she dived for it. knowing it would be Justin. "Want me to pause it?" said Sally, in a tone that made it clear she should make it quick, but Lola batted her hand like it was an irrelevance and scooted out of the room to pick up the line in the kitchen. I thought it was only me who could hear the secret language that Sally layered under her words, but looking back I think Lola heard it just as clearly. She simply had the good sense to let it wash straight down the drain.

Sally rolled mascara-laden eyes at me as I popped the receiver down.

"This is fun."

"She can't help herself," I said, and Sally snorted with laughter, hearing my comment as an acidic aside, when what it actually was awe. Lola's open-hearted adoration of Justin was deeply sweet, so sweet that I envied it. Matt had hesitantly told me he loved me on Valentine's Day, like he'd reached the appropriate page in his romance manual, and I'd sort of said it back. "Me too," I'd muttered, because I didn't know how to tell him that I wasn't sure what I felt. I wished for the first time in my life that love was an exact science, that you could bubble it up in a test tube and drink down the draft. I wanted to be with him, felt deeply fond of him, but I didn't feel that obsessive excitement I felt around James, like I'd do anything *to wring out a few more minutes with him, like the rest of the world could turn to rubble and I wouldn't even notice. But was that real, or a fantasy version of love that could only exist when the relationship took place in my fevered imagination? Looking at Lola I could see there was a third way, a version that rendered both of mine fatally flawed. I vowed to concentrate really hard on all the things about Matt I liked and admired in the hope it would jump-start my heart: perhaps love could be a choice, rather than the gift bestowed by fate that I'd always believed it to be.*

Lola came back eventually, full of apologies, her face flushed. "Would it be weird if he came up tomorrow night?" she said. It would be weird, no question, but I could see how much she wanted it, and it was, after all, her family's house.

"Course," I said.

"Whatever you want," said Sally, her words clipped, her eyes fixed on the remote control.

"Honestly, girls, tell me if it is. It's just he was meant to be going to a gig, and now he isn't, and he'd love to see it. You can keep the room, we'll sleep down here . . ."

"It is a little bit weird," I started, "but it's honestly fine. I mean—"

"It's settled," said Sally, cutting straight across us both. She pressed play very deliberately. "Eyes forward."

We got into bed, me dressed in thick, mismatched pajamas topped off with a pair of woolly socks, Sally in an oyster-colored baby doll nightie that looked like a major fire hazard. The concept of dressing down was not one she ever dallied with. She was holding cotton wool pads to her panda eyes, soaking off the last of the black gunk.

"You're not going to spring a Bagpuss surprise on me are you?" she whispered. "Not packing any emergency Whiskas?"

I giggled, then felt a bit sad. I wished that I couldn't bear forty-eight hours apart.

"No Whiskas," I said.

"Thank Christ for that," said Sally, continuing in her stage whisper. I was sure Lola wasn't asleep yet. I imagined her, lying in that single bunk, wondering what we were saying about her. She slid under the covers, looked up at me. "What's up?"

"With Francesco," I started, making sure to speak at a normal volume so I didn't make Lola paranoid; Francesco was Sally's Spanish older man, "was it like you couldn't live without him?"

She looked at me, sucking up every single bit of it without asking a single thing. That's what I loved about her: it felt like she was the all-seeing eye, like she knew every scrap of me better than I ever could.

"You thinking about James, yeah?"

I nodded sheepishly.

"I was fucking crazy about him," she said, speaking normally again. A naughty grin crossed her face and I knew exactly what she was remembering. Matt and I mainly had sex with the lights off, a companionable exchange of orgasms followed by an affectionate postcoital cuddle. She stared at me, knowing just as well what I was thinking about, even though I'd never betrayed Matt by opening our bedroom door. Not until now at least.

I felt like we were back in the bubble, floating off somewhere high and far away. We talked and talked, like the well was bottomless. I told her how much the ghost of James stalked my relationship, even when we hadn't spoken in weeks and then, as she heard it how I wanted it to be heard, confessed my bigger, darker fear that my parents' awful marriage had infected me somehow, like an airborne virus, fatally altering my relationship DNA. Sally laughed, but kindly this time, found the words of comfort I needed to hear, then told me what she'd learned about love from her romantic misadventures. It was a well-spun story, no more than a beguiling narrative, but there in the darkness it sounded like ancient truths written on parchment. Every time one of us stopped, the other would pipe up with something else that just had to be said, or a stupid joke that had to be told, until eventually even the birds joined our conversation. There was no way I'd be getting up bright and early to study.

It was time we got some sleep. She rolled over toward me, planted her lips on my cheek, her body momentarily pressed against mine through the thin, synthetic fabric. She lingered there for a couple of seconds.

"Night, Livvy," she said, her voice soft and thick, laced with something I hadn't heard before. I knew I didn't know it, but I didn't know what it was.

"Goodnight," I said, a quaver in my voice.

I don't remember much else about that weekend.

CHAPTER NINE

THE BACK OF MY HAND IS A CRIMSON, STICKY MESS. Twice I've applied a coat of lipstick, twice I've sloughed it off like it's laced with arsenic. I look at my pallid face in the harsh yellowy glow of the strip lights that illuminate the office loos: not flattering. Not that it matters: it feels so wrong to be making myself look pretty—to be making myself look more alive, in a way—so that I can slip into an evening that should belong to no one but Sally. Right now I'd do anything to get out of it. I scrabble around in my handbag for my phone.

"Hi."

"Where are you?" says Jules. "You sound like you're underwater."

"I wish I was." I can feel my voice rising, that petulance I sometimes get with my big sister. "Why did you say that stupid thing to me when we went to the museum?"

"Because sometimes I've got a really big mouth." She's not laughing at me, but she's soft with it. I feel my heart start to slow, the tide of my fear receding a little.

"Yeah, you have. Now I'm feeling totally paranoid. What if he thinks that's what I'm doing? Hanging around waiting to pounce?"

I rub at my lips again, making sure every last trace of color comes unstuck. I think of that high-pitched vibrancy that Sally had, like life was an extreme sport that she could play better than any of us; how can it have been simply ripped away from her? I can't even bear to consider the other option, the idea that the game had become such an endurance test that she was the one who blew the whistle on it. Is the piquancy of it not just in the tragedy but also in the insane, egotistical thought that I somehow could have stopped it? As though somewhere inside me my twenty-something self still endures, like a Russian doll held inside the shell of a larger one, stubbornly insistent that she is the one person who could have dragged Sally from the rapids that were pulling her down? I think of Madeline, the greatest casualty of all of this, marooned on the floor of the gift shop, and sharp tears start to prickle. I'm really not sure I should be doing this. I've no right to this grief; the last thing I want to do is ask him to comfort me.

"He invited you!" says Jules, pulling me back to the moment.

He did, it's true, but since then I've only heard from him once, via a businesslike e-mail that arrived two weeks ago asking me to meet him on the steps of the Royal Courts of Justice in—I look at my watch—thirty minutes' time. Oh God.

"This is the last time I'm seeing him," I say, meaning it. It's too complicated, too hard, the danger of doing more harm than good too great. It was all very well feeling sentimental when I thought I'd never lay eyes on them again: now the reality is here I'm fairly sure I can't handle it.

"Just get through tonight. You'll be fine. Call me from the loos again if you have to. We'll have a debrief tomorrow."

I hang up, pull down the dress I'm wearing, a shapeless black cotton thing that's normally banished to the furthest recesses of my wardrobe where it belongs, and go out in search of a taxi.

I'm a few minutes late, and I scramble out of the taxi, thrusting a note at the driver, anxiety turned back up to maximum. He's standing by the impressive stone archway of the building, the collars of his camel cashmere coat turned up to take the edge off the biting wind. I feel an illogical surge of guilt for abandoning him there, this almost stranger, waiting in the cold for me to deign to make an appearance. He doesn't see me approach.

"I'm so sorry," I say, touching his arm.

He turns, looks down at me. For a second it's almost as though he's surprised to see me there.

"No need to apologize," he says, turning on a smile that I sense requires some effort. "It's lovely to see you again. Very decent of you to submit yourself to this."

He leans down to kiss me on each cheek, and I feel a blush rising up in response to the almost imperceptible brush of his lips. I try and breathe out my paranoia, find my center. I take in the impressive building, steeped in history, fiery torches blazing at the inner entrance. There's a fierceness about the welcome it offers.

"Are you ready?" I ask him, hoping that he hears in my voice that if he wasn't, if he wanted to turn tail and run,

I'd run with him. I somehow think there's a glimmer of recognition, a second where he strains toward my almost imperceptible offer, but then his sense of duty reasserts its iron grip.

"As I'll ever be." He looks down at me. "If you find it too ghastly for words I won't be offended if you make an early exit. Sally always despised this kind of thing."

A little ripple of shock runs through me, making it hard to breathe, the past tense still so brutal.

"No way," I tell him. "It's one for all and all for one."

One and one and one makes three.

"Shall we?" he says.

We arrive into the genteel scrum of a drinks reception, held in an elegant, high-ceilinged function room. It's dove gray, with elegant white cornices, a warm light shed by the heavy chandeliers that overhang us. I take off my coat and pass it to an attendant, realizing as I do so how badly I've pitched my frock. It looks like I should be picnicking in a park, while all the other women are swathed in great puffs of taffeta and velvet, like they've knocked off a ball gown from the curtains hanging in their stately homes. I knew in my heart it was wrong, but the wrongness is born out of respect, not disrespect. I long to tell William so, but he's too distracted to notice, surveying the scene with something that looks like trepidation. I wish that I'd gone further outside, made absolutely sure that he knows that he's not alone with his grief. I spot a few people shooting darting glances in our direction, looking away before they're duty-bound to come over and acknowledge what's happened. There's a few double-takes at the fact he's with a woman, but he seems utterly oblivious to it. I sense a certain innocence about him, that same innocence that refuses to allow for the possibility that Sally could have ended her own life. Because he is a million miles away from thinking of any woman but the wife he's buried, I'm sure he imagines that no one else would jump to such a sordid conclusion.

"Let me find you a drink," he says, but as he moves away he's assailed by a frightening brunette, hair lacquered into a rigid helmet. She must be about my age, but you can tell instantly that she's the kind of person who came out of the womb middle-aged, most likely clad in a padded water-proof vest.

"William, my deepest commiserations," she booms. The fact that her voice is indeed so deep almost makes me want to giggle. I keep wanting to laugh at the most inappropriate moments, the pressure searching for release.

"Thank you very much," he replies automatically. "And thank you both for your card. It was much appreciated." He looks over to me, but she runs on before he can introduce us.

"Such a shock," she says. "I was saying to Rory, is it worse to watch someone suffer, but have time to say goodbye, or have them taken in an instant but know they didn't endure too much?"

"I don't think I could answer that question," says William evenly, as I try not to gasp at the sheer insensitivity of it. Now Rory appears, a squat, gingery character with a bald patch that he's attempting to conceal with a fierce commitment to side-combing.

"So sorry," he says, awkwardly clapping William's shoulder. "Such a shock."

"Yes, yes it was," says William. "This is Olivia, she was a great friend of Sally's. She's been very kind to Madeline and me over the last couple of months."

The bad-hair couple turn in unison, finally forced to acknowledge my hovering presence, taking a long hard look at me before they deign to address me.

"I'm Trixie, pleasure to meet you," says helmet-head, hand shooting out like she's launching an attack. She gives me a long look, woman to woman, exuding suspicion from every pore.

"Hi," I say, cringing.

"Rory," says Rory abruptly, with a stiff nod, before settling in to stare a bit more. He turns back to William. "So I gather you're here a few more weeks? Waiting for the dust to settle?"

"In a manner of speaking," says William, grabbing a waiter and pulling a couple of glasses from his tray, his hand shaking as he passes me one. For a few weeks? I look at him, surprised, and he gives a small nod, acknowledging the truth of the fact. I can't quite work out if it feels like a good thing or a bad thing. "If you'll excuse us, I've just spotted Graham Fox over there. I must just go and have a brief word."

He draws away and I follow, Trixie's beady little eyes boring into my back. I'm half expecting him to duck out, to need a breather to discharge the awkwardness of that horrible encounter, but it turns out Graham Fox really does exist. He's a little less charmless than the BHC but he's hardly a bundle of laughs. He deals with the messy business of Sally's death with a couple of brief sentences, then moves to grilling William on various incomprehensible transatlantic power wrangles.

As I stand there, shifting from foot to foot, I'm suddenly blindsided by a bolt of grief so much less complicated than what I've felt so far. Perhaps it's because Sally feels so close right now, as if I haven't taken her place here, but squeezed in tight next to her. I miss you, I think. I miss the fact that you would have found these people even more gruesome than I do, that if you were here we'd be trying to score as much free champagne as we could, getting increasingly, inappropriately hysterical at the horsey wives and their terrible outfits. I miss you—I always did, even when I hated you. Did you miss me?

I'm more than ready to sit down by the time they summon us through for dinner, having spent the best part of an hour skulking in William's shadow like a ghost at the feast. He's tried to include me, but everyone he's spoken to has approached the conversation like a bullet-pointed meeting, and I haven't made the agenda. I may be being an inverted snob, but they've also made me feel like some kind of serf. Did Sally keep that estuary twang she had? I can't imagine her without it, and I certainly can't imagine it landing well in this cloistered, privileged enclave. I hope she stuck it right back to them.

William pulls out my chair for me. "Are you surviving?" he asks.

"Are *you* surviving?" I ask.

"Yes, thank you," he says, reaching for the menu, and I feel an unexpected stab of anger. How can he be so calm, so measured? This is hideous, these people are hideous, their sympathy so bloodless. "May I pour you some wine?"

"Sure."

My anger softens as I watch him endure a carbon copy exchange about Sally's death with some emotionally constipated suit that's seated to his left. I don't think I could manage it, if I were walking in his polished, expensive brogues, but I can see that it's exactly what's expected of him, that there's no choice, even though there is. Is this his privileged, twisted version of destiny, a life laid out for him when his name went down for Eton while he was still in diapers? I shake the thought away. We're more than that, surely we are, more than a sterile sum of our experiences: fate has to be the magic ingredient we can't predict?

"So what made you extend your stay?" I ask him, sensing a break in the conversation that I can slip into.

"I think perhaps you had a point," he says, a little wryly. "I decided that boarding school was a little premature, but I did want Madeline to spend some time in England. And," he looks away, his jaw tight, "let's just say that New York doesn't feel like a home away from home right at the present moment."

"What actually . . ." I start, then trail off. He's closed himself down, shut me out, the mechanism invisible but the effect instantaneous. He shifts gear, pulls on a smile. "And how about you? What news?"

"A chance to talk" was how he billed tonight, but the opposite seems to be true. It might be the public setting, the exhaustion of fielding people's clumsy attempts at sympathy, but it feels more fundamental than that. It makes the thrum of fear start up in me again, makes me wonder what unfolded between his warm phone call and touching back down in England a month later. I know that I can't ask, so instead I let him lead the dance. I tell him about the project—how much I wanted to make it work, and how frustratingly elusive Flynn Gerrard has proven to be ever since that fateful night.

"I just muffed it so badly in the apartment. I'm worried he thinks I'm an incompetent schoolgirl and he doesn't want to let me near it."

"It doesn't sound nearly as bad as you're painting it. Anyway, you've done the hardest part. You won the pitch. Was the ice queen suitably humbled?"

"Maybe. Something's happened to her."

It's odd. Ever since then Charlotte has been much nicer; so much nicer that I almost wonder if James was right. Neither of us have mentioned her since, so I haven't given him the satisfaction of telling him so. Besides, I don't really want to venture back there. I didn't like where it took us.

"And the other competition?"

"Did I tell you about that?" I say, blushing with embarrassment. I'm starting to notice how he hoovers up facts, absorbs tiny details that I barely remember shedding. I reread the story on a lonely Sunday when I was feeling particularly sad about Sally; perhaps it was the mood I was in, but it felt too structured and crafted, lacking in heart. I tried again, poured all of the emotion that was whirling around inside onto the page, and sent it off before I could waste any more time prevaricating.

"Well done," he says, when I tell him. "If it's anywhere near as accomplished as the poem you wrote for Madeline, I'm sure you'll surprise yourself."

"Thank you," I say, touched by what he's said. It feels meant.

"Will you excuse me for a minute?"

As William heads for the bathroom, I turn to my other side, where I've got a kindly, patrician civil servant who I've already spent a little time chatting to. It makes me realize I've been a little harsh about the crowd: he asks interested questions and gives me enough insight into Number Ten to keep me agog, while deftly avoiding any real revelations. William's back in the banqueting hall now, but he's talking to a group on another table.

"And how do you know each other?" asks Jasper, nodding to him.

"His wife was my best friend at university."

"And beyond?"

I smile, say nothing.

"Terrible business. I gather there's some outstanding questions around the circumstances?"

I nod, trying to mask how little I actually know, hoping my face won't give me away.

"Frankly I'm surprised he's been able to stay, considering how it seems to be unfolding."

I bite my tongue, determined not to gossip. I won't talk about you like this, I think, digging my fingernails into my palm to try to stop the tears springing to my eyes. If only William would come back.

When he does sit down, shortly after, I find myself almost asking him with my eyes. He either doesn't see, or chooses not to see, looking instead to the gray-haired man who's rising to his feet, his army uniform weighed down by a battery of medals.

"Who is he?" I whisper.

"Sir Richard Fothergay." I look totally blank. "He's the ex-head of the British Army. Retired last year."

Watching QVC and playing Scrabble clearly doesn't give him enough to do, as he gives a speech about the importance of transatlantic interdependence that lasts approximately two hundred years. My concentration waxes and wanes, so much else circling around my mind.

"Finally," says Sir Richard, and I start to sense escape, "I know that you will all join me in expressing our deepest condolences to William Harrington who recently lost his wife in the most tragic of circumstances. Our thoughts and prayers are with you and your family at this difficult time."

All eyes turn in our direction, the room silent. William looks at his plate, surveys the petits fours like they're lost treasure, and then forces his gaze outward. "Thank you," he says, then returns his gaze to the plate.

Then we're finally released from the table, and pushed back through to the ballroom. Horror of horrors, they've turned it into a disco, complete with a cheesy deejay standing poised behind a pair of decks. I look at William, embarrassed: the celebratory mood seems like an anathema. He manages a weak smile, then leads us through the chattering throng of people, but before we can make our escape, we're waylaid by Trixie and Rory.

"Marvelous speech," says Rory.

"Without question," agrees William while I'm stuck with Trixie, groping for something to say. She swivels toward William, turning her back to me.

"You must come for dinner before you flee back to the US of A. You just pop up the A40 and you hit Henley in no time."

"Thank you. Very kind."

"Be warned I'll be holding you to it."

"She will," agrees Rory.

She will, I can tell. Jules is right, the fix-ups will start in no time. Even if it's too soon, the Trixies of this world will be making sure their single girlfriends are sowing the seeds for when the clouds of grief have cleared and they can respectably make their move. I look at his profile, wondering if he realizes what the agenda is here. It makes me sad, the thought of it, even though logically I know that his life has to go on: time is so merciless, the way it scatters earth over the past and builds the new over its bones. And yet—I can't see Sally letting go that easily. Whatever the second Mrs. Harrington chooses to believe, I know she'll never be able to escape the shadow cast by the first.

"If you'll excuse us, Rory's promised me a boogie," says Trixie. Now this I've got to see, oddly comforted by the realization that I'm still me, in the midst of all of this. Again that absence, that sense of Sally, the outrageous nickname she'd have damned Trixie with by now. William's stopped, is staring at the dance floor, watching the couples who are starting to flood their way over. We're marooned on the periphery—a couple of people, most definitely not a couple.

"Do you . . ." asks William, his expression strained. I swatted him away.

"Oh no, I . . ."

"Trust me, you've been spared," he says. "Dictionary definition of two left feet."

Jasper crosses toward us, distracting me from the sight of Trixie doing little high kicks and finger clicks to "You Sexy Thing": Rory is most definitely the least sexy thing I've ever seen in my life.

"Would it be inappropriate to steal you for a song?" he asks.

"Please do," says William, and I feel an illogical shard of rejection.

Jasper turns out to be a surprisingly good mover, although I don't much like the way his hands are taking the scenic route. I look back toward William, an isolated figure at the corner of the dance floor. I might be imagining it, but it seems as though his eyes are trained on us.

"He's brilliant, you know," says Jasper. "One of the finest minds of his generation."

"Is he?"

"He can spin anything. Turn it into gold."

And finally we're out, hit by a gust of bracing night air, blowing away the stultifying atmosphere of the past four hours. I gulp it down, aware how suffocated I've felt.

"Please don't be polite," says William. "I know what an endurance test that must have been." He pauses, hesitant. "Thank you."

"It was a bit, but nothing compared to how it must have been for you. I can't believe . . ."

"They were trying to be kind."

We stand there a moment, looking at each other, and I try and summon up the courage to articulate the questions that are plaguing me.

"Shall we find you a taxi?" he asks, before I get there.

"Yes, or . . ." I want to ask him if he wants to get a drink, but it's hard to get the words out.

"In fact we could probably share one. The new digs are in Battersea."

"Great," I say, as he flags one down.

William perches awkwardly on the uncomfortable flip up seat, leaving me to luxuriate in the spaciousness of the back seat. If this was Sally, she'd just dive right in there and not worry about the consequences. I'm so scared of hurting him, or alienating him, or getting an answer that makes everything somehow worse.

"So what does the rest of the week have in store?" he asks.

I don't think I can stand any more small talk. As words start to tumble out of my mouth, I realize that I'm a little drunk. Maybe the lack of inhibition is what I need, or maybe it's the absolute opposite.

"William, you might think this is none of my business, or that I'm being as inappropriate as all those chilly snobs in there, but can I ask you what's happened the last few weeks? Something Jasper said . . ."

He looks at me, then turns away, his jaw set, his eyes fixed on the night skyline. I'm shaking, my nerves jangling. I should never have gone here. I wouldn't have done, if I'd had any choice. I felt like I owed it to her in some stupid way.

"She died, Olivia. On June the eighteenth 2012 my wife died. At this precise moment in time I can't see what else matters beyond that fact."

"I thought maybe you wanted to talk about it. You said you wanted to . . ."

A coldness comes over him, quite different from the reserve that I've become accustomed to.

"And if I did, don't you think that I would do so?"

"Okay, okay, I'm sorry." Silence reigns for what feels like forever, before some kamikaze part of me blunders on. "It's just I knew Sally, not just knew her like a mate. She was my person."

The silence continues, but then, as I look at him, I notice a lone tear slither down his face. He doesn't attempt to wipe it, just continues to stare straight ahead.

"Your person," he repeats, a hollowness about the way he says it.

"Yeah, she was," I say, almost defensive.

He looks at me for the first time in ages, a deep sadness in his eyes.

"Your person." He waits a while. "Do you honestly believe that such a thing was possible?"

"Coming up on the left, mate?" says the cab driver, his voice cutting its way into the intensity of the moment.

"Look, I'm just down the road. Come back and have a glass of wine, or a cup of tea, or something."

I don't even know where that came from, but it felt so abrupt for us to part ways like this. I don't think for a moment he'll agree, but to my surprise he does, and a few minutes later we're drawing up outside the apartment. He insists on paying, then follows me up the dingy stairs that you have to race up in order to avoid the stinge light, as James calls it, snapping off to save the visor-wearing landlady's electricity bill. To my relief, the door is double locked. I definitely don't think I need to be making any formal introductions right now.

"Home sweet home. What can I get you to drink?"

"Is there any remote chance you've got whisky?"

James does, and I sit him at the kitchen table and pour him a largish measure while I make myself a cup of peppermint tea. As I watch him swallow it back in a couple of gulps it occurs to me how frequently he seemed to need his wine glass topping up. I leave the whisky bottle on the side, but he goes and finds it, motioning to me to check it's okay for him to pour more. I smile my assent, wishing for his sake that he wouldn't.

"I didn't lure you back here to grill you. We don't have to talk about it . . . we can just have a drink."

"You say that," he says, voice thick with alcohol, "but all I'm seeing is a steaming mug of dull. Don't abandon me now, Olivia."

"I hate whisky."

"Nonsense, you just need more practice."

I reluctantly pour myself a tiny measure and take a sip. It's like fire burning down my windpipe. I cough, wrinkling my nose. "Courage." He clinks my glass and knocks back more of his. I watch him, wary. It feels too intimate somehow, him sitting in the chaos of my ramshackle kitchen, expensive coat flung over the back of his chair. He's almost a stranger, and yet I feel like I know things about him that I have no way of knowing.

"Fire away. Ask me anything," he says, tipping more whisky into his glass, an edge to him.

This isn't right. This isn't how it should be. What was I expecting? That I'd be able to heal him with the golden balm of my sympathy?

"Are you sure you don't want a cup of this instead? You're going to feel like shit in the morning."

He gives a mirthless laugh at my abject stupidity.

"Sorry." He sits there, waiting, and I feel duty-bound to carry on. "I just wondered what had happened since you'd been back." He watches me. "With the investigation and the whole . . ." Exhumation is the word in my head, but I can't say it. It sounds like something from a horror film.

"The insurance company is mounting a case. They've got witnesses. A family who say they saw the car zigzagging between lanes." He looks up from his glass, gives a sort of grimace. "Which they claim makes it less and less likely to be a momentary loss of concentration."

There's a taste of metal in my mouth, a coldness spreading through me. I grope for something to say, grope for that same level of control that he seems to be able to exert over himself.

"It's not proof!" I say, my voice rising. "It might not even have been her car. They can't prove anything!"

I hate these shadowy vulcans who are putting William through this ordeal, putting Sally's final hours under the microscope. Suddenly truth feels like a bad thing, an unnecessary debt to run up that one can never hope to repay.

"I suspect it is. They're searching for CCTV now, appealing for more witnesses."

"I'm so sorry."

He looks at me, those hooded eyes making his gaze seem very distant. We sit there in silence for a minute, the sense of something more hovering between us.

"Was there—is there anything else—"

He cuts across me.

"I don't want you to think badly of her," he says, emotion surging through his voice. That clenched control has gone, his face cleaved open, eyes pleading. "That was always what she feared, Olivia."

I look at him sitting there, his body straining toward me—he's hopelessly in love with her. There's something painful about it, above and beyond the obvious tragedy of her death. I might be imagining it, but I sense that he's as mired in quicksand as I always was.

"I won't," I say, knowing as I say it that it's a promise I can't sign up to.

"There's debts, Olivia, credit cards I didn't even know she had. There are thousands of dollars on them, all unpaid."

"But surely—won't they just write them off?"

"It seems not. There's big cash withdrawals too, that I had no idea about. It could bankrupt me if I lose the case. It's hard not to live in fear of what the next revelation might be."

What a master of understatement. I smile at him, putting my hand very gently on his arm. I don't think about it before I do it, it's just an instinct, a need to reach through the bars of his prison. It lies there like a dead thing, his arm rigid to my touch. It seems like an age before he speaks.

"I don't think I made her very happy," he says, his voice no more than a gruff whisper.

"You can't possibly think it's your fault—"

"It's simply an observation."

"Oh William . . ." I pause, trying to choose my words carefully. "The Sally I knew—she was a thrill-seeker. She was always craving something just out of reach."

That was her rocket fuel, what powered her forward. It propelled her out of her humble suburban beginnings, demanded that she found a sophistication and poise that was self-taught. I'm guessing it took her all the way to that upscale life in Manhattan—what did she crave once she'd finally arrived?

"I should go," he says, rising heavily to his feet.

I've gone too far. Who am I to sit here, tarnishing her memory?

"Are you sure?" I say. He nods, heading for the door. I feel terrible, like I've ripped open the wound without anesthetic, then left it exposed. I follow him down the passage.

"Can't I call you a cab at least?"

He turns, bats my offer away.

"I'll be fine."

He looks anything but fine.

"William . . . sometimes I've got such a big mouth. Please ignore anything I said."

He suddenly puts his arms around me. I tense, waiting for what must surely be a kiss on the cheek, but instead he holds me. I can hear his heart beating through his dinner jacket, my head pressed against the warm expanse of his broad chest.

"You're lovely, I want you to know that."

I look up at him, nervous energy shooting through me. I should extract myself, and yet something stops me. He's staring at me.

"So are you," I say, uncertain.

And then he leans down and kisses me, our lips meeting for a few seconds before I pull away, almost pushing him backward. It's just in the nick of time.

"I'm alwayth lothing my keyth," says a familiar voice from the other side of the door.

"William—" I say, but he's already opened it and started down the stairs, pushing past James and Charlotte without so much as a backward glance.

Charlotte stares after William, wide-eyed, as James looks at me in disbelief. "I'm going to bed," I say, refusing to meet his eye, and disappear to my room as fast as I my shaking legs will carry me.

I stare at myself in the mirror, my fingers raised to my lips, tracing the pressure of our kiss. What was I doing? What stopped me from pushing him away before his lips reached mine? Guilt floods through me—has some awful, rogue part of my personality gone AWOL and decided it's time to wreak revenge on Sally? I stare at my reflection a second longer, almost as though I'm watching a stranger.

It's then the truth dawns, a truth that might be worse. It wasn't revenge, it was something much simpler and yet so much more complex. Slowly, stealthily, feelings have sprung up, like weeds left to rampage their way around an untended garden. I've missed him, I realize, thought about him more than I've admitted to myself. A flash of Trixie springs up, that suspicious scowl she shot in my direction when he wasn't looking: how awful to think that I am the girl she thought I was, the one I hated too—the stupid, conniving girl, foolish enough to try and inveigle her way into Sally's place.

I can't bear the thought that William might have seen what I've denied before I saw it myself. What if he thinks I threw myself at him, luring him back here to seduce him? Of course good manners would dictate that he'd never tell me so, but secretly he'll think I'm a predatory vulture, picking at the carcass of his marriage, my concern for him and Madeline no more than a strategy.

I fall into a feverish sleep, punctuated by the sound of glasses clinking down the hall, Charlotte's lisping falsetto tinkling away. It's worse when it switches to a pregnant sort of silence. The front door clunks shut at two-thirty, waking me up, and I notice the red light on my phone blinking away. *Please accept my sincere apologies for my appalling behavior. Best, William.* I read it three times, hoping it will sound less pained, less awful. I can't bear the thought that he might be lying there feeling every bit as guilty as me. Once I feel strong enough I'll text him back something equally polite, and then stage an emotional lockdown until the scorching embarrassment cools. A wave of pain sweeps across me. Now I've truly lost him; now, when I finally know that losing him is not what I want. It's my rightful punishment.

CHAPTER TEN

JAMES HAS ALREADY LEFT FOR WORK WHEN I DRAG myself up, hopelessly late, having hit snooze at least three times. When I get to the office Charlotte's already at her desk, as perfect and groomed as someone who's had twelve hours of dreamless sleep. She gives me a big, imaginary smile of welcome.

"There's a latte waiting for you on your dethk," she says loudly. "I hope it won't have gone cold!"

Mary looks up, her eyes swiveling toward the wall clock, silently racking up the ten minutes I've missed in her mental ledger.

"Thanks," I say, terse.

"Maybe we could grab a thandwich later, talk about the Flynn campaign going forward?"

Is this just a ruse to get me alone, or is she trying to muscle in on it?

"Yup, sure, fine," I say, not yet out of my coat.

Mary struts down the office toward me. She's wearing a gigantic gold cuff that clanks as she walks, like she's a particularly glamorous jailor.

"Yes, let's have a catch-up on that today," she says, gaze boring into me. "I'd like to hear where you're up to." Panic sweeps across me as I think how little progress I've made—bleating that he won't return my calls is hardly a defense.

Just then Mungo strolls in, a panama hat perched on his head at a jaunty angle, utterly unconcerned about the clock that's hovering above his head.

"Morning Mimi, cool jewels," he says.

"Why thank you!" she says, jiggling her laden wrist at him, and giving that girlish smile. She looks back at me. "In fact," she adds, coldly, "there's no time like the present."

She turns abruptly, and I scuttle after her, trying desperately to order my thoughts. When we get into her office she shuts the door, settles into the sofa, and simply looks at me, a vaguely bored expression on her face.

"Well it's early days . . ." I start. "And we haven't completely worked out the brief for production yet." On and on I ramble, waffling on about platforms and demographic reach, Mary's expression completely inscrutable. Eventually she raises a perfectly manicured hand.

"Enough." I must seem so ragged and unprofessional, my excuses paper thin. She came across me in the loos last night as I was pulling on my disappointing dress and I stupidly told her where I was going. Looking at her face now I feel like she can see every single lump and bump, inside and out.

"Mary, I know I messed it up that night. It was a stupid thing to say, and it didn't sound at all like how I meant it.

He's just not returning my calls. I think he might be back in LA . . ."

"He's not. Me and Charlotte took him for dinner on Monday."

I try desperately to keep my face neutral, hoping my eyes won't fill up. It's over before it begun, snatched away without me even having had the chance to try.

"How . . . how was he?" I say, wondering how quickly I can thank her for the opportunity and make a dignified exit.

"Oh, you know Flynn, full of beans. Charlotte felt a little understretched so I've created a new role for her alongside her main job. Creative director of Talent Relations."

Vintage Mary—if one of her shiny stars shows any sign of jumping ship she throws money and status at them like confetti: I can just imagine Charlotte's downcast eyes as she expressed her "dithappointment" at not winning the pitch.

"Will she be running my campaign or hers?" I say, trying to keep the petulance out of my voice. It's so utterly humiliating that I've been bombarding him with messages when the conversation's moved on without me.

"You will be running your campaign. We made that very clear to Flynn."

A complicated kind of relief floods through me. I'm glad I haven't been thrown off the job wholesale, but if I'm still part of it, why did they have to cut me out? Even if they'd told me the dinner was happening, but not invited me, it would have felt better than this. Mary's studying me, waiting for my reaction. I get hold of myself: I can't lose this job. She wouldn't sack me, I don't think, but I've watched what happens when people fall out of favor, the wind-chill factor growing ever greater until they admit defeat and fall on their swords.

"Fantastic. I just want to get stuck in."

"Come on, Livvy, we all know the truth," says Mary, looking amused. "There's very little to do here. It's a vanity project, a mutual backscratching exercise. Your main function is to fan the flames of Flynn's ego."

"Really?" I say, crushed. "But . . ." I pause, not wanting to contradict her. "I want to try and make it work. It's a great cause."

"Obviously," she says, witheringly. "It's hardly like my heart's desire is for African women to die in penury, but that's why we've got Oxfam. He'll raise a few quid, waste most of it paying some airhead hanger-on to administer it, and feel a toasty glow of self-satisfaction. But if we can keep him onside, who knows what could come out of it? Film campaigns, work on all those international brands he promotes. There's a huge opportunity here."

I try not to look utterly gutted, even though I feel like a child who's spotted Mom extracting their milk tooth from underneath the pillow. Maybe I would have agreed with her when she first announced it, but, until Flynn's radio silence, I'd bought it hook, line, and sinker, not least because of her passionate declarations. It felt like it had been meant to land in my lap at the exact moment I needed a sense of meaning.

"So what do you need me to do?" I ask, hoping I don't sound sullen.

"Become a willing slave." She giggles. "There's no need to look so navy-knickered Livvy, I just mean that you need to keep in constant contact with him, make him feel involved every step of the way."

"But you said . . . I mean, I'll mainly be finalizing scripts and briefing the agency. And anyway, that's if he returns my calls."

"He will now," she says confidently. Paranoia rages through me like a forest fire. What have they said to him to convince him that I'm up to the job? If he doesn't want me on it, I don't want to do it, but looking at Mary's steely expression, I know that a graceful exit is not on offer.

"Great."

"Go and write it with him. You know what those illiterate thesps are like, always aching to screw around with the words on the page. We can get him involved on the casting, picking a director. Make him feel indispensable. You never know, it might be fun!"

"I'll call him now."

"Are you all right with that? Do you foresee any problems?"

"No, no. It's fine," I say, starting to stand up.

She brushes my hand with her long, painted fingers, pulling me back down onto the sofa.

"How was last night?" I try to smile, not trusting myself to speak. I can see her next meeting standing impatiently at the door, a cockatoo-haired Swedish director brandishing a couple of mood boards.

"You just take a minute," she says, smiling kindly. I take a couple of deep breaths, sitting there until I feel like I've collected myself.

"Thank you," I say, again readying myself to leave.

"Go well," she says, watching me. "It sounds like a cliché, but time can heal the most unhealable things."

She's like a good witch, or maybe a goodish witch, the way she seems to read the undertow in the slightest thing.

Just for one, insane, second I want to pour out everything about last night, ask her what I should do, but then I come back to my senses. I hold the door open for the visibly irritated Swede, and she gives me one of her funny, conspiratorial little eye rolls at the ludicrousness of his hair.

Once I'm sat back down at my desk I decide I've got to reply to William. I hate the idea of him beating himself up about it. *Please don't worry,* I write, *you've got nothing to apologize for. We'd both had too much to drink. Take care, Livvy.* I look at it a second, then change it to *Olivia,* in case he thinks I'm being overfamiliar, then change it back because my logic seems so ridiculous.

I look over to Charlotte who's on the phone, waiting for the other person to finish speaking, her eyes narrowed as she computes what they're saying, body hunched over it like she's waiting to pounce. I hope she won't hurt him, I think, even though an awful part of me hopes she does, just so I'm vindicated; I wish I was a nicer person.

Next stop Flynn Gerrard. I don't have the slightest expectation that he'll answer his phone, but he picks up on the second ring.

"Berrington, Olivia," he says. "What a pleasant surprise. I've been meaning to call you."

"Hi!" I say, trying to sound sunny and upbeat and professional. "I was just calling you with an update."

"Update away. Actually, hold on a sec. How are you? What's happening in Olivia-land?"

"Um, well, I went to a very posh dinner last night. The head of the British Army had a lot to say for himself."

"Did you dazzle them? Bet you did."

"I wouldn't say that."

"You're modest, I already know that about you."

Oh God, I hate the way he tries to steamroll me into flirting with him. And anyway, while I can see he's ludicrously handsome, I don't actually fancy him—it's like admiring a work of art rather than a visceral pull on my heart.

"So, let me tell you where I'm at. Though I'm sure Mary and Charlotte will have already briefed you."

My eyes unconsciously move toward Charlotte, who's off the phone now and trying, and failing, to look like she's not straining to hear. I recycle my spiel about the research I've done on demographics and reach, then tentatively mention the script. Mary might be able to pull him into her slipstream, but I'm not sure I've got the same powers of persuasion.

"I'm sure you won't have time, but if you did? You're so passionate about it."

"It's my baby, Olivia, and it's the one baby that's not an eleven-hour flight away. Certainly keeps me awake."

"I know. So to be able to harness that passion, and really mold the script out of it . . ."

"I do like to have a wee scribble when I can." Bingo. "You know, we're the ones who understand the words from the inside out." He pretends to mull it over, lasting approximately two seconds. "Can you get yourself out to Pinewood on Monday?"

"Of course."

"Then I think we've got ourselves a date."

I go and tell Mary, who seems suitably reassured, then ready myself to do battle with Charlotte. I think it's going to take more than a slick of MAC lipstick in dangerous red, but unfortunately that's all the ammunition I've got.

"How do you feel about thushi?" asks Charlotte, as we step out onto the street.

Hmm, how do I feel about sushi? I feel like Madeline does—that it's slimy and suspicious—and also that Charlotte would be advised to stick to lunch options she can actually pronounce, but I can't be bothered to negotiate, and before I know it we're stuck in a hole in the wall somewhere off Goodge Street, surrounded by hordes of Japanese businessmen shouting at each other across the tiny Formica tables.

"What do you like?" she asks, scanning the menu with that frightening focus she brings to all endeavors. This is the moment to fess up to my total raw-fish ignorance, but it feels desperately important I don't concede anything—instead I stab wildly at the tiny, repellent pictures on the menu like I'm playing a deranged game of pescatarian bingo.

"Wow, you mutht be really hungry, I'll get the waiter."

Now I'm going to have to eat the world's remaining fish stock just to save face.

"Tho," says Charlotte, once the waiter's left, "tell me all about your converthation with Flynn."

Is she literally going to pretend that last night didn't happen? I scrabble around, trying to work out the best plan of attack. I could come over all 1950s-Dad and ask her what her intentions are, but it'll look distinctly weird, and I'm also worried about the speed at which her robot brain computes information: if she somehow worked out how complicated my uncomplicated relationship with James really is, I'll be left living on a knife edge. The thought of her whispering it to him in some cozy postcoital moment, fake concern masking the poison, is too much to bear.

"Yeah, it's going well," I say, bright smile plastered across my face, rattling through the contents of the call.

"Tho you're going to write the thcript *with* him?" she says, a doubting look on her face. Did they not agree this strategy when they went out for their stupid, cozy dinner?

"Well, sort of, that's what Mary asked me to do. I think it'll be more about making him feel he's involved."

"I wish you the betht of luck," she says, in a tone that makes me very much doubt she does. "And ath you know, my new role meanth I'm there to back you up every thtep of the way."

"Yeah, thanks for that," I say, leaden. Then we simply stare at each other for a few seconds.

"Can we talk about what'th been happening?" she says, and I nod, not trusting myself to speak. "I want you to know that I do really like James," she continues, her voice as flat and robotic as it was when she was ordering a tuna roll. "The thituation is obviouthly really complicated and the latht thing, the very latht thing, I want to do is compromithe our working relationship."

"Me too," I agree. What else can I say? I'm staring at the hideous, fiery green slime that surrounds my so-called lunch, terrified my face will give me away. I wish that I was a big enough person to wish that it would work out, instead I just want it to go away, melt into the ether like it never existed, or explode horribly so the debris settles into an approximation of how life was three months ago. I glance at my phone, arranged at the top of my bag so the screen's visible: no message. "You guys just need to work it out."

"Exactly," agrees Charlotte, signaling for the bill, task successfully completed. "Life's never thimple. Thertainly not for your friend," she adds, watching me carefully.

"No." I can't bear that she's got access to me, a spyhole into my life. I look at her hand wrapped around the bill, diamond twinkling like the northern lights. "Let me find my card."

"My treat." A treat's one word for it. "You can get it next time."

Next time? Oh joy.

I stand, shivering, outside Northfields tube, waiting for Jules's red Nissan Micra to turn the corner, hoping there's no such thing as the Ealing strangler. Eventually she pulls up, tooting its tinny horn, shoving baby paraphernalia off the passenger seat and apologizing. Then she sees my face.

"God I'm really sorry, Livvy, he was just really colicky and grumpy. And I've got to be back by ten."

"It's not that," I say, a solitary tear trickling down my icy cold cheek.

"Oh, little one!" says Jules. It was her hated childhood nickname for me, but right now it's music to my ears. "Tell me!"

And I give her a brief synopsis of last night, while simultaneously urging her to drive. Dad hates lateness, it makes him go all hurt and huffy, and I'm not in the mood for humoring him.

"Listen, we'll talk about it properly later," she says, turning left into Dad's road, "but I seriously think it'll be fine."

"Don't be such a Pollyanna mentalist. To recap—'best, William,' and he hasn't replied to my text. I just feel like such an idiot."

She pulls up, switches off the engine and turns to me.

"Livvy, he's a mess. Of course he's a mess—he's just found out his wife would most probably rather kill herself than live her life with him. In the nicest possible way it's not about you."

"No, I know that . . ."

She studies my face, her expression gradually registering that my stupid, slavish heart has caught up with her prediction.

"Oh, Livvy."

"Yeah, cheers for that." I smile at her, telling her I'm not blaming her. "There's no future in it. It's ridiculous that I'm even giving it house room. It's done, over. Didn't even begin."

"Just don't jump to any conclusions," she says. "Let's just see what happens."

"Absolutely not," I say, blood surging through me. "I'm not doing that to Sally." I pause. "I'm not doing that to myself."

Jules grabs my hand as we walk up the path to Dad's terraced house, telling me with a squeeze that she didn't mean to be crass, and I squeeze back. We ring the doorbell and eventually the energy-saving lightbulb in the hallway springs into feeble life. Dad opens the door, a look of controlled disappointment surfing his face. He's wearing a striped butcher's apron and a pair of unpleasant beige Crocs, and is brandishing a spatula.

"Sorry—" starts Jules, about to fess up, but before she does, I jump in.

"I was moaning on to Jules, and we just got held up," I say, leaning in to kiss him, and handing him the bottle of decent but unflashy red wine I picked up from M&S en route.

"Can't be helped," says Dad, still slightly Eeyore-ish. "It's just that I'm trying out a nut roast that I downloaded from the Internet and it specifically asks for forty minutes. Let's all just keep our fingers crossed it's still edible."

We grimace at each other as we follow his Crocs down the dingy hallway that leads to the tiny kitchen. We started out with a distinctly ordinary family home in Northwood, which melted down into two modest parental apartments in the molten fire of the divorce. Mom bought wisely in an up-and-coming area, did it up, and sold it for a healthy profit a few years later, while Dad bought this unprepossessing rat run in order to minimize his mortgage. I worry he'll be carted out of it in a box, as I can't see anyone ever taking it off his hands. Not that he'd even want them to—he's most definitely a creature of habit.

The nut roast looks more like a brick than dinner: it thuds onto the serving dish and sits there, menacingly, while Dad prods at it inquisitively with his spatula.

"Right then, girls, pull up a pew," he says, tucking my wine into the wine rack and pulling out a dodgy-looking bottle of cabernet that he's already opened. We squeeze ourselves along the bench that runs down the side of the ancient pine table, and sit there, pinioned, waiting for him to carpet-bomb our plates. "We'll need to tuck in, as the concert starts in, let's see," he peers at his watch, "fifty-seven minutes."

"Concert?" I say, trying to keep the horror out of my voice. I know where this train is headed.

"Did you forget to tell her?" says Dad, admonishingly, to Jules.

"She's run off her feet with Nathaniel," I say, taking a slug of my wine. Big mistake. It tastes more like mouthwash than anything a person might drink for pleasure.

"Oh Livvy, don't be so melodramatic! I'm fine." I wasn't being melodramatic, I was defending her: why is it that we automatically revert to bickering adolescents the minute we enter our parents' airspace?

"It's nice, isn't it?" says Dad proudly. "It was on special at the cash and carry, so I thought bugger it, I'll invest in a case."

I think about telling him the truth but it will just feed his conviction that I'm a profligate wastrel, permanently channeling my inner Marie Antoinette. Don't get me wrong, I love my dad with the kind of boundless affection that makes my heart almost curdle with the need to protect him from a world he always feels out of step with, but he also drives me stark raving mad.

"Mmm," I say, my "mmm" dragging on slightly too long to be convincing. "Tell us about the concert."

"What you'll be enjoying tonight is a soupçon of modern jazz, played by the very finest musicians of the Ealing music society. You girls are in for an aural treat."

Looking at Jules is too great a risk. Instead I take another gulp of mouthwash and try to look on the bright side: while modern jazz is surely one of the most heinous inventions of the modern age—right up there with novelty ringtones and Quorn—it at least saves us from too much conversation. If Dad asks me if I've met anyone I seriously think I might cry, and romantic advice from a parent who hasn't had a relationship since John Major was leading the country is not what I need right now. Instead we pass round Jules's iPhone, looking at the footage she's shot of

Nathaniel, Dad marveling at the technology. A video camera would have been far too extravagant a purchase for the Berrington family, so all that exists of me and Jules are such photographic delights as the school picture he has framed on the kitchen wall, my gappy, protruding teeth offset by Jules's shaggy blond pudding bowl. Poor Madeline, I think, my eyes fixed on it. How much easier it is, even if you don't know it when you're pulling out each other's hair and barricading yourselves in your bedrooms, if there's someone else roughly the same size to negotiate your family with.

We try and gnaw our way through a respectable amount of the brick, Dad's eyes constantly darting to the clock.

"We really ought to get on the road," he says eventually, casting that permanent look of disappointment at our unclean plates.

"It was lovely," I say, wanting to walk around the table and hug him back to happiness. Since he retired, I feel like the little intricacies of his days have taken on even more importance than ever. He was a manager for the council's education department, which gave him the perfect outlet for his fussy precision and a decent gang of people to boss around—now he's just got us.

"You haven't finished your wine, Julia."

"Oh, you know, breast feeding! Don't want Nathaniel getting a taste for it."

He bustles off to get our coats, handing them to us as he pulls on his windcheater.

"How's your mother?" he asks, faux casually, his gaze trained on the zip.

"Fine," we chorus, a little too fast.

"Good, good."

"She's been getting into Zumba," says Jules. He looks blank. "It's a kind of dance exercise thing."

Is it better or worse to give him detail? He looks even more crestfallen now, but simply saying "fine" makes it sound like she's run away with a multimillionaire Italian count and we can't bear to tell him.

"She always was a bit of a mover," he says, doing a peculiar wiggle of his hips.

The concert venue is a good fifteen minutes away, but Dad insists we walk, despite our protests about the drizzly weather ("don't be so lily-livered!"). We arrive in the drafty community hall with only a couple of minutes to spare, the foyer empty but for a ruddy-faced woman frantically waving a handful of tickets at us. Gray frizzy hair erupts from her scalp, untamed by any kind of styling product, and she's clad in a tent-like dress, offset by a pair of flat, red Jesus sandals that might give Dad's Crocs a run for their money. It's funny, I'm surrounded by women fighting aging as if it's as lethal as nerve gas. There's something refreshing about someone who's sinking into it like it's a warm bath.

"Thank you, Margery" says Dad, snatching them from her. "I do apologize: the girls were late."

If it were Stone Age times and the car was yet to be invented I'd have some sympathy—I start saying as much, before Jules nudges me to shut up. She's right: I shouldn't be taking my bad mood out on him.

"Hello!" says Margery, casting a darting look between the two of us, radiating nervous energy from every pore. "We can't chat, it's starting." She bodily chases us into the hall like a great big flapping bird. A ragtag group of amateur musicians are "tuning up": either that or a squadron of cats are being strangled. She plunks herself down next to me and leans in uncomfortably close.

"So, Libby, your dad tells me you do something very exciting!" she says. I try to explain my job in a hoarse whisper but it ends up sounding faintly ridiculous, even to me. Then the "music" begins. Saxophones screech, snare drums bang without any discernible rhythm, and Dad, sitting the other side of Margery, jerks and bobs his head around like a demented sunflower. Honestly, the people sitting behind him must be seasick by the time it finally, mercifully, stops. Margery has a beatific smile on her face when the lights come up. She swivels her head to him, and then to me.

"It's so transporting!" she says, face pinker than ever.

"Isn't it?" agrees Dad, equally blissful.

"I need to get going," says Jules, before realizing her mistake. "I mean it was brilliant, utterly brilliant. But I have to be back for Nat's night feed."

"And the car *is* about ten miles away," I say, unable to stop myself. I am literally thirteen years old.

Once we're ensconced in the car, goodbyes said, I suddenly don't want to leave Dad. I look at the closed door, the patchy glow of the energy-saving light bulb feebly shining, and feel a surge of that illogical desire to save him from something.

"Do you think he's okay?" I say, wistful.

Jules is already turning the key in the ignition. I put my hand on her arm, make her pause.

"William?" She turns to look at me. "How could he be?"

"No, Dad." Jules looks at me, mildly exasperated. "Go on, drive," I say, sensing her impatience: this is a well-worn conversation. "He just seemed a bit sad, the way he talks about Mom . . ."

"They were married for twenty-five years. Course he wants to know what she's up to."

"He's not just asking, though, is he, he's pining. What if he's a swan?"

"I can't think of anyone less like a swan, Livvy."

"They mate for life, swans. If a swan loses his wife, that's it. It's game over."

"He's fine, he's just Dad, don't overthink it." We've stopped at the light, and she turns to look at me, gives me that big sister look that brooks no argument. "Think about William instead. If you do have feelings, you shouldn't just write it off."

"I've got to, Jules." I look at her, trying to turn a raging torrent of emotion into a logical, coherent thought. "I can't not."

She shifts into gear, slides off. Is it selfish or entirely human that I feel a stab of longing for the days when we'd have snuck off somewhere for last call and a proper, unhurried conversation, which wasn't dictated by traffic signals?

"But given a bit of time he will move on, and I don't see why it shouldn't be you. I hate to say it, but the fact he kissed you kind of proves it."

I can't deny the logic of what she's saying, but nor can I buy into it. It makes love sound like bond trading: stock seized at an all-time low with the expectation of a healthy return. Again, I feel that sense of Sally, so strong that it's almost as if she's here in the car. My heart starts to pound and I grip the seat, trying to slow it down, trying to breathe my way back to reality.

"Doesn't prove anything. He was drunk, people do stupid things when they hit rock bottom. Besides, I'm the absolute last person he should move on to. The last."

Do you hear me, Sally? If I say it loudly enough will you believe me?

March 1996

"Close your eyes and make a wish," said Sally, bursting into my room, a burning candle stuck lopsidedly into the top of a boiled egg.

I struggled to wake up, disoriented. She was standing at the end of my single bed struggling with a laden tray. In addition to the eggs, there was a posy of flowers, a round of toast, a cafetière of coffee, and a beautifully wrapped present.

"No Bagpuss?"

I should've been loyal enough to remind her of his real name, but I'd learned by now it was a waste of breath. I used it to blow out my candle instead.

"I'm meeting him at ten in the library cafeteria." Did she know he wasn't here? If she didn't then the ambush was quite a risk. But then, I thought guiltily, I'd shared enough for her to know he wasn't a great one for morning nookie. "Thanks,

Sally." I felt warm and toasty inside at the thought of her going to all that trouble.

"It's only the beginning," she said excitedly. "Go on, open your present."

I sat up, ripping open the paper to reveal a silky teddy, with soft cups and poppers at the bottom. It was only from Marks and Spencer, but to me it felt like it had tumbled straight out of a Jackie Collins book.

"Thanks!" I said, trying to imagine how Matt would react to it. He'd have to keep the light on to get the full effect. I held it against myself, enjoying the feeling of the slinky fabric. This was the new me, nineteen years old and ready for anything.

"You're going to look a right minx in that," she said, flopping down on the end of the bed and pouring the coffee. I looked to the small stack of cards on my desk that I'd diligently saved to open on the day.

"Want me to chuck them over?" said Sally. There was a $40 gift card from my dad, a brooch from my mom that I knew I'd never wear, and a large, pastel pink number from Jules, with two small girls sitting on a swing. FOR THE WORLD'S MOST SPECIAL SISTER it said.

"What's that?" said Sally, picking it up by the tip of her red painted fingernails like it was radioactive.

"Oh, me and Jules have this thing where we always try and get each other the most schmaltzy card we can find." I was reading the appalling poem inside by now, which clunkily rhymed "sister" with "miss you," but I felt too self-conscious to laugh. I'd got to the bottom of the pile now. There was one more from home, sent by my—I could no longer call her my best friend I realized, it wouldn't be true—my old best friend Sara who was studying biology at Cambridge. The sight of her neat, rounded vowels, so familiar from the endless studying

we'd done together, made me feel immediately guilty about my neglect, my broken promises to visit. Cambridge seemed so far away, so irrelevant. I felt a little winded, looking at the scattered cards. Nothing from James. He's a boy, I reasoned, boys never remember things like this, even though last year he'd remembered enough to plan a day trip to Brighton.

"What's up?" said Sally, noticing my pensive expression. I teetered on the brink of telling her, then thought of Matt and stopped myself.

"Nothing." I hugged her. "Thank you!"

"So I'm gonna take you for lunch in town," she said, grinning back excitedly. "Browns or something. You need to be properly spoiled on your birthday."

"That's so sweet of you," I cried. I loved that sentiment, so far from the loving briskness with which birthdays were treated in my family. "But you've given me this lovely breakfast, and I'm meeting Matt at ten. I won't have room."

"Liquid lunch!"

I grinned back, her glee utterly infectious. I felt torn, as I often did. I wanted nothing more than to be swept up in her whirlwind of sparkly plans, but I couldn't ignore the fact that I had a doggedly loyal boyfriend who might have his own ideas about how today should be spent.

"I might have to play it by ear," I said, then saw a flash of anger erupt across Sally's face. What I'd learned by now was that she hated to feel thwarted: you had to disguise any refusal in something more appealing, like burying a toddler's zucchinis in a spoonful of mash. "I'm sure it'll be totally fine! You know Matt," I said, rolling my eyes disloyally. "He's always got some kind of extra-curricular activity that can't wait."

"Doesn't he just," said Sally, warming up again. "You've gotta tell him he's got to share you tonight."

"Why?"

She tapped her nose with a knowing smirk, refused to say more.

Matt's card was one of those Monet pictures you've seen a hundred times, bought from the Student Union bookshop. To Livvy, happy birthday, wishing you a really great year! Much love, Matt. I looked at it, faintly disappointed, even though I'd done nothing to merit a more extravagant declaration. But perhaps it was exactly that, if I'd only had the humility to see it. I was becoming addicted to a life lived as a rollercoaster ride, the swooping highs and lows where everything upended and then spun back in a dizzying twist, and in the process become immune to any pleasures that were more subtle and finely wrought. He'd look at me with such vulnerability at times when he thought I wasn't watching, but I wouldn't acknowledge it, wouldn't give him the courage to bring his feelings out into the light, even though I liked knowing they were there. I guess in this relationship he was the one who had to hide the zucchinis.

"Thanks," I said, turning my attention to the small package that accompanied it, neatly taped, edges perfectly lined up. It was a black cotton V-neck jumper that I'd seen when we'd been shopping for a pair of pants for him in House of Fraser.

"You said you liked it, so I went back and got it," he said, his happy smile telling me how pleased he was to have pulled off this daring act of subterfuge.

"Thanks, Matt, that's really sweet." I'd glanced at it, thinking it would be a good layer of extra insulation against the Yorkshire winter, then decided it was too dull to waste my

puny clothing budget on—I was more interested in shiny scraps of fabric from Topshop nowadays. I felt myself blush at the thought of Sally's gift, which came from a different present-giving universe. Would it repel him, make him recoil in disgust at me trying to be something he didn't want me to be? I felt a stab of irritation as I looked down at the drab pool of black fabric. Why wasn't he the one with the imagination to buy me sexy underwear?

"I've got to finish my Keats essay today," he said, and I gave a little internal cheer at the bright colors flooding back into my afternoon, "but we're going out for dinner tonight, my treat. Thought we could try out that new pasta place."

"That'd be great," I said, reaching for his hand across the plastic table, "but . . ."

He looked at me, deflating. He knew what was coming.

Sally and I got ready together, makeup passed back and forth, Take That blasting out between our two bedrooms. We sung "Pray" at the top of our voices, Sally clutching her heart melodramatically at the chorus. Lola was dressing too, but she soon worked out it was too much hassle to run up and down from her room on the second floor—I don't know why we didn't just bring all her outfit options upstairs and make space for her. That's not true—I know exactly why we didn't.

Sally took a critical look at me when I thought I was ready, all dolled up in a dress from Oasis that cost more than I'd ever spent on one item. She'd told me I had to have it, that it was a "no-brainer." I felt myself wither under the weight of her gaze.

"Yeah," she said, head tilted to one side, makeup thick and professional-looking. "Almost."

I felt a surge of anger. If it was only an "almost" why had she persuaded me to spend so much on it that I'd had to live on pasta and Dolmio for a fortnight? But my anger disappeared in a puff of smoke when she offered me a red dress that I'd never seen before, with an expensive-looking label that I couldn't even identify. I had to slither into it, the fabric clinging like a second skin.

"Perfect, apart from the VPL," she cried, a delighted look on her face. "Get your new slinkies on, Livvy-toilet."

She didn't leave the room, simply waited. I turned away, trying to reveal the minimum amount of naked flesh, but I could feel her eyes tracking me, knew on one level that she was enjoying my discomfort. I ignored the fact, concentrated on the difference that the smooth lines of the teddy made to the look of the dress. Sally added a pair of her high heels, the toes stuffed with tissue paper, and there I was, good to go. I barely recognized myself, something I felt with increasing regularity.

"Gorgeous," she said, standing behind me in the mirror, our eyes meeting in the reflection. I remember that image as clearly as if we'd snapped it for posterity.

Sally instructed the cab driver in a whisper. Every time I asked where we were going she'd say "It's a surprise!" and I'd feel that addictive, heady sensation of being celebrated just for being me. The three of us girls squashed up in the back, sharing a wine cooler that Sally had stowed in her handbag, increasingly loud and giggly.

"Will Matt know how to find us?" I asked, responsibility temporarily puncturing my euphoria.

"Yeah it's fine. I called Bagpuss mission control," said Sally, taking another swig, her tone telling me how low it was on her list of priorities.

We pulled up at a bar right in the city center, too upscale to be frequented by students. *"We're on the list,"* said Sally, sweeping past the meaty bouncer without a backward glance. She led me through the bar to a back room, a happy birthday banner strung across the back wall, a bottle of cava already chilling in an ice bucket. There was a crowd of people there, most of whom I knew. The fact that many of them were only sort of friends made me realize, just for a second, how much oxygen Sally took up. *"Surprise!"* she shouted, bubbles cascading into my glass, leading everyone in a chorus of *"Happy Birthday."* Matt was there in the crowd, smiling shyly, relegated to a bit part. She must have been planning this for at least a week, I thought, but unless it was a double bluff he didn't know this morning. I pushed that thought away too, irritated by the fat bluebottles of negativity that were buzzing around my mind, marring this amazing moment.

"Thanks, everyone," I said, raising my glass as they toasted me.

"Shit, have I missed the toast?" said a familiar voice. I turned slowly, my legs shaking at the shock of worlds colliding. There, present in hand, stood James.

CHAPTER ELEVEN

Jules's words whirl around my head the next few days, stubbornly refusing to quietly retreat into the ether. I'm so confused by now that I barely know which way is up. I know that William and I could never be, whatever she says, but I also know that he is a soul in torment, a man in need of a friend. And yet, who am I trying to kid? Every time I think of his kiss I feel a hot rush of shame at the fragment of time where I allowed myself to fall. The shame doubles as I remember how self-righteous I was back in the day, how quick to judge, the irony too bitter to contemplate. Until I know, absolutely know, that the urge has gone, then I must keep myself quarantined.

Not that there's a shred of evidence that he wants my friendship—I haven't heard a peep from him since I sent the last text. Perhaps it really is over, done, finished, back to the place where news comes via occasional updates from Lola, but some place inside me balks at believing it—the secret, hidden part that feels connected to him, drawn together by her and yet irrevocably held apart.

I can't help thinking that James is avoiding me. He's conveniently away for the weekend, but come Sunday night, I find him standing at the stove, holding a wooden spoon as if it's a hockey stick. James is not a natural chef.

"Hi!" he says, crossing the kitchen to kiss me as if I've just arrived at a dinner party. "Spaghetti bolognese coming up."

"You always put massive lumps of carrot in it," I say, sullenly.

"No carrots!"

"Stop talking in exclamation marks," I say, glugging a large glass of wine out of the extravagant-looking bottle he's bought. "It won't stop me hating you."

"Hate's a very strong word, Olivia."

"And don't call me Olivia."

William always calls me Olivia. Why is that?

"Livvy." He abandons his station to clink glasses with me. "Sorry."

He is sorry, I can see that, but there's also an irrepressible glee that lurks behind it. Sometimes I wish I didn't know him quite as well as I do. I think back with the minimum possible enthusiasm, and peer into the frying pan, poking at the bolognese with maximum disdain.

"Charlotte said you had a nice lunch together."

I spin on my heels, enraged. I hate that they're talking about me offline, that there's already an "us" and a me. It was bad enough being the sex police, but this is worse.

"Oh did she?"

"Y-yes. I thought—"

"Whatever you thought, you thought wrong. This is a terrible idea, James. She's engaged! She works with me. And even if those things weren't the case, she's not a nice person."

Disastrous approach. He scowls at me, fire flashing in his eyes.

"I'm indulging you here, Livvy, it's not actually any of your business what two consenting adults decide to do. And don't go thinking you've got any right to the moral high ground." That hits me where it hurts. I sit back down, winded. "Sorry," he says again. I look at him, hoping that if my eyes are a window on my soul, the blinds are down. "I shouldn't have said that."

"I'm sorry too." The fight has all but left me. He looks at me, a softness about him that I rarely see, that macho jokiness turned down low. "Do you like her?" I say, even though I know the answer, the very asking of the question almost masochistic. At least I'm not thinking about William anymore.

"Yeah," he says, a helpless smile unfurling across his face like a welcome banner. "She's . . . she's totally different from the others."

Harder to get, I think, remembering the parade of ninnies who've tripped through our house, leaving any shred of resistance at the door. Is that all it is, or could it really be something more profound? I don't think I can bear it to be the latter.

All these years I've told myself that James isn't a man who can commit, that I've captured the best of him like a butterfly collector trapping the perfect Admiral—if it was just that I didn't make the grade it will hurt more than I could ever admit.

"Just be careful, okay?" I say, leaning across the table and squeezing his hand. "Is she saying anything about leaving him?"

I look around our skanky kitchen, thinking about that oversized rock weighing down Charlotte's spidery left hand. The Postbox is a banker, the kind of man who wears red pants but manages to get away with it thanks to the size of his bank balance. I bet her no-fat yogurts live in a top-of-the-range Smeg fridge, her unused oven some kind of self-cleaning masterpiece of German engineering. I can't help worrying that James is the equivalent of the handsome tennis coach servicing a bored trophy wife until she can't stand the heat.

"She'd leave tomorrow if she could, but he's totally emotionally reliant on her."

The idea that that phrase has sprung from the lexicon of James's mind is patently absurd. A flash, a fragment, a shard of the past: Sally sobbing in my arms about Gabriel. That's why—the very reason—I won't let my feelings for William gain any kind of purchase on my heart: unavailable equals agony. James is the proof—both the fact of him and the state of him at this very moment. I spring up, cross to the stove.

"I knew there were carrots in it!"

I set off for Pinewood at the crack of dawn, hoping that tinted moisturizer will pass for a good night's sleep. James and I stayed up until gone midnight talking, the subject of William inevitably rearing its ugly head. I totally downplayed it, repeated my line that it was an error of judgment born out of grief, leaving out the part where something within me reared up to meet him. The fact I omitted that vital piece is probably why he didn't warn me off.

"Poor bastard," he said. "I bet he feels like a total tool, on top of everything else he's getting thrown at him." I thought of William that night at the Berkeley, the self-punishment that lurks inside him, and knew that it was true. "I'd give it a couple of days and text him again, put him out of his misery."

Perhaps I will, I think, swinging James's ancient Golf up to the Pinewood security gates—he always tells me if he thinks I'm behaving like a loser, so if he's actually advising a course of action it can't be so disastrous.

After I've submitted myself to the kind of questioning you might expect if you were crossing the Iron Curtain, the security guard finally waves me through and I go and park. I've been told Flynn's assistant will be meeting me, and after a couple of minutes a stressed-looking girl in the skinniest of skinny jeans comes speeding across the parking lot clutching a sheaf of papers and gabbling into her phone. Her conical face is scattered with freckles, dark auburn hair hanging loose around it: she looks like a fox, pursued by a pack of hounds.

"Bye, bye," she barks in a cut-glass accent, then turns to me. "So sorry, I'm Katy."

"Nice to meet you."

"Follow me," she says, bejeaned legs scissoring off at ninety miles an hour. "I'm afraid they're running over. Flynn suggested you might want to come down to set."

To set? Would I ever! They're shooting an exterior scene on a back lot, the crew all standing around waiting for the lighting to be adjusted for the next take. Flynn's sitting on a canvas chair with his name on it, like an old-fashioned film star. He's studying his lines.

"I don't want to disturb him," I say, sensing Katy's anxiety levels rising, but just at that moment Flynn looks around.

"Olivia!" he says, springing up, arms held wide. He wraps me up in a warm hug.

"Hi!" I say, my face crushed against his stubbly cheek.

"You just give us a few minutes and I'll be all yours," he says. "Have you got Olivia a drink?" he asks Katy.

"No, I was just about to," she says.

Flynn grins and shrugs in mock despair.

"Can't get the staff these days."

"I'd love a cup of coffee if that's okay," I say, trying to tell her with my smile that he's joking, that I'm a fellow serf. "Milk, no—" but she's already left.

A gorgeous French actress who I've seen in a couple of art-house films prowls onto set, all long limbs and flicky dark hair. The scene is only a couple of lines, but the dialogue has to take place in the midst of a rain shower.

"It's always been you," she pleads. "You must know that."

Water buckets over her, as Flynn replies.

"If only I could," he says, crossing to kiss her and then striding out of shot.

You'd think we'd be done in ten minutes, but the crew have to shoot it from every possible angle, the actress getting more and more frozen on every run-through. Eventually the director shouts that it's time to move on.

"One more guys, one more," insists Flynn.

"We've got it," says the director. "You nailed it."

His costar is already wrapped up in a blanket, gratefully climbing into a warm pair of Uggs. Flynn's expression changes to one of grim determination.

"I can do better. We can do better. You've gotta trust me on this."

The director looks at him, the tension between the two of them palpable. I can feel a knot of anxiety forming in my stomach, even though it's not my drama. Eventually she forces a smile.

"Reset for Flynn's close-up."

It's a good hour before they finish, what with the retouching of Marie-Claire's ruined makeup and the lighting being adjusted to best serve Flynn's emerald green eyes. Once they're done he claps me on the arm, full of bonhomie.

"Let me get showered and changed and then we can get to work."

Half an hour later I'm tentatively knocking on the door of his trailer.

"Enter," he calls, and I swing open the door. He's got a shirt on but it's still unbuttoned, toned six pack displayed to perfection.

"Shall I . . ."

"No, no. Come in, make yourself at home."

I can't help but feel a little disappointed: the trailer's huge and everything, with an impressive-looking minibar, but it's still faintly reminiscent of those rainy Welsh caravanning holidays Dad used to subject us to.

"Have you had a haircut?"

"No, not that I'm aware of," I say, self-consciously patting my windswept mop. "Um, I washed it."

"Glad to hear it," says Flynn, gazing at me. "The washing, I mean." I try my hardest not to get flustered, distracting myself by pulling the pages of script out of my bag. "Snap," he says, reaching into a perspex folder and bringing out his own version. At least I think it is: it's so covered in scribbles that it looks like a troupe of inky-legged spiders have staged a line-dancing contest across it.

"Lovely job you've done here. Lovely. Had a few wee thoughts on where we could go next, if it's any help."

"Of course! That's why I'm here—fire away."

"I wanna bring everything I can to it, you must understand that," he says earnestly. "So I'm thinking, shouldn't I be on camera, out there in the field? So my fans can see I'm not just another celebrity piggybacking on some cause for their own glory."

My heart sinks as heavily as an elevator plummeting fifty floors. I can't bear for Mary to be right, for this to be no more than a vanity project. I suppose the writing was on the wall if I'd just chosen to read it.

"That's so key, of course, but the whole idea is that it's from the point of view of the young girl, the contrast between the two outcomes."

He sits back in his seat, crossing his arms.

"And you think if my ugly mug pops up people suddenly won't care?"

I laugh nervously.

"Of course not. I just wonder if it might be a more immersive experience if we enter her reality unadulterated." He stares at me blankly, and no wonder—I sound like I've walked off Newsnight Review. What would Mary do, what would Mary do? She'd flirt, in that special patented Mary way that I can't begin to emulate. "Your face would always be a bonus, but I just wonder whether your voice-over would do the same job."

"That's settled then," he says, getting out a thick, black pen. "Open on Flynn, in a shanty town, wee children playing in the background." He stares off into the middle distance. "I was thinking I could maybe direct it too, save us a few quid. It's *imperative* the money goes to where it's most needed."

I grit my teeth, a wave of anger rising up inside. A stubborn part of me still won't let him throw away the chance to do something that's genuinely good. I look at him, smile as warmly as I can. Surely, on some level, that's what he wants too?

"Yes, and that would be great, but we do have some excellent directors we can call on. Spending money on making the best film we possibly can will mean we'll pull in more cash in the long run."

"And you don't think I want to do that?"

"Of course I do!"

"Then you've lost me," he says, a tight smile on his face. "Not sure what your point is."

"I'm..." I pause. I know I should just back off, admit defeat and bow to Mary's superior understanding, but something won't let me drop the bone. "I'm just trying to advise you. Professionally." Wrong tack—I can see his hackles rising as he feels himself being patronized. I hold his gaze, try and find the "jumped up gypsy" with no airs and graces who I liked so much. "Flynn, we can do something amazing here, we can really make a difference. I just want the finished product to be every bit as heartfelt as your vision."

"And who better to deliver that than me?"

I might as well have brought a sleeping bag. By the time we've reached the bottom of page two, three hours have passed, Flynn questioning every single line, me refusing to play dead. There are repeated demands for him to go back to set, but he ignores every one. When the third knock comes, he flings the door open like he's being tortured.

"I will *be there* once this is done," he snarls at the hapless walkie-talkie-wearing assistant director. "You cannot control me with a schedule." A couple of minutes later his phone rings. "It's my agent," he mouths. She's obviously been alerted by the producers, as he starts to get red in the face as he listens to her. "I'm about to go," he snaps. "You know how important this is to me. It's not like I'm just writing a check, why won't people appreciate that?"

As I look at his earnest face, I realize that it's true; in his Alice in Wonderland celebrity world, this is the closest he gets to duty. Now I'm close to it, it's looking increasingly like an enormous playground, with grown-up-sized children playing an extended version of let's pretend, every whim indulged until they're barely able to feed themselves. What happens when something truly terrible happens, when the sky turns from blue to black in a way that no amount of money or sycophantic assistants can fix?

"Shall we wrap this up?" he says, casting me a black look, like it's all my fault.

I look at the raddled version of the script I'm holding, covered in endless adjustments and counter-adjustments and wonder how I'll ever make sense of it. I should have just admitted defeat three hours ago, listened to the tune he was humming and sung along—that's what Charlotte would have done. I can see Mary in my mind's eye, almost feel the *froideur* that will ooze from her when news reaches her of my latest idiocy.

"Yes, sure. Just give me your last few notes."

I take them down as diligently as I can, even though the kind of sickly, maudlin lines he's come up with are nothing like the message of empowerment that I wanted to get across. And then, finally, it's over.

"Thanks very much for taking the time to do this," I say. "I know how fierce your schedule is." I look at the script again, the prospect of imminent freedom giving me a surge of hope. Perhaps it can still mean something, achieve something out there in the big bad world. Flynn's eyes are narrow and frosty as he looks at me.

"It's my project, Olivia, there's no 'taking the time.' I should be thanking you."

Finally I'm back at the car, shaking my limbs out to get rid of the sticky energy of the last few hours. Mary's texted me: *Did you wow him?* she's put, with a gratifying string of kisses at the end. You can always tell you've committed some unmentionable sin when she damns you with a single *x*, left hovering, lonely and friendless, at the end of a message. Something tells me I'll be back in that particular wilderness pretty soon. *I think it went OK* I write, then let loose with a string of x's of my own. I look at it for a minute, blindsided by one of those rushes of fearfulness—that sense of the world as a place that's perilous and fragile—that have dogged me ever since I first heard that Sally had been killed.

I couldn't name exactly what it is that makes me decide that now is the time to contact William again—it feels like a force that exists outside myself. Perhaps it's the knowledge that he must feel it too, that our kiss might have heightened the nightmarish, surreal quality that the world has taken on. I want to at least make that tiny piece of it all right again. I don't want to send some stupid, abbreviated semblance of a message; instead I call him.

"Olivia," he says, his voice shot through with embarrassment. "Thank you for calling."

"Thanks for picking up."

"I've wanted to call, to apologize properly for my atrocious behavior."

"Please don't. Apologize I mean," I add hurriedly. "You've got nothing to apologize for."

"That's very generous of you, but of course I have." Is it more than the inappropriateness of it—is the very idea of kissing me truly horrific, something that could only happen *in extremis*? Holding me for those brief seconds must have made him blindingly conscious of what it is that he's lost forever. Maybe I shouldn't have called, should have let that stupid, stolen kiss be the stop sign. "But please, let's stop talking about me for a minute or two. How have you been?"

There's something in his voice, something that catches me before I make my excuses and run for the hills. Instead I let the stress of the last few hours come tumbling out, relieved to have a tiny window of normal, rather than the relentless narrative of life and death.

"She's a tricky customer, this Mary lady," he says, once I've vented my frustration.

"She's brilliant though," I say, hotly. "And she was right. I can't believe I've screwed it up all over again."

"There is no right, Livvy," he says, his tone softer. I think it's the first time he's called me that. "And you tried to do what *you* thought was right. I'm worried about that text though."

And something unfurls in me against my will, like a cat stretching out as its tummy's tickled. It moves me that he cares about something so small in the midst of everything.

"Hang on, I've not actually sent it. I . . . I wanted to call you," I say, hoping he doesn't hear something in my voice that shouldn't be there. I fiddle with my phone, find it saved to drafts, then let him help me come up with something that's not exactly a lie but won't send Mary apoplectic.

"Thank you," I say, once it's done. "And . . . William, I can forget what happened, I'm a brilliant amnesiac. I don't want you to never call me again."

"You've been a very good friend these last couple of months," he says, his voice infused with that softness. "I can see why Sally . . ."

He doesn't finish the thought. Instead it hangs there, until I feel I have to fill the silence.

"Maybe we could take Madeline on another outing. The Saturday after next?"

"I can't," he says, his tone suddenly cold. Oh God, I've totally misjudged this. He was going for a gentle landing, an easy exit, and instead I've taken him at his word.

"Okay. Look just call me when you can—"

"No, I mean I *can't*," he says, emphatic, somehow detecting the hurt in my voice. "I truly can't, not that I don't want to."

And then he tells me why. The personal effects from his New York apartment are being shipped back to the family home in Dorset, and he must spend the weekend sorting through them. His parents are abroad, and I picture him alone in some gloomy country estate, subsumed by the pieces of a life that's lost, holding each one up to the light and trying to decide if it means enough to make the cut. It's too awful to contemplate.

"I should have done it all when I was there, but . . ." He trails off again.

"It must have been so horrible being in that apartment."

"We tried, but it was too much. We turned tail and went and stayed with Richie and Mara, they oversaw packing it all up. They've been incredible."

I feel instantly guilty at the way I bristled when I met Mara, competing for Sally's affections even in death. She said she'd be there for them and she's been true to her word.

"William, please tell me to piss off if you want to, but . . . I could help you." The words are out of my mouth before I can think too much about what they mean. I pause, tense, wondering if I've overstepped the mark again. He doesn't speak, but then there's a clicking sound. "Are you smoking?"

"Possibly," he says, taking a drag. "That's a very kind offer but it's not your responsibility."

"I know that."

He can take it or leave it.

MARCH 1996

I could feel the blood draining from my face and I reached a hand toward the bar to steady myself. He was sporting a hat, a navy trilby, pulled to a bit of an angle, which he somehow managed to pull off, and a jacket far trendier than anything I remembered him wearing.

"Gimme a hug," he said, "I've traveled halfway across the British Isles to be here."

He was staring at me, waiting for me to bridge the gap, his look of appraisal impossible for me to miss. I knew him too well, knew that while he wasn't sleazy, he couldn't help but weigh up every situation that presented itself—too young, handsome, and horny to lose out on a round of what he saw as a numbers game. He wasn't a bastard, he was an opportunist, and it was only now, from the vantage point I was squarely standing in, that I could admit to myself that I'd never previously elicited much of a charge. I could see in his eyes what I already knew—that the Livvy that had packed up her Greenpeace-badged backpack five months before had ceased to exist. I wrapped my arms around his neck and pulled myself toward him, my whole body sparkling and rippling at the feel of him. One thing certainly hadn't changed. I pulled away as fast as I could bear to, immediately guilty.

"I can't believe you came!" I said. "This is Matt, my boyfriend"—I turned toward him and he gave an awkward half-grin, still not stepping forward—"and this is Sally."

Sally was beside herself at the sight of her plan coming together.

"Feels like we've already met," she laughed, leaning in and kissing him on both cheeks, branding him with her plum-colored mouth. He looked at her a little too long for my liking, though I couldn't entirely blame him. She was skinny again, dressed in a floor-length green sheath with a halter neck, her hair expertly tonged into an up-do: combined with the thick black flicky eyeliner she had a kind of retro glamour that felt almost unnaturally sophisticated, her ability to transform herself into more than the sum of her parts more pronounced than ever. In fact, if you entered the room cold, you'd doubtless put money on her being the birthday girl.

"How did you do it!?" I asked, throwing my arms around her. My heart should have returned to a normal rate by now, but it didn't seem to want to play ball.

"Called your mom," she said. "Happy birthday!"

I squashed down the voice in my head that urged me to subject her motives to some forensic analysis. She obviously took on board how much James meant to me, and thought I'd love him to be here. She was right too. I smiled at him. "You need a drink," I said, exactly in unison with Sally. The three of us looked at each other, and cracked up laughing.

It's hard to enjoy your own party, especially when the love of your life and the love of the moment are within ten feet of one another. It was utterly different from any birthday I'd ever had before—I loved the way people bought me drinks and made me feel special—but I felt bad that I couldn't pull Matt into the center of it all, his tortoise-like demeanor totally at odds with this kind of forced sociability. It wasn't like we didn't have lovely times when we were alone—we could talk endlessly about the books that had defined our adolescence, and he would remember every small detail about my life, quietly protective of me— but somehow it didn't translate. We stood at the bar, awkward, our conversation as stilted as a couple of foreign exchange students thrown together with only a phrase book to get them through. James was having an animated conversation with Sally, her fingers lightly dusting his arm for emphasis.

"Let me properly introduce you to James," I said, embarrassed by the way my eyes kept straying toward them.

"You haven't mentioned him before," said Matt carefully.

"Haven't I?"

"Nope."

"Really? We went to high school together."

Matt didn't respond, but he was no fool and I felt sinful, even though my sins were shadowy and nebulous. James must have noticed we were talking about him, as he chose that moment to come over.

"Hi, mate," he said, pumping Matt's hand. "How you surviving?"

"Surviving?"

"Life with this one," he said, a smile playing around his lips, an intimacy about the way he said it.

"I wouldn't call it survival," said Matt, trying to defend me, even though he didn't need to. In principle I loved him for

it. We stood there for what felt like an age, three statues, before Sally crashed into the circle. She grabbed both my hands, seemingly oblivious to the two boys, even though I knew with Sally that oblivion was only ever a pose.

"We need proper dancing," she cried. "I brought some CDs."

James cleared his throat theatrically.

"Ladies," he said, "stand aside and await musical greatness."

James loved his music; one of the first things that had triggered my romantic delusions was him making me a mix tape, although I soon found out it was no more than an excuse to show off his precociously eclectic record collection. I remember what he put on first—"Modern Love" by David Bowie—and we threw ourselves around, screaming the chorus, before Depeche Mode came on. I'd never known Sally to like anything remotely indie or retro, she was very much a chart girl, but she seemed to be loving it, and so was everyone else. Soon the whole party was jumping around, with me getting drunker and drunker, reveling in the frenzy of it all. Matt danced too, but we didn't dance together, even though we were close by— we'd lost our phrase book again. When it got to midnight, he pulled me aside.

"Would you hate me if I made a move? You can come back to mine later, I just can't miss training tomorrow."

"Course, I understand," I said, a little too quickly. Perhaps my eyes even flicked back to the dance floor. "I mean, I wish you'd stay, but if you have to go . . ." I smiled at him, trying to smooth the hurt from his face, but it was as if the wind had changed and it would stay that way forever.

"Goodbye, Livvy."

"Don't say it like that!" I said, hoping that if I played dumb, I could row the boat back to the shore.

"It's not right," he said simply.

I gripped hold of his hand, not remotely prepared, even though I should have been. It was all I deserved. "I don't not love you," I said.

Who could blame him for walking away from that tangled clump of words?

"Goodnight, birthday girl," he said, making a speedy exit, too kind to give me a rundown of my multiple sins right in the middle of my own party. If I could find that version of Livvy again, part of me would urge her to run after him, win a couple of years of being safely held, and avert the trauma that was hurtling down the track, but perhaps neither he nor I deserved something so vanilla. Instead I stood there, staring after him, unable to work out if the pain in my chest was hurt pride or a wrecking ball of loss.

Sally came and found me, giving me a massive hug when I told her what had happened, filling my nose with the familiar combination of Marlboro Lights and Chanel No. 19—for years my head would whip round on the tube when that cocktail of smells seeped from a nearby body. "Twat," she kept saying, "how could he do that to you on your birthday?" At first I stood up for the truth, protesting that it was more complicated than that, but gradually I sank into the warm bath of her unconditional support, wiping my eyes and bravely reentering the fray on the dance floor like the wounded heroine she'd painted me as. Sally wasted no time telling James what had happened, and he too puffed up with outrage, until we were like the Three Musketeers, a trio who had existed forever, bonded by blood.

Sally started flirting with a guy from the ex-poly, Shaun, who'd sneaked in from the main bar, and James and I found ourselves dancing together more and more. It wasn't that we were slow-dancing—it's hard to do when the song's "Come

*on Eileen"—but it was more than dancing separately in close
proximity. I felt high on it, the shock of Matt's abandonment
somehow fueling the intensity of the moment —his fingers
would brush me more than necessary, his smiles slow, lan-
guid invitations, and soon I was physically yearning for him
to kiss me. I shudder now thinking about it: I hope it was
youth that made me so callous, that there isn't some switch
buried deep within me that could still be flicked to off.*

*Eventually the lights went up, and we struggled to adjust,
mole-like and disoriented. "Sally said I could crash at your
house," said James, his eyes fixed on me, and I felt my old
anxieties flooding back, a painful reminder that they were
more than just a coat I could shrug off at will. I tried to ignore
them, tried to force the inside to tally with the polished shini-
ness of my outside, impulsively reaching for James's hand.
He squeezed it back, flung an easy arm around my shoulder,
and we went to look for Sally, me trying my best not to betray
how much my body shook. She was out the back with Shaun,
sharing a cigarette, and soon the four of us were piling into a
cab back to our halls, waving a cheery goodbye to Lola, left
stranded on the pavement with Justin. I remember Shaun
was relegated to the front seat, forced to make conversation
with the driver, while the three of us continued our love-in—
now I'd got over the shock, it felt amazing to be bumping
around between the two of them, the two hemispheres that
made up my world.*

*When we got back I showed James my tiny little room
and left him making a pretense of unrolling his sleeping bag
while I went to the bathroom. I locked the door, looked at my
face, makeup smeared by tears and sweaty dancing. I didn't
take it off, I adjusted it; I would never have had the courage
to face James without its protection. It made me miss Matt*

suddenly, who was never happier than when we were hiking around the moors, my cheeks colored only by the biting wind. The booze was starting to wear off, an early onset hangover kicking in, along with that tinge of melancholia that it often brings. It brought me up short, made me question what I was walking back into, but I didn't have the strength to turn away: I'd longed for this, and it felt like if I didn't seize this chance, I'd lose him to all those other girls who were the real deal rather than the imposter that I was. Courage, I thought, giving myself a wide, artificial smile in the mirror. Was I homesick for the Livvy that had gone absent without leave?

I slipped into bed, and James propped himself up on one elbow.

"I know it's cold, but are you really going to bed in your party dress?"

I felt utterly silly. He smiled at me, sensing it, perhaps relieved I was still my same old awkward self when I was put under pressure.

"Do you want a cuddle?" he said. "You know I'm an excellent cuddler."

I nodded mutely, holding the duvet up to give him room to slip into my bed, part of me hoping he meant it literally. I wish I'd the courage to speak, to tell him that for all my bravado, it was much too soon for us to jump into the grave of my relationship with Matt. I wish even more I could have told him how much more intimidating the reality felt in comparison to my love-soaked, sepia-tinged daydreaming, in which I always maintained directorial control. The feel of him in my arms, flesh and bone, was almost too much to bear.

As he kissed me I felt myself floating above us, critiquing my performance. He peeled off my dress, revealing Sally's present. "Wow," he muttered, kissing my neck and shoulders around the straps, and I felt that yawning gap between inside and outside, my sexy underwear signing me up to a contract I was terrified to deliver on. I kissed him back, stroked that body I'd longed for, but I couldn't abandon myself to it. Now I wonder why that felt so wrong—why shouldn't we have needed to travel the runway before we took off, to have got to a place where it was born out of a relationship rather than a collision of circumstances—but then it felt like abject failure. We were naked by now, but he must have sensed my body stiffening to his touch. I wanted to coil myself around him like a sinuous serpent, but instead I felt like a plasticky curl of garden hose. He drew back, stopped kissing me, his hands withdrawing.

"We don't have to do this."

"Perhaps if we just slow down a bit," I replied, kissing his face like an overeager puppy, full of apology.

He kissed me once more, little more than a brushing together of our lips, and then we lay there, neither one of us asleep, neither of us venturing back over the line. Did he know that it was because I wanted him so much, rather than because I didn't? Even now I still don't have the courage to ask.

He looked like he was asleep when I woke up, and I crept out of the room, wrapping my nakedness under all the clothing I could grab. As I left I saw him surreptitiously open one eye, then shut it again. Shaun and Sally were in the kitchen, sipping coffee from her cafetière, giggling away as if they'd known each other for years. "Hang on," said Sally, racing after me to the bathroom and shutting us in.

"So?" she said, searching my face. I tried to bat her away, wishing I'd been able to close the door quicker.

"It's not like that with us," I said, trying my hardest to sound breezy. "I should've known that. We're meant to be mates."

"Well at least you know now," she said, her voice comforting. "It's better, isn't it? To know?"

How quick she was to agree, even though my protestations wouldn't have convinced a four-year-old. I don't believe for a second that they convinced her.

CHAPTER TWELVE

AT EIGHT-THIRTY A.M. HE TEXTS TO SAY HE'S ARRIVED, and I clatter down the stairs, weighed down by the picnic I stayed up until midnight assembling (I needed a distraction, there was no way I could sleep). I look up and down the street, but there's no sign of him, until he unfolds himself from a tiny yellow vehicle that looks more like a gob of phlegm than a car.

"Don't say it," he says, smiling ruefully. "You try hiring a car at six o'clock on a Friday." Some part of him must have fought tooth and nail to escape from this.

"It's very—colorful. Who'd you rent it from, Ronald McDonald?"

He's wearing jeans, actual jeans, and his face is covered by a light peppering of stubble, which seems to somehow smooth out that rigidity that often imprisons his features. He's wearing a green sweater over the jeans, which brings out the hazel flecks in his deep-set eyes—at the very second I notice them, I remind myself who most likely picked it, think of her rifling through my student wardrobe, the "chuck" pile turning into a tower, deaf to my protests. "It's the new you, Olivia Berrington!" she said, holding up a brown turtleneck like it was nuclear waste.

"It's my sister's—they keep it in the garage for dire emergencies. If it breaks down, I'm relying on you to push."

I flip the passenger seat forward so that I can deposit my goods and chattels in the back.

"Traveling light?"

"Oh," I say, embarrassed. "I brought a picnic in case we didn't have time to stop—they're like, the law, on long journeys in my family."

"So what's on the menu?"

"I hard-boiled some eggs, which I know can smell a bit farty, but with celery salt they're really nice. And there's some hummus sandwiches, and tangerines. And some Green and Black's for pudding."

I stand there, swinging my carrier bag of boiled eggs, suddenly feeling like the world's biggest nerd.

"Thank you," he says, his eyes soft, and the feeling transforms into something far sweeter. Until . . . until I remember what it is we're here to do.

William drives fast, but I don't feel remotely unsafe.

"Is it weird?" I ask, tentative. "Driving, I mean?"

"I can't start thinking like that," he says, effortlessly moving the spitball of a car into the path of a BMW, proximity perfectly judged. "I've only ever had one, stupid accident. Madeline doesn't need me turning into a neurotic wreck."

"What happened?"

"I hit a rabbit," he says, smiling. "Near my parents. I could see it, hopping off, half dead. I couldn't bear it, so I went in pursuit."

"What, to finish the job? What would you have done?"

"It was just instinct, I hadn't thought it through. Anyway, the police came past and saw me crawling around on a grass verge, with the car door hanging open. One breathalyzer test later I finally convinced them."

I love that you did that, I think, that the welfare of a single rabbit mattered that much. I put on the radio, swallowing the thought before I accidentally say it out loud. It's tuned to Magic: William's sister clearly has excellent taste. I'm about to swivel the dial to something more fusty and impressive but William stops me.

"No, leave it on. This is definitely one of my desert island discs."

It's "Wichita Lineman," that mournful, heartbreaking ode to an ordinary love affair. We listen in silence, until I have to break it.

"I love it too," I say, "but it's too sad."

"It's too romantic to be sad."

"How can you say that? He wants her more than needs her. I can't think of anything worse."

My flesh crawls at the very thought of it, a life lived in codependent torture with someone you know isn't the love of your life. Who wants to be a prisoner who tossed away their own key?

"But he needs her for all time," says William, insistent. "That's impossibly romantic. Despite the fact that he knows her flaws, he's pledging to be there for eternity. He's not giving up."

"Only because he needs her, not because he wants her. He'll probably be sat in the basement glued to a PlayStation, scratching his balls and demanding his dinner. For all time."

William laughs as he looks over, and with just our eyes we agree to differ.

After we've listened to more Phil Collins than even I can stomach, we finally get off the M3 and start driving up the coast. I had no idea how beautiful and windswept it would be, the beaches deserted, the sea choppy. The sky is that crisp autumnal blue that only lasts a few short weeks.

"Shall we stop for a hard-boiled egg break, or do you think it's too cold?" says William, who's been increasingly quiet since we left the motorway, his dread silently mushrooming as we get closer to the house.

"I'm hardier than I look," I say, and he swiftly swings into a beachside car park.

I grab the picnic from the back seat as he rummages in the trunk, reappearing in the world's most hideous jacket. It's a sludgy tan, cut to just below the waist, cinched in with plastic toggled strings. I forgot to adjust my face quickly enough.

"That bad? Bonfire worthy?"

I can't believe Sally let him wear that in public.

"It's . . . it's quite brown."

I see him visibly cringe, and I automatically reach out and squeeze his sludgy arm before drawing back.

"I don't know what possessed me. My parents just sent it to me." He gives a sheepish smile. "I think my father might have one."

Man, I'm glad my parents don't dress me anymore: I was always pleading to pick my own look, rather than being subjected to Jules's washed-out hand-me-downs. But then, I'm thirty-five, so it's no great surprise they've given up trying.

"They must really want to keep you warm," I say, setting off down the beach.

We sit on the rocks, exhaling steamy puffs of dragon breath, our sandwiches balanced precariously on our knees.

"You're right about the celery salt," says William.

"It's my secret picnic weapon."

Neither of us are in any rush—despite the biting wind, we last a good half hour chatting companionably about nothing very much.

"Are you ready?" asks William eventually, his face suddenly blank and distant.

"When you are."

"Two more minutes," he says, pulling me to my feet and running to the water's edge. He skims a couple of stones with fierce concentration, rewarded with a satisfying series of bounces.

"You try."

"No point. I'm hopeless," I say, throwing one at the water and watching it sink without trace.

"It's all about the wrist," says William, and just for a second James jumps to mind, with his four hundred male euphemisms for "I'm wanking over you," and I have to stifle a giggle. "May I?" says William, putting a stone in my hand and taking my wrist before I've replied. His grasp is firm and gentle at the same time, and I relax into it despite myself. "Now, go." And with his hand encasing mine, the stone surfs the water, bouncing through the surf like a joyous fish. "Told you!" He is grinning with satisfaction. I smile back, my gaze meeting his for longer than it should, before I'm poleaxed by the reality of today. I spin away, look to the car. He follows my gaze, and we start the walk back up the pebbly beach, feet sinking into the stones. The distance feels like an eternity.

The road squiggles and twists like spaghetti, a thick canopy of foliage overhanging us. I can sense my mounting anxiety as we drive ever further from home, from everything that's familiar, but it seems too insensitive to articulate it, even though the words might chase the feeling away. Instead we drive the last few miles in silence, without even the radio for company.

When we reach the house I try not to gasp. It's not just its size—it's big, very big, with outbuildings and stables visible in the distance—it's also the sheer magnificence of it. It's old, Victorian I think, but perfectly preserved, the gray stone gleaming like a well-fed cat, the leaded windows polished until they sparkle, with a wide gravel drive that sweeps up to the heavy doors like a swishing tail. I stare up at it, dwarfed.

"First things first," says William, coming around the car to open my door for me. "Let me find you a cup of tea."

We walk through the dark, high-ceilinged hallway and into a large, well-appointed kitchen, dominated by an Aga along one wall. There's no note, nothing left behind to ease William's journey, but he doesn't seem to notice. He flicks on the kettle and opens the fridge.

"Ah, Doris has left some milk."

"Doris?"

"Lady from the village who helps out."

He turns out to be terrible at tea, the bag steeped too long and with the merest dash of milk, but I don't have the heart to tell him; instead I sip it politely, sitting at the bare pine table, dread wriggling around my solar plexus. Sally would have sat here, at this very table, looking out onto the barn which now holds the debris of her life.

"Are you sure about this?" he says, his strong hands clasped around his mug.

"Yes," I say, trying to sound stout and certain.

He gives me a tense smile, then hauls himself to his feet. He leads me across a beautifully tended walled garden, to the barn, which has been converted into something much smarter than the word would suggest. Stacked inside its cavernous interior is box upon box, HARRINGTON written in marker pen, with the rooms marked underneath. BEDROOM reads one, and I feel a shudder go through me, assailed by memories of makeshift student moves, our possessions shoved into flimsy boxes from the corner shop, then piled up in the back of Sally's tiny hatchback until she could barely see out of the back. And now I'm here, unpacking her life, with her torn out of it. I sense William steeling himself, before striding forward and stripping the packing tape from the first box.

"Madeline's toys," he says, a smile of relief wreathing his face. A stern, old-fashioned-looking doll emerges, and he pushes it back in the box, scanning the rest of the pile.

"These will be her clothes," I say, spying some wardrobe boxes, trying to keep my voice from shaking. He rips the tape off like a Band-Aid coming off a livid scab. It's dress after dress, packed in tightly, suspended from a rail. William bunches the fabric of one up in his hands, and I turn away, look out of the window; perhaps he inhales her scent, buries his face in it, it's not for me to know. By the time I turn back he's standing away from them, surveying them critically.

"I shudder to think how much these cost," he says. "Do you want . . ."

I shake my head, before he can say it. I step forward, pull out a sapphire blue sheath, the fabric cut into a deep V at front and back. It's a size zero. How beautiful she must have looked in it.

"Oxfam," I say, swallowing. "Oxfam know how to get a proper price for designer clothes. Or eBay." I pull out a couple more dresses, catching the top note of Chanel No. 19 and struggling to continue. "Or you could keep them for when Madeline's older."

Now it's William's turn to shake his head, his face set.

"Oxfam's the answer. At least they'll be doing some good." He writes it in large capital letters, the nib of the marker pen biting into the cardboard. "Let's keep going." He's barely looking at me, his gaze turned inward, the fleeting ease of the car journey a distant memory. A wave of fear breaks over me, a sense of being so far out of my depth that the shore is no more than a pinprick. I feel the fabric scrunch between my fingers, the smell of perfume catching in my throat and it gives me a fragment of comfort, a sense of a time when, rightly or wrongly, she was my anchor. He's pulling open a box full of toiletries now, face creams and body lotions, abandoned half used—I feel almost sorry for them.

"This one's easy," he says, starting to tip the contents into a rubbish sack. I can't stand it—I feel my hand shoot out before I can rein myself in.

"William, wait. Please . . ."

"Do say if there's anything you want."

"It's not that!" I say, trying not to sound harsh.

"I'm just mindful of the fact you've got a train to catch," he says. I can see the rigidity in his jaw, how tight it is.

"Here," I say, making my voice as gentle as I can, taking the bag from his clenched fist. "I'll do it."

And I lay them in the bag, bottle by bottle, consciously feeling the solid presence of each one as I hold it in my hand. I open her face cream, rich and thick, the peaks and troughs created by the pressure of her fingers. I rub some into the back of my hand before I consign it to the bag, inhaling its smell.

There are boxes and boxes of books, and William kneels on the floor, sifting through them. "Shall I carry on with the clothes?" I ask, but he doesn't respond. I stand there, awkward, looking down on his bowed head, the subtle recession of his hairline. He looks so vulnerable to me.

"Sorry," he says eventually, looking up, a hardback in his hands. After a few seconds he turns the cover toward me. It's *The End of the Affair* by Graham Greene, a beautiful old copy. "One of my favorite books. First edition. I gave it to Sally on our first Valentine's Day." I wouldn't know how to receive that, I think, however beautiful the edition. He's staring at the inside cover, the inscription out of my sight line. "Yes, do please carry on." He is distracted. "We'll stick with the Oxfam plan."

I work my way through a box of beautiful knitwear. I should probably just scrawl Oxfam on it and move on, but it seems disrespectful somehow. I lift each piece out, then stack it up, lifting the pile back into the box at the end. William is going through her jewelry now, holding up beautiful necklaces and earrings. I watch him, unsure if he wants to feel there's someone here, or prefers to work in bleak isolation.

"They're beautiful too."

He doesn't even turn, and I go back to the boxes, cowed. He grabs a rough handful of necklaces, and pushes them back into a jewelry box. It takes all my will power not to cross the barn and detangle them, lay them carefully in their velvet case.

"Surely you're going to keep them?"

"No. No, I'm not," he says, his voice as cold and black as oil.

I feel my hackles rise, and try to breathe myself back to an unsteady calm. Why is he being like this? He thrusts the jewelry into a cardboard box and starts pulling out magazines.

"Why did they even pack these?" he says, angrily.

I open the next box, running my fingers across another rack of perfect dresses. My eyes roll upward, almost unconsciously; I hope you're glad I'm doing this, I think. You'll either be glad or enraged, there'll be no third option. I pull out a black velvet dress with a fishtail hem and a boned bodice, the kind of outfit she must have worn to accompany him to those god-awful functions. It makes me feel unexpectedly close to her, something we've shared without ever having been able to share it. I gather it close, my heart beating against the fabric.

"She had such lovely dresses," I say, my voice thick. "She always did. Do you remember her wearing this one?"

He glances over briefly.

"Not specifically, no."

I feel stung, and by proxy that she too has been stung. It suddenly feels so important that the dark is not allowed to eclipse the light—surely we need to remember the ways she shone as we plow through the pieces of her life? I pull out the green one.

"She was wearing a green dress on my nineteenth, the year she threw me a surprise party. She looked like some kind of sea creature."

"She was certainly a big fan of parties," says William, terse.

"Yes, she was," I say, sharp, reacting to the judgment I hear in his voice. "She could've made a party out of a couple of packets of crisps and a Bacardi Breezer."

"You're right," he snaps. "It's just that at some point the music has to stop." He stands up, face turned away, but even in profile I can see he's boiling. "Excuse me a minute" he says, walking swiftly out of the room. I stare after him, shocked. How did we move from the gentle companionship of the journey to that kind of spitting rage? I look around the room, Sally's life heaped up around us, the stage set—of course it wouldn't be without drama. Part of me wants to bolt after him, apologize profusely for my clumsiness, but I worry it will only make it worse. How little I know him, even though sometimes it feels like the opposite.

I cross to the box with the jewelry and take out the necklaces that lie there, tangled up together like strands of bindweed. I tease each one out and lay it down, until the velvet interior starts to feel like a coffin. I swallow down a tide of nausea, suddenly wanting nothing more but to run down those lanes, my heart lurching in my chest, until I'm somewhere far from here. I sit down, gather myself.

After a few minutes I carry on, sorting determinedly through more boxes of sweaters, and exquisite pants, and perfect pairs of heels until I eventually reach a box full of heavy winter coats, bought to withstand chilly New York winters. I pull each one out individually, take a proper look at it, imagine the life it's lived. One attracts me like a magpie alighting on a jewel: it's scarlet, with a sweeping collar and ostentatious black buttons running down from a scooped neckline. That same smell of Chanel No. 19 clings to it, perhaps even the underlying odor of a secretly puffed cigarette, and something compels me to slip it on, even though doing so leaves me light-headed. I twist my body around, feeling its luxuriant swish, and go and look at myself in the bathroom mirror, almost expecting it to be Sally who stares back at me. Who were you in this? Where did it take you? I don't know why, but something tells me it was a favorite amongst all those others that are stuffed together, as tight as sardines.

As I stand there, I feel something hard in the pocket, and my hand tightens around it. I pull it out: it's a numbered plastic tag with CAPRICORN HOLDINGS written down the middle. It sits there in my palm, significance unknown. I'm suddenly desperate to get the coat off, terrified of William coming back in and finding me in it. I put the tag in the pocket of my jeans, away from the mess of boxes, ready to show him. I try to move on to the next box, but there's a gnawing sensation that won't allow me to lose myself in the task at hand. The tag digs into my upper thigh, hard and pointed, until I feel I've got no choice but to go and find him.

It's raining outside, the lawn wet and spongy under my feet. The kitchen door is stiff, and water pours down the back of my neck as I try to jiggle it. I shout William's name, but there's no response. Eventually I shoulder my way in but the house is still, with only the solemn ticking of the grandfather clock in the hallway punctuating the silence.

Where is he? I take a doorway off to the right of the hall and find myself in a dark dining room, tall wooden chairs positioned around a rosewood table like jurors trying a case. I can't help but inspect the family pictures displayed on the sideboard, my eyes drawn to a school picture of William aged around twelve, dressed in a striped school blazer with a large crest, his hair cut into a severe short back and sides. He's looking straight into the camera like he's trying his very hardest, like he wants so much to deliver on what's been asked of him. I take a quick look over the rest of the pictures—the interchangeable shots of infant grandchildren, the wedding photos—rites of passage that prove you've left your mark on the world. His parents' wedding photo is a sight to behold, his dad dressed in a spotless morning suit, body held rigid, unsmiling gaze directed outward, as if the pretty, smiling bride holding his hand wasn't even there. I'm not sure there's a single image that hasn't been formally composed.

I go back into the hall and call William's name, not trusting myself to open any more doors. There's no response, just that maddening ticking sound. I'm cold and damp and alone, somewhere in the depths of the countryside, living out my very own version of *The Shining*.

"William!" I shout, more sharp, trying to quell the irrational fear that's starting to creep through my veins like a slow-acting poison.

There's a pause, and then the creaking of a door.

"Here," he calls, voice broken.

I stand there, frozen, wondering if it's an invitation. I trip-trap up the long staircase that curves around the entrance hall, arrive on the landing and head for the one open door. It's like I've stepped through time; he's sitting in his boyhood bedroom, perched on a single bed, surrounded by cricketing trophies. There's a small wooden desk under the window, replete with a dictionary for homework duties, and a bookshelf full of *Tintin* books, with a few *Star Wars* figurines scattered across it. He's looking at his iPhone, but he dumps it on the bedside table at the sight of me.

"Sorry," he says, voice flat. "I didn't mean to abandon you."

"It's okay," I say, sheepish. "I just wanted . . ." I'm about to pull the tag out of my pocket, but when I look into his hollow eyes I can't force the words out. "To know if you wanted a cup of tea."

"I should be making you tea, Olivia," he says, half rising, our apology exchanged in the most English of ways. I sit down next to him, hoping it will keep him here—I don't want him to switch back into autopilot. This room is like a shrine. Even if my parents hadn't sold the family home, I know Mom would've taken roughly five minutes to turn it into a stinky, incense-ridden meditation den.

"Are you a batter or a bowler?"

"Batter, though I only get about a game a year these days," he says. "Got—that might change now."

"*Tintin* not *Asterix*?"

"I've never trusted the Gauls." He gives a half smile. We sit there in silence for a few seconds, the rain pitter-pattering against the glass. "Tell me about *your* room," he says.

"Then or now?"

"Either. Or both."

I look out of the window, aware of the gathering dusk, the piles of boxes yet to sort. Perhaps he'd rather do it alone, perhaps my presence has left him too vulnerable.

"I had lots and lots of books."

"That's no great surprise."

"Yes, but they weren't all highfalutin! I had *Hollywood Wives* hidden under the mattress so my mom wouldn't find it." I look round the tiny bedroom. "Come on then, where are your *Playboy*s?"

He crosses the room, opens the wardrobe door with a flourish.

"Top right-hand corner, under the rowing gear. At least I hope they're still there." He sees my face. "Not for that! For the sake of Mom's modesty."

"I didn't know your mom was a centerfold."

He rolls his eyes at me, and I giggle, despite myself.

"What else?" he asks, the bed shifting as he sits back down next to me. "Actually, revise that. What's it like?"

"*Hollywood Wives*? Oh, terrifying if you're me," I say, and then curse myself for accidentally tripping over the truth. He looks at me, quizzical. "You know, all those waxed dominatrices with their bedroom acrobatics."

I'm suddenly very aware we're on a bed, even though you can 100 percent guarantee no Jackie Collins heroine would be caught dead strutting their stuff on this beige candlewick bedspread.

"I see. Sounds very intriguing." We smile at each other again, the silence an unexpectedly gentle one. "I need to get you to your train relatively soon."

"I know, I'm sorry. I feel like I've hardly done anything," I say, feeling that hard chip of plastic digging into me. This peace feels too fragile and hard-won to take an ax to just yet.

"Not at all," he replies, heartfelt, and I realize that somewhere along the way I've learned the difference between his meaningless reflexes and the moments in which his real feelings peep through. "Let me organize that cup of tea."

"And then we can do some more . . . if that's helpful."

"You're very kind," he says, turning those soft, dark eyes toward me, and a glow of satisfaction spreads through me like molasses.

One disgusting cup of tea later, accompanied by a stale ginger snap, I start steeling myself for the final push. I can't help but wonder why there's no more than a stale ginger snap, why his parents didn't try to take the edge off the abject horror of this task, but perhaps I'm reading too much into the damn cookie.

"Shall we?" I ask, tentatively, swallowing down a mounting feeling of dread. I've decided to wait until we're back out there, and I can show him the coat I found it in. He doesn't reply, gaze lost. Maybe he'll know exactly what it is—a facility they used when they moved to the US, a family hidey-hole for excess furniture—and I'm making a fuss about nothing, but some sixth sense is whispering to me that it's more. And if it is—how can I abandon him here, surrounded by the ashes of a life he's struggling to know how to grieve? His head snaps back in my direction.

"No," he says. "You've done enough. If we leave now we'll get you to the train in plenty of time, and I'll push on through until it's done."

Relief winds me—the knowledge that I won't have to go back into that makeshift mausoleum and pick through Sally's life like a thief—but it's mixed with an illogical sense of hurt. I want so much to shoulder some of the burden, to breach his isolation. A horrible thought strikes me—do

I want that for him, or is some sly, perfidious part of me wanting it as much for myself?

As he busies himself finding my coat, I pull the tag out and hold it in my hand, ready to offer it up. He holds my coat out, and I step into it, liking his old-fashioned courtesy. Once I'm successfully swaddled, I turn to him, to spit out the words that have kept catching in my throat, but his phone rings before I get there.

"Hello, darling," he says, and signals for me to follow him out with that natural authority that he has.

It's Madeline's bedtime, and I hear him asking about her day with her cousins. "I see," he says, a number of times, sounding a little like he's on a conference call, before he starts to wind up. "I'm afraid I've got to go. I'm taking Olivia to the station."

I wave a hand, try to tell him there's no rush, but after a "night-night" he hangs up. I feel a pang, imagining her clad in her white nightie, little hand clinging on to the dead receiver; I hope she doesn't feel abandoned, like I've stolen him away from her.

"Righto," he says, coming around to unlock my door—the spit gobbet is from an age long before central locking. He turns the key in the ignition, and it emits a low rumble, before puttering back to silence. He tries three times, each less successful than the last.

"Bugger," he says, striking the steering wheel hard with both hands. "I'm dreadfully sorry."

"It's okay, it's not your fault," I tell him. And suddenly it is okay; suddenly it feels too soon to go, to abandon him to the chilly embrace of this big, gloomy house.

"I'm afraid it is." His tone is stern, his inner headmaster in overdrive. "Let's just hope Belinda's got breakdown

coverage," he says, heading for the house. The unfortunately named Belinda's managed to disappear off the face
of the earth—her cell and landline elicit no response—and
William resorts to searching for a cab number. He looks at
me, stricken.

"They're an absolute nightmare to track down on a
Saturday night, and it's a good thirty miles to Poole. I feel
wretched about this. Have I ruined your plans?"

The rain's bucketing down by now, wind blowing the
trees into oblivion. It's emphatically not a night to be
screeching around hairpin bends on the back of a combine
harvester praying I'll make the last train. And I have no
plans.

"William . . ."

"Mm?" he says, rootling through the kitchen drawers.

I feel utterly exposed, but I tumble on before I can censor
myself.

"I could just stay," I say, feeling myself blushing. "There's
tons of room, and I can get a cab in the morning if we can't
get the car fixed. I won't get home till God knows when if I
go tonight."

I study his face, desperate to capture his true reaction
before good breeding suffocates it. He smiles a real smile.

"We might starve."

"Man up, we've got ginger snaps."

William opens a bottle of highly superior wine from his
dad's cellar and gives me carte blanche to look in the lar-
der. I find some tinned tomatoes and some ancient-looking
chili flakes, the beginnings of some kind of scratch supper.
I look through the window at the barn, the lights glowing, a

constant reminder of why we're really here, and survey the paltry ingredients, acutely reminded of the student suppers I'd rustle up from the shelves of the Happy Shopper. Sally never cooked, never ate anything that didn't come from a packet, a can, or a waiter, unless I made it for her. She was like a baby bird, waiting to be fed, and I was happy to oblige. I liked taking care of her—did she learn to find that same satisfaction from looking after them?

"Pretty pathetic," I say, going back to the kitchen, dumping the ingredients unceremoniously on the table.

"Ha! Not if I dig you up an onion," says William, looking pleased with himself.

"But you'll drown!"

"I'd rather drown than have you starve."

I smile more fondly than I should, and out he goes, reappearing ten minutes later, ruddy-faced and bedraggled.

"M'lady," he says, bowing, and presenting a huge white onion and a handful of chives.

"You're soaking!" I scrabble around to find tea towels.

He shakes himself like a big dog, rubbing hard at his sopping wet hair and as he does so, it feels like something is being sloughed away, like he's losing that layer of pristine rigidity that keeps him so untouchable. My heart squeezes in my chest, beating its way into my consciousness, and I have to look away, busying myself with finding a knife and a chopping board. He sits down at the table, half an eye on the paper, his glass of wine at his elbow. Again, that yawning gulf between what it looks like and what it is.

"I've got to call James if I'm not coming back," I say, digging my phone out of my bag, stirring the sauce as it rings. It's Saturday night, so I'm expecting to leave a message, but he actually picks up.

"Hi," he says, voice flat. "You at the station?"

"No. Where are you?"

"Living room. I'll come get you if you like."

I don't think I've ever known James to stay in on a weekend night without either a promise of sex or a deathly illness. Charlotte, I think, heat rising, but he would never have picked up if she was there.

"No you won't, not from here," I say, glancing at William. He's ostensibly reading the paper, but I get the sense he's tracking me. "I'm . . . I'm still in Dorset. With William," I add. "There's a storm raging and the car's broken down."

"How Gothic," says James, an edge to his voice.

"At least it means I can give him some more help." William raises sad eyes toward me, and I start to feel awkward. "Listen, I've got to go, I'll see you tomorrow."

I hang up, oddly flustered. "Sorry about that." William pushes the paper away.

"It's very kind of you, but I meant what I said earlier. Just helping me start the task made all the difference. I'll worry about it tomorrow when you've gone." He reaches over, filling our glasses almost to the brim, clinking his against mine. "And I don't mean to take issue with the cook, but something's burning."

It's not my best effort, the onions more blackened than browned, the tomatoes sharper than I'd like, but William pronounces it delicious on his first bite.

"But William it's not," I say, surprised to find how much it matters to me. I want to know that he is able to tell me the truth, rather than feel like he's tossing out platitudes the way he'd throw bread to the ducks; I suspect he spends most of his life telling people what they want to hear.

"I'm enjoying it," he insists.

"That's different from it being objectively delicious. You don't have to flatter me." Where's my edginess coming from? It's guilt in part; that plastic tag still digging into me, the sense I'm sitting opposite Sally's husband, her seat still warm. "I was always the cook when I lived with Sally," I add, looking at him. Was it wrong to mention her? She feels so strong here that I couldn't not, couldn't risk him thinking I'm trying to obliterate her.

"I can believe that," he says, his fingers gripping his glass a little more tightly. "She was a great one for eating out."

"Did she ever learn to cook?" I ask, the atmosphere palpably shifting, an icy dampness engulfing us.

"No." Our forks scrape against our plates, every sound magnified by the pregnant silence. Sometimes it's as though he disappears when she appears, like they're two tiny figurines in a weather house; maybe he can only stand to be alone with his memories. "She hated it," he adds, emotion surging. "Which was her prerogative, of course, I'm not some kind of Victorian patriarch."

"She didn't have the patience for it."

"Sally was never a fan of delayed gratification," mutters William, his face a mask. I wish I'd never gone here, stumbled from the warm and friendly path we were ambling down. There's nowhere to go, nothing to distract us, the silence an ocean.

"Fancy splitting a ginger snap for dessert?" I ask, hating my feeble attempt at levity.

He turns his heavy-lidded eyes toward me.

"I'm sorry, Olivia, I don't know why you're putting up with me."

"It's not a sufferance," I say, my voice catching. "I promise you that."

He stares at me, as if he's holding up what I've said to the light.

"And I'm sorry I snapped at you earlier. It was totally unnecessary."

"Don't worry. You're under so much stress."

"It's just . . ." He's looking at me, but his eyes don't seem quite able to see me. "There's something not right."

"What kind of not right?" There are so many kinds of not right that it's hard to pin one down. He pauses as if he's weighing up whether or not to speak. When he does his voice is low and hard to hear.

"There's things I can't seem to find. There's a pair of diamond earrings I gave her for our anniversary, an S necklace she used to wear all the time. I don't know where they can be."

He looks at me, his face an appeal, pain etched there. My suspicions start to swim to the surface.

"There's something Madeline said to me, at the museum. About her and Sally having a secret place. I just wonder, if there are things missing—"

"It won't have meant anything," he says, quick as a flash, his face shutting down. "That's what they were like together. She often used to treat Madeline more like her best girlfriend than a little girl. Sometimes when I got back from a trip it was as though I was intruding."

His eyes are burning, that fat worm of stress throbbing in his temple, and I know instinctively that I've gone too far. It's so confusing the way he'll venture toward opening the door on whatever secrets Sally might have had, but then slam it shut like he can't bear to look inside. No wonder he won't entertain the idea of suicide: if she had taken her own life, he wouldn't have the luxury of keeping the door locked.

"Oh William . . ." I feel out of my depth again, suddenly longing for a platitude of my own to throw into the lake of his grief. "I'm sorry. Perhaps Richie and Mara will know?"

He looks at me again, his gaze intense, my words lost somewhere between us.

"Can I show you something?" he asks.

"Of course," I say, anxiety clawing its way up my spine.

He crosses to the counter, picks up his phone. Then he tells me what it is—the footage of Sally's last minutes. The very idea of it makes bile rise up my throat, but I can't refuse to watch it, because to do so would be to abandon him. I reach out a shaking hand, and he presses play. It's CCTV footage that the insurance company has tracked down, the car a tiny speck, zigzagging its erratic path through the traffic, almost like a video game. You can see other cars swerving to avoid it before it jackknifes down a ramp and then barrels into the median strip, driving straight for it, the impact all too obvious from the way it crumples. I look up at him, the blood drained from my face. I can't speak.

"Livvy, I'm sorry," he says, his face filled with concern. "I shouldn't have thrust that on you. Let's get you some brandy."

He pours me a measure and I gulp it back, the fire of it bringing me back to the here and now.

"It's all right," I mumble, my teeth chattering with the aftershock. I'm searching for something to say, but I'm all out of answers. Seeing the car's haphazard progress it's hard to believe that it could be an accident. I look at him, my eyes welling up with tears. He crosses around to me, and puts his arm around my shoulder.

"I know how shocking it is. It was too much to expect of you."

I'm so grateful to feel the living warmth of him, it anchors me in this universe, makes the ground feel solid again. I sink a little further into him, and he settles into the chair next to mine. I can feel his body breathing, his sweater soft against my cheek.

"Are they saying it confirms it?" I whisper.

"They can say whatever they choose," he says, hotly. "It means nothing of the sort."

How can he be so sure?

"No of course, but . . ."

"It certainly helps their case. The police haven't yet agreed to reclassify it, but a hearing looks increasingly likely."

"And . . . are they . . . the exhumation?" I say, my voice still little more than a whisper. I hate the thought of that, of them rousing her from where she lies and pulling her around like she's no more than a carcass.

"I won't let that happen," he says, his whole body tensing.

We sit there for a little while, alone with our thoughts.

"Was it like that?" I ask him, my voice soft, the question coming almost unbidden.

"What do you mean?"

"Being married to her."

He stiffens, and I wonder if I've crossed that invisible line, but then he speaks.

"It was lots of things, it could be the most incredible fun, but . . . she used to say people were drains or radiators, and I think I know what category she thought I fell into."

"You're not a drain!"

"Coming from you, that's a huge compliment," he says, smiling down at me. "Certainly not a deserved one."

I reach for his free hand, almost unconsciously, and he doesn't pull it away. I press my thumb into the palm as he continues to talk, hoping it will stop him from floating up and away.

"I suppose my job's not one you can do by half measures. I wasn't around as much as she'd have liked." He looks exhausted even talking about it.

"Did you ever think about doing something else?"

"We had quite a lifestyle," he says, and I think of the clothing mountain that's sitting in the barn, each item a piece of art. "And she'd given up so much." I see her there, arms flung wide, "Manhattan!" Sally was never one for self-sacrifice, whatever he believes. I stay quiet, my thumb still tracing his palm. "She took me away for my birthday last year, booked this beautiful hotel in the Catskills. We had the most incredible dinner on the first night, we . . . it had been a long time since we'd made love." I can feel him blushing, without even needing to look up. "We . . . we did . . . we walked in the mountains and then . . ." He swallows and I turn my gaze to him. "It was like a switch flicked, like I was someone else. She was so distant all of a sudden. I kept going over and over in my mind what we'd done that day, where I'd lost her."

"She was just like that, William. It wouldn't have been you." He gives me that reflexive smile of acknowledgment I've come to know so well, but I can see my words aren't touching the sides.

"It felt like that happened more and more the last few months. I'm sure it was deeply unattractive, me begging her to tell me what I'd done wrong. Sometimes I felt like . . ." his voice drops, "like she despised me."

I feel a surge of anger on his behalf, then realize that it's not just for him, it's also for that younger version of me, blindsided by those swift, brutal changes of mood. I want to reach back in time and tell her what William won't yet believe—that it wasn't down to some horrible inadequacy that only Sally's X-ray vision could see. I grit my teeth, search for the right words.

"Of course she didn't despise you."

"I did actually ask her straight out, a couple of months before—before it happened—if she wanted a divorce."

"What did she say?"

"She was distraught. I'd seen her upset, but never like that. It took me hours to calm her down."

"And what did *you* want?" I ask, tentative.

"I didn't want to carry on as we were, but I certainly didn't want a divorce. It's not . . . it's not what I believe in."

There's such a determination about how he says it, like he's the last little boy in the class who believes in Father Christmas.

"It does happen—cases have been recorded," I say, then hate myself for the sarcasm of it.

"I'm well aware, but to my mind there should always be a solution once there are children involved."

"But what if you've married the wrong person? That's what my mom and dad did. I wish they'd got divorced a hell of a lot sooner. It was like living in a phony war."

I think about it, about Dad's routine little life. I'm not sure it's what he believes. I wonder if he did find his one, but then found he wasn't the one for her.

"I don't think my mother's had it easy with Pa, but she's never faltered."

"How so?"

"Oh . . ." He shakes his head, like he doesn't want to go there. "Besides, I'm sure it was an ordeal for you when it happened."

"Yeah it was, of course," I say, thinking of Sally, how she would laugh me out of my moments of melancholy, keep me wrapped up in the fun of my new life. I push my thumb into his palm, embarrassed by how far we've strayed from the path. "Did it get better after that?"

"Without question. She seemed happier. We had some lovely family time. And then . . ."

He looks away, lost in his own personal hell. It must make those final moments all the more torturous: was that brief second honeymoon an illusion, a fantasy that Sally was weaving as she plotted her next move, or was it a tantalizing glimpse of what could have been? I draw my hand away, suddenly seeing us from above, his arm around me. What would she think of me? To my surprise he pulls it back.

"Thank you," he says, burying his head in my hair, and drawing me toward him. I feel as though I'm stiffening and softening all at once. He pushes my bangs out of my face and I risk raising my eyes toward his. "You're the only person I feel any vague semblance of myself with."

That's what we all want, isn't it—the person who sees all our lumps and bumps and loves us anyway? At least, that's all I've ever wanted.

"You're an angel," he breathes, tilting his face downward to kiss me. I put the flat of my hand against his chest to push him away, but then I accept him, let logic and context melt into a puddle of nothing. He pulls back and looks down at me.

"Olivia," he says, his eyes full of concern, "is this acceptable?"

"Yes, but . . ."

"What?"

There's too much to say. If I start to say it I might never stop.

"Please will you call me Livvy? When you call me Olivia it makes me feel like I'm in trouble."

Whatever he calls me, there's no doubt I am in trouble. The very fact I couldn't bear to sacrifice the moment to hear the truth is all the proof I need.

"Livvy it is," he says, giving me a smile that warms me. "Come next door, we'll be more comfortable."

We end up on a long, maroon sofa in the living room, loomed over by an enormous mahogany cabinet full of priceless-looking china. There's a scattering of occasional tables, littered with more silver-framed family pictures and a TV that looks like it was bought in the late eighties. As he drops soft kisses down my neck I have to twist my face away to stop my gaze catching his wedding picture, his smile of joy radiating out of the frame—and next to him Sally, that smile that I could swear doesn't quite translate. Why am I doing this? I sit up sharply, winded.

"Just . . ."

"I'm sorry," he says, sitting up straight, starting to recover himself. I can see that encroaching tide of guilt rolling toward us like a tsunami, but something inside me wants to stem it a little longer. It's me who kisses him this time, who pulls him toward me, who feels a different tide start to rise up and take him. It's as if we make a silent agreement to quiet down the voices for a while, to simply exist within the moment, our kisses all the feeling that we need. If I could abandon fully it would be heaven—I'd be shedding clothes as naturally as a snake slithers from its skin—but of course I can't. He pauses, sensing it, and pulls me into his chest. I love how safe I feel here, even if I know that it's illusory.

I stroke his stubble, unable to find any words that won't make the situation worse.

"I like . . ." he starts, then pauses, fingers playing with the neck of my madly unglamorous stripy sweater. I try not to feel inadequate at the thought of all those silken, seductive outfits that are lying unworn in the barn.

"What are you trying to say?"

He twists round and looks down at me, a smile on his face.

"I suppose what I'm trying to say is how can something so wrong feel so right?"

"You've totally missed your calling, you realize. You should be writing country and western songs."

"I know, it's deeply unjust. Why don't they have graduate training programs for jobs like that?"

We hold each other's gaze, so much going unsaid, and then he kisses me again, more fervent than before. I lose track of time as his hands gently caress my body, never venturing too far, but never stopping their exploration.

"Do you think you've found your calling?" he asks me, propping himself up on one elbow. I stop to think about it.

"I feel grateful to be doing something fun," I say.

"When you describe it it sounds more like the fun's in principle."

"No, it isn't," I insist, a little defensively.

"This is just a blundering observation, but it's when you talk about the writing I see you light up. Have you heard back about your story yet?"

"No, nothing," I say, embarrassed. "Anyway, it was like getting blood out of a stone." It was until I let myself go, poured all of this sharp truth into it. "I'm not a natural.

Don't you think that's a page one requirement for your calling?"

"They say that about me sometimes," he says, gruffly embarrassed.

"I'm sure you are."

"But I certainly don't feel it's my calling. Or maybe it is my calling. No one ever promised your calling would be something you liked. It might just be the place where you can make the greatest contribution."

His voice changes as he says it, as if he's parroting someone else's words. My eyes slip, unconsciously, toward a picture of his beakish father placed pride of place on the occasional table.

"Of course it is! That's why it's your calling. It's your heart's desire." He looks at me like I'm the village idiot, and I reach up and grab his face, which is becoming increasingly handsome to me as time goes on. "Go on then, Kenny Rogers, what would you do if you could do anything in the world?"

He pauses, looks away. He's ashamed, I think.

"Tell me," I say, more gentle.

"I'd be a gardener." I try not to laugh, imagining him in a pair of denim dungarees, tilling the earth. "Proper gardening, landscaping. I designed that whole vegetable garden, planted it with my own fair hands," he says, holding them up. He's actually got lovely hands, well turned without being effeminate. He shrugs. "It's nonsense, of course."

"It's not nonsense. If it's really what you want to do."

"You're sweet," he says, kissing me on the nose.

I lose all sense of time lying there in his arms—or rather, I throw it away, conscious that this sweet moment of intimacy, laced as it is with a strange kind of naivety, will not be something that we can keep hold of. Right now I feel like I can ask him anything, and so I do.

"What did she say about me, William? Did she really say we drifted apart?" He pauses, the cogs whirring, and I trace his temples with my fingertips. "Just tell me the truth. I can take it."

"You're not how I thought you'd be."

I feel myself tensing.

"Neither are you."

"Touché," he says, smiling. We're quiet for a couple of minutes, both of us holding back our cards.

"She said you were the best friend she ever had, but it got too intense." He pauses, watching my face, I think to see how far he should go. "She said you had a terrific row, and she couldn't ever forget what you'd said. She tried, but it wasn't quite the same, and you didn't seem to want her in your life."

I shudder at the very memory of it, but I shudder more at her blatant reframing of events to cast herself as the innocent victim.

"That's not fair," I protest, shaking my head, blood coursing through me. "I don't want to go into it all now, but . . . she dumped me."

I hate that even after all these years, when I talk about Sally I still resort to the language of lovers without missing a beat.

"She was thrilled when you sent the card, after she hadn't heard back from the wedding invitation."

"She didn't *invite* me to the wedding," I say, my voice rising despite myself. I wish I hadn't started this conversation. He doesn't contradict me, but I can see in his eyes that he's not convinced.

"I thought you saw each other in England, when Madeline was small. I could almost swear she told me so. It was the card you sent that made us give her your name. She promised me she'd call you when she was home, rather than simply crying about it."

"She cried?"

"Oh yes. She was overcome."

"It must have been sleep deprivation," I say, then curse myself for my insensitivity. I can sense his retreat, even if he doesn't withdraw his body from mine. I shouldn't be asking him to choose between our versions of events, not now when he must feel so guilty about holding me in his arms.

"She struggled, Olivia. I don't think friendship was always easy for her, she felt so much. Even with Mara—I saw it dropping off in the months before she died."

"I know," I say, trying to make good. "And when she was on form she was the best friend I've ever had."

It's true. She was.

The atmosphere shifts a little after that: how could it not? About half an hour later, William looks down at me.

"I'm exhausted," he says, and I feel myself withdraw, so cripplingly unsure of my place. "Don't worry, you'll be quite safe. Just as you said, there's plenty of spare bedrooms."

I follow him up the stairs, not feeling safe at all. Most of all I don't feel safe from me.

"Where are you going to sleep?" I venture.

"Ma's only made up the one room, so I thought I'd give you that, and sleep in here," he says, indicating his boyhood bedroom.

But somehow we're miraculously transported inside, squashed into his narrow single bed, so close that we're almost one entity, the awkwardness of the last hour having melted away. Perhaps the room entraps us in its teenage innocence: we strip down only as far as our underwear and sleep entwined, my head nestled into his bare chest. If only we could stay here indefinitely, floating in this bubble—the outside world poses far too great a risk for our fragile hearts.

CHAPTER THIRTEEN

I HARDLY SLEEP A WINK. MY THOUGHTS ARE CHURN-
ing, my body squashed against William's unfamiliar bulk,
the intimacy of it almost painful. I can smell him, male and
unfamiliar, feel the soft hair that mats his body, and yet,
once the reassuring stream of conversation has stopped,
every shred of me screams that I've committed a crime. I
drift into a fitful sleep in the wee small hours, then wake
what feels like five minutes later to find William surreptitiously easing himself out of the bed.

"Don't get up," he whispers, "I'll be back very soon."

I must slip back under, because when I wake again, an
attractive sliver of drool escaping from the left side of my
mouth, he's reappeared. He's sitting at a desk at the far
end of the landing, fully dressed, with his laptop open. I sit
up, wrapping the bedspread around my body, cripplingly
self-conscious.

"Hello. Where did you go?"

"Mass."

"Church?" I say, trying not to sound like a heathen. I picture him in the confessional, pouring out the sin of letting another woman into his bed, or on his knees, begging Sally for forgiveness. How could I have done this?

"I try to go most Sundays," he says, matter-of-fact. He's sitting up, ramrod straight, dressed in a shirt, as if he's been transplanted on a magic carpet straight from the office. And yet, despite the invisible fence he's built around himself, something still stirs in me as I look at him. My heart opens to him, the first insistent tremors of a feeling that could engulf me if I gave in to it. I can almost hear Sally's laugh ringing in my ears, the way she'd mock me instead of felling me with a clean right hook. She'd laugh at me now, I'm sure of it. I pull the covers tight around me and swing myself out of bed.

"I just need to find a bathroom."

"There's one up here. Third on the left," he says, his gaze pulling toward his e-mails.

I scuttle around the back of him, the bedspread tripping me up, last night's clothes screwed up in a tight bundle under my arm. I slosh my body with the feeble jet that emerges from the shower extension that hangs from the claw-footed bath, water more cold than hot, soaping myself with a bar of Pears that I find on the sink. Despite the inadequacy of the pressure I try and get into every crevice of my body, wanting so much to feel sparkling and bright, then dry myself piecemeal with a hand towel. The fact I have to put on yesterday's outfit is a major drawback; I didn't even like it then: it protested too much with its willful androgyny, a message from my conscious to my subconscious that I should stay vigilant. My face looks drawn and plain in the mirror, the few scraps of makeup I have marooned in the bottom of my handbag down in the kitchen. I'd do anything for a change of clothes, acutely aware of the irony of those endless, perfect outfits that lie quarantined in the barn.

When I open the door, William is standing in the hallway holding out a cup and saucer.

"I made you tea," he says, handing it to me. I'm sure it's just that the mugs are dirty, but to me it feels like a tiny step backward into that cloying formality. "And I also went to the farm shop. We've got eggs, among other things."

"That's great, though I really should start making tracks soon. I'm assuming a cab . . ."

I hope he doesn't think I hate him. I hope even more that he doesn't think the opposite.

"The auto club has been here, so there are no problems on that front," he says, setting off down the stairs. He hasn't touched me once, not even brushed my fingers when he passed me the cup.

The kitchen table is scattered with papers, and I hide behind them as he scrambles eggs and fries bacon. When he lays a plate down in front of me, he holds my gaze.

"There's something I need to ask you."

My whole body freezes, waiting for the blow.

"I won't tell anyone, if that's what you mean."

I hate how sharp I sound, my guilt turned acid.

"It wasn't that," he says, shaking his head. "I actually wanted to ask if you'd consider becoming Madeline's godmother. We're going to have the christening in November, back in . . ." he falters, "in the church. Sally would have approved of my choice, I'm sure."

"Even after last night?"

The words are out of my mouth before I can stop them. He looks down, embarrassed.

"She never forgot you." It wasn't what I asked. Does he not feel the same throb of guilt that thrums through every shred of me? Or did last night mean so little to him that he can simply shake it off like a dusting of dandruff on an old man's collar?

I almost say no, I really do, but then I realize, that for all the complications, I don't want to. I care about Madeline, and if I can help make the next few years less bleak, then I should at least try. Is it more than that though? Is it the sense of an enduring connection, however painful it may turn out to be?

"Why wasn't she christened when she was a baby?" I say, the thought suddenly striking me.

William pauses.

"We never quite got around to it," he says, carefully.

Is this what you even wanted, Sally? Am I adding another piece to a structure that's being built over your very bones?

"If you're sure," I say, the questions catching in my throat. "I'd be honored. I know Lola would too though . . . I don't want you to feel obligated."

I'm meant to be seeing her in a couple of weeks, our first meeting since the funeral. I was looking forward to it before last night.

"I don't," he says, simply. "Now why don't you get stuck into those eggs before they go stone cold?"

My heart sinks lower and lower over the next hour, the easy intimacy of last night seeming like a delusion. I've already tried to talk about it, and been rebuffed. Besides, my feelings are so contradictory and infuriating, so laced with self-disgust, that I don't trust myself to articulate them. By the time we're back in the car, I've almost started to hate him, his good manners feeling like a benign dictatorship. He turns to me before he starts the engine.

"Olivia—"

"Livvy," I correct him.

He pauses, his hands holding the bottom of the steering wheel.

"I wanted to say . . ." he starts, hesitant, "I've very much enjoyed spending this time with you, despite the context."

"You don't have to do this—"

"Please let me finish," he says. "So perhaps you'd let me take you for supper?"

I look at him, utterly thrown.

"Yes, I mean, I suppose so."

We're like two people doing a dance without having learned the steps. Or maybe it's just me who doesn't know the steps.

"I'd like that." He smiles a real smile that makes my heart soften and mulch. I shouldn't be here, and yet I've somehow lost the strength to pry myself away. "Ready?" he says, turning over the rumbly engine.

It all feels so abrupt all of a sudden. I grip the foam of the seat, my fingers digging in.

"Do you mind . . . I just need to go back to the barn for a second."

I step out quickly, too fast perhaps for him to stop me, gulping in the clean country air, so different from the closeness of the car. I feel that light-headed sensation as I open the door, suddenly conscious how similar it is to the way I used to feel when Sally would push me too far, force me to look over the edge of the precipice.

It's almost a shock to find everything piled up as I left it. The sense of her is so acute, so vivid: I wouldn't be surprised if she'd found some wrinkle in time and space and come back to remind me who's boss. I wish you had, I think, a lump in my throat at the inconvertible evidence that she's not coming back. The half-empty boxes and stacks of clothes form a strange kind of imprint of yesterday. So much has changed since I last stood here, or perhaps it hasn't—perhaps it's only changed for me.

Something draws me back to that scarlet coat. I pull it out, hanging it on the outside of the box where I can contemplate it. I never wore color until I knew Sally—it was her who taught me how much a vivid shade could infuse your state of mind and change the way the world reacted to you. I hold the tips of the sleeves outward, almost like we're holding hands, my eyes brimming with tears. "I'm so sorry," I whisper. "Please don't hate me."

It takes a supreme effort for me to collect myself: twice I get as far as the door and have to stop and simply breathe. The coat hangs there like an exclamation mark—before I leave I push it deep into the box it came from.

William's staring straight ahead into the middle distance as I slide into the car.

"I'm sorry, I just needed to—"

He cuts across me.

"I called National Rail Inquiries. There's a train leaving Branksome in thirty-five minutes, so I'll need to put my foot down."

My head swivels toward him, but his gaze is still firmly planted on the drive, his jaw clenched shut to stop anything untoward from escaping.

"I'm ready."

March/April/May 1996

The winners and losers from the holocaust of my birthday were as follows:

LOSERS—Me and James. When I'd got back to my bedroom he was fully dressed, sitting bolt upright on the side of the bed as if he were waiting for sergeant major to come in and do an inspection. He took me for a heartbreaking, rushed "birthday breakfast," en route to a train he claimed he had to catch in order to write an urgent essay. I found the paucity of the excuse almost worse than the fact he felt he needed to make one—it was as if I'd crossed into the enemy camp, become a generic girl to be managed, the whole sweep of our confusing, unruly friendship destroyed by one disastrous mistake. I knew him far too well to think he'd ever have abandoned a chance for fun in favor of academia: he'd have written it, pepped up on ProPlus, until the early hours of Monday morning, then handed in to his tutor with the kind of smile that would have charmed them into an A.

Breakfast reflected my new diminished role. He was offensively polite, not stealing a single chip from my plate, swallowing down a burp as though he couldn't bear to offend my delicate sensibilities. He even asked me about my course. Needless to say, neither of us mentioned the fact that he'd been crawling over my naked body less than twelve hours earlier. When he got back to Norwich I didn't hear a peep, and neither of us contacted the other for the entirety of the Easter holidays.

I think my shame and hurt would have completely done me in but for the fact that I had Sally to distract me. Though not as much as I'd have hoped.

WINNERS—On the winning team we had Sally and Shaun. As the door slammed shut on Matt's and my relationship, it swung gloriously open on this fledgling love match. "Timing's a bitch," giggled Sally as she disappeared off on yet another date, reeking of Chanel No. 19 and something else that I couldn't quite put my finger on: she was emitting some kind of musk, like an animal does when it's in heat, a sexual energy that radiated off her until she almost glowed with it. It only increased my sense of inadequacy: I couldn't help thinking I'd been punished, sent back to the geeks' corner where I belonged, my virginity supersized and handed back to me as a life sentence. The timing was indeed a bitch and I nurtured an illogical resentment about it. I felt like I'd in some way sacrificed my relationship with Matt for my relationship with Sally, only for her to spirit herself away on a magic carpet, tantalizingly out of reach. Matt meanwhile was resolutely avoiding me, dodging behind the shelves in the library if he caught so much as a glimpse of me. I didn't know if it was because he hated me or if it was the opposite, but I was too much of a coward to find out.

Shaun was perfectly nice, a hulking, sexy bear of a man who was studying photography at the less prestigious university down the road. Watching her with him was a master class for a novice like me. She would fix her big, limpid eyes on him across the kitchen, hold his gaze just long enough and then look away. She would flick her hair, giving the kind of girly giggle that should have been like nails down a blackboard but was clearly music to his ears. Her voice would turn all sugary too, scraped clean of that abrasive edge it usually had. "Mom" became "mommy," "dog" became "doggy" and my friend became unrecognizable. Is that what men want, I would think, the feminist credos my mother had drummed into me ringing in my ears, then take one look at Shaun, hopelessly caught in Sally's slipstream, and admit defeat.

I never would have chosen it, but having room to breathe was the best thing that could have happened to me. Lola was no sex kitten, she and Justin were happily committed rather than obsessive, and she and I started to knock around more, taking ourselves off to afternoon films and working opposite each other in the library. It was second best for both of us—we didn't give each other the same heady thrill that Sally provided—but it was comforting and solid, and it meant I'd started to feel good about the fact that we were going to be sharing a house the next year.

When Sally invited me to spend the last few days of the Easter holidays at her parents' house I was thrilled, any residual sense of abandonment consigned to history. On the train there I worried that the visit was the consolation prize, that she was bringing me there to tell me that our second-year plan was off, that she was moving in with Shaun, but it wasn't the case. It was like the semi-estrangement of the last few weeks had been a mirage. She picked me up at the station, hugged me like she never wanted to let me go.

"We've got so much to catch up on," she cried, giddy with it all, and my heart leapt at the joy of having her back. I didn't have much to share, truth be told—I'd been mooching around Northfields, trying to fit back into a life that no longer existed since we'd all scattered, hoping to bump into James but dreading the very real prospect that if I did, he'd be wrapped around someone every bit as beguiling as Sally. I'd started the slide back to my pre-Sally wardrobe of corduroy skirts and ill-fitting jeans, but she soon put paid to that, heaping me with gorgeous, alien clothes that she claimed she never wore anymore. She introduced me to her mom as her "best friend Livvy" and I almost burst with pride, loving their colorful, overheated house with televisions in every room, so different from our muted, drafty family home.

Sally was still Sally, if I'd chosen to see it, but of course I didn't. When Gina produced spaghetti carbonara for dinner she acted like she'd assaulted her—"you bloody well know I'm not eating carbs!"—until she gave up and shuffled off to make her a salad. Her dad, a quiet, withdrawn kind of character, simply let it play out like he was immune to it. I wonder now if he was a bit of a depressive, if some of Sally's problems came from him. I sat there, squirming in my seat, not knowing where to look—nothing like that would ever have happened in our house, it would have been seen as the height of bad manners—but perhaps that was what was good about it; emotions were expressed, played out in all their flamboyant glory, rather than swept under the carpet in an orgy of middle-class restraint.

"How's it going with Shaun?" I asked her, once we were holed up in her room with a bottle of wine she'd casually plucked from the kitchen cupboard. I was determined not to fail this time. I would ask all the right questions and respond with womanly knowingness.

"Good, yeah," she said in a way that somehow failed to convince.

"Has he met your parents yet?"

"God, no!" she said, and I felt a rush of pride that I'd got there first: Sally's special skill was weaving a triangle out of thin air. *"It's fun, you know?"* she added in a tone that tarnished it. I couldn't help but wonder why she'd bothered to make him fall head over heels in love with her if she was so neutral. *"How about you?"*

"No, no one since Matt," I said, blushing for no earthly reason.

"That's not strictly true," she giggled, poking me in the ribs. James and I was not something I could giggle about yet: I summoned up a weak smile, hoping she'd leave the subject alone. *"You still not heard from him?"* she said, cocking her head and turning her full attention on me.

"No," I said, curling in on myself like a snail. It was so tender, so private. I didn't even understand my feelings, was nowhere near being able to articulate them, even if I'd wanted to.

"You should just call him."

"I can't."

"Why not?"

"I just can't."

"Yeah you can," she said, playfully picking up the phone in her bedroom.

"No Sally, don't," I said, panicky. She put the receiver down and then stared at me until I broke. "I just feel like such an idiot. I always knew he didn't feel the same way. I should've just kept what we had, not messed it up by becoming another notch on his stupid bedpost."

"But you thought you loved him."

I didn't speak. It wasn't a past tense, but I didn't want to say so.

"I know it sounds totally pathetic, but I'm just not the kind of girl he'd ever feel like that about." Not like you, was the unsaid end to the sentence. "It's hard to explain to someone like you . . ."

"Someone like me?" said Sally with a hysterical laugh even though she knew exactly what I meant. I'd temporarily snuck past the velvet rope, forgotten my place in the pecking order, before being summarily sent back to the end of the line. I just wished that I didn't miss him so much, that it wasn't a constant, savage throbbing, a mixture of loss and trepidation about what I might hear next.

"Let's not talk about it," I said hurriedly.

"Okay, if that's really what you want," she said, leaning over and giving me a spontaneous hug. "But we're gonna fix it. I can't have you going around feeling like this."

How comforted I felt, how held. I loved that my problem was her problem, like we were twin souls, all our woes merged and halved. It didn't occur to me to think about how little interest she'd taken over the previous weeks when I'd been skulking around our house, blatantly miserable, mummified by layers of sex-repelling corduroy.

"Anyway, I've got something to tell you that'll cheer you up," she said, glugging wine into my glass until it nearly erupted over the brim.

"What?"

"Shauny's got a house for us!"

Some other third years were moving out of a wood-floored, light-filled apartment that they rented from someone's dad, thus bypassing the list of scuzzy, student-friendly hovels that the local landlords peddled. Sally had Polaroids, which she laid out on the bed, getting increasingly excited as each one slapped down. I pored over them, loving the prospect of our sophisticated, urban existence. I was so aspirational then, so ready to slough off my parents' values and speed in the opposite direction. Then I went through them again more carefully.

"Where's the third bedroom?" Sally pulled a face. "We can't . . . we've promised Lola."

"But it's perfect! And she's got Justin, anyway. I wouldn't say it if she didn't."

"I don't think she wants to live with Justin." I knew she didn't now we'd spent more time together. They had that certainty they'd have the rest of their lives for that, wanted to wring the best out of their student years. "We can't!" I said, then saw Sally's black expression and started to wither. "I mean, I really don't see how we'd do it."

Those three little words—"we'd do it." I was toast.

Sally had a plan. "The last thing I want is to hurt her," she'd said, face arranged to convey this self-evident truth. "But it'd be criminal to turn it down." I would have to pretend that it had unexpectedly appeared via some family friends—it would link too obviously back to Shaun if she said it—and that we'd been offered it for such a bargainous rent that we couldn't say no. Every time I thought about talking to Lola I felt physically sick, but every time I thought about disappointing Sally I felt even worse. I was a terrible liar, and I told

Sally as much. "Sometimes a girl's got to do what a girl's got to do," she said cheerfully. "We'll tell her together, if you like." Another hideous choice. I hated the idea of us ganging up on her like that, iron fists in a pair of velvet gloves, but I couldn't bear to have to absorb her disappointment alone. It all happened so fast. I was still silently wavering at the point when Sally went ahead and put down the hefty deposit, leaving me with no way out. Of course there was a way out, if I'd developed a backbone, but I was too far gone.

It was both better and worse than I'd imagined. Lola didn't scream or swear, she simply flushed a deep red and asked us to leave her bedroom. "Lola, don't be like that," said Sally, trying to step toward her and stifle her distress with one of her patented hugs.

"I mean it," said Lola, more dignified than I ever could have been. "I just want you to get out."

I looked at her, stricken, and she stared back with an unwavering gaze. It was the look of one suburban girl to another, and it cut me to the quick. She was telling me that what I had done was unforgivable, that she and I were not cut from this kind of cloth: Sally's vividness couldn't help but breed this kind of mercurial reversal, but I had not earned the right. When we got to the kitchen I burst into tears and, seconds later, so did Sally. I question those tears, I think they were of the crocodile variety, but at the time they bonded us even more tightly together. Sally's hug was unleashed on me and we clung to each other like we were the victims.

"Wanna hear something that will cheer you up?" she said, once our sobs had subsided.

"Go on."

"We're going on a little weekend jaunt. We're off to see your friend James."

CHAPTER
FOURTEEN

James is standing at the train barriers waiting for me, even though I told him I didn't need a lift. I didn't think I wanted to see him, but now he's here I can't help but be comforted by his presence.

He looks gray, his mouth a thin line, which only serves to illustrate how well he normally looks.

"You look terrible," I tell him, as he grabs my bag from me.

"Cheers," he says. "Nice outfit, by the way." I think the excitement of not having to vet every word that crosses my lips made me veer too far the other way. He looks down at me, fixing me with a hard stare. "So what exactly has been keeping you?"

"I told you, there was this massive storm and William had borrowed his sister's car, which is pretty much a Reliant Robin and . . ." I'm talking too much. "How come you were home alone, anyway?"

"Oh," he says, swinging his keys a little too casually. "Charlie was trying to get out of this shit-awful dinner party in Chelsea, and we thought she'd managed it, but then she had to leave."

"She came over again?"

"Don't get all Mrs. Danvers on my ass. Yes, she was in your home," he says, doing a stupid, spooky voice.

"It's not about me. It just doesn't look like being a mistress is making you very happy."

"Tell me what's going to cheer me up," he says, opening the car. "Little Lisbon."

Little Lisbon is an utterly rank tapas bar on the Oval Road that I only ever go to when it's past last call and I've got a death wish.

"You're the one who says the chorizo is made of dogs' willies."

"It is," he agrees, pulling out. We approach Waterloo roundabout and he looks at me expectantly until I shrug my agreement, as he always knew I would.

"One drink," I tell him.

"One drink," he agrees.

Sangria is a truly disgusting invention, but at least the lemonade disguises how vile the cheap red wine really is. We've got most of the way through the jug now, accompanied by some of the dog willy chorizo and some Spanish omelet that tastes and smells of sick, stuffed together on a tiny bench at the back of the bar. There's a loud foreign soccer match going on on the widescreen TV, and every now and then the swarthy crowd of men at the bar emits either a loud cheer or a groan.

"It's nearly finished," says James, banging the jug on the table.

"Don't do that, they'll think we want more."

We make disgusted, drunken faces at each other, competing to see who can twist their face into the most ludicrous shape.

"Let's do a tequila shot," says James.

"It's a school night. And you've got the car."

"I'll get it in the morning. Right now, I don't even care." He keeps swinging from bonhomie to melancholy, and right now the pendulum is ricocheting back toward abject gloom. I've successfully blocked the subject so far, but now there's no stopping him. Poor Charlotte. Apparently when they go on long car journeys the Postbox "barely thpeaks" and he never tells her she's beautiful. There are various other outrages, including not supporting her professionally, but by now it's just starting to sound like noise.

"Sorry to sound like a stuck record, but is she going to dump him?"

"Yeah, course. It's just not gonna be instant." I look at him, biting my lip. "What?" he says, prickly.

"It can't carry on indefinitely. You might have to give her an ultimatum." He gives a dismissive snort, and I realize he's just as deluded as all the other poor fools having an affair, just as convinced that this is the real deal, existing in a separate romantic biosphere. In fact, he's probably even more deluded, because he's never had any kind of heartbreak. He won't be able to recognize the signs, like a person who gets rushed to intensive care on the brink of death because he stubbornly insisted the stabbing pains in his chest were indigestion. Two glasses have appeared now, and, even though I can think of nothing worse, I find myself downing my shot. James puts a drunken arm around me, signaling for the waitress with his free hand.

"Stop changing the subject. Come on, William."

I look at him—his stupid, puppyish excitement fighting against the painful truth that the object of his affection is nowhere to be seen—and suddenly I decide that I'm not going to lie or downplay: he's not the only one with a story. I tell him all of it, as I do so, realize that it's everything and nothing all at once. We've barely done more than kiss, and yet in the moments of intimacy, it's felt more intimate than whole relationships have felt.

"You know it can't go anywhere, right?" he says, when I've finished. That's my line: I'm surprised how much it cuts when it's thrown out by someone else.

"Yeah, no, obviously," I say, dipping my fingers in the wax of the candle, and making hot little fingerprints on the greasy paper tablecloth.

"You're just too nice sometimes, Livvy."

"What do you mean?"

"I can see how it's happened," says James breezily. "I mean, I can't imagine what he's going through." It's such an easy phrase, and it's one I know I trotted out early on in all of this. It's a get-out-of-jail-free card, an effortless way to swerve from engaging with a tragedy too brutal to contemplate: it's just that now I don't want to leave William to rot in his cell. James suddenly bellows a loud cheer into my ear, making me jump out of my skin. "They scored," he says, digging me in the ribs.

"Who?"

"Maritimo!"

"Oh. Okay." I'm finding it hard to reach the desired pitch of enthusiasm, despite the back-slapping and hugging that's going on between the men at the bar. James raises his glass in a toast, and they toast back, welcoming us into the fold. It's typical James: he swims upstream so easily, finding the positive in every situation, the world holding up a mirror to his inner reality. I've always loved that about him, but I guess it comes easy to him, a person who's never had to struggle for anything, or anyone, very much.

"And I tell you what I really can't imagine," he adds. "Him and Sally."

It's the absolute opposite for me—not only can I imagine it, I can't stop imagining it, and when I do, I see him utterly consumed by her, the flashes of darkness only heightening her power over him. Did she pull off the ultimate seduction by exiting his life in such a spectacular way? Perhaps she sensed that even he would eventually lose patience; now his heart will be left in suspended animation, trapped by questions that he'll never be able to hold her to account for. My fingers reach subconsciously for the tag, caught in the pocket of my bag. I'm going to Google Capricorn Holdings as soon as we get home.

"I guess they're proof that opposites attract," I say neutrally, hating the subterfuge.

"Do you really believe that though?" asks James, that teenage smile spreading across his face. Right now, all roads lead in one direction.

"Isn't it the point?" I say, feeling inappropriately emotional about it. "If someone's going to complete you they've got to have qualities you don't have."

"Nah," says James. "It's about what you've got in common. You want them to complement you, not complete you." Here we go. "That's what's so great about Charlotte— she's got balls, she's not going to let me get away with anything." He looks wistfully into the distance. "I've met my match with that one."

And then it hurts again. Why didn't he ever think that the person sitting beside him pulling faces and slamming tequila and cooking his dinner three nights out of seven might somehow complement him? Was I just too nice?

"We ought to go you know," I say, signaling for the bill. He grabs my waxy hand and squeezes it, cocks his head to consider me. It's not just tequila that's making him sentimental.

"I just . . . I dunno, I want you to find the same thing. You deserve it, Livvy, you really do."

I haven't told James about the tag, I'm not quite sure why. It feels like a secret, a secret between me and her. Once I'm back in my room I lay it on my dressing table and stare at it, steeling myself to do a search. I can't help but feel guilty, like I'm overstepping the mark, but this may prove that it's innocuous, something that William doesn't need to worry about. And if isn't—at least I might be able to help him with the fallout.

I tap *"Capricorn Holdings"* + *New York* into my ancient laptop and wait for the results. A correction comes up: *Capricorn Holdings, New Jersey*. There's a picture of a gloomy-looking building, with a screed of text running across the bottom of the screen: CAPRICORN HOLDINGS, STORAGE SOLUTIONS. FOR WHEN YOU NEED SOME SPACE IN YOUR LIFE.

Maybe that's exactly what she needed. I look at my watch, work out the time difference and fire up my Skype account before I can lose my nerve. A brusque-sounding woman answers the phone.

"Hi," I say, trying to channel Sally's unshakeable confidence. "I've got a storage unit with you. I just wanted to check . . ." Check what? ". . . if it's there." That doesn't even make sense.

"Name?" barks the woman.

"Sally Harrington," I say, a shudder passing through me, unable to rationalize the feeling that I'm walking on her grave.

"Please hold."

She goes away for what feels like an eternity, while I try and breathe through the waves of anxiety that keep knocking me to the curb. Finally I hear her coming back.

"There's no account in that name."

"Are you absolutely sure?"

"Sure I'm sure!" says the woman, aggravated by me questioning her competency.

"Would it show up if there was a previous one that was closed down? Anything in the name of Harrington, period?"

"There's no such account, never has been. You've made a mistake, lady."

She hangs up without even bothering to say goodbye, and I sit there, transfixed by the small lump of plastic I'm holding in my hand, all out of answers.

JUNE 1996

Sally drove us all the way down to Norwich, even though I'd rather have taken the train. She drove like she was in a computer game, zooming up behind cars to force them to move over, and violently slamming on the brakes at the sight of a speed camera. I wasn't a driver yet, but I knew it was a far cry from my dad's painstaking signaling and ponderous crawl.

It added to my unvoiced sense of unease about the trip. I still hadn't contacted James myself, and yet the two of them had been in touch. Sally was thrilled at her own cleverness, casting herself as the UN peacekeeping force, but I felt intruded on. I tried gently to say as much, but she blasted me out of the water. "You'd have sent him a billet-doux from your nursing home if I hadn't stuck my oar in. You need to get out of that clever head of yours and live a little!"

She was right about that, no question, so I squashed my doubts into my backpack and hoped for the best. Besides, it was good to have an excuse to get away. Lola had been added to the roll call of people who weren't speaking to me—she mainly stayed at Justin's but the couple of times I did run into her, her look of betrayal made me feel like an insect. When I told Sally how bad I felt she agreed. "We'll make it up to her," she said, but to me it felt like we'd broken something that was too delicate to be repaired.

We got to James's digs about eight o'clock, my heart speeding in my chest like it might make a bid for freedom, my palms cold and damp. She hugged him first, then looked back at me as if she were encouraging her toddler to step into the nursery rhyme circle.

"Hi," I said uncertainly, submitting myself to a hug. He gave it freely, putting his whole self into it, and I allowed myself to relax. Maybe this would be okay.

"I've got big plans for us, girls," he said, rubbing his hands together like an evil genius, and I realized that I was as in love with him as I'd ever been, only now I'd taken aim and missed the target. Was it worse to be here—so near and yet so far—or to not have him in my life at all? I didn't know yet.

We went to a student club, the kind of place that Sally would usually have turned her button nose up at: tonight she seemed perfectly happy to throw herself into the sweaty vortex. We drank copious vodkas and multiple shots, dancing to Happy Mondays like it was our last night on earth. Sally had that wild brightness about her that sometimes came upon her, like the moment after a firecracker's been lit and you know you need to jump back. James couldn't help but react to it—to ask him not to would be like asking a bird not to fly—and I tried my hardest not to mind the way he looked at her. At least he was back by my side, within touching distance, and I knew she would never dream of doing anything. She

*was just being herself, the self I adored, and any trace of jeal-
ousy was a sickness I had to eradicate.*

*I was pretending to be happy, self-medicating with shots,
even though I knew I didn't have Sally's iron constitution.
Fatal mistake: I threw up outside the club at chucking out
time, and the three of us piled into a cab, me desperately hoping that James couldn't smell it on me, that it wouldn't com-
pound his lack of desire. Sally fussed over me when we got
back, putting me to bed in a room that one of James's roommates had vacated, and helping me wash my hair to ensure
there were no rogue traces. I felt cosseted by her, and fell into
a fitful, muzzy sleep.*

*There were streaks of blue in the sky when she climbed into
bed beside me.*

*"Sorry," she whispered, "go back to sleep. You need your
rest."*

"What time is it?"

"Late. We just got chatting."

*I felt a prickly feeling inside myself, sleep suddenly a dis-
tant memory.*

"About what?"

*"Oh, stuff," said Sally, her voice thick and heavy like she
was almost unconscious.*

*Was she? Maybe she was: her breathing certainly implied
it. As for me, no chance, I just lay there, trying to get my
heartbeat to return to a normal pace, my imagination stag-
ing a riot.*

*There was an ease about them the next day—they no lon-
ger needed me as a conduit, they had an intimacy all of their
own. I convinced myself that my fears had been nothing but
the kind of paranoia that strikes in the wee small hours, but I
was still discomfited by the subtle change of tide: a triangle*

was a dangerous toy to put in Sally's eager hands. James suggested a country walk—he's always loved anything vaguely sporty or outdoorsy—and Sally readily agreed, even though I'd barely ever seen her out of a pair of high heels. As we trailed behind him up a hill, she linked her arm in mine.

"You feeling better? You look a million times better than you did last night."

"Yes, much better thanks."

"You having fun?"

Sort of was the honest answer, but truth was a commodity I'd learned to sacrifice in favor of peace.

"Yeah, totally."

"Good! She looks better, doesn't she, James?"

"Man, you were green. You were like, bile colored."

He made a face, and I laughed, and felt an intense rush of gratitude for the fact that normal service had finally been resumed. He was pink from the wind, his blue eyes twinkly and warm, and I tried not to let the longing unseat me. I could do this, I always had, I'd just have to relearn the steps.

By the time the weekend was over I genuinely thought I'd enjoyed it.

"Goodbye, You," said Sally, flinging her arms around him theatrically.

"Bye," he said affectionately, hugging her back.

"You'll have to come stay in our lush new pad," she added, without a trace of guilt about how it had come about. Then it was my turn to hug him.

"It was lovely to see you," I told him, hoping my voice wasn't soaked through with too much feeling, like a Christmas pudding doused in brandy.

"Yeah, you too," he said, our gaze meeting for a second, a silent acknowledgment of what had kept us apart.

"Come on, the traffic's shit on Sundays," said Sally, impatiently tossing her keys between her manicured hands, the nails red talons.

Once we were on the road she put Beverley Craven on full blast.

"Say thank you to your Auntie Sally," she said, grinning at me.

"Thank you, Auntie Sally," I parroted, trying to squash down the uncomfortable feelings that were threatening to bubble to the surface. She laughed, high with it all, then stamped down on the accelerator so sharply that a truck swerved to avoid us, leaning on his horn in outrage.

CHAPTER FIFTEEN

"SALLY WOULD HAVE LOVED IT HERE," SAYS LOLA, already welling up.

We've met in a French wine bar behind Oxford Circus that's a particular favorite of mine. It's quite low-key, despite the location, the only light coming from the stumpy candles that are allowed to melt over the tightly packed wooden tables, the wine served in basic glass beakers. There's not a martini to be had for love nor money: I can guarantee Sally would have hated it.

"I know," I say, squeezing her hand. I'm lying already and we've only been here five minutes. It is a white lie, at least, born out of my determination that we don't get dragged back into the savage triangle that defined our years at Leeds. Already the two of us together without Sally feels totally weird.

"Look at you," says Lola, smiling a tear-sodden smile. "You've got a real glow, Livvy."

"Have I?" I say, guiltily. I know logically that William and I is pointless and hopeless, but I'm seeing him on Sunday, and I haven't been able to smother a tiny spark of excitement that burns away unbidden. At least, not until now. Lola looks careworn, dark circles ringing her eyes, her concealer applied so thickly that it only serves to draw attention to them—she radiates sadness like the candle between us radiates light. "You look well too," I say, because to say the opposite would be cruel.

"Still can't believe it," she says. "I keep expecting my cell to ring, and it to be Sally calling me from Saks, or some other stupidly glamorous place, while I'm doing a three-point turn in the Guildford Tesco."

"I know," I say. I don't know that exactly, but what I do know is how it feels to wait for a call from Sally that will never come. How stupid I was, the way I always thought that there'd be more time. But then, even if I had pushed, would I really and truly have wanted her back?

"Mesdemoiselles, are you ready to order?" says the dark-haired smoothie of a waiter, approaching us with his pad in hand. We're mesdames really, but it feels delicious to be flirted with. We order a bottle of warming red, accompanied by some stinky cheese, and settle into our corner. I feel very sentimental all of a sudden, tears pricking behind my eyeballs, the years concertinaing back to the time when we really were mesdemoiselles. I should have fought harder for my friendship with Lola, made good the damage I did, and established a relationship that wasn't about Sally anymore.

"It's lovely to see you," I say, clinking my glass against hers. "I'm still—Lola, I'm sorry for the way I behaved back then. It was so selfish . . ."

A flash of anger crosses her face, a tiny sign that the hurts of the past still exert a grip on her too, but then she forces her expression back to neutral. Is it simply human nature that the deepest cuts must leave a scar, or are our wounds more raw because of the intensity that Sally brought to everything?

"I can't stop thinking about William," she says, sidestepping everything I said like it's a dirty puddle. "You know he's moved back here?"

"Yes, yes I did know that," I say, my voice sounding high and artificial.

"I called a couple of times, but I didn't hear back. But now . . ." She looks at me, embarrassed, and a tiny, awful part of me feels smug that for once I'm not out in the cold. "He's getting Madeline christened next month."

"Yes, I know. I'm actually going."

"Great! That's great," she says, trying and failing not to sound surprised. Should I tell her I'm going to be godmother, or will it just draw us into territory too murky to risk? "Have you spoken to him at all?"

I look at her, trying to formulate a response, the words choking in my throat.

"Yeah, I have. He wanted to meet, actually." Why do I keep saying actually? "To talk about back then. You know, what I remembered about . . . about Sally."

"Oh. Right."

"He's a nice man, isn't he? I'm glad she did so well."

"I think he thinks *he* did pretty well," says Lola, quick as a flash.

"Yeah, no, I didn't mean it like that. I just meant that he's a nice man. You must have got to know him properly with all those trips to New York."

"I only went a few times." Everything we say to each other seems to land as though it's barbed, even when it's not intended that way. I wish we could just clear away the silt and start again, the waters clear. But what I've done—I've lost even the possibility. "But yeah, they were great together."

"Were they?" I say, sadness seeping through me. I need to hear this, need to keep remembering that William could never be mine, not truly.

"I mean I'm lucky if Justin gets me a bunch of daffodils on Valentine's Day!" says Lola, her own infatuation with Sally shining through her open face. She never took her off the pedestal, I can see that. "I remember the last time I went to see them, they had this thing that he had to get her a proper present when he went away for work, not like duty-free chocolates or perfume. So he'd been to Milan, and he'd spent the whole of the last day literally walking the streets, looking for the perfect thing. He had to beg them to let him on the flight."

"What did he get her?" I ask, trying to sound wistfully curious, to not let her see how ravenous I am for details that I know will hurt me. But it's not just about William, I want to know who she became: if I know who she became, perhaps I'll know why she left.

"It was this beautiful handmade photograph album. I think he slipped a picture of Madeline into it before he gave it to her." Lola looks across at me, eyes bright. "It was so romantic."

"Did she like it?" I say, feeling a little queasy, like I'm some kind of hustler playing a confidence trick.

"Yeah, of course she did."

It would have been a matter of weeks before she died. William still pushing himself to the absolute edge to try and win her approval. Did she love him for it, or despise him like he so often seemed to fear?

"And they were happy?"

"Yes, Livvy, she was happy! She had a lovely life. What's your point?"

"It's just . . . you know what she was like. She liked to keep them on their toes, didn't she?"

Lola gives an angry little shrug.

"Did she? We were kids, Livvy, it's a long time ago. She was a wife and mother. She'd grown up."

Just for a second I wish with all my heart that Sally was here. She'd get the gray areas—that you can have a lovely life on paper and still be unhappy, that being a wife and mother might not change your essential nature. She could always see through people and situations like a hot knife slicing through butter, it was what allowed her to keep pulling the strings. I lost my naivety to Sally, but perhaps some of it needed to go, for my very survival. She taught me truths about human nature with those sly, perceptive little observations of hers. I don't think she'd want to be airbrushed; I know that I wouldn't. You truly are gone when the stories people tell about you become as sweet and artificial as synthetic icing, the messy reality of who you really were too complicated to keep alive.

Lola's arms are folded across her chest now, the warmth of earlier all but evaporated. I should probably back away, but she was too close to Sally's final months for me not to try a little harder.

"I'm not trying to be harsh." I pause, trying to find the words. "It's just, there's still a lot of unanswered questions about what happened. This is really horrible but I think you will want to know. The insurance company is trying to say that it could have been suicide."

Lola's face drains of color, her eyes as round as saucers. I shouldn't have told her. It's fifteen minutes or so before she can make any kind of sense, the shock too overwhelming.

"It's rubbish," she keeps saying. "How can they be so callous?"

"I know."

"William knows it's a lie, doesn't he?" she says.

I think of that footage, the way the car pinballs between the lanes like it's got a mind of its own. Knowing it's a lie is his truth, but whether it's the actual truth is a different question all together.

"Yeah, he's fighting every step of the way. But he's having to comb through absolutely everything. She had big debts," I add, tentatively, watching her face. "All these credit cards he didn't know about."

My breath has grown tight in my chest, my body telling me what my mind refuses to acknowledge—that I am wading out into quicksand.

"She loved beautiful things," says Lola, a certain desperation in her eyes.

Just for a second I see us from above, both stretched as tight and tense as the skin on a drum, each new piece reverberating as it hits.

"I'm sorry to drop all of this on you," I say, smiling at her, hoping that she knows that I care about her, that my being here is about more than Sally. She grabs my hand across the table.

"I'm glad you told me," she says, her eyes filling again. She pauses a second, and I can see the cogs starting to whir as the shock recedes. "Have you spent quite a bit of time with him then?"

"No, not that much. I think it's just that he doesn't have that many people to talk to."

I pause a second, my words echoing in my head. I meant it as an excuse, but perhaps it's the truth.

We have one more glass of wine, trying with all our might to find some kind of normality in the midst of chaos. She tells me a little about her life with Justin and their two boys, the contentment and the exasperation sitting side by side, and I try to describe my life to her, unable to convince her that hanging out with a film star isn't all it's cracked up to be. The way she hoovers up the details makes me realize how much she'll miss the flashes of glamour that Sally gave her, those New York trips a highlight in the calendar. When I tell her I'm still single the balance is redressed. "I'm sure you're going to meet someone really soon," she says, a kindly sort of pity in her eyes, and I nod my assent, conscious of the loneliness of keeping so much padlocked inside. *How can something so wrong feel so right?* That's what William said. Did he mean it, or was it just the trauma and the red wine that were talking? Now Lola's sitting across from me, Sally so present again, I can't imagine a time when anyone would believe the right could justify the wrong.

We say our goodbyes at the tube, both of us tearful again.

"I'm so glad we had tonight," she says. "It was . . ." she looks at me, her grief overwhelming, "it was lovely, sort of."

"I know what you mean," I say, hugging her so close I can feel the contours of her solid, well-padded body through her coat.

"Soon!" she says.

"Soon," I agree.

"Anyway, we'll see each other at the christening, whatever happens."

I feel my stomach start to drop at the very thought, but I force a smile.

"Course."

As I'm walking toward my escalator, our goodbyes over, Lola suddenly calls out to me. She runs over, grabs my arm.

"She was trying, you know," she says, emotional. "I just thought. The last time I was there, I went barging into her room to take her a cup of coffee, and she was pulling all these gorgeous things out of her wardrobe and packing them up. I remember because she really snapped at me, but I can see why now. She was selling them, she said. She must've been trying to pay back the money she owed."

OCTOBER 1996–MAY 1997

I'd spent the summer holidays hanging out with James, our uneasy ease reestablished. He was a nineteen-year-old boy, he wasn't going to overanalyze anything, he was just pleased that normal service had been resumed. I advised him about other girls, determinedly swallowing the lump in my throat, and then cheerfully accepted his last-minute cancelations when my excellent advice paid off. I took what I could get, too craven and devoted to think about the price that I was paying; I was like any addict, only my drug was James, and I was prepared to put my heart in hock to get a fix.

Then it was back to Leeds, and time to guiltily move into the apartment that had cost so much in every sense. I'd rung Lola three or four times over the holidays but she'd never returned my calls. I'd tried to write her a letter, but our story was peppered with lies, and anyway, I couldn't even justify my behavior to myself. I remember I tried to tell Jules about it, and found myself lying again, almost unconsciously, too embarrassed to tell her how shameless we'd been. How lonely I'd made myself, how dependent on one person. I missed Lola far more than I could have predicted, held on to the hope that all those clichés about time's healing properties would turn out to be true.

Sally arrived back before me, had already been to Habitat and bought a bleached wood coffee table and a chrome magazine rack and all kinds of other fancy pieces that looked more befitting to a Martini advert than a student apartment.

"Looks amazing, if I do say so myself," she said, grinning at me, her face alight with triumph.

"Yeah, it does," I said, dropping my bag, and drinking it in. I wanted to revel in it, but it was hard for all kinds of reasons, not least the thought that my grant check had already disappeared in a puff of smoke. She'd said we should have a shared bank account for house things, and I hadn't been nearly forensic enough about what that meant. "But how are we going to afford—"

She waved an airy hand.

"Don't worry about it, you can pay me back. Now get some glasses, my friend, Mr. Bubbles is in the fridge."

And there you had it: whichever way you looked at it, she owned me. Perhaps it was the way I liked it.

Sally insisted we threw a housewarming. She loved a party, but also I knew she wanted to show off the apartment. She draped it in fairy lights, carefully planned a playlist, worked out how to mix a lethally strong strawberry margarita in our brand-new blender. The party was thronged, but I realized, as I did on my birthday, that while I did have other friends there, their friendship was a weak, insipid thing compared to my bond with Sally. In fact the friends I had that weren't also hers were always at risk, her sharp eyes seeking out their faults and finding a way to write them on a banner across my consciousness. A lot of people there that night were friends of Shaun's, an older crowd I didn't really know. By one a.m. the neighbors were starting to complain—after all, it wasn't a student block—but Sally was defiant.

"They're just being uptight," she said, her limbs wrapped around Shaun like an octopus's tentacles.

I turned the music right down, ignoring the howls of protest.

"Jesus, Livvy!" said Sally sharply, streaking across the room to turn it back up. I felt like everyone's eyes were trained on us. "Don't be such a killjoy."

As the volume peaked, a cheer went up, and I retreated, furious, to my room. There was a couple snogging on top of a pile of coats, and I kicked them out, dumping the coats outside in an angry heap. An hour later it was still as loud, and I got back up and found her. She wasn't in the living room, wasn't in the kitchen. I knocked on her bedroom door and eventually, after much giggling, the door swung open. "Hi, Livvy," she said, hugging me too tightly. Her pupils were like round, black buttons in the center of her bright blue eyes. Shaun and a couple of other people were squashed up on the bed, silent, like a line of naughty children.

"Are you taking drugs?"

"No!"

"I don't want people taking drugs in my house!"

"Did you hear that?" said Sally. "Livvy doesn't want people taking drugs in her house." She turned back to me. "Okay,

Livvy" she said, in a sing-song voice. "I'll make sure no one takes any drugs in Livvy's house."

"I mean it, Sally, I'll call the police."

The four of them started laughing, their laughter growing uncontrollable, and fear began to grip hold of me. I was out of my depth, being punished for pretending to be someone it turned out I didn't even want to be anymore. What if a neighbor decided they'd call the police—could we be arrested? I thought of my dad, the profound disappointment he would feel, and grabbed her arm, imploring.

"Sally, please, I don't want it to be like this."

Sally hugged me, dropped a wet, lipsticky kiss on my cheek.

"We're having fun! You should have more fun. You're my best friend and we're having a party."

Suddenly I wished more than anything that I was in a big, messy house where baked beans encrusted an ancient range, and I could sit around a kitchen table and bemoan our essay deadlines with my fellow geeks like they really were a matter of life and death.

I missed my innocence, so carelessly squandered and so impossible to regain.

She was right though: we did have fun. The nights I really loved were the ones where I would cook—Sally full of praise, even though all she'd do was nibble a few bites and then push the food around the expanse of her plate—our dinners perched on our knees so we could watch whatever TV program was our current obsession. Sally could create a sense of occasion from a tiny thing, and for a few months the weekly episode of This Life was like a stadium event. Thursday night was sacred, and we'd huddle up close on the sofa, a bottle of cava on the coffee table, agog at the latest twists and turns, lusting after Miles and Egg like they lived next door.

But other times the closeness would seem like a mirage. I lived in fear of Sally stepping into the dark forest that sometimes took her away from me, and turned her into someone unrecognizable.

Those times, she would come home from college and barely utter a word, shutting herself in her room, her birdlike eating replaced by a diet of junk food. I'd noticed it in the first year, but I'd been able to minimize it in my head. There'd been Lola for one thing, as well as a whole houseful of other people, all there to provide a distraction or share the responsibility. Now I couldn't help feeling it was my fault. She often wouldn't say what was wrong, but if she did, it often seemed to be some kind of romantic bruise from the past that surely should have healed by now. I would feel helpless, naive, without resources. The storm could blow in so many different ways; she could be cold and aloof, want me nowhere near her, or she could be wracked with sobs, her white fingers wrapped tightly around me like they were claws, me trying to somehow hug her back to happiness.

But the storm could blow over as swiftly as it blew in. Shaun might appear, and she would plaster a happy smile on her face, her foundation a little thicker than normal to cover the ravages of her tears. One weekend James was due to visit, and I warned him in advance of what he could be facing, knowing he was absolutely useless at dealing with emotional girls. But sure enough, as soon as he tipped up she put on a face and poured the drinks, for all the world like a sunshiny cocktail waitress. It should have troubled me, the way she lit up around him, but self-preservation prevented me from registering it. After all, we were each other's life support.

When I think about it now, I realize that she always did make sure she had backup, even while she tried to keep my options to an absolute minimum. I remember bursting back through the door one This Life night, my stint in the library longer than I had intended. "It's starting!" I shouted, running into the living room, only to find Lola, stockinged feet neatly tucked underneath her, sitting on the sofa.

"Hello, Livvy," she said, giving me a brief, polite smile devoid of any warmth.

"Oh . . . hi! Lovely to see you."

I walked toward her, hoping she'd let me hug her, but she might as well have been wreathed in barbed wire.

"We've got a house guest!" said Sally, sailing back in, a bowl of Pringles in her hand, not a trace of discomfort. I don't know what she said to her, I never asked, but she somehow managed to lure her back into the fold. But now the fold was only big enough for two. They would hug and shriek and go for drinks, and occasionally I would go along, but it was abundantly clear who was making the bed sag in the middle now. Lola would tolerate me, but no more than that, and to go out with her on my own and lay it on the table would somehow have felt like going behind Sally's back. Neither of us would have dared do that.

It wasn't just Lola. It sometimes felt like she got crushes on people, girls as much as boys, and she'd suddenly want to see them all the time. She might invite me along, but it was always in a way that told me she was doing me a favor rather than relishing the idea of my company. After the first couple of times I learned not to be jealous. These people were like fireflies, their tenure brief, the friendship burning out before it gained any real momentum. And then it would be me and her again, almost as if I'd imagined it.

That apartment left me broke. The rent was sky high, and that was before you took into account how much it cost to survive the cold of a Yorkshire winter. We'd divided up the bills when we first moved in, putting a few in each of our names, but Sally would leave hers until they were red and angry, final demands and threats of court action. I'd beg her to pay them, and she'd laugh.

"They're messing with us. They won't do anything. I'll pay it next week."

She was right, of course, but I didn't like the menace of it, the sense that we were in trouble. It gave me a feeling of living in the last days of a dying empire, like we were squatting in Buckingham Palace.

I dated a bit that year, but it was halfhearted. The real romantic punctuation came from my time with James. His visits got more frequent as the year rolled on, and any remaining awkwardness trickled away. It was still a pose on my part, but like I said, I was craven.

It wasn't just me who was excited when a visit was imminent. "I love James," Sally would say, and I would try and be pleased that my two favorite people liked each other so much. It seemed petty to not be happy about it, but I couldn't help but resent the way she'd never give us any time alone. I knew that if I asked there'd be all manner of trouble, and even the act of asking seemed to contradict my breezy assurances that we were no more than friends.

She hardly ever invited Shaun on our nights out with James, even though it seemed obvious to make it a foursome. Instead we'd be a sharp-cornered little trio, jumping on a virtual trampoline, competing to see how high the fun could take us. One time we somehow ended up in a house club, full of bare-chested ravers sweating all over us and blow- ing whistles in our faces. It was the last place I wanted to be. Sally disappeared off somewhere, and after an hour me and James started to get worried. I finally tracked her down in a corner by the loos, snogging someone I could barely see, beyond knowing for absolute certain that he wasn't Shaun. I waited until I started to feel like a Peeping Tom, then gave up. When she got back I managed to make myself heard over the bass line.

"What were you doing?"

She looked at me, blank-faced, and then danced a little bit harder. Once we got home, I tried again. We were in the kitchen alone, waiting for James to sort out the music.

"Who was that guy?" I said, trying to stop myself from sounding disapproving. I didn't think Shaun was the love of her life, but nor did I think he deserved her cheating on him. He'd wanted to come out with us, but she'd claimed it was a girl's night. She'd told us conspiratorially, said how much she was looking forward to us being the three musketeers, and I'd swallowed my irritation at the way she acted like she'd been there from the beginning.

"What guy?"

"The one you were snogging."

"I dunno what you're talking about," she said, pouring boiling water into our mugs, her eyes refusing to meet mine.

"You so do!" I said, trying to keep it light.

"Why are you saying that?" she said, blue eyes flashing ice.

"I saw you."

"Shut up, Livvy," she hissed, spotting James coming back into the room. "Hello, You," she said, honeyed. "Cup

of tea, or shall we go for one last cheeky vodka? You know it makes sense."

It wasn't really working. I'd always longed for me and Sally to be more like sisters than friends, which just goes to show, you should be careful what you wish for. Sally saved her worst behavior for her family, and I think that, once we'd moved in together, that was what I'd become in her eyes. Living with her made me anxious, the whole atmosphere dictated by the violent seesaw of her moods, and my grades were suffering as a result. I'd got a part-time waitressing job to help fund my rent, which made it even harder to focus. I started to wonder if my rackety finances might provide me with the life raft I needed. Perhaps I could plead poverty, move back into a shared house, and keep the good bits of my friendship with Sally and slough away the bad.

"That sounds like a fantastic idea," said Mom, when I told her, her relief palpable. "You're only a student once in your life, so you should jolly well be one."

It was nice to feel that my family was there too, that not everything was dictated by my relationship with Sally, each experience taken back and pored over in the lab of our friendship.

I put off mentioning it for a couple of weeks, rehearsing it again and again in my head. In the end I broached it on one of our sofa supper nights, hoping that the chilled domesticity would soften the blow. As soon as she grasped what I was saying she burst into hysterical sobs.

"You're my best friend," she said, burying her face in the cushions. "Why wouldn't you want to live with me?"

"It was only an idea!" I said, helpless in the face of her grief. "I just thought, we've only got a year left. It might be fun to share again."

"If it's about money I'll pay more! It is about the money, isn't it?"

I paused, trying to muster up enough courage to tell her that it was about more than that. That I couldn't give her everything. That if I did there would be nothing left for me.

"Forget it. Forget I said anything. It'll be fine."

CHAPTER SIXTEEN

SUNDAY DOESN'T QUITE LOOK LIKE I THOUGHT IT would. At eight a.m. I'm sitting at the kitchen table, the pages of the script spread out around me, giving it one final polish before it goes out to directors tomorrow. It's gone back and forth between Flynn and me over the last few weeks—every time I think it's finally done he comes up with one more nit-picking tweak that he's convinced is pure genius.

My dinner with William has metamorphosed into a trip to Windsor Castle with Madeline with dinner tacked on at the end, a reimagining that is hard not to take as a slight. I haven't spoken to him since we said a hurried goodbye at Branksome station a fortnight ago, communication limited to a few e-mails he's sent from what seems like an endless merry-go-round of work trips. At least it's meant my heart's been forced to start catching up with reality—I'm going to be a godmother, a godmother he once shared a teenage cuddle with, and hopefully, given time, it will stop pining for a future that could never be any more than a fantasy.

I think I've done all the pining that any one person deserves to do in a single lifetime. At this precise moment in time Charlotte is ensconced in James's bedroom, the Postbox safely dispatched on a stag weekend. The fact that I'm still putting my all into these tired pages is because it's all the ammunition I've got left against her. A few days after that fateful trip to Pinewood Mary sent me a six-thirty a.m. e-mail. *Fancy a coffee?* it said, with the lone *x* of doom that I've come to dread. Honey called me an hour later to tell me to skip the office and go straight to the Charlotte Street Hotel, and I waited there, quaking, for Mary to arrive. Twenty minutes later she swept in, dressed in a scarlet kaftan and a miniskirt, leaving her sunglasses on for a disconcertingly long time.

"What's wrong?" she said, her voice deceptively warm, a smile of faux concern on her face that swiftly evaporated., "I did think that the task I'd set you was relatively simple."

And then she finally pushed her glasses up onto her head, turning that minesweeping gaze on me so she could study me for any signs of weakness.

"Has Flynn said something?"

"Flynn's always got plenty to say for himself, but it's you we're here to talk about."

"I didn't mean to offend him," I said, pleadingly. "I just wanted to help him make it the best it could be. I was trying to support him."

"Support him? It's a lovely sentiment," she said, with a rictus grin. "I'm wondering if it's *you* who might need the support. I haven't talked to her yet, but I'm sure Charlotte would consider taking the whole thing over. She's certainly going to need to calm his ruffled feathers."

I knew from the way she said it, that it was a lie, that it was almost a done deal, Charlotte poised and ready to feast on my carcass.

"No!" I snapped, all tact burned away. "I mean, I can handle it. I'll do whatever it takes."

"Whatever it takes? Take a moment, Livvy. I don't want you to turn around and find you've made another empty promise."

It hurt when she said it; the idea that I'm a person who doesn't keep her word. I pleaded with her, pledged my loyalty, while she simply watched me twisting on the hook.

"I do wonder if your friend's—what happened—has hit you harder than you realize," she said. "I can't help thinking that you haven't been yourself. Do you think you might need some time off to gather yourself?"

That was when I went into overdrive. I know how it works, weakness made flesh so it can be thrown back at you when things have reached the point of no return. Losing my job is not part of the plan.

"Okay," she said eventually, her red sleeves flapping in the breeze like the wings of an elegant bird, her expression inscrutable. "There's not long until he disappears back to the US. I hope you realize that you'll have to give this absolutely everything you've got."

She stared at me as she said it, challenging me to break, but I didn't flinch. If one thing started to break, I don't know where it would end.

William is late, a full fifteen minutes: if William time is like dog years then that's the equivalent of three hours from a normal person. I stand in front of the mirror in the hallway fiddling with my lipstick and trying to stop the left side of my hair from looking like a lopsided Princess Leia do. I've made much more effort with my outfit this time, but not too much effort—I'm trying to pull off something that straddles the shaky line between homespun and attractive. I've gone for a fitted blue corduroy skirt with a gray cashmere V-neck and the gold heart pendant that Jules gave me for Christmas. Once it's close to half an hour I call him. Apart from anything I need to make sure I'm out of here before Charlotte starts draping herself around my kitchen.

"I'm so sorry," he says, sounding harassed. "We're actually just outside."

"Oh! Okay, I'll come down."

He's parked in a black Golf, and is standing on the pavement, the passenger door flung open. Madeline's sitting there, a look of total fury on her face. I gingerly approach.

"Hello there," says William, barely looking at me, their frustration like a heat haze that's crackling between them.

"Hi," I say, hanging back. Madeline's fists are balled up in her lap, her cheeks aflame. Looking at her I feel deeply trepidatious.

"Hi, Madeline," I venture.

"Go AWAY," she snarls, not even deigning to look at me. I take a couple of steps backward, like a novice lion tamer stepping away from the cage.

"You will not speak to Olivia like that!" snaps William, voice sharp. Hearing his tone, how shaming it might be, makes me step a little closer.

"It's fine," I tell him, trying to make eye contact with her. "What's wrong? I thought we were going to go to a castle."

"Nothing," says Madeline, folding her arms across her chest and staring determinedly into the middle distance, looking for all the world like a tiny little version of her dad.

"You need to get in the back seat this instant!" says William. "That's Olivia's seat."

"I can sit in the back, it's fine."

"No!" shouts Madeline. "I don't want you in my car. Go back to your house."

Does she have some kind of sixth sense about me, an innate need to protect her mom's patch?

"Maybe I should go," I ask William. "She really doesn't want me here."

"No," he says, loud enough for her to hear, voice steely. "She's just taken leave of her manners."

It's like a red rag to a bull. Madeline rips open the glove compartment and grabs the contents, flinging them into the road, her face scarlet. "Right, that's it," says William, lifting her out of her seat and holding her arms by her sides. "You need to apologize," he tells her, the vein at the side of his face throbbing. Madeline wriggles and screams, her red buckled shoes stamping on the pavement. I can't bear it: her rage feels so justified, so understandable, that part of me longs to scream along with her. I should probably back away, leave them to it, but instead I crouch down so I'm at eye level with her. It's no more than instinct: I've got no idea what to do now I'm down here. I swallow my nerves, telling myself how ridiculous it is to be this intimidated by a seven-year-old.

"What about the castle?" I ask her, though I can barely hear myself above her screams.

"I don't want to go to stupid Windsor Castle," she says, turning her furious gaze on me. "I already went to stupid church. It doesn't even have any princesses."

"How about if we went somewhere else?" I ask.

"With you?" she says, scorn in her voice. It takes all my self-control not to shrink away.

"If you'll let me come."

She pauses, sizes me up, like we're two cowboys facing off across a Wild West saloon.

"Where would it be?"

Don't fail me now, brain. Where would be near enough and fun enough to rescue what has so far been a very bad day?

"Brighton! There's a pier, and a beach, and fair rides. And we can get them to make us doughnuts. They're properly yummy and I can't eat a whole bag on my own."

I love those doughnuts. Even now James and I sometimes jump on the train and spend the day mooching around. I look up to his window, the curtains still drawn. Madeline still hasn't replied.

"I will do that," she says, eventually, her eyes narrowed, "as long as there isn't a silly, boring castle."

"Good!" I say, standing up, beaming at William, my satisfaction melting as I take in his icy gaze. "I'm sorry..." I say, uncertain.

"I appreciate your efforts, but I'd prefer you leave the parenting to the parent," he whispers curtly, jerking past me to buckle Madeline into her car seat. I stand there, stung, on the verge of running back to the house and calling it quits. He's right: I should've thought, but instead I just acted and left him feeling completely undermined—it's not like I know how it is day to day, or what preceded her tantrum—he's the one negotiating the barren reality of life as a single parent. Is it more than that, though—a barrier thrown up to remind me that this isn't a job interview, that Sally's death has not created a vacancy?

He gets into the driver's seat and I sneak a peek at Madeline, sucking her thumb, for once seeming so much younger than her years. I don't regret it, I tell him silently, hoping it somehow punctures his rigid cranium. There's no sign it registers: his hands are tightly gripping the steering wheel, eyes fixed on the mirror, that vein still pulsing away, beating a tattoo through his fine, pale skin.

I've loved Brighton ever since James first took me there on my eighteenth birthday—I love the smell of the sea, I love the nausea-inducing rides on the pier, I even love the unromantically pebbly beach. We park in a big multistory near the seafront, and I step out, too mulish to make any suggestions about what we should do. William has been infuriatingly courteous throughout the journey, triggering a level of resentment in me that doesn't make me like myself very much. I think it's because I know that my resentment is about more than the last hour, it's about what he cannot be for me, a fact that I'm still struggling to accept. He put on a tape of Enid Blyton stories for Madeline, which at least spared us from too much conversation—Timmy the dog's intuitive woofing at swarthy gypsies was far safer.

"I'm hungry," announces Madeline. "And I'd like my lunch to be a hamburger."

She knows she's got the upper hand; even a nonparent moron like me can divine that fact. William concedes, and then turns to me.

"Do you have any suggestions? You seem to be something of an expert."

"I can think of a couple of places," I say, addressing myself to Madeline, and lead them off toward the Lanes, immediately starting to feel a bit ashamed of myself. The last thing Madeline needs is adults throwing silent poison arrows at each other—who knows how much of that she's already had to endure? "Have you been here before?" I ask William, as cheerily as I can muster.

"I think I toured the university, but Durham won out in the end."

Sometimes William sounds approximately one hundred and five years old. Maybe this is perfect. Maybe what I need is to start finding him ridiculous, devote myself to becoming the world's best godmother and leave him to be picked over by whatever ghastly parade of young yuppies Trixie shakes out of her address book. But as soon as I think it, my body tells me a different story, reminds me how it felt to be pressed up against him in that tiny bed. I look at him, trying to sense whether seeing me again has brought it to the fore, but he's involved in an earnest conversation with Madeline about a Dalmatian on the other side of the road. Normally I can tell if someone loves me too much or too little, but he's got that same distant stateliness that his parents' house had.

"Here we are," I say, drawing up outside Browns.

"Excellent choice," says William, and the three of us walk in, looking for all the world like a perfect little family. Madeline happily eats her hamburger, chatting away to both of us as if her furious tantrum was a figment of our imagination. "What was wrong?" I quietly ask William, as she reverently studies the dessert menu. I still feel a little scared of her, like she's a bomb that might blow up at any moment, the detonator hidden from view. He shrugs, a bleak expression on his face.

"I don't know, Livvy. Please don't take it personally. That kind of thing has been a regular occurrence recently."

Who was I to be so judgmental about how he handled it? I touch his hand for the briefest of seconds, and he reaches under the table, interlocking his fingers with mine, squeezing them in a way that makes warmth spread through my whole body. I look at him, then look away, feeling momentarily so close to him that it takes all my reserve not to reach out to stroke his face.

"Chip?" he says, nodding to his plate, giving me the sweetest of smiles.

"Thanks," I say, grabbing one and smiling back.

"I want a chocolate brownie," Madeline announces, stabbing at the menu with her finger. "And then doughnuts," she says, turning to me, the world's foremost doughnut oracle.

"Is that okay?" I ask William.

"Just this once it should be absolutely fine."

The day ends up being sort of lovely. I say sort of because every second of it is infused with the awful absence of Sally, the two of them—no, the three of us—struggling to find a way to acknowledge her without being destroyed by the weight of her loss. Madeline manages it best. When I ask her if she wants to come on the swinging teacups she tells me that her mommy says tea is like fish wee, and she only ever drinks coffee. I can imagine that: Sally only liked things that gave her a kick. When she asks if we can go on the ghost train William looks stricken. "Mommy won't be in there!" she tells him, looking at him like he's a complete idiot. "She up in heaven with the other mommies who died." We both stare down at her, and look at each other, but she's already running off, heading for the queue. William strokes my hand again, and leans in.

"Thank you for being here," he says. "Despite this morn-ing's performance, I promise you it's an enormous help."

"I'm glad," I say. What am I to you, I think, or rather, what could I be? I hope he doesn't see the question in my eyes.

Madeline gets to the front of the queue before us.

"Three tickets please," she says, passing the man in the booth a handful of tokens.

"That for your mom and dad?" he asks. "Can't come in on your own."

"That's my daddy, but she's not my mommy," says Mad-eline, pointing to us. "She's Olivia. My mummy's dead."

The man in the booth is lost for words. William steps forward, taking the tickets.

"Thank you," he says. "Sorry about that."

"But she is," says Madeline, her bottom lip starting to go. William's getting that look again, like a rabbit caught in the headlights. Public displays of anything are not his strong suit.

"Yes she is," I agree, trying to convey to her in my look that I can really hear what it is she's trying to say. "And it's really, really sad."

Perhaps the ghost train is exactly what she needs. Even though the phosphorous skeletons are completely phony-looking, she screams and howls, and holds on to William like she never wants to let him go. After that we give up on the rides, treating ourselves to some huge puffs of cotton candy, eating them as we walk down the pebbly beach, dappled by the setting sun. William shows Madeline his stone-skimming trick, holding her hand so delicately that she really believes that the multiple bounces are entirely down to her. She jumps up and down, cheering, her face a picture of delight, and I marvel at her ability to hold so many extremes of emotion within herself, moving between them as though she's surfing a wave.

"Do you want to know something very exciting?" says William once she's calmed down.

"What?" she says.

"When we have you christened, guess who's going to be your godmother?"

My palms feel cold and sweaty, stage fright completely overwhelming. I'm going to feel completely humiliated if she rejects me out of hand.

"Princess Kate?"

"No, guess again," says William, tapping her on the nose. "Besides, she's a duchess."

This is painful. Madeline turns round slowly and considers me.

"You?" she says, one word imbued with so much meaning; in this moment she is so like Sally that it winds me.

"Yes," I say, cautiously. "If you'll let me?"

She looks at me for a few seconds, and then tears away down the beach, dark hair flying behind her like a familiar. I watch, helpless, as William sets off in pursuit—it feels utterly symbolic, like the universe is sending a thunderbolt crashing down from the heavens, warning me off. The idea of my own child, my flesh and blood, is one thing, but the idea that this broken, angry little person would ever let me come anywhere close is utterly unimaginable. I'd be a shadow, a wraith, a human reminder of what's been lost.

They're talking now, William kneeling in front of her. I hope to God he's not telling her off. Eventually they walk back toward me, holding hands. Madeline's gaze is direct as she addresses me.

"Godmother is not the same as mother."

It's like she can read my thoughts, my flights of fancy utterly transparent—I feel too exposed to risk so much as a glance in William's direction. When Sally died she made damn sure she'd left a gatekeeper in place.

"No, it isn't," I tell her. "But it means you'll always be special to me."

"I will let you then," she says, solemn.

"Thank you," I say, my voice cracking. Now I look to William, but it doesn't reassure me, his smile more like facial scenery than an expression of his thoughts. Perhaps he thought it too, in those seconds he went running down the beach, perhaps he knew right then and there that there would never be space for us. For someone else maybe, a clean skin, but I come with too much written through me for my presence to ever stop sending out an echo from a painful past.

CHAPTER SEVENTEEN

IT'S DARK BY THE TIME WE GET BACK TO THE APART-
ment, a mansion block positioned right on the corner of
Battersea Park. Madeline is half asleep, but is still groggily
insisting she's not tired as William gently lifts her out of her
car seat and hauls her inside, her dark head lolling over his
broad shoulders. I trail behind them, wondering if I should
politely make my excuses and slip off home. William turns
to me, whispering.

"Let me just pop her into bed. I'm sorry, I should have
mentioned I had to give the au pair the night off. I thought I
could call out for takeaway."

"Oh," I say, trying not to look stricken. It's not that I
wanted to be wined and dined, it's what it says to me. I take
a deep breath, determined to let him lead. "Great. Shall I do
some Googling?"

"Please don't worry about it," he says, and I feel myself shrink and contract. It's like I've woken up in a parallel universe where I don't know how to be me, where every step I take is as likely to be wrong as it is to be right. "The kitchen's just through there."

"Bye-bye, Olivia," says Madeline, giving me a contented little wave from the cozy nook she's found in William's shoulder. "I think it's your bedtime too."

The kitchen is large and gleaming, fully equipped with top-of-the-line appliances, but it feels more like an operating theater than a piece of a home. It makes me realize how important my kitchen is to me, how much I've always found my center by cooking. It's so many things; a way to silently convey to a person that you love them, a necessity in order to survive, and a way that I get out of my stupid, thought-ridden head and lose myself in something creative and physical (to hell with stupid old Zumba). I take a sneaky peek in the fridge. It's full of ready meals from Waitrose, all arranged in neat stacks, a surprising amount of wine and beer, and the kind of pre-prepared basics I'd never think to buy. What kind of sloth needs a supermarket to grate their cheese for them?

"Are you pouring yourself a glass of wine?" says William, and I jump out of my skin.

"That was quick."

"Cursory brushing of teeth and then straight under the covers. She was exhausted. Besides," he says, swiftly crossing the room, "I wanted to get back to you."

He gathers me up in his arms, his surety utterly intoxicating. For a few, delicious minutes it banishes all my doubts and insecurities, the world telescoping down to the two of us, wrapped around one another, his body a shield against any wolves that are howling at the door. Eventually he pulls away, looking down at me.

"I've been wanting to do that all day. I kept watching you, thinking how beautiful you looked."

Did you? Is it that I can't read you, or that you're trying to tell me what I want to hear?

"Thank you," I say, reaching up to stroke his face, too frightened to stay in this moment. "Now what are we going to do about supper?"

It turns out I misjudged him. The reason he didn't want me to Google Pizza Pronto was because he was one step ahead, having somehow found a service that delivers from any restaurant in a five-mile radius. As we wait for our delicious-sounding Italian to arrive, I ask him for a tour of the apartment. It turns out the kitchen is a microcosm, each room large and well appointed, but utterly lacking in personality.

"This is the sitting room," he says, and I look at the immaculate cream sofa, which I can't help thinking would be improved by a few scuff marks. The dreary Impressionist reproductions on the beige walls are the only punctuation the room has, other than that picture of Madeline and Sally in New York, which sits in state on the mantelpiece. The room overlooks the park, and he gestures out to it.

"We certainly can't complain about the location."

For some reason it feels more sinister than scenic to me. "How did you find it?"

"The embassy arranged it all. They found a nanny for us too." I might be wrong, but it feels like every element of his life is controlled by outside forces. Even though he's escaped from New York, the authoritarian tentacles of his job have stretched across the pond, slyly trapping him in another gilded cage.

"Is she live-in?"

"No, she comes as and when she's needed. Let me show you the rest."

There's a small spare room, endless bathrooms, and Madeline's room, which has her name emblazoned across the door in wooden, purple letters. "And this is my room," he says, nudging the door. I can't resist a quick look inside. It's perfectly ordered, the watch and cufflinks on the chest of drawers the only sign of life, entirely devoid of that soft, feminine clutter willfully escaping from drawers and wardrobes that I'm sure characterized his marital bedroom. It makes me feel cold. "That's quite enough of that," says William, sliding the door closed, and I wonder what he means. Is it that he feels exposed, or that he's giving me another red light?

He looks at me expectantly, with a trace of that earnest little boy I saw looking out of the school picture.

"It's nice," I say. It seems too cruel to flag up its failings, when they're no more than tiny mirrored fragments of a bigger explosion. I want to wreak havoc—go through it with a paintbrush, shower it with brightly colored cushions and splotchy paintings of Madeline's and elusive grains of rice that have snuck behind the stove when a hot, delicious curry has been cooked with the radio turned up loud—but it's not within my gift. We sit there for a couple of awkward minutes, entombed by the sterile kitchen, before the doorbell rings, heralding the arrival of a smartly dressed delivery man with a stack of boxes. William's about to dish it all out when I stop him.

"Let me warm the plates," I say. It feels important somehow.

"As you wish," he says. "I'll open some wine. Red, I presume?"

He does notice things, I think, more gratified than I should be—there is a world beyond the mental hamster wheel he's stuck on, those terrible questions driving him around and around.

"That'd be lovely," I say, hoping my eyes don't communicate too much. Sometimes I feel like he's a rescue animal that I can only approach with the softest of steps for fear he takes flight.

He seems particularly fragile to me today.

"I was thinking, about Madeline. About how angry she is. Maybe it would help if she could talk to someone. A professional, I mean."

"I appreciate your trying to help, but I tend to think such things do more harm than good."

I think of the way his face twisted when he talked about Sally's therapy sessions—it was a stupid thing to suggest. Probably in his family it's roughly akin to having a crack habit. I pause a minute then try again.

"Tell me to shut up if you don't want to talk about it, but how was the rest of the packing?"

Part of me hopes that he found something else, that there is a trail of breadcrumbs leading to her secrets. I could be wrong, but I'm sure there's a whole wealth of them to find.

"Ghastly," he says. "There's no other word for it."

"You poor thing."

He looks away, troubled.

"What?"

"She had so many clothes, but there are certain favorite pieces that she wore so much that I'd recognize them. It was a source of irritation, I'm afraid to say, that she'd endlessly shop and then simply recycle the ones she loved." I think of what Lola said about those heaped up outfits. The words rise up in my throat, but then I swallow them down. Why would she sell her worn out favorites: the real money would come from all the priceless frocks that were left hanging, tags often still attached. "And then the jewelry—there are the pieces that are gone, but also a couple of things that look, even to my untrained eye, like they would have cost a small fortune. And I've never seen them in my life."

"Oh William," I say, unconsciously pulling back. I'm starting to feel like a Peeping Tom, watching the marriage unravel before my eyes. I remember Shaun, his entire grant check gone, because Sally had somehow persuaded him that she needed a diamond-studded cuff that she'd scoped out in Harvey Nichols. There's no way Sally would buy expensive jewelry for herself—it was too good an opportunity to make some hapless man prove how much he loved her.

"Was I really so stern that she had to hide what she'd bought? If she really loved them, I wouldn't have denied her."

I love you for your innocence, I think, my eyes threatening to fill. I'm pretty sure where this trail is leading, even if he's heading for a completely different part of the forest.

"I'm sure you weren't stern. You're not a stern person," I say, putting my hand back in his. He gives me a look that's infused with such sadness that I almost can't meet his gaze. He squeezes my hand.

"I'm very sorry for how I spoke to you this morning, it was unacceptable."

"No it wasn't! You were stressed. Please don't apologize." It's like he carries a pack on his back filled with his imagined crimes, the weight of guilt constantly pulling on him. "Have you spoken to Richie and Mara about whether things could have gone astray?"

"Mara promises me they sent everything. There's an appointments diary too, that I thought would be in the contents of the desk. It's one of the things the investigators have asked for."

I hate thinking about them, those hawk-eyed suits poring over Sally's behavior and trying to understand why she would have done what she did—someone should tell them how futile a task that has always been.

"Have you heard more from them?"

"There's definitely going to be a hearing," he says, that cold combativeness coming over him. "Most probably the beginning of December back in New York. That's where they'll decide about reopening the police investigation."

"Oh!" I say, my hand flying to my mouth. "Will you have a lawyer?"

"Yes, behind the scenes, but I'll handle the hearing myself. There's no one better qualified to speak about my wife than me."

He looks almost broken, sitting there, his shoulders slumped, his hand wrapped around his wine glass. I squeeze his other hand because there are no words.

"If there's anything I can do, William, you know . . ."

"I do," he says. "You're doing a great deal right now. I only wish I could be more use to you."

"Use? I don't need you to be useful."

"I think you do," he says, considering me, his expression holding within it the intimacy of the time we spent in Dorset. "Would you like a top-up?"

He reaches for the bottle, pouring with a wobbly left hand so his right can stay connected to mine.

"That's useful!"

He laughs, and clinks his glass against mine. If it was allowed, I'd be falling in love with you, I tell him in my head. In fact, I think I might have already fallen in love with you, stored the feeling away for a longed-for time when the terrain is less bleak and brutal, like a squirrel building up his winter store of nuts.

"She did have some money of her own last year, with this job she got, so I do wonder if she just thought she'd treat herself."

"I didn't know she'd gone back to work."

"It was for a fashion PR firm. I thought . . . I was very pleased when she got it. I thought she might feel better about my traveling once she had a focus of her own. And she did get off to a flying start, but it seemed to crumble very quickly."

For a highly intelligent man, he seems almost incapable of connecting the dots: that was surely the story of Sally's life. In fact, horribly enough, it really was the story of her life. The thought makes me shudder: is that true for all of us, our small arcs representing our bigger ones, if only we could fly up overhead and see where we're headed? I look at him, his gaze lost somewhere in the warp of the table, and try not to take the thought to its logical conclusion.

"Is the financial situation looking any better?"

He gives me a look that tells me the exact opposite.

"If the worst comes to the worst I'm sure my father will help. It's just . . ."

"What?"

"I feel treacherous even saying this."

"You can say it," I tell him, as gently as I can.

"They never wanted me to marry her," he says quietly. "They wouldn't have dreamed of saying it directly to her, but she was too sharp to miss it. They threw down a gauntlet, in a way. What I said in my eulogy was perhaps a slight reimagining of events."

There he goes again, sculpting truth into a convincing shape. Is that his arc, the road he blindly retreads again and again?

"How so?"

"She was in a desperate rush to marry. There were lots of tears every time we had to attend that endless merry-go-round of weddings. And meanwhile my parents were desperately keen that we didn't."

"Why?"

"They couldn't see what she brought to the table," he says, his face giving me the translation of their horrible, snobbish judgment. I'd hoped it was better than that, understandable parental concern about how Sally treated him, but I'd suspected as much. I can just imagine her donning her spurs and going into battle.

"And what did you want?"

"I loved her, but I knew it would never be easy." He's smiling at me, but his gaze feels like it's fixed on a point far in the distance. "But I also knew it would never be boring."

Recently I've started to wonder if boring is somewhat underrated. Maybe life's meant to be a little bit boring sometimes, skeins of ordinary events that quietly accumulate until you've made a canopy of shared experience to take shelter under. The moments of ordinariness I've shared with William have felt as precious as diamonds—watching him read the dreary bits of the *Sunday Times*, his gently balding head bowed over it, munching our boiled eggs on that windy beach—but maybe that's down to context: ordinary feels pretty good when extraordinary looks like this. I hope he values them too. I hope they're more than fuel for the tank, that he won't go hurtling back into orbit in search of another shooting star once he's filled up.

"I bet it wasn't."

"Certainly wasn't," he says. "And I think she did value it." He pauses. "Let me qualify that. Mostly I think she valued it, in a Sally-ish way."

Sally-ish. The fact that for him her name is still an adjective is why I should probably get my coat and make a dignified exit.

"Enough," he says, coming around the table and leaning down to kiss me. This is the moment for my dignified exit, but I can't muster up the strength. "All we ever seem to do is talk about my woes. Let's take our wine next door and you can tell me things for a change."

As I stand up he reaches out and holds me, his face buried in my neck. "Thank you," he whispers, and I pull him close—it still surprises me how natural it feels to be squashed against him, despite all of this. As he kisses me I realize I'm a little drunk—I hadn't noticed how often he'd topped up my glass. I steady myself against the table, and he moves himself close against me, his grip on me forceful, his fingers slipping into the V of my sweater. I fleetingly think of Madeline, her quick changes of mood: I'm not sure I can change gear quite as easily as they seem able to do. I let him slip it over my head, deeply relieved that my bra didn't get chosen from the stern outreaches of my subconscious. I felt like I was tempting disappointment by putting a pretty cream lacy one on, but now I'm standing in the harsh glow of the light from the stove I'm grateful for my foresight. This is ridiculous.

"Are you okay?" I ask, but it's like he doesn't hear me, his quick fingers seeking out the side zip on my skirt while passion and insecurity duke it out for my attention. It's flattering, no question, but there's something deeply unnerving about it too. I don't want to lose him to the excitement; I want to feel that he's still here with me, Livvy, not venting some kind of primal need for which I'm only a bit-part player. "William," I say, a little more sharply than I intended. He steps backward.

"Sorry," he says, fingers playing with my hair. "You're just so distractingly beautiful." I'm so not, by the way, but I defy anyone not to have their heart melted by a statement like that. I smile up at him, all resistance lost. "Shall we take this next door?" he says, the battle already won.

I have to admit that by now I have devoted a smidgen of mental imagining to how this moment might go, but I was way off. We land in his big, corporate bed, my skirt lying in a puddle on the floor before I've had time to notice its exit. I decide to just go with it, to let him set the pace, and he seems more than willing to take command. And it's good, more than good, his stuffy way in the world bearing no relation to his way of being in the bedroom. I think I imagined he'd be a little more awkward, a little more bumbling, and perhaps in a weird way I would have felt on safer ground if he had been. I stroke his face, look into his eyes. He does gaze back at me, his eyes full of something—I'm just not entirely sure what that something is. Of course it's impossible to lose myself in the moment, to do so would be almost sacrilegious. Like everything else about this relationship, there is a price.

As we lie there afterward I give myself a firm shake: from a glass-half-full point of view we've taken a huge step forward. And thank God he's not some guilt-ridden sexual robot without a trace of feeling. He wraps his arm tightly around me, and pulls me into his surprisingly hairy chest.

"Thank you," he says again, his voice thick with an emotion I wouldn't like to call.

"You don't have to thank me! Thank *you*."

"No, really," he says, kissing my nose, as he's wont to do. "That was wonderful."

I nearly say it back, but I can't quite do it. If I said it was almost wonderful I'd crush him, but that's the truth of it. Instead I nuzzle a little further into the woolly expanse, my thumb running up and down his jaw. Love wells up in me like a fountain spurting out a jet of water, fear boomeranging back with equal force.

"I should probably go home at some point," I say, holding on a little more tightly. "It'd be super weird for Madeline . . ."

"Are you sure?" he says, stroking my hair. Beg me not to, I think, but he doesn't. "Please don't feel like you have to," he continues, and I die a little inside, damned by faint praise.

"No, I should," I say, starting to very gradually unpeel myself, mentally and physically. "When she said it was my bedtime I don't think this was what she meant. And anyway, I don't have a change of clothes."

"I'm guessing Mary would wither you with her fabled death stare if you went in wearing those?" he says wryly.

"Got it in one." My voice is flat. I don't think it registers.

"Stay a bit longer at least," he says. "Can I get you anything?"

"A glass of water would be lovely."

"Righty ho." He leaps out of bed and grabs a robe from the back of the door. He's actually got a very nice bottom, but I'm too shy to tell him.

It feels like it takes forever for him to come back; I don't know if he's checking on Madeline, checking his e-mails, or simply carving out a moment to recover from the extraordinary strangeness of doing what we just did with someone who isn't Sally. I have to take a gulp of breath, the impact of it hitting me full force. All those times I worried about being compared to Sally and found wanting, or made that cruel comparison myself, and here I am, playing some kind of ill-judged game of snap with my heart, slamming it down, raw and exposed, right where hers lay.

"As promised," says William, coming back in with the totally unwanted glass of water. He puts it down on the nightstand and perches on the side of the bed. I take a self-conscious sip, wrapping the sheet a little more tightly around my décolletage, wishing he'd get under the covers, wishing I felt safe enough to simply pull him back in. For some reason I'm stabbed by the memory of that long ago night with James: I hate it when I don't know what the rules are, it turns me into such an incompetent moron. My fingers unconsciously seek out the heart pendant, the only thing I'm wearing—Jules would laugh at me, but I do think Regency romance had a lot to recommend it. You might reach your wedding night without the faintest idea what to do, but at least you wouldn't be faced with this kind of emotional minefield.

"Thank you," I say, swinging my legs out of bed. "But now I really ought to get back."

He reaches over, cupping my face in his hands and kissing me with a gentleness that makes me shudder. I almost roll back the way I came, but the ground feels too unsteady beneath my feet. Instead I ask him to call me a cab, which comes at such supersonic speed that I'm still putting my tights on when it pulls up outside.

"Dinner soon?" he says, when we're on the doorstep.

"When?" I ask, determined I won't be waiting for his call.

"This week's rather a challenge, so could we say the following Thursday?" He kisses me as he says it, and I nod politely, while a part of me wonders if I should play a bit harder to get. Maybe it's naive to think normal rules do not apply just because the circumstances are so extreme.

"I can't wait," he says.

Perhaps waiting is exactly what we should have done.

August 1997

I should've known: Sally was never going to let her twenty-first go past without celebrations of a magnitude roughly akin to the Queen's Coronation. She set such store by birthdays, and I felt bad for my sense of trepidation. She had been so generous on my nineteenth, even though it wasn't a significant one, and I didn't want to let her down.

What she'd asked for was a "girls trip," a long weekend in Malaga. I knew I couldn't afford it, and racked my brains for something else that would satisfy her sense of occasion, but she was deaf to my arguments. "My Dad's mate's got a place," she'd say, "I'll get the flights, so it's just meals out." I tried a feeble excuse about coursework, knowing how coruscating she could be about stinginess, but that fatally weakened my position. "You can read on the beach," she said, then booked the flights, stealing my passport from my bedroom in order to do so.

Something had started to shift for me by then. We'd been back in Leeds for much of that summer, me not wanting to lose the waitressing job I now desperately needed. The cracks that had opened up had not gone away; if anything they were getting bigger. Sally's moods seemed more fragile than ever, and the fact she'd split up with Shaun meant that there was little respite. I'd caught myself making up shifts, just so I could have a valid excuse to be away from her. I was planning a secret trip to East Anglia too, determined to spend some time with James far from the reach of her batting eyelashes. And yet it wasn't like I didn't love her anymore. She was still my best friend.

A couple of days before her birthday we climbed off a sweaty budget flight onto the Spanish tarmac, the intense heat hitting me like a steamroller. I was far from well traveled, and it was very different from the shabbily middle class bits of France that we'd occasionally gone camping in. I thought it was the unfamiliarity that made me feel so unsure of myself, but it was more fundamental. It was having only Sally to rely on, with no real way to make contact with Mom or Jules or any other friends who might give me a point of reference outside our tiny, suffocating little clinch.

The first night was fun. The apartment was nothing to write home about, a concrete drawer inside a big concrete box with only one bedroom, but it was absolutely fine. We dumped our stuff, took a cab into town, and had one of those drunken, laughter-fueled nights that were Sally's specialty. I tried to resist her entreaties to have shots, but she cocked her head and said, in a little girl voice, "It's my birthday" and I didn't feel I could refuse. As a result, the next day we felt utterly heinous, struggling to even get as far as the pool downstairs from the apartment. I think Sally rather enjoyed the extremity of those hangovers, they were like battle scars that proved the war had been won, but they made me feel melancholy and faintly ashamed of myself.

Her mood had also changed, made one of those subtle shifts that were invisible to the naked eye, impossible to call, but devastating in their effect. She said very little, but it wasn't a comfortable kind of silence. I found myself searching for conversational titbits that would bring her out of herself. When I was talking she would study me as if I was an alien creature that had landed, inexplicably, in her orbit.

"I'm going to move that umbrella over here," I said.

"I thought you said you wanted a tan."

"I'm not that bothered, to be honest. My skin's so stupidly English, I don't want to burn."

"Then why did you say it?"

I paused, waiting for my heart rate to slow, studying her profile, the purse of her painted lips. She'd lain back down, offering up her xylophone ribcage to the burning sun.

"Are you okay?" I asked.

"Yeah, I'm fine," she said, reaching over and deliberately pushing her headphones into her ears.

My heart still wouldn't return to normal, anger pacing around my body like a prisoner left too long in solitary confinement. I'd become so well adapted to this kind of thing, my coping strategies seamless—I would go to the library, or call my friend Catherine, or Jules, or simply retreat to my room and wait it out, knowing that in a couple of hours the scudding clouds would have blown through and Sally would be like a different person—but why was I putting up with it? I knew it was fatal to open this can of worms when I was such a sitting target, but perhaps it was that very fact that allowed me to start tunneling my way out—it was too starkly apparent to ignore. No one said it would be easy.

Our friendship was killed by a version of death by a thousand paper cuts. Ordinarily my flashes of anger flared up and burned out, cowed by her superior levels of passion, but now all her small crimes were lit up in neon letters.

She was the one who'd brought an adaptor plug, pulling me onwards when I tried to get my own at Gatwick. "We've got one, it's fine," she said, but now she was hoarding it. When it wasn't in use, I was convinced she was hiding it. She would force me to ask for it, then behave as though she was doing me an enormous favor. For all her sanctimonious chat about stinginess, she was more than capable of withholding when it suited her.

She'd take forever to get ready in the evenings— straightening her hair, curling her eyelashes, all things that now seemed vacuous and shallow rather than fascinatingly glamorous—so that by the time we'd got out I'd be ravenous and grumpy. Food was an irrelevance to Sally, but I couldn't starve myself the way she did. "Come on, Livvy, smile, you can do it," she'd say, implying my badly disguised irritation was nothing but pettiness.

I longed for my own bed, wondered why I'd allowed this stupid tradition of us doubling up to become an accepted wisdom. I thought about retreating to the uncomfortable sofa, but I knew it would start World War Three. Instead we fought about having the fan on or off, the window open or closed—there was nothing we seemed to agree on anymore. Or maybe we'd always disagreed on things, it was just that I'd never let the words cross my lips.

By the time we got to her birthday, even the eighty-degree heat couldn't overcome the permafrost that had sprung up between us. I was determined to make it nice, my moments of internal liberation interspersed with waves of enormous sadness about the way in which the gold plating was scuffing its way off our friendship.

"Happy birthday, birthday girl!" I cried, as she woke up, a sentence that didn't make sense. Nothing really did. We went out for breakfast, as she'd requested, but the local cafés were a bit scuzzy, the menus lined with pictures of fried eggs and rashers of bacon. For once it was a good thing that Sally didn't eat. She had black coffee and I slurped down some Frosties, wondering how to make today feel sufficiently different from the other days. I drew out her present, trying to do it with a flourish.

"Oh. Thanks for that." It was a tube of the plum Chanel lipstick that she always wore. I'd imagined that it would seem thoughtful—something expensive and luxurious that I knew she used—but because Sally never denied herself anything, it just seemed unimaginative. I'd thought that my coming on the trip would count as a bigger present, but that seemed irrelevant now, my lone gift lying there, feeble and paltry, on the plastic tablecloth. Sally gave me a big, empty grin. "Shall we go down to the pool?"

I wished we could sometimes go to the beach, but Sally didn't see the point when we had the pool on our concrete doorstep.

We lay in the sun, me reading Wilkie Collins, her reading Jilly Cooper, the day stretching out interminably. I kept talking to her like a Butlins Red Coat: to be fair, I was annoying myself.

"What would you like to do this evening?"

"Dunno. Surprise me."

Oh God, Challenge Livvy was a game show that could run and run.

"Do you fancy some lunch, birthday girl?!"

"I'm not that hungry. Wouldn't say no to a glass of vino, though."

I knew I'd have to have one too, even though drinking in the heat made me feel like an alcoholic colonel in the dying days of the Raj. By the time it got to dinner time we were both drunk, a fatal start to proceedings. I suggested an overpriced fish restaurant down by the water, desperately checking my balance to make sure I'd be able to cover it. I knew that I had to pay. She wouldn't say anything out loud if I didn't, but she'd say it in other ways.

We ordered more wine, and I kept up my relentless chatter while Sally looked out to sea or across the restaurant, her eyes moving back to me just slowly enough for me to know that I was boring her. I couldn't shake my feeling of guilt. I kept remembering my party, my basque, the exquisite breakfast she'd put together. I snuck off to the kitchen and briefed them that I'd want a candle in the dessert I knew she'd barely touch.

"Well cheers!" I said.

"Cheers," she replied, voice flat, and then we returned to the odd small talk we'd been reduced to. How had this happened? I was too drunk and young and confused to diagnose any of it, resentment mixed up with love and with my whole fragile sense of who I was since I'd left home.

"I brought you something," she said, as the waiter cleared our mains.

"Have you?" I said, surprised.

She reached into her handbag and pulled out a beautifully wrapped box. I nervously unwrapped it, revealing a little silver charm bracelet.

"It's lovely," I said, my heart starting to speed up. "But it's your birthday, not mine."

"I know. But it was a stretch for you to come out here, and I wanted you to know that I appreciate it."

She looked at me, unsmiling, her face not remotely tallying with her words. I desperately wanted to believe her, but she didn't really give me that option. What I suspected was that she wanted to grind my feeble efforts into the ground, trump my present and remind me how grudging I'd been. If she'd had to be genuinely grateful she'd have seen it as handing me something, and Sally couldn't bear to give the smallest drop of her power away.

"Thank you," I said, slipping it back into the box and into my handbag. "That's really kind." I awkwardly squeezed her arm.

A couple of lads had been watching us from the bar, and now was the moment they chose to send over a round of drinks. I was grateful for the distraction but not for their attentions. They were plump and burned and stupid-looking, their white shirts only serving to magnify their redness. Besides, the all-day drinking had made me feel dozy and crave my bed. Needless to say Sally was having none of it, and as it was her birthday, it had to be her call. She made sure she paired up with the better-looking one, not that there was much in it, and we all ended up in a cheesy basement club, the two of them snogging on the dance floor. As so often happened, it gave the ugly friend confidence, and soon I was desperately spurning his advances, pleading an imaginary boyfriend. Surely I'd done my time? I waited until Sally came up for air, then tapped her on the arm.

"Look, would you mind if I made a move?"

"Of course I'd bloody mind."

"We're only five minutes away. I'm past my peak, and I really don't want to cop off with his mate . . ."

Her eyes narrowed, the build up of pressure visible. It was like coffee whizzing through a machine, gaining heat, waiting to spurt forth, black and scalding. I nearly backed down, but my own pressure gauge had reached its maximum.

"Fucking hell, Livvy. It's my birthday!"

"Strictly speaking it's not anymore. It's quarter to one."

Her eyes flashed, disbelief on her face.

"Don't you fucking dare . . ." she said, grabbing my arm.

"Get your hands off me." I couldn't stand her controlling me a second longer.

"Well cheers for that, Livvy. You've already destroyed my birthday, thanks for making it even more of a fucking disaster."

"What? How exactly have I done that?"

"Watching you drop my bracelet in your bag like it was a piece of shit, not good enough for your precious wrist. You destroyed me."

"Oh come on . . ." Again, she had a point, but how could I explain how loaded and toxic it had felt? "Don't be so oversensitive."

I hated myself for that. It was a crime I'd been accused of my whole life, but a row like this doesn't allow for nuance, it's little better than hand to hand combat, and we were right in the throes of it.

"Don't you dare say that to me. I invite you out here— poor little Livvy, who can't afford it—I pay for most of it, and you spend the whole time walking around with a face like a slapped ass. You've ruined it, like you ruin everything. You are the biggest killjoy I've ever known."

"So why have you spent the last two years hanging out with me then?"

"Not a clue," she said, with a sneering shrug. The boys were watching us, wondering whether to approach, but I didn't care. We were locked in our own private vortex, the intensity of the last few years turned into something nuclear and life-threatening.

"I see you," I hissed. "Don't think I don't. You think no one knows what you're like, but I see you twisting people round your little finger and laughing at them behind their backs. You killed my relationship with Matt, you killed my relationship with Lola—the only person you give a fuck about is you."

"That is bullshit," said Sally, the shock in her face telling me I was hitting home.

"It's not, and you know it. I'm taking my life back, Sally. I'm not your slave anymore."

"You're just some stupid little dork who sucked up to me so much I felt sorry for you."

"Not anymore. It's finished," I said, struck by the words I used—the language of a love affair. "You've done nothing except cause me grief." Another gross, unfair simplification. "You've bullied me, and cried on me, and trashed my reputation. And . . . and you've nicked my best friend."

"What's that supposed to mean?"

"James. Don't think I haven't seen how you look at him. All that pouting and wiggling and 'hello, You' bullshit. You'd do anything, absolutely anything, to anyone if it meant that you'd won."

"Don't try and blame me for the fact he doesn't want you. That's all you."

She knew. She always had. I could see triumph in her eyes, the knowledge she'd hit me where it hurt the most.

"I don't know why anyone would want you," I spat back. "If they saw what I saw they'd never go near you. You're poison."

That was it. She let rip with a stream of expletives that even now I can't bear to think about, and stormed out. I ran back to the horrible apartment, shoved all my things into my bag, then used the last of my cash to rent what must have been the most horrible hotel room in Spain. We didn't speak a single word to each other on the flight and when we passed through customs she stalked off, her body as sharp and stiff and lethal as a blade, refusing to look back.

CHAPTER EIGHTEEN

"Congratulations," says William, a smile wreathing his tired face, and we clink our glasses of champagne.

We're out to dinner somewhere incredibly posh and French and garlicky in Mayfair and, as I look around the ranged lines of couples, I realize that, at least for tonight, we're part of their ranks. Dinner last week got canceled at the last minute, but at least now we're finally on a proper date, not something born out of duty or contrivance.

"Thank you," I say, unable to stop myself beaming. I heard today that my story is a runner-up in the competition—I still can't quite believe it. It wasn't a win, but it at least suggests I might still have some kind of talent for writing stuff that's less disposable than a punchy slogan. The Flynn project seems to be going better too. Amazingly, directors are responding favorably to the script, and at the moment he seems happy to keep his grubby little paws off it and let someone else take the helm. It's not long until he goes back to the US, but Mary's mooted the idea of me going to New York to meet a couple of directors he's suggested, a prospect I can't quite get my head around. The bitter irony of it seems too great—to make my virgin trip there so soon after Sally's death seems almost cruel. I dug out the tag when I heard, looked at it again. I'm thinking that if I'm there I might as well go and find Capricorn Holdings and see if showing it to them elicits any more answers.

"Are you going to let me read it?"

"Oh no, you don't want to do that. You've got enough to worry about."

The very idea makes me cringe, particularly when I think how much of the emotion of recent months I poured into it. It's an old woman looking back on her life, but still, I'm sure he'd be able to pick out some of me and Sally in the talk of jealousy and loss.

"I do," he says, simply.

"Okay, I'll think about it."

Tonight's definitely infected with that awkwardness that's written through the DNA of a first date. I think partly it's the sex: what was once innocent and tentative has now been made flesh—made of flesh—and cannot be reshaped into something that leaves us both feeling whiter than white. I notice him looking at me a couple of times when he thinks I'm not aware, a watchfulness about him that I haven't seen before. He's making an effort to ask me questions too, the kind of biographical detail you'd expect to have down pat after this many meetings, but which have been swept away by more primal exposures of the heart. It should be a nice thing, a sign that he's genuinely interested in me, but in my paranoia it's making me feel like I'm on a job interview with the most terrible odds. I realize, as I'm falteringly describing my relationship with Marco, that I'm giving it more weight than it deserves. He's been married, had a child, and here I am with only a few months of cohabitation under my belt—I don't want him to think I'm some kind of emotional invertebrate.

"Relationships do tend to get to that point, don't they?" he says. "Where you have to commit or call it a day?"

"Totally," I agree, all the time knowing that I've never even got close. James creeps into my consciousness without me having invited him in—I don't like to overanalyze the why of it.

"That's one of the good things about marriage. It forces a decision, stops one from drifting."

"Didn't you say that . . . that you were under quite a lot of pressure to get married?"

Why did I say that? The last thing I want to do is sound like I'm chipping away at her, a wicked stepmother waiting in the wings.

"Undoubtedly, but it doesn't mean I regret it," he says, stoutly. "Now I don't know about you, but I'm in the market for some dessert."

I offer to go dutch, but he won't hear of it—my relief mingles with a painful awareness of that towering pile of debt he's facing. Before we leave I scoot off to the toilet, and frantically chew some gum to try and dissipate the overwhelming taste of garlic from the snails he persuaded me to share. Once we're out on the pavement he grabs my hand.

"Shall we walk?" he says, and I nod, though I don't really know where it is we're walking too. We pass through one of those elegant squares with the fenced off gardens in the middle, then past the Connaught: I wonder if he'll suggest a last drink, but he doesn't.

"Something came up at work this week," I say, tentative. "It looks like I might be going to New York for the Flynn thing."

He looks at me, shock on his face. I don't know if it's the very mention of New York, or it's the thought of me in it.

"I see."

"I just thought—if it does coincide, if there's anything I can do to support you . . ."

"That's very kind," he says automatically. "Have you ever been there before?"

"No, never."

"You met Mara, didn't you? I'll put you back in touch. It can be jolly overwhelming first time around. She and Richie will gladly take you out."

I don't care about Richie and his scary wife, and I certainly don't care about sightseeing—I care about you. I look at him, his features tidied back up into a neat formation, and know better than to say it.

"Thank you. That'd be great."

"I meant to ask you, we've been finessing the christening details today," he says, the subject of New York firmly closed. "I wondered if you'd like to bring Julia along?"

The christening: the very sound of those words fills me with a deep sense of dread. The idea of having to feign cool detachment—in front of Lola, in front of his parents, in front of the rest of Sally's friends—while all the time they wonder why I've been elevated from bit-part player to godmother, is horrific. I need to call Lola and tell her up front, but I've been too chicken. I worry that she'll put two and two together, think about how much information I had, how much I pumped her for, and start to have her own suspicions. I wish I could talk to her—about the tag, about what Madeline said, about the heaped-up clothes—but she's so in Sally's thrall that I suspect she'd think it treasonous.

"That's a lovely thought."

Of course he wants me to bring Jules, she's the perfect beard. I feel a stab of illogical hurt, then remember that of course we couldn't be seen to be together so soon. I know how it would look to me from the outside—it looks that way from the inside much of the time too. I should head for the tube, keep some kind of distance, at least for the next few weeks.

"I'd love to invite you back," he says, leaning down to kiss me. I try not to lose myself in it, to keep some kind of detachment. "But I've got to be up at sparrow's fart for a meeting in Westminster."

"No, of course," I say, trying to convince myself that this was exactly what I wanted.

"I was going to say, Madeline's staying with her cousins this weekend. I wondered about going away for a night?"

"Really?" All my doubts fragment in the face of my stupid feelings.

"I did enjoy . . . I liked how we were able to get to know each other a little better when we were in Dorset. I'll ask my assistant to come up with some options."

Me too. Much as a proper date is gratifying, I can't help but miss the rawness of our tangled, complicated encounters, where truth always ends up dashing across the plane like a naughty little dog.

"Great!" I say, trying not to sound too pleased.

This time, when he kisses me, I let go of the crash barrier. Perhaps all I need to do is trust.

I'm going to text him Wednesday morning to thank him for dinner, but then I remember his meetings, and wait until lunchtime. It's pathetic, I want him to get it at a time when he might have time to reply, but for all my futile strategizing, I don't hear anything until ten o'clock. *It was my pleasure, William*, it says, with no kiss. He never puts kisses on his messages, but at least he doesn't write *best* anymore. I stare at it, trying not to feel disappointed. I'm a fool if I ask for more than he can give, a callous fool at that. And we've got our night away to look forward to, a prospect that gives me a fizzy feeling whenever I think of it, despite everything.

By Thursday lunchtime I'm wondering if I should call and ask him what the plan is so I know whether to bring an overnight bag to work tomorrow. Something stops me. Instead I go and buy travel sizes of products I can't afford, then trail around the Selfridges lingerie department holding silken scraps of nothingness up to my body. I get halfway to the changing room before that nausea starts to rise up; the memory of that birthday teddy smashing into the present moment—the moment in which I'm considering trussing myself up like a Christmas turkey to seduce Sally's husband. "I'm sorry," I mutter, yet again, shoving the bra and knickers onto the nearest rack like they're on fire. I bet when she did deign to sleep with him it was amazing: I know what she's like, what she was like, she would have put in a *Hollywood Wives*-worthy performance to ensure that he pined like an abandoned dog until the next time she chose to bestow her sexual largesse. That's probably why he's got some moves, she will have taught him everything he knows. I push my way to the escalators, suddenly desperate to get out, the air close and stifling.

By Friday morning I'm properly desperate, my insides as taut and stretched as harp strings. "A night"—such a cruel distinction, if he'd said "the weekend" I could demand clarity without looking like a fool. I'm terrified of bothering him, of making him take flight from a relationship that he can only approach through half-closed eyes.

And then, finally, as the fat black hands of the office clock crawl their way to four p.m., he calls. At that precise moment I'm in the corridor, trying to have a sotto voce emergency confab with Jules, Mary's eyes boring into me from her vantage point behind her big glass desk. I can't face speaking to him with her in plain sight, so I take the elevator to the ground floor and call him back. No answer, and he's left no voicemail. I can't risk being out here long, not after leaving the office at lunchtime yesterday, so after five more minutes I force myself to go upstairs, where I find his e-mail.

Hi Livvy, just tried you, but no success! I'm afraid the weekend plan is off. Madeline is firmly ensconced with me, and now I've no childcare. Would you mind if we had another kitchen supper next week instead? Thursday at 8pm? Looking forward to it! William.

I aim a vicious kick at my stupid, hopeful overnight bag languishing underneath my desk, trying my best not to cry. Mary's still watching me, and Honey's warned me that she's hoping to get ten minutes with me before the end of the day. I hate that he called on the hour, like he knew he couldn't leave it a minute longer without his precious manners being called into question. I hate that he uses exclamation marks to make the lack of kisses less glaringly obvious: Sally threw kisses at messages—at life—like they were confetti, and I don't believe for a second she'd have let him get away with it. I hate the fact that the writing is most likely on the wall, but that I'm too cowardly and lovesick to turn back, the thought of ripping the bandage off too much to bear. And most of all, I hate that I can't say any of this to him. But I guess he feels like that every day—haunted by a million questions he wants to ask the one person who will never reply.

Then Mary calls me in.

"You've literally watched it a thousand times, you know what happens," says James, coming into the living room to find me stuck on the sofa, *All About Eve* playing, marooned in a sea of Kleenex and Quality Street wrappers.

"It's not the film."

"Has he changed it to tomorrow?" he says, then looks at my face. "He's canceled, hasn't he. Livvy . . ."

"Stop, hush. I know what you think, there's no need to say it."

"He's having a complete fucking nightmare, I get it," says James, his fists balled up with frustration, "but he's taking the piss." James hates it when a man hurts me, doesn't see any irony in the countless hearts he's broken over the years. I like it, and also I hate it: if I needed any proof as to how he sees me, it's right there in capital letters.

"He can't help it. He's in so much pain." James looks at me, his expression saying it all. "If it carries on like this of course I'll finish it," I say, unconvincing even to myself. "Anyway, it's not just that. Your bloody 'whatever she is' totally screwed me over today."

The ten minutes Mary wanted were to tell me that she and Charlotte have decided I'm "too sensitive" to deal with

Flynn's "artistic temperament" and she's sending her to New York single-handed. It's utterly humiliating, particularly considering the stream of e-mails he and I have been swapping about what we were going to do.

"Why didn't you just tell me?" I said, the tears that were already threatening starting to spill. "If you were always going to do this, I wish you'd just done it weeks ago."

Mary's eyes flashed with anger at me questioning her management, and I shrank back into the pink velvet sofa.

"I've been trying to give you a chance," she said, tone icy, and then smiled at me. "Come on, Livvy, you've no idea how much you've learned. You'll thank me for it in a year."

The gratitude hasn't started to kick in quite yet, just a glum sort of relief that she's talking about me having a future a year hence. I watch James as I'm telling him, convinced he's trying to suppress a surge of glee at the thought that he might get a dirty weekend in New York out of the whole sorry business.

"That's utterly shit, Livvy, but I don't see how it's Charlotte's fault."

"She's been scheming and manipulating—"

"Mary always treats you like dirt, you just don't like admitting it to yourself. You're too scared of biting the hand that feeds you."

"No she doesn't! I've learned everything I know from her. She's like . . . she's my Yoda."

"If you say so," says James, rootling futilely in the Quality Street box—only the ones with weird-tasting cream centers have survived my self-pity-fest. I find a hazelnut one that I was stowing behind the cushion and silently hand it to him, thinking about what he just said. I'm not saying it's true, but it's not not true either.

"Anyway, I don't know why you're sticking up for Robot Girl. You wouldn't be hanging around here on a Friday night if it wasn't for her. What's the latest on her leaving?"

James looks quietly gutted, but then he rallies.

"It's fine. We went for tea—well, green tea—on Wednesday afternoon at some Japanese place. It's good to try new things."

"An hour in the day does not maketh a relationship," I tell him, pompously.

He looks at me—the crowning glory of my Friday night outfit a pair of bright green Toastie slipper socks—and doesn't say a word.

"Come here," he says, flinging one of his long, springy arms around me. "We're gonna be all right. It's all gonna to be all right. Promise."

I snuggle into him, smelling that familiar smell of him, and just for a second I believe him.

OCTOBER 1997–JUNE 1998

It couldn't last. It was never going to be that simple. Even if I'd been ready to truly throw her off—like a snake effortlessly shedding its mesmerizing, jewel-colored skin—we were signed up for another year in that expensively furnished prison.

I'd thrown myself on the mercy of my friend Catherine when I'd gotten back to Leeds. Even though she and I were closer, I was careful to be circumspect, as she also had tutorials with Sally. Besides, I didn't feel so sure of myself now I was out of the fetid prison of the so-called holiday, and when I tried to articulate it, even to myself, it sounded like the worst kind of hair-pulling pettiness, the sort of catfighting that gives girls a bad name. It wasn't an easy landing. I was too blighted by confusion and guilt to appreciate the longed-for camaraderie of a shared house, but too ruined by luxury not to recoil at the skid-marked toilet and leaning tower of washing up.

By the time I ran into Sally, a week or so into term, I was a broken woman. We were both in the common room coffee queue, a painful reconstruction of the many other times we'd stood there, snorting with laughter and shushing each other as we came up with grosser and grosser suggestions for what the coffee actually was. She pretended not to see me, but I knew she had; she was standing a little more straight, shoulders flung back, her fingers tightening around her red vinyl purse. It was my heart that tightened; it wrung out tears for the loss of something that felt suddenly precious and irreplaceable. I remembered the awful things I'd said to her, that last tirade, somehow defusing all the grenades she'd lobbed in my direction until they had no charge. I think it was more self-protection than altruism. It was easier to take it on myself—incinerate it in the well-stoked fire of my anxiety and self-doubt—than to leave it lying outside on the periphery where I would be forced to read the small print. My sense of who I was still so fragile, a thin canopy that I'd stretched over the pain of my family breaking apart, and I didn't want to risk its destruction.

She was ahead of me and she got all the way to the top before she acknowledged me, interminable minutes in which my stomach mulched and rumbled like an angry monster. Then she spun on her high heels, two paper cups held close to her body, a magician pulling a rabbit from a hat.

"Hello, You," she said, grinning, mouth painted that familiar shade of plum. "Fancy a cup of sewage?"

I moved back in that night. Sally had bought a bottle of champagne, not cava, and she hugged me almost to death as she popped the cork. "Let's not talk about it," she said, eyes stretched wide with the horror of it all. "Can't go there." As a solution it suited me just fine—what was there to be gained by going back over it, I reasoned, cowardice and confusion holding me fast.

And there was no doubt that Sally was nicer to me. She took to stocking the fridge with more than just alcohol, thinking about the things I actually liked to eat. She stopped turning her back on me as soon as a man floated across her orbit and also stopped undermining all the friends I had who weren't her. She started treating me like an equal all the time, rather than just when it suited her.

As we settled down in front of EastEnders one night, Sally turning around for a cheery toast with the red wine she'd bought even though she preferred white, I allowed myself a moment of self-congratulation. Maybe that was all it needed—a line in the sand, an opportunity for me to hold my ground and tell her that she was not the boss of me. Spain, for all its grimness—self-created, perhaps? I didn't know anymore—might have ultimately reaped dividends. Now our friendship had been handed back, polished and restored, and I could pour myself into it without any of the traces of wariness that had dogged it before.

Sally insisted on driving me to the station to get the train home for Christmas. She was teary as she hugged me good-bye, and I was ridiculously touched.

"It's gonna be so freaky without you down the hall."

"I know."

"Don't ever forget how much I love you. You're my best, best, best friend."

"Me too," I said. "You I mean!"

And I set off for home, my heart soaring with that velvety, vivid, magic carpet ride of a feeling.

I hadn't heard from James much that term, but I suppose I'd been too caught up in my other twisted version of a love affair to pay too much attention to his absence. Perhaps subconsciously it had been a relief: it would have been infinitely harder for Sally and me to maintain our collective amnesia if the cornerstone of our anger had pitched up on the doorstep. As soon as I got back I was dying to see him, but it took a few calls before I got hold of him and pinned him down to a night in the White Horse, the pub we'd always tried to sneak drinks in when we were underage.

"Hello, stranger," I said, aware as soon as I said it that I sounded more like Sally than like me. Although what did "me" actually mean? Of course phrases and habits drift back and forth between people when they're close, a constant shifting osmosis making a strange kind of whole somewhere in the middle.

"Hi," he said, not sounding like James. Who did he sound like? I felt a sinking feeling in my stomach, terrified at the thought of what shady ventriloquist might have winkled her way in during the autumn term; this relationship was so fraught with danger. I don't know why, for an intelligent girl, I was so incapable of realizing that what I desperately needed was a relationship that did exactly what it said on the tin. We looked at each other, wary. "Gin and tonic for the lady?" he said, tugging an imaginary forelock, and I finally allowed myself to breathe out.

But when he sat back down it still didn't feel right. We tried to reminisce, tried to swap news about last term, but nothing took flight.

"How's Sally?" he asked carefully, and I felt the hairs on my body stand to attention.

"Oh, fine."

"Great. Send her . . . send her my best."

We'd known each other too long and James was too lacking in guile.

"What's she told you?" I demanded, blood rushing to my face.

He looked at me, helpless.

"I said I wouldn't talk about it."

Fury slammed into me so hard that I couldn't form a sentence. He shrugged, sheepish.

"She came to see me, bit before the beginning of term."

"What, did she call you?"

"No, she just turned up. She came from Gatwick." He looked scared by the memory. *"She was in a fucking terrible state. She was bawling, Livvy. Her face . . ."* He gestured, and I could see it, as clear as if she was standing right in front of us; her face, awash with mascara, those crocodile tears painting a canvas out of her distress. *"She told me that you'd had that horrible argument, and she didn't know what to do."*

"Did she tell you what happened?"

"Yeah."

Stupid question: she'd told him what had happened in a fantastical scenario that suited whatever agenda she was pushing. And I had a horrible, fatalistic certainty about what that agenda was.

"She was a total bitch to me all week."

"She said she didn't understand what she'd done." She was too clever to leave any scars. It was all spiteful pinches that hurt like hell in the moment but wouldn't bruise. *"She just kept going on and on about how much she loved you, and how she'd never had a friend like you."*

"So why couldn't you speak to me?" I said, my voice sharp and brittle. He looked into his pint. "Just . . . just spit it out."

"She kissed me," he said, and I felt the bottom drop out of not just my world, but the world. It contained so much, this betrayal, but it was also a trapdoor into all the other times he'd looked past me to the girl a few feet behind.

"And you kissed her back," I said, voice rising. Right then I wished fervently that I didn't know him as well as I did. Denial would have been a warm bath in comparison to this.

"Just for like, a minute. I didn't let it go any further. I promise you." He looked more distressed than I could ever remember, far more than he had the morning after our ill-judged hook up. It was she who'd done this to him, not me.

"What, so she wanted to?"

He nodded, and I threw myself back against the padded seat, trying to control myself. I didn't swear, or shout. "How could she?" I said, my voice as shrunken as the rest of me. He looked at me, trying to measure out his words. My eyes were trained on his beautiful mouth, waiting for them to land; I'd never kiss it again, I felt sure of that.

"I'm so sorry I didn't tell you. I was a total shithead to keep it secret. It was just she said . . ." And again, I knew what was coming. I steeled myself, like a tennis player angling himself for his opponent's killer serve. It tumbled out in an awkward rush. "She said that you were in love with me, and that you'd be completely gutted." He watched my face, but I was ready.

"She's just saying that, 'cause of what happened, and Matt and everything."

And that's when I saw his face, the way relief spread through it like the bliss of a sunrise. That might have been the worst bit of all.

"*Course, I know that!*" He shook his head. "*She's unbelievable—we're gonna be all right aren't we, Livvy?*"

"*Yeah, we will,*" I said, forcing myself to smile. I couldn't afford to hold on to any of this with him, not even for a single night—the stakes were too high. If I lost him again, it would be for good.

"*I should've told you straight off. At least you know now though, you can kick her into touch.*"

He threw his arm around my shoulder, and I tried to minimize the tremor that was pulsing through my body like a riptide.

"*She's not worth a fucking tenth of you, Livvy. She's dirt on your shoe.*"

Yes, but you still wanted to kiss her, even when she looked like a war zone. You still wanted to sleep with her, if only you hadn't had to stop yourself. There is still a tiny little piece, out there in the ether, which is just about you and her, not about me and you.

I went ballistic. I didn't waste any time on hurt, or sentiment, or self-doubt—I opted for pure, unadulterated anger. I sat on the stairs of my mom's apartment, and screamed at her like I'd never stop. She tried to get a word in edgeways a couple of times, but I steamrollered her. When I finally stopped, my throat raw and hoarse, she was lost for words. Or at least I thought she was lost for words.

"*Have you finished?*" she asked, her voice clipped.

"*Yes.*"

"*And it didn't occur to you for one single second that he might have been lying? Or, I dunno, that there might be two sides of the story?*"

"He's not a liar, Sally," I said, my tone loaded.

"Okay, so he's not a liar. He's right that I went to see him. You'd cut me, Livvy, so deep. The things you said to me . . . I've never had a friend like you. I couldn't believe what I was hearing. I felt like you'd gone mad, and there's no one except me who knows you better."

"Right."

"Yes, right!" she said, with a flash of anger. "And it was him who kissed me, for your information. You know what he's like." I hated her insider knowledge, the way she'd forced her way on to our patch. I was well aware what a hopeless tart he was—that's why I knew he'd have kissed her back—but I also knew he was telling the truth about who had started it. I said as much to her, but she dismissed me.

"And you're right, I shouldn't have told him how much you like him, but he was . . . he wanted me, Livvy, and I was so fucking upset, I didn't know what I was saying, I just knew I had to stop it. It was hard, you know?"

I didn't believe her version, and yet the film still played in my head, looping around and around like some kind of instrument of torture. I couldn't stand it anymore.

"I'm going to go," I said, fight replaced by resignation, by a sadness that stifled and suffocated me, like a fire blanket extinguishing flames.

"Get some rest. I'm sorry, Livvy, I am. But it only happened because I love you. 'Cause you hurt me so much."

Isn't that what wife beaters say? You drove me to it. I only did it because I love you.

I didn't hear from her for the rest of the week. I stayed, holed up in my tiny box of a bedroom, listening to Kate Bush and *hoping that the tide of deep, coruscating sadness would roll back and reveal something different. I didn't feel able to call anyone from Leeds or from school—Leeds because of Sally, home because of James. Instead I wrote great big serial rants in my diary, the ink sent haywire by my tears. Then the letter arrived.*

Dear Livvy,

I'm writing because I can't face another horrible row. The last phone call we had left me so destroyed that I couldn't eat for two days and my mom thinks it's better we don't talk again. I'm sorry that I upset you, but like I said, it was a reaction to the unbelievably cruel and spiteful things you said to me on the holiday I took you on. I'm sorry too that you chose a boy over me, and trusted his word instead of mine. I guess there really is no such thing as Girl Power. I loved being your friend, and I loved you, but there is no point in a friendship where the trust has gone. I must have had you/it all wrong, which is very hard for me to cope with. We got past the last row, but this feels like too much to come back from.

I wish you well with everything. I hope you get the first I know you want so much. See you around I guess!

Sally x

I read it time and time again, hoping that it would become less devastating. It was like a puzzle, traces of truth threaded through a maze of lies, emotion, and manipulation so inter-mingled that I couldn't tell them apart. I thought I hated her, but of course it wasn't that simple. You cannot simply exterminate love like you can an unwanted infestation. Its absence is bigger than its presence: you stare into the crater, wondering what it was that filled it. I went over and over those last few months, trying to work out what was real. Was it all only about Sally trying to build up her defenses so that when it did ultimately come out, she'd have a chance of keeping me on her side, or was it altogether darker? Was she enjoying my happy oblivion, laughing about the fact she'd taken my most secret longing and vandalized it?

Soon it was Christmas. Jules's visit was a fleeting one, and she had Phil in tow, so it was hard to talk. Besides, I knew when she'd visited me in Leeds, she hadn't particularly taken to Sally, had worried about how all-consuming the friendship was, and I feared a big sisterly "I told you so." Christmas Day was a stressful parental merry-go-round. We started at Dad's, listening to carols on Radio Three around his dwarfish tree, a single package of mince pies to share between the four of us. Then it was Mom's, the table heaped to the point of collapse with food, her jollity so fearsome that it felt like a battle cry. It brooked no nostalgia, it was propaganda designed to inform us that she'd made the right decision and all of us were happier for it. There was truth in that, but it wasn't the whole truth, and I found myself falling down the cracks. The fact that Jules had Phil in tow gave her an easy buffer between then and now, but I felt the contrast like a physical ache.

I had become a magnet for any kind of sadness—a homeless man begging in the snow, a child trailing behind his indifferent brother—any hint of pain chimed off me and shook me by the scruff of my neck.

And then it was time to go back to Leeds. I told Mom a little of it, but I felt ashamed of my part in it, not just my recent part, but all the other moments when I'd trampled on people because I couldn't take my eyes off the prize. I'd seen James a few times by now, but that was also hard. He was a boy—as far as he was concerned, the situation was dealt with and we knew who the enemy was. He made me feel, even more than ever, like one of the lads, and for now that was too much to bear.

There was no room at the inn, a fact Sally must have known. Catherine's house was so packed to the rafters that I'd slept on an air mattress in her room, and everyone else I could think of was already sorted. I'm not sure how she managed to unseat Lola from her situation midterm, but she had so much will, that of course she found a way.

I, meanwhile, didn't feel that there was much will coming my way. Catherine let me stay while I sorted myself out, but it was so grudging that I agreed to move in with a bunch of second-year medics just to get out of her hair. I'd tried to talk about what had happened, but she'd just listened, volunteering very little, responses of the infuriating "I'm sorry you feel like that" variety.

I soon found out why. Sally had ambushed everyone early, right when I was still barricaded in my bedroom, tearfully ringing them to pour her heart out. The picture she drew used that brilliant fusion of lies and fact, the landmines laid in such a way that when I tried to defend myself, she'd already rigged the explosion. "It was her birthday, Livvy," said our old first-year roommate Jasmine, her eyes full of reproach. I'd been the one who made an effort with her, listened to her dull tales about her year off backpacking around Thailand while Sally rolled her eyes from behind the *fridge door, but it counted for nothing. Birthdays became my bête noire, a perfect opportunity for Sally to force a choice that I always seemed to lose. I would see her in the common room, and my whole body would surge with adrenalin, while she seemed entirely unmoved, her eyes sliding over me like I was a piece of furniture that had been carelessly left in her path.*

It was too much for me, my sensitivity a disease I couldn't find a cure for. So much of my Leeds life—my life period—was about Sally, and now I had been condemned to the wilderness. It turned out to be a blessing in disguise that I had landed up with a houseful of medics. One, a timid girl called Hayley who I would sometimes meet late at night in the kitchen when insomnia had driven me to the fridge, stopped me one day in the hallway.

"I know it's none of my business, but I think you might be depressed."

The fact that I burst into tears on the spot rather confirmed her theory, and soon I was at the university doctor's, crying into his scratchy, budget tissues, and telling a story that didn't stand up to much retelling. To my surprise it got bigger, and wider, until I felt like Jonah and the Whale, my whole self disappearing into the black mouth. I wept about my fears for my dad, about how angry I felt with my mom for abandoning him, about how little trust I felt in the whole damn universe. How unsafe it was, how ready it was to turn on a sixpence and rob you of any kind of certainty. How it made me want to stay inside with my well-thumbed books and the albums I'd listened to thousands of times; at least with those stories I knew how they would end.

He wasn't so great, that doctor, but even articulating it had helped. He offered me antidepressants, but I vigorously refused, and instead I went for counseling. She was a motherly woman with a rug-strewn, softly lit office who let me go around and around in circles until I was ready for her to gently steer me out of the maze. With her help, I found my academic fire again, got the First that Sally rightly divined I longed for, and made it through a difficult year with some understandings that have helped me forever more.

But I never forgot Sally. I never subscribed to the idea that she was just a symptom of a bigger malaise. Somewhere in my heart I always believed that there were answers, if only I could find out where they lay.

CHAPTER NINETEEN

I'M DELIBERATELY, CHILDISHLY, LATE—A FULL HALF hour—but I don't think William even notices. Madeline's in bed, and he's been working at the desk in the living room, his laptop flung open, a glass of wine perched next to it. Meanwhile every available surface seems to be covered in stacks of paper and plastic folders. He moves some from the sofa to the floor, and takes a glass of wine from the cooler on the window sill. I can't help but notice it's already two thirds gone.

"It's white, I hope you don't mind. I've got a nice bottle of red we can have with dinner."

"Of course," I say, awkwardly lowering myself into the nest of papers.

"Excuse the chaos. I've got to courier the last of the documentation to my lawyers in the US so they can make sure we've got our ducks in a row before the hearing."

I feel my righteous anger start to seep away, the reality of what he's going through too much to contend with. Neither of us have mentioned the fabled night away.

"It's a couple of weeks after the christening, isn't it?"

"Well remembered. Will you still be . . ."

"Oh no. That's all off now. Charlotte's going."

Is it relief that crosses his face? I don't know, that might just be my paranoia. He crosses to me, hands me the glass, and leans down to give me a funny sort of half kiss.

"It's rotten luck. Do try not to take it personally, I know you did a first-rate job. The man's a monster, clearly."

I make a funny roaring sound, make my hands into claws, then wonder what on earth it is I'm doing. It seems so pathetic to moan about Flynn, about my bruised ego, when we're surrounded by the cold paper trail of his marriage.

"Thanks. I'm trying to be Zen."

The tag still remains a permanent fixture in my handbag, even though I'm not going to New York. I'm sure the truth of Sally's last months doesn't lie in these dry stacks of documents. My eye catches that picture, that smile of hers.

"I was going to call out for dinner," he says.

"Why don't I try and cook us something?" I suggest, trying not to think about the strange, sterile contents of his fridge. "I can always go to the corner shop if I need to."

It doesn't seem like the kind of area that would stoop to something as useful and ordinary as a corner shop, but it's the principle of the thing. I want to make something, from scratch, with my bare hands, rather than have him throw money at the problem.

"That would be great," he says, his face lighting up. "Could you forgive me if I did a little more work while you do that? I'm writing this speech for one of the Washington bureau chiefs, and I haven't quite cracked it. I should have done it earlier, but Madeline was in a fearsome temper at bedtime."

"Yes, of course," I say, wondering if I should ask more, but he's already turned back to the screen.

I can't work out if it's progress—the two of us coexisting in companionable harmony—or yet another stop sign that I'm choosing to ignore. I know what James would say.

I was too hard on the pre-grated cheddar, it turns out to be my kitchen supper lifesaver. With the addition of some penne, I've got a fairly decent macaroni and cheese, and I find some salad that's just about within date at the bottom of the fridge. I put Magic on very, very quietly, singing along under my breath, and try not to finish the large glass of wine he poured—I've been too nervous to eat all day, and even half of it has left me tipsy. I hoped that William would come find me, but by the time the cheese is starting to turn from brown to black there's still no sign of him. I venture next door to find him sitting at the desk, the chair swiveled toward the view of the park, staring into space.

"Hi, it's nearly—"

"Great," he says, giving me one of those smiles that by now I know is nothing but an attempt to throw me off the scent.

"What is it?" I ask, tentative.

He pauses, looking into the dark expanse of trees, then turns back to me.

"I can't fucking do it!" he says, hand striking the desk. I don't think I've ever heard him swear before.

"I know. It's so cruel, but you've already done so much. When this has gone back to America, you've only got the hearing to get through. Which I know you're dreading, but—"

"No, the speech! I've never had this before. Writer's block, I suppose you'd call it. It just won't come."

He's steaming with anger.

"What's it about?"

"Diplomatic immunity."

"Do you believe in what it is you're saying?"

"I don't care, Livvy, that's the problem. I simply don't care. All the facts are there, I just can't seem to make them mean anything."

I'm still in the doorway. I cross the room, sit on the edge of the coffee table so I'm within touching distance, but I don't touch him. It's one of the many baffling things about death, how differently you can wear it. It can make anything mean more than it's ever meant before—every drop of life something precious, to be savored—or it can render it meaningless, a game we don't know the rules to, that can be savagely halted by a whistle that's blown in another dimension. For all his faith in God, I don't think he's got any answers.

His anger, normally so tightly held, is palpable right now. I think Madeline's got the right idea with her shouting and stamping—at least she's letting it pour out of her and drain away.

"You expect so much of yourself," I say, stroking the back of his hot hand with the pads of my middle fingers. "I think you're trying to do too much. It's okay to not be able to cope; Madeline and the hearing are enough to deal with. Can't you just tell them you need some time out?"

For a second he softens, his body unraveling a little, but then I see his jaw clamp shut, as if he's shutting himself off from any encroaching self-pity.

"I'm perfectly able to cope, it's just a question of staying focused." He looks at me properly, gives me one of those smiles that goes to the heart of me. "But thank you. I appreciate your care."

"I do care." I'm trying not to let my face say too much. I pause. "I know this sounds mad, but do you want me to have a go?"

"Have a go?"

"If all the facts are there, I could try and give it a polish."

He stands up, his hand automatically reaching for his glass.

"Can't do any harm."

"Don't count on it."

I feel quite proud of myself. I didn't really know what diplomatic immunity meant until an hour ago, but I managed to weave together a couple of paragraphs that gave him the bridge he needed to build to a rousing conclusion—it's funny, my sort-of win in the competition seems to have infused me with a new kind of confidence. I tried inhabiting it as I typed, like trying out a grown-up molar once you've lost your baby tooth. We look at the completed speech, chink glasses, and for a second I don't give a toss about Flynn or Mary or any of it. William takes me in his arms.

"You're a marvel," he says, kissing me properly. I wish in a way that it didn't feel so lovely: the moments when it feels like this are like the last day of the holiday of a lifetime.

"Congealed macaroni cheese is no one's best friend," I say, eventually, pulling away.

There's some moments of real jollity at dinner, a sense of us having come together and achieved something. He apologizes for our fantasy night away, and I promise him that I understand. He asks me properly about what happened at work, and listens to my answers with attention.

"You can't stand for it indefinitely," he says. "You need to have a sense of whether there's a real future for you there. You need to be valued."

I look at him, then look away.

"I know."

Then I ask him, as gently as I can, about the paperwork that litters the apartment, whether it's revealed any more. He sighs, searches for his strength, and I wonder, yet again, what impels me to keep digging.

"There's perhaps more of a pattern to the cash withdrawals than I first realized. There's more of them too."

"What kind of pattern?"

"They seem to take place in the first five days of the month, as a rule. Perhaps when Bergdorf's have got their best pieces!" he adds, attempting an unconvincing smile.

I think again about the tag: could it have been when she had to pay her monthly fees? But the kind of amounts he's talking about are way beyond what you'd pay on a storage unit.

"I just wonder—what Madeline said about the secret place, you don't think she could've had somewhere?"

His face shuts up like a clam, anger buried there, and I draw back. I keep thinking about telling him about the clothes, about the tag, but I know he won't want to hear it. He can't face deviating from the script, the shadowy drones from the insurance company a convenient enemy. I can't help wondering what will happen when they've slunk back into the shadows, whatever the verdict is. I worry he'll be left permanently stranded in this no-man's land, his brilliant mind recast as the worst enemy of all, torturing him with unanswerable questions about his elusive, impossible wife. Surely no one wants to be married to a ghost? Or perhaps that's exactly what he wants.

"Trust me, Livvy. I know my daughter, and I . . . It would have just been one of their silly games. Yet another little trick to get one over on Daddy. And anyway, it's hardly Manhattan real-estate money."

I wonder why they only had one child? It sounds mad, but I can't help thinking that the lure of a triangle, a triangle that she would undoubtedly reign over, would have tickled Sally's fancy. We sit there in silence for a minute or so, sipping our undeniably delicious wine. I say sipping—I can't help but notice, yet again, how much William seems to get through. The thing is, however hard you hold down the lid, pain has to find a way to rise to the surface.

"Delicious wine," I say, my voice a stranger's.

"Thank you." He pauses. "There's something I wanted to ask."

"What's that?"

He looks at me, struggle in his eyes.

"What she said about me," he says, his voice low. "I know what she said to me about you, but . . . when was the last time you saw her?"

I feel sick, tears prickling, the memory of it almost too sharp.

"Um, I think it must have been a few months before you got married." My voice a liar's voice. As if I didn't know—as if it wasn't what it was about. I'm wrong, it wasn't just about that: it was the final round, but this time the umpire's whistle didn't come from another dimension. He's looking at me, appeal in his eyes. "She said that you were very kind, that you would look after her." That's not enough. I hate her for a second, hate her for making me do this, then remember no one forced me at gunpoint into this insane version of a relationship. "She was excited, you know—she was a bride-to-be."

We end up back in his big bed, the room as uniform and characterless as I remember it. There's a hardback book about the financial crisis on the nightstand, and what looks like a vacation picture of the three of them on the chest of drawers—I almost ask him if I can turn it face down, but it feels like the kind of thing a wicked stepmother in a fairy tale might do. Instead a part of me stays in the corner of the room the whole time, vigilant and watchful, making sure we're alone. I'm not entirely sure we are.

I hold onto him afterward, trying to feel close. I didn't even feel close to him when we were as close as it's possible for two bodies to be—we were closer when we were writing his speech. Why does everything feel so upside down?

"You'll stay, yes?"

"Yes," I whisper, my head on his chest. His breath feels constricted inside there, and I gently roll myself sideways. "Goodnight, Livvy," he murmurs as he falls asleep. I lie there next to him, his face softening and relaxing as he loses consciousness. It feels like I'm keeping guard.

If there are owls and larks, I am the tawniest of tawny owls. The alarm on my phone goes off at six, but I somehow manage to turn it off in my sleep. The next alarm that greets me is seven years old, and carrying a copy of *Fifth Formers at St. Clare's*. I try my very best not to yelp.

"Good morning, Olivia," she says breezily. "Carlotta is a very naughty girl. Would you like me to read to you about her?"

William shoots bolt upright, his face a picture of horror. I mummify myself with the sheet, trying desperately to regain some composure. The clock reads six thirty-seven a.m.

"Good morning, Daddy. I have packed my lunch box. Secretly there are two Penguins but also an apple for my teeth."

"J-jolly good. Now why don't you go and brush those teeth and I'll organize some breakfast? It's still very early."

"But I'm reading to Olivia!"

"Tell you what, why don't you read to me when we've all brushed our teeth?" I say, blood rushing in my ears like Niagara Falls.

While Madeline trots off happily, William seems much less happy. I smile at him, but he can't drag his mouth even slightly upward.

"She doesn't seem too traumatized," I say, reaching my hand across the bed toward him.

"Hopefully not," he replies, yanking a robe around himself and heading for the en suite.

I try and breathe, willing the paranoia to fly past me and wrap its black wings around someone else. When he comes out I take his place, his eyes barely meeting mine. I look at his electric toothbrush, gleaming and pristine, wondering if I dare use it, hating that it's even a question after all the places his mouth has met me. I rub some toothpaste over my gums with my finger, jump in the shower, and climb into the clothes I rolled up small in my big handbag so he wouldn't think I was being presumptuous.

Madeline's having a bowl of porridge, the book weighted open by the toast rack.

"Chapter Five," she announces self-importantly the moment I appear.

"We don't read and eat," says William. "Finish up your porridge, please."

Madeline and I catch each other's eye, and I struggle to keep my face completely neutral, William's mood as stifling as a fire blanket. All I want to do is leave, but I feel like I've made her a promise.

"Coffee?" he says, that wooden smile wheeled back on to the stage of his face. I slightly want to slap it.

"Lovely," I say.

"Mommy doesn't always make me eat everything," says Madeline mutinously, spoon jabbing fiercely at the porridge, molding it into turrets. "Not when my tummy's full."

A look of supreme weariness crosses William's face, which he swiftly suppresses. Suddenly I've lost all desire to slap him.

"Three more big bites and then you can stop."

I might be wrong, but I don't think that that was what she was trying to tell him.

"Did your mommy like porridge for breakfast?" I ask her gently, even though I could have a pretty good guess.

"No-oo," says Madeline, giggling at the very idea. "Mommy likes coffee, like you, but not with milk, and one slice of toast, no butter. Butter is for fatties."

"I like butter," I say, horrified by the message, and then remember that the last thing, the very last thing, I should be doing is contradicting Sally's diktats. Madeline's got so little to hang on to as it is.

William gives us both a bleak smile, then gives Madeline leave to stop. She reads me four pages of *St. Clare's* before I can escape, her progress slowed by the frequent pauses she makes to fill me in on the intricacies of the back story ("she is the naughtiest girl in her whole class, and the French Madame had to make her write 'I will behave' in class two hundred times"). "That was great!" I say, when she takes a momentary pause for breath between scenes. "But I'm afraid I've got to go to work now."

"I understand," she tells me in that solemn way she has, and I leap up, relieved, grabbing my bag. "Why didn't you sleep in your bed in your house, Olivia?" I freeze. My eyes swivel toward William but his face is carved out of granite. Just for a second it gives me a sense of complete and total aloneness. "Well, it was very late—"

"Were you very, very tired?"

"She was," agrees William. "And now we need to let her get to work and get you to school."

"And you to work!" adds Madeline. "To Germany."

"Not until Monday." He turns to me. "Sorry, I should have mentioned. I'm off to Frankfurt for meetings."

"Oh! Okay."

Why didn't he tell me? Not that he has to tell me. Maybe the question should be why am I expecting a duck to walk like an elephant? Applying a cold compress of logic doesn't seem to stop it hurting though.

"So the likelihood is I won't see you until the week after. The christening itself in fact."

"And then we are going to my nanny and grandpa's, not my grandmother and grandfather's, and then I am going to be christened, and then you will be my godmother."

"I will," I say, the words catching in my throat. I take a risk, leaning in to kiss her goodbye, grateful to be able to hide my face behind the thick curtain of her dark hair.

CHAPTER TWENTY

THERE'S NO OVERSLEEPING TODAY. I'VE SET THE alarm for seven, but I wake up at five-thirty and then lie in bed, rigid with fear. Thank God I'll have Jules by my side, whatever William's motives were for inviting her. I've barely heard from him since that fateful morning—there's just been a couple of texts and a phone message early enough for a cynical part of me to think he'd worked out I'd still be asleep, telling me all the plans for the christening were "shaping up nicely." We haven't even talked properly about how we'd handle today, beyond a tacit agreement that it's too soon for anyone to know. I e-mailed Lola (the coward's way out) to tell her that I'd been asked to be godmother, and got the briefest of replies; a reply that made me worry that even if she doesn't suspect that anything's happened, she'll be asking herself if that's what I'm angling for.

I'm massaging conditioner into my hair when a series of crashes erupt from the kitchen next door. I swaddle myself in a towel and run through: James is hurling saucepans at the floor, bright red in the face, his favorite coffee mug in bits around him.

"What are you doing?!"

"That fucking bitch!"

"Calm down," I say, grabbing his arm. "Come sit down." He slumps at the kitchen table, pushing his iPhone toward me, his face a picture of misery.

James, you have made my life very difficult, and hurt Peter very badly. The calls you've been making, at such funny times, made him suspicious so he got into my e-mails. He knows everything. When it looked like it was over, I realized how much I would be throwing away—I thought you were a great guy, but me and Peter share too much history. To divide up our lives would cause so much upset and turmoil and I have begged him to give me a second chance. What we had was infatuation, but love is about the long haul—I hope you find someone to go on the long haul with. You mustn't contact me again, under any circumstances. I wish you all the luck in the world, Charlotte.

Divide up our lives—I knew she'd never uncurl her grasping little claws from the Smeg fridge. She's right about one thing, though, love is about the long haul, not about the fizz of a firework that burns out before it's begun. James has never quite grasped that fact. I look at his disbelieving face, the pain that cuts into it, perhaps he finally had, if only she'd chosen to hear him.

"Oh, sweetie," I say, putting my arm around his broad shoulders and, as he feels the pressure his head drops onto his arms, a sob erupting from somewhere deep and guttural within him. I stand behind him, rubbing his back, a little freaked. I don't think I've ever seen James properly sob: he shed discreet tears at Sally's funeral, but it was me who was howling, shredded tissues littering our pew. A wave of dread hits me at the thought I'm going to be back there in a few short hours. I cast a guilty look at the clock, aware I can't comfort him for any more than twenty-two minutes.

"It'll feel better soon," I say, knowing that it will, but also knowing it sounds like nothing more than a pat phrase trotted out by a person who's too short of time to really try. I hope that Sally's death hasn't hardened me, turned me into some kind of self-appointed moral arbiter, making sweeping judgments about what is and isn't a valid excuse for grief.

"I love her, Livvy, like properly love her." No you don't, I think, you don't even know her, but to say it would be wildly unhelpful. "Couldn't stop thinking about what you said, about it not being a proper relationship, and I knew I had to get some answers, or I'd have started to feel like a total fucking fool."

"Is that why you kept ringing her?"

He nods, shamefaced.

"That went well," he says, and I know, in that instant, that he'll bounce back.

"I know how much it hurts, but just give it a bit of time."

"I should fight for her."

"Don't do that." He looks at me, mutinous. "She was never good enough for you, not ever!" He's not ready to hear it, still swinging between rage and adulation, and I endure a long rant about all her wonderful qualities, even though I know they could be written on the back of a stamp. In capitals. Then he sinks back into gloomy torpor.

"Let me get you a cup of tea," I say, "and then I've got to finish getting ready. I'm really sorry."

"Don't go!"

"I have to, it's Madeline's christening."

"You could say you're ill."

I look at him in disbelief. He actually means it.

"I can't do that."

"I need you, Livvy."

"Call Ed. Or call your brother. You know I'd be here in a heartbeat if I could be, but I really, really can't."

He glowers at me.

"He's not right for you."

"Don't. Just don't, okay? I have to get through today. It's not about me and him, it's about Madeline."

"I just don't want you to get hurt."

There's that, and also the fact you don't want to lose Livvy On Tap, I think, looking at his handsome, slightly spoiled face.

"I'll call your brother."

"He's not you," he says, voice breaking, and I realize, in a blinding flash, how long this has been my prison. The shocking thing is that in the old days his plea might have been enough; I would have made my excuses, pulled on a pair of jeans, found a DVD we both loved and settled into comfy oblivion. Not now—not now.

Jules and a sleeping Nathaniel arrive on the doorstep at ten-thirty, simultaneous with James's little brother Christopher. "Come up," I say, makeup half done, trying to zip up my fourth change of outfit.

"How's he doing?" whispers Christopher, trying not to wake the baby. Nat makes a little snuffling sound, but then settles back down.

"He's not great," I reply, directing him toward the kitchen where James is still reading and rereading his e-mail like the content might miraculously transform before his very eyes.

Jules is carrying Nathaniel in a sling, and I quietly show her my selection of outfits, while she thumbs up and thumbs down around the sides. Nathaniel slowly, sleepily opens his eyes and gives me one of those gummy smiles that you'd need to be a psychopath to resist.

"Definitely the green one," says Jules, stroking his soft blond head.

"I feel weird about green . . ." Jules fixes me with that clear gaze of hers, and I sink heavily onto the bed, pausing to collect myself. "She looked amazing in green, but the black ones feel funereal, which is the last thing I want to be. And they all look a bit cheap."

"No they don't!"

"You should see the things she had in her wardrobe . . ."

"And think how they made him feel. All they added up to were debts." Jules takes my hand, squeezes it. "You look amazing in green too, and if we don't leave in the next ten minutes you won't even *be* a godmother."

She's right, but part of me needs a moment. I sit there for a few more precious seconds, then yank the green dress over my head and grab my makeup bag.

"Ready?"

"As I'll ever be."

"You'll be fine," says Jules, pulling out of the end of our road. "It'll be over before you know it."

I foolishly text William to tell him we're on our way, even though I know it will create a gnawing sensation inside me until I hear back.

"It's full on, Jules. I have to renounce Satan."

"That's fine, he's a boob." I roll my eyes at her. "Sorry. Is he properly religious, do you think?"

"Yeah, I haven't really talked to him about it, but I think he's pretty Catholic. Like the guilt's always there around the edges, you know?"

It's exactly the kind of Achilles' heel that Sally would have sought out and transformed into a deadly weapon, as fatal for him as my insecurity was for me.

"I know I'm a stuck record, but give him time. Of course this is extreme, but I think there's always a trace of the last person, anyway."

"What do you mean?"

"Phil still calls me Lisa about once a year." I look at her quizzically. "He went out with her in the first year, and she dumped him. Remember we called her 'double decker ass' when I started going out with him?"

"Oh, her!" I say, remembering Jules making me look at three separate pictures of her in forensic detail so we could be absolutely sure that she was prettier. "Still?"

"Yeah. It doesn't mean anything. It's just she was the last. I still Facebook-stalk Bradley a bit."

Bradley was her entirely forgettable high school boyfriend: I can't imagine anything remotely interesting has happened to him in the intervening years. I think about what she's saying, but I can't help thinking it's a symptom of her unnaturally optimistic world view.

"But what if William never recovers? What if he stays with me, but he's never really there? It'd be like loving a hologram."

Did a part of him leave with Sally? Did she spirit a little bit away with her over that invisible divide: some vital piece, infuriatingly invisible to the naked eye, but utterly imperative to the clockwork of his heart? I've tried to convince myself that she'd want him to be happy, but it rings false, nothing more than a get-out clause. That wasn't how Sally loved, and, if some part of her remains, as some primeval part of me believes it does, it won't be how she loves now.

"Livvy—" says Jules, gearing up to offer more comfort, but I talk over her, everything so close to the surface.

"I'm scared I'm just hopeless, like Dad. What is this, just a dressed up, fancy version of me pining for someone who's never going to want me back? I don't want to be like that anymore."

I hear my voice break as I say it, my deepest, darkest fear dragged into the open. It's been sitting there for so long, like an ugly great heirloom you can't bear to get rid of; instead you cover it up, squeeze past it, do anything you can to avoid acknowledging how much it blocks out the light. Jules turns to me and gives me exactly the smile I want. It's not a "buck up" smile, or a "Livvy, you're being ridiculous" smile, it's an "I hear you, and although I think you're wrong, it doesn't mean you as a person are ridiculous" smile.

"Okay, firstly, that's just not true. And secondly, Dad is fine. I think he wanted to tell you himself, but I took Nat around there on Monday and guess who was there?"

"Mom?"

"No, Livvy, of course not Mom. Margery! They're totally doing it."

"Margery with the bright red face?"

"The very same. It was kind of obvious that night, when you think about it."

Not to me. I sit there in silence for a couple of junctions trying to absorb the idea. It shouldn't be a big deal but somehow it feels seismic. Poor, lonely, heartbroken Dad is nothing of the kind.

"Do you think he's in love?"

"Hard to say. He's hardly going to become Rhett Butler overnight, but he definitely has a spring in his Crocs."

"She is quite scarlet."

With the unfunniest pun in the world ringing in my ears I give in and look at my phone. Nothing from William. I take my lipstick out of my purse and very, very carefully apply another coat, the tremor in my hands just about within my control.

Time does one of those weird backflips when I see that sign for the turnoff, the months since Sally's death spiraling and contracting inside me like an elastic band. So much has happened, so much has changed, and yet it also feels like yesterday that James and I were making this very journey. "More rescue remedy," says Jules, patting my knee, and I shake a few drops under my tongue. My phone finally beeps, but it's only Mom.

Nathaniel screams like a police siren for the last couple of miles, a piercing, relentless sound that seems like it will never end. I clamber inelegantly over the passenger seat and try to soothe him, my useless cooing and toy-waving counting for nothing. Finally, just as we're nearly there, his wails subside; he pauses, gives me something akin to a smile and then projectile vomits right down the green dress.

"Oh Livvy . . ." says Jules, horrified. "Let me just get the wipes."

I can't speak; I just stand there on the pavement out-side the church, looking down at the sticky white mess that covers me, wondering if it's a sign. It's right then that Wil-liam's parents come past. I drop my eyes, hoping his father won't see the state of me, and try and signal to Jules that we should move closer to the car, but he's anyway too grimly focused on hectoring his wife to notice. He's more broad and imposing than I remember, his features granite-cut: he should be handsomely distinguished, but he's too hawklike for that, master of all he surveys. William's mother scuttles behind, a slim, elegant woman perfectly turned out in a dove gray skirt suit. That's what I should have worn, gray or navy, something that straddled the divide between fune-real and celebratory: everything about my outfit suddenly feels wrong, even without allowing for the coating of vomit.

"I specifically warned you about the traffic around Bish-op's Stortford," says Mr. Harrington, swiveling his head around so he can fix his wife with a stern gaze. "You would have had ample opportunity to . . ."

As they sweep past I whisper to Jules who they are, feel-ing a little jet of warmth toward our own hopeless, infu-riating parents. I've never for one second doubted that either of them loved me, whereas I can't imagine that man being capable of any kind of human warmth. I'm sure he loves his children in principle, but sometimes a word and the actual meaning of a word can be hopelessly adrift of each other.

The next person I see is Lola, her whole family in tow. She stares, wide-eyed, at my still sicky dress, and then comes up and hugs me. If nothing else, it's broken the ice.

"Oh you poor thing," she says, her natural warmth van-quishing her pique. "Justin, have we got anything in the car?"

Soon she's helping Jules to mop me down while I tell her adorable little boys what Nathaniel did, and just for a minute life feels normal. I love those moments, those brief wisps of time when I get to catch my breath, but then the inevitable backwash begins, my body tensing as if it's preparing for a blow. Jules and Lola survey their handiwork. "You'll do," says Jules, holding my gaze. And then it's time to go in.

William is already inside the church, standing near the front with his parents and his in-laws. Our eyes meet down the length of the aisle, both of us momentarily frozen. I'm sure my face tells him everything: all I can hope is that no one else is there to decode it. And what do I read in his eyes? I can see the deep pain that runs through him, the mammoth effort it is taking to keep this show on the road, but maybe that's something that any old person walking in off the street could see. Maybe I don't have the special insight I think I do. He comes toward us.

"Olivia," he says, grazing a barely-there kiss against my cheek. "Julia, thank you so much for coming. And Lola, Madeline will be so pleased you brought the boys."

"Where is she?" I ask, my voice high and false.

"I've left my sister in charge. She's brought a little friend from school and it's all we can do to stop them starting in on the communion wine."

Everyone laughs politely and then falls silent.

"So it sounds like she's finding her feet!" says Lola, overflowing with concern. Because we've been existing undercover, I'd forgotten how forced and unnatural everyone is around him—it's exhausting to even witness.

"So far, so good," he says genially. "Now I'm afraid I'm going to have to steal Olivia away, her services are required at the front of the church."

I'm cringing as I walk up the aisle with him. I can't help feeling that everyone's watching us, even though of course they're doing nothing of the sort. Is he fighting to not be dragged under by the memory of Sally walking toward him on their wedding day? How glamorous she looked, her dress cut low, cinched in tightly around the waist she fought tooth and nail to keep tiny—"Takes more calories to eat it than it's got in it," she used to say, crunching theatrically on a celery stick, ignoring my entreaties that she was looking dangerously thin. And here I am, walking alongside him, a cheap, too-bright dress clinging to my podgy upper thighs, a top note of vomit detectable, at least to me.

I look to the front pew, feeling like I'm walking into a trap. There's Sally's mom, trying to keep it together, a fistful of tissues clasped tightly in her hand, her son and husband kept close. William's parents stand next to them, his dad's back ramrod straight in his charcoal pinstriped suit, his mother exuding the nervous energy of an exotic bird captured midflight. "Are you okay?" I whisper, knowing as I say it that it's an inane question, to which he can't possibly provide a real response. I hope he knows that it's not really a question, more a squeeze of his hand that I'm sending him through the ether. "It all seems to be going to plan so far," he says, not breaking his stride. I will him to look around—to give me some tiny sign that he's here with me in spirit, that in some parallel universe we're facing it together—but he won't allow a single chink of himself to peep through the carapace.

Madeline comes rushing toward me once we reach the front of the church. She's dressed in a beautiful white lace frock, hair neatly plaited, a small blond girl trailing in her wake.

"Thank you for arriving," she says, imperiously. "I would like you to say hello to Francesca. She is my best friend now."

It's the sight of Francesca's reaction that sends me close to breaking point: she can't hide her delight, a gap-toothed smile spreading across her chubby little face, her hand instinctively reaching out to find Madeline's. The memory of how it felt is suddenly so painfully acute—the sense of finding a different version of a soul mate, a person who shows you back to you and makes you better. Of course William couldn't meet my eye: Sally's presence is overwhelming—quivering, intense, permeating every single molecule and atom and particle that surrounds us, the present drowned out by the crashing cymbals of the past. I look around at her mom, our eyes filling with tears at the sight of each other. She gives me a look of such welcoming warmth that it's almost unbearable, shame and guilt knotting up inside me until I can barely breathe.

Madeline submits to Francesca's handhold for a couple of minutes, then violently shakes it off.

"I have to become very prepared," she says sternly, gluing herself to William's side, utterly oblivious to her friend's crestfallen expression. I smile at Francesca as kindly as I can, wanting so much to take her in my lap and tell her everything I know about what she's got left to learn, but instead I find out where her mom is sitting, and make sure that Madeline says goodbye to her properly before walking her over.

"When we are friends afterward I will be christened," she tells her proudly.

And now it really is time. The same solemn priest takes his place at the front of the church, his words sensitively acknowledging what it was that we last gathered here to mark. I look across at Madeline, acutely protective of her, but her face shows nothing but fierce self-possession. William is equally stoic, his features arranged in an expression of earnest attention. I look over to him a couple of times during the service, but his gaze is still fixed straight ahead, one hand on Madeline's shoulder, the other gripping the pew so fiercely that his knuckles are blanched white.

The priest summons us to the font, Madeline racing ahead, her excitement palpable, loving being the center of attention. Sally breathes past me, the memory of her ostentatious glamour at my nineteenth birthday party, all eyes trained on her. The four godparents step forward: me, William's friend Ronan, Sally's brother and Belinda, a handsome-looking woman who displays the same impressive self-control as the rest of the family. The rest of the guests gather around, and I force myself to find my center, giving my responses as clearly and confidently as I can. William smiles at me as I do so, his gaze finally lingering on me. I feel warmed by it, hoping my face won't shout out a truth that cannot be so much as whispered. The priest performs the final ritual, bathing Madeline's upturned face with the holy water, and then, finally, it's over, the drop in tension palpable. "Well done," mouths Jules, simultaneously jiggling the fractious baby. William turns to me, Madeline's hand in his.

"Thank you," he says, a careworn but lovely smile on his face. "Say thank you to your godmother, Madeline."

"Thank you," she says, grinning up at me, and my heart scrunches up with hope. Maybe with time they could be as happy to have me around as they look right now. Maybe the fact that I truly understand how sad it is will make it less crass, more truthful.

"No, thank you for asking me," I say, gabbling with relief. "I didn't get to tell you, Nathaniel threw up all over me when we were coming in and—"

Belinda comes up, laying a hand on William's arm.

"We do need to ensure all the guests know where to go," she says, voice terribly far back in her throat. She smiles at me in a brief, absent way that fulfills her obligations.

"I'm so sorry, you must excuse me," says William, sliding off. "I'll catch up with you at the reception." I stand there, looking after him, trying not to feel crushed, trying not to feel like I'm one pebble on a shingly beach. Today is not about me.

The reception is in the function room of a lovely old country pub, all oak beams and roaring fires. They're playing *The Best Christmas Album in the World . . . Ever*, even though it's more than a month away, and in my weird, altered state I actually start to think I like Slade, when in fact it's Christmas that I like. Christmas: I glance at William, who is surrounded by earnest-looking guests, all wearing versions of the same sympathetic smile. He must be dreading it.

"Shall I get us some mulled wine?" says Jules, eagerly eying the tureen.

"See if you can nab a mince pie too."

"Here, you take Nathaniel," she says, plunking him in my arms. I hold him a little gingerly at first, wary of any more projectile vomiting, but he seems perfectly content to chew on his rubber giraffe. I squeeze him a little closer to me.

"Who's this little bundle of joy?" says Claire, another one of our gang from halls, who I haven't seen in years before these last few months. We exchanged only the briefest of hellos at the funeral.

"Oh he's not . . ." I pull him closer toward me, loving the feel of his warm body snuggling against mine, his big eyes looking up at me in mild surprise.

"That gorgeous boy," says Lola, appearing at my other side, "is her nephew."

I look over to Jules, who's fallen into conversation with someone over the other side of the room, and signal to her that she doesn't need to rush, that I don't want to hand him back quite yet. When Claire wanders off Lola gives me a spontaneous hug.

"It's so nice to see you," she says. "I'm sorry if—"

"Don't worry," I say, cutting her off. I don't want to pick over anything too forensically. "It's lovely to see you too." I feel overwhelmed, the causes too multiple to list; the Christmassy-ness, the sight of William, so close to me and yet so far away, the mirror effect of Sally—shockingly, horribly absent and also so present. "Let's make sure we go out again soon."

"It's a deal," laughs Lola.

It seems like forever before William and I get to talk to each other. He comes over to me and Jules, deftly pulling me aside.

"Sorry," he says, smiling down at me, his eyes crinkling. "There seem to be a million guests at least. You look lovely, by the way."

I try not to smile at him in the wrong way, a thank-you muttered under my breath, the moment broken by Madeline appearing at our elbows, grinning from ear to ear.

"Nathaniel really, really likes me. He smiled twice and I fed him some banana."

"That's great!" I tell her. "He doesn't smile for everyone."

Then William's father appears, pushing his way into our little group like a papa lion returning from a kill. William seems to stand to attention somehow.

"I thought that went off very well," he says, surveying the scene. He looks down at Madeline. "Well done, little miss."

"Without question," says William, his jaw tightening in that way I've become so familiar with, one of those tiny tells that he can't quite control. I can feel myself straining toward Lola, standing nearby with Justin. I don't want to abandon William, but equally I don't know if it's exactly what he wants—is it having me in his father's airspace that is making his vein throb?

"It does still seem a great shame that you didn't feel able to use the family chapel. Your mother at least seems to understand your logic."

A bolt of anger strikes William's face, but he quickly represses it.

"As I explained, I felt the symmetry of it was important. The main thing is that it went off without a hitch." He turns to me, eyes flashing. "Pa, have you been properly introduced to Olivia? She was a great friend of Sally's. I think you might have met her . . ." he stumbles a little, "at the funeral."

His father's eyes minesweep their way across me, not a shred of warmth in his expression. Just for a second I imagine living the rest of my life within range of that gaze.

"Of course," he says, extending a large, strong hand. It wraps itself around mine, establishing complete dominance, and then drops back to his side as fast as it appeared, his interest spent.

"Olivia is my godmother," says Madeline, almost as if she's protecting me from his indifference.

"I know she is."

"That means she can stay at my house whenever she likes. On Sunday she got very, very tired and she went to sleep in Daddy's bed and in the morning I read to her all about St. Clare's."

Just for a second it feels like someone's pressed an enormous, metaphysical pause button and the world has stopped in its tracks. William's father's appalled face looms over me, his interest well and truly reignited. An anarchic part of me wants to stick two fingers up to him—tell him he's got it all wrong, that what we've shared is something sweet and important—but then I see William's stricken face and the fight drains out of me. My bravado was nothing but stupid, misplaced hope—the childish part of me that secretly longed for the truth to be our deliverance, our liberation from building a relationship on a mess of lies.

"We're not going to talk about that now," William says, voice strangulated. He leans down to Madeline. "Why don't we get you some more cake?" If he even so much as looked at me, made it a moment shared, there might still be a way back, but instead he leaves me there, humiliated and abandoned. I catch Lola's eye, and she whips her head away, fury in her eyes.

"William?" says his father, as the rest of the family start to notice the disturbance. I wish so much that Jules was here, but she's taken Nathaniel away to change him.

"I'd prefer not to talk about it now," says William, almost pleading. Sally's brother's watching now, looking between the two of us, his eyes like flint. William sees it too, and visibly flinches. His voice drops, but not far enough. "Besides, there's very little to talk about."

I break away, my eyes fixed on the door.

"Olivia . . ." he calls, but he doesn't try to physically stop me.

Lola grabs me as I'm desperately pushing my way out, her fingers gripping the flesh of my arm.

"You're unbelievable," she snarls, two flashpoints of color burning her face. "I hope you can sleep at night."

"I know what it looks like," I plead, "but it . . . it just happened." It's so impossible to explain, the delicacy of it turned to something callous and brutal as soon as it's dragged into the open. I look back to William, who now seems to be involved in a furious conversation with his father. "It wasn't against Sally."

"Bullshit. You had to get your own back, didn't you? She was right to dump you, but it was all poor little Livvy, butter wouldn't melt. Everything she said about you was true."

There's no coming back from this—it's the ultimate betrayal. I know that better than anyone.

"What's that supposed to mean?"

"The way you made her move into the apartment in the second year. Pleading with her to take it."

"She was the one who found it!"

"That's not what you said at the time . . ."

"No, because she said we couldn't tell you . . ."

Lola looks at me, an expression of complete disgust on her face. Not only have I tried to steal Sally's husband away, I'm trashing her memory. One of her sons approaches, finally giving me the opportunity to make a run for it.

"If she could see you here she'd turn in her grave."

Jules is in the car, on the phone to Phil. I climb into the passenger seat, tears streaming down my face. I'm sobbing so much I can barely speak.

"We need to go, right now."

"Little one! Tell me what happened?"

"Seriously, Jules, let's just get go."

"Livvy, wait . . ."

William is running toward us, his hair askew. I lean out of the car.

"Don't bother." The very sight of him sends a tidal wave of grief and anger flooding through my body.

"I cannot apologize enough."

"That's right, you can't. So don't . . ." My voice breaks, a sob hiccupping out of me. "Don't even bother."

"Livvy, get out and talk to him," implores Jules.

"Olivia . . ."

That feels like the last straw, the final insult. I step out of the car.

"It's Livvy. We have slept together, in case you hadn't noticed. What was it, a shoulder to cry on that went a bit too far?"

"Of course not."

"That's how it feels." I look at his helpless face, more etched with pain than ever—what did I really expect? "It's my own stupid fault," I say, "I shouldn't have—" I stop, not wanting to humiliate myself any more than I already have.

"Shouldn't have what?" he says. His hand almost moves toward me, but then he pins it back down by his side, his gaze unconsciously pulling toward the pub.

"I shouldn't have had feelings for you," I say, enunciating carefully, the words as dry as sawdust in my mouth.

"Please don't think I don't have feelings for you too."

Feelings, feelings, jolly old feelings. It's how you make those feelings flesh that matters; if they're no more than a cerebral concept then they're no good to anyone: they're as magnificent and dead as Madeline's dinosaurs.

"I'm not sure I believe you." I should turn on my heels and go, but my legs won't quite obey—once I've left then it will be truly over, this whole interlude nothing but a memory—and yet I know that life will refuse to return to normal. Normal no longer exists in any meaningful sense. "If you did, then you would have stuck up for me in there."

"I'm so sorry to have failed you so spectacularly," he says, his whole body slumping under the weight of it. "What you've done for me, for us, these last few months. I can't put into words how much having you there has helped."

"Thanks, but I don't want to be your aspirin. I never did."

"Aspirin?"

"Just some *thing* that makes you feel better. What you said about Mary, it's the same thing. I'm worth more than that."

"Of course you are! If you were to give me a little more time . . ."

I think about what he's asking; the long road stretching forward, me tiptoeing down it as quiet as a mouse, trying to win his heart by stealth and patience. The very thought of it makes my guts contract, like they're already preparing to make themselves smaller to suppress their messages. I think of the ropes around his heart, the way Sally can still twist them and tighten them at will, and how powerless I am to untangle the knots. There's more there too, I know it, and when and if the unexploded bomb goes off, I don't want to be its first casualty.

"I don't have more time," I say, lightly touching his fingers.

All these years I've spent pining for a perfect version of love, the love that will make all the missed opportunities feel like no more than lucky escapes; it's only now I can see that it's a version of love that only exists inside the covers of my dusty hardbacks. It's time to stop pining, fruitlessly and safely, for the men I can't have, and find the messy reality of one that I can.

"If that's what you feel then of course I'll respect it."

I look at him, those even features so perfectly arranged, and start feeling infuriated all over again. I hate it when he sounds like a press release.

"That thing you said about Sally, that sometimes it felt like she wanted to be married to you and sometimes it felt like she really didn't. That's how I've felt with you."

"Oh, Livvy." He looks utterly devastated, his carapace well and truly punctured, and for a second I feel like I've been too cruel. And yet I was right to tell him: the worst thing is to walk away from a relationship not knowing what the other person's truth really was. He steps forward, enfolds me in his arms, and I let him. His words disappear into my hair like they did that day in Kensington, the first time I thought I was saying a final goodbye. "I wish with all my heart that it was different. I *do* know your worth, sometimes I've thought I know it more than you, and if I've made you feel otherwise then I'm desperately sorry. If anyone's worthless it's me. I'm no more than a husk."

"Don't say that! You're not a husk. You're a proper person, dealing with the absolute worst thing I can think of, with more courage than I could ever have." He grips me more tightly now, the solid thrumming of his heart reverberating through every last corner of me. I'm fighting to store this feeling, the imprint of his body squashed up against mine, for the long skein of time that expands ahead.

"Is there nothing I can say?"

"No. I don't think there is. We both know, don't we? That it's over?"

I wish that I could tell you that I love you. I wish that that one simple truth was allowed, not just the harsh ones.

"You're lovely, in the truest sense of the word, and I will miss you infinitely more than you realize."

I'm crying in earnest now, holding on to the bulk of him. He's a rock, a rock from which my fingers are sliding.

"I'll be thinking of you, William. I'll hold you in my heart."

It takes all my strength to pull away, to admit to myself that we've reached the end, but eventually I do. I look up at him, his eyes swimming with tears. It's now, in this moment, that I can see in his face what I've hoped to find, but there's too much against us. "Goodbye," I whisper, and then I summon up all the strength I've got left, turn on my heel and walk back to the car.

PART THREE

"How do you like the Queen?" said the Cat in a low voice.

"Not at all," said Alice: "she's so extremely—" Just then she noticed that the Queen was close behind her listening: so she went on, "—likely to win, that it's hardly worth while finishing the game."

Lewis Carroll, *Alice's Adventures in Wonderland*

CHAPTER TWENTY-ONE

"Can I get you more tissues, honey?"

This time it's the blond stewardess who approaches, her kind, motherly face full of concern. We're an hour away from landing, which means I've been crying for approximately six hours and thirteen minutes.

"Thank you," I say, smiling gratefully and grabbing the wad of serviettes she holds out to me.

Trust me, this is not how I imagined my first trip to New York. I spent the entire weekend sobbing, my wretched grief coming from a place so deep that it started to frighten me, its pull so strong I felt like I was being pulled into some kind of underworld. I thought of what William said, of feeling like a husk, and I understood, finally, in my bones, why he had to push me away. And yet somehow the knowing didn't make my heart ache any less, the loss coming in savage waves that left me breathless.

And then on Monday, my face defiantly red raw, my Mary-pleasing mask thrown in the bin where it belonged, I found myself summoned to her office. Charlotte had rung to tell her that she needed to skip the trip for "personal reasons," a phrase she spat out like she had a cockroach lodged in her mouth, and I was now back in the Flynn Gerrard hot seat, due to fly to New York a week later. I thought about throwing it back in her face, drawing an angry line in the sand, but something stopped me. Something told me that I should simply follow the path that was opening up, accept the fact that the final whistle was yet to blow. "I'll make my arrangements," I said, smiling sweetly. She started with the crocodile concern, her fingers snapping at my wrist like a bony handcuff, but I snatched it away, dismissing my blotchy face as no more than a reaction to a rogue moisturizer.

William doesn't even know I'm here. I look at my watch, still set to London time. It must be nine or so: I picture him at that brand-new kitchen table, *The Times* laid out before him as he forks his ready-made dinner into his mouth, the fourth glass of wine of the night never more than a few inches from his ready hand. Has he shut down from me already, preserved his strength by cutting out any unnecessary drains on his resources? He hasn't contacted me once, not so much as a text, and I wonder if the relief of no longer having to try trumps whatever pain he feels at losing me. The thought stings too much, and I push it away.

The cab swoops over the Brooklyn Bridge, the New York skyline spreading out before me for the very first time, and a starburst of excitement goes off inside me, despite everything. But then, the backwash of sadness. I think of Sally, her arms flung wide, "Manhattan!" I always thought it would be her I'd lose my New York virginity with—I remember talking her out of an insane plan to spend our entire student loans on a couple of plane tickets, sure there'd be plenty of time to do it when we were grown-up enough to have salaries to use. I take out the tag and put it in the center of my palm, thinking of it sitting in hers. Now, suddenly, the most obvious thought occurs.

"Capricorn holding company," says a bored-sounding woman.

I take a breath, the words sticking in my throat.

"Hi, my name's Sally Atkins. I just wanted to find out if my storage unit is still active."

"Can I please put you on hold?"

It's so obvious. If there were times when she didn't want to be married to him, then why wouldn't she have taken it to its logical conclusion?

"Ma'am, you're in arrears. You won't be permitted to access anything without clearing your debt."

A surge of triumph hits me, until I remember what it is that I'm actually doing: walking another mile in Sally's high-heeled shoes, my gait unsteady, destination unknown.

"Of course. How much is it that I actually owe?"

"Three hundred and sixty-six dollars. To be settled in cash."

I want to go there right now, but they're only an hour from closing, reopening at eight a.m. tomorrow.

Flynn is yet to share his schedule, but all I can hope is that his pathological flakiness will win me a few precious hours.

My hotel is in what I think must be midtown, a nondescript concrete shell, indistinguishable from business hotels the world over. The gray-haired concierge—a warm, friendly

New Yorker who can't believe it's my first time—directs me across the sidewalk to a bustling Italian trattoria, where I eat my supper with a copy of *Grazia* propped open, trying and failing not to think about William. I will see him again, I know that—neither he nor I will let the fact that I'm Madeline's godmother become an unkept promise—but the thought of having to make polite conversation on the doorstep, while a woman who knows less than I do about how scarred his heart truly is bustles around in the background, makes my own heart feel like it's breaking.

Still, the next morning when my phone rings three times while I'm stuck in the tiny shower, I can't help but give in to the plea-bargaining: "if I leave my conditioner in until I count to sixty it will be him"; "if I soap between my toes it will be him." Of course it isn't him, he'd never be so rude as to call three times in succession, it's Flynn.

"So you've landed?" he says, petulantly. "I didn't know."

"I did try and call last night, there was no answer."

I'm sure he's horrified that Mary's fobbed him off with the girl from the subs bench.

"Well I've found you now. We'll be meeting our first girl at Pastis at midday. Reckon you can manage that?"

"Yes, of course," I say, with absolutely no idea what or where Pastis might be. I say my goodbyes and yank on my clothes. It gives me three hours—the sane thing to do would be to wait until afterward, but sanity doesn't really come into it.

William was right about New York being overwhelming. It's boggling my mind; the long avenues, the tall buildings, the ancient, fur-swaddled old ladies in huge sunglasses tottering along with their tiny dogs. Part of me wishes I could savor it, but savoring it alone seems like such cold comfort.

It takes forty minutes in a smelly cab to get to the huge, brick mausoleum of a building, buried deep within an industrial estate. I stand there looking at it, my legs shaking, my heart thumping in my chest, and then lean on the heavy door. The sight of the stern, gray-haired man behind the desk makes me realize how ill prepared I am. Whatever Lola might have said, I hate lying. I mustn't blush and stammer like I usually do, mustn't arouse any suspicions that I'm a fraud. I hope he never saw her. You wouldn't mistake the two of us, not for a second.

"I'm Sally Atkins," I say, sticking out a confident hand. I do have more confidence now, there's no denying it, and some of that is thanks to William. "I've been in England, and I stupidly got myself into arrears. Let me find you some cash."

"Should ask you for ID, but I'm a sucker for an English accent," he says, grinning.

"Really?" I say, counting out the money as fast as I can before he has time to change his mind. "That should be all of it. And here," I say, adding a ten dollar bill, "take this."

"Very kind of you, ma'am," he says, his meaty paw landing on the notes. "Will you be closing it up?"

"Yes. Yes I will."

"Lucky you remembered. Your goods nearly ended up on a garbage truck."

I climb up three flights of stairs, anxiety and breathlessness competing for possession of me, then walk the length of a long, dark corridor until I finally reach the door.

I don't know what I expected—perhaps that I would be like Alice, falling down her rabbit hole and entering a parallel universe full of clues—but all I find is stacks of cardboard boxes, far flimsier and cheaper than the professional packing boxes that filled the barn. It's more like the hap-hazard chaos of our student moves, with clothes erupting all over the floor. The lack of time is probably a godsend, as I don't have the luxury of melancholy. The clothes seem like a mixture of well-worn favorites and brand-new pieces, the tags still attached. It feels like her clothes are endless, a taunting trail of nothingness that speaks only of how much she loved to shop. I carry on, frenzied, determined to sort my way through every box. The last stack is shoved into the corner against the tiny window. As I lift the top one up, its flaps messily taped shut, the bottom gives way and a cas-cade of papers spills out, a haphazard shadow of the paper-work that William neatly stacked. A cloud of dust chokes me, covers me in its grayish fog. There's an official-looking document in a reinforced document wallet, a Post-it note stuck to the front—*For You x* it says, in Sally's scrawly, impa-tient handwriting. I trace it with my fingers, tears springing to my eyes, remembering all the notes and cards she gave me in that curly-wurly script of hers. It's yet another piece of her imprint, her unique way of being in the world, that's been lost forever. The shrill ring of my phone shakes me back to the present. It's Flynn.

"I'm here, twiddling my thumbs," he growls, restaurant noise loud in the background.

I look at my watch. Eleven forty-five. Shit.

"I thought we were meeting at twelve?" I say, scrambling to my feet.

"The meeting's at twelve. I would have thought it would be obvious to any idiot we'd need time to agree on our questions."

"I'm so sorry, I'll be there as soon as I can," I say, pulling the papers from the folder.

"Where exactly are you now?"

"Closer than you think," I lie, slamming the door of the unit shut.

I open the folder as I'm running down the stairs, and a set of keys comes tumbling out. I chase after them, then frantically scan the paperwork. It seems to be a lease—*12 months, Sally Atkins, Montana Avenue, New Jersey.* I shove it all in my handbag, stopping briefly by the security guard.

"I'm not quite ready, I'm afraid. I'll be back this afternoon."

"No problem," he says. "I've had a look at the system anyhow. You can't close it on your own. You'll need your husband to countersign."

CHAPTER TWENTY-TWO

I WISH I'D TAKEN MORE WITH ME WHEN I LEFT. THE contract, which looks shop bought, reveals little more: she rented the apartment in May, three months before she died, from someone with handwriting even more unintelligible than her own. I weigh the keys in my hand, wishing I could go straight round there, wondering if I should call William. "Your husband"—perhaps he did know about this all along, and the use of her maiden name is nothing more than some kind of minor tax dodge? But then I think of the forensic attention he gives the broadsheets, or the righteous analysis he gives me of world affairs, and I'm sure that he's not a person who would brook even a small dishonesty. Besides, there's something about that *For You x*—it's not a *For You* for a husband, it's a playful invitation to a lover. I'm going to go, find out all I can, and then decide if it's a hurt that he needs to have inflicted on him.

My fingers are still tracing the words when the cab draws up outside Pastis, an achingly trendy French bistro in what

I'm told is known as the Meatpacking District. Meatpacking really doesn't seem to be the point anymore—the street is lined with eye-wateringly expensive-looking clothes shops and boutique hotels—but there's no time to gawp, I'm nearly half an hour late.

Flynn's got a prime corner table, and is taking up an entire velvet banquette, the hapless interviewee perched on a stool opposite him. She's a slight, dark-haired little thing, who looks a few years younger than me. Heavy, dark-framed glasses dominate her face, a cunning piece of kit that lulls you into thinking she's a plain, earnest type, rather than the pixie-featured beauty that's revealed on closer inspection. I introduce myself, hoping she won't notice how much my hand is shaking. I turn gingerly to Flynn, who flashes me the kind of big, leonine grin that never quite reaches those famous green eyes—they remain as cold and lifeless as a dank pond.

"So sorry to be late."

"Get yourself comfortable, Livvy, I'll grab us the waiter back. Fancy a glass of the bubbly stuff?"

I can't think of anything I'd like less, apart from the fact that I feel the very opposite of celebratory; it seems faintly icky when we're discussing a film about women living in abject poverty. I take a couple of tiny sips and try and engage with the meeting, one hand tracing the outline of the keys in my handbag. *For You*—the phrase keeps pinballing around my head, its meaning as soft and fluid as melting wax.

Kirsten is a first assistant director. While this means that she is extremely good at bossing people around, it doesn't mean that she's actually directed anything of her own, a fact I accidentally root out of her in the first five minutes, earning myself a glare from Flynn. The two of them had a "to-tal ball" on *Sh*t Happens 2*, the nature of which I'm starting to wonder about, as I notice the flirtatious looks they seem to be casting each other when they think I'm not watching. I ask her what kind of films influence her, and then surrender myself to a verbal barrage.

"*Taxi Driver, Chinatown, GoodFellas. . .*" she says, striking them off on her fingers, nasal New York drawl landing like machine gun fire, Flynn hanging off her every word. She seems to have entirely missed the point, this film bearing absolutely no relation to a gangster movie, but I've most definitely resigned from fighting a battle I know I can't win.

"Great," I say, trying not to fixate on my watch. Couple more questions, another toast to Flynn's general munificence, and then I should be able to get myself to the apartment. A cold, damp chill suddenly spreads through me: what if the *You* is actually resident there?

"Livvy?" snaps Flynn.

"Yes, no. It's great," I say, trying to focus.

"What, you actually think it's right that one percent of the population control ninety-nine percent of America's wealth?" says Kirsten, her lips, painted an unusual shade of hipster brown, pursed in sanctimonious astonishment. She wraps them around the champagne glass and awards herself a generous swig to deliver her from the shock. I've had enough of pretending. I stand up, reaching for my coat.

"I'm so sorry, I know I'm not doing this meeting justice. I've had some rather shocking news from home, and I need to go and deal with it. I'm sure you'll do a wonderful job, and you've got Flynn here to tell you all you need to know."

I hoped he'd be relieved—after all, they clearly want to get a room—but me walking away is like the equivalent of the Emperor's New Clothes, and this particular emperor does not want to be exposed as the naked fraud he really is.

"We still need to interrogate what this film is really saying."

I should probably try for a lightning save, but I've got nothing left to give.

"I can only apologize."

"There's two more candidates."

What joy to think I won't have to go through the charade of meeting them. I'm probably going to lose my job, but I don't much care about that either. Not right now at least.

"Lovely to meet you, Kristen," I say, ignoring him.

"It's Kirsten."

"Kirsten! I'll call you later, Flynn."

The cab draws up outside a gloomy-looking seventies apartment block, the frontage peppered with a handful of lit windows. I scan the second floor, that sense of cold dread tracking its way through my veins like an injection. I ring the buzzer for 211, but there's no response, and I tentatively turn the key in the lock of the outside door. The lobby smells musty, the dingy beige carpet covered in a patchwork of stains. Why would Sally want to cross the tracks to somewhere like this?

Blood pounds through my ears as I turn the key in the second lock, but as soon as the door is opened I know the apartment is deserted, the stillness eerie in its completeness. I step into its force field, calling out a meaningless hello to try and slice my way through it. I'm in a narrow hallway, with an ugly little galley kitchen coming off it. I open the door of the tiny cube fridge, and find a lone carton of milk. I pick it up: it's heavy, the milk long since curdled into yogurt. I look at the date stamp, June 11th, the week before Sally died. Nausea rises within me, the smell worsening its waves. I shake it out down the sink, running the tap on full force, flecks of soured milk flying up at my face. Why am I even doing this? I twist off the tap and blunder on, switching on all the lights to try and break up the gloom.

The small, square living room looks out over the river; there's a portable TV balanced on an ancient, dusty chest of drawers and a tasteless, pinky velour sofa. I sink into it, needing a moment's respite. I look around at the room, remembering how Sally would sneer at the full-on student houses our friends lived in, smug about the chic little bolt hole she'd found us. What would draw her to this fetid prison?

I look outside to the gathering darkness, holding my coat a little closer around me, feeling more alone than I can almost ever remember. No one knows where I am, no one in the world. But then my eye catches an empty tumbler, a desiccated piece of lemon barely recognizable at the bottom, an ashtray with a single Marlboro Light butt lying by its side. Now I'm less alone. I don't know which is worse.

I get to my feet, pushing open the next door off the hallway. It's like stepping into a different apartment. There's a big, comfy-looking bed with a deep red bedspread on it, and a copper lamp on the white, painted bedside table, which gives out a warming glow when I flick the switch. There's a chaotic heap of clothes lying on a squidgy little armchair, almost as if Sally's just stepped out of them and slipped between the sheets. I know immediately that this room is the heart of the place, the reason for its very existence.

A tiny top note of Chanel No. 19 catches in the back of my nose, the smell taking me everywhere and nowhere, more a feeling than a specific memory. Just for a second I'm eighteen again, smelling that smell for the first time, ready to be taken on a magic carpet ride of someone else's making. I look down at the bones and sinews of my thirty-something hands, the turquoise ring that I always wear on my right middle finger, needing to reassure myself of my own solidity, of the fact that I can no longer be dissolved, like a soluble painkiller that's dropped into water and fizzes its way into nothingness.

There's a pile of things lying on the bedside table: I sit, shakily, on the bed and pull it toward me, suddenly feeling like a thief. Have I any right to do this, to be here, unpicking what she left behind? Some stubborn bit of magical thinking is still insisting that she led me here, but maybe that's no more than my own need for closure dressing itself up as something noble and brave.

It's a jumble of stuff, reminiscent of the permanent chaos of Sally's student bedrooms. A cheap-looking phone flies out and lands on the bed, the screen blank. There's what looks like a prescription, and an A5 hardback book which, when I open it, turns out to be an address book. A strip of passport photos fall out—it's Sally with her arms wound tightly around Madeline, both of them sticking their tongues out, laughing so hard they're unable to pose properly. My tears fall onto the page at the sight of them, that freeze-frame that tells you so much about what it is that Madeline's lost—she'll never get that exhilarating silliness with William, the joy of laughing until you have to cross your legs and hope for the best. I think of how he stood there, sober, at the side of the dance floor, politely waiting for me to return to my senses.

I find a charger inside the bedroom cabinet and, while it's powering up the phone, take a closer look at the prescription. "Sally Atkins" it says, the doctor's address also in New Jersey, with an instruction that I can't read. Now the phone is spluttering into life, giving out a few beeps.

I need to pee and, perhaps, I just need a moment to prepare myself for what more I might find. The bathroom is as small and poky as the rest of this place, the toilet shoved in close against the plasticky shower. There's a roll of paper at least, abandoned halfway. I tear off a piece, absurdly spooked. It's so strange, all these fragments of an unfinished life.

I wash my hands, looking at my white, drawn face in the smudgy glass of the bathroom cabinet. I swing open the mirrored door; moisturizers, lipsticks, baby wipes— and a pair of pill bottles. I hold one up, peering at the typed label: lithium. The word rings a bell, but I can't quite place it in my panicky state. I go back next door and retrieve the charging phone. Despite its cheap look it seems to have e-mail capacity.

Whether or not there was someone else, I get a profound sense of Sally's loneliness here; it doesn't feel like a room or an apartment that was filled with love or affection—the chaos isn't built from two people slamming against each other, it's peculiar to her. It was always so, I suddenly realize; she swung between those intense connections, but when the pendulum finally stilled at center, she'd sloughed them all off, ready for the next clean swing.

From: MissAtkins@bmail.com
To: Riskiwager@hotmail.com
12/12/11
Can't stop thinking about yesterday. I can feel you on my skin, don't want to wash you away. Wish it could be Wednesday NOW! Call me if you can get away xxxxx

From: Riskiwager@hotmail.com
To: MissAtkins@bmail.com
12/12/11
You are so sexy and beautiful and fuckable. If I could I'd drive over right now and trust me, I'd be anything but a gentleman. No way I can get away from Madam, but when I can, I'll call. xxx

I drop the phone like it's red hot, bile rising up in my throat. I feel worse than a Peeping Tom. There aren't that many messages at least; did she edit them down, keep only the ones that were most meaningful?

From: MissAtkins@bmail.com
To: Riskiwager@hotmail.com
2/17/12
That was close!! Did you like what I did? Mrs. Gale wouldn't know what hit her if she knew. Meet you at BG's on second floor. I'll be in lingerie changing rooms. Come find me if you're man enough xxx

From: Riskiwager@hotmail.com
To: MissAtkins@bmail.com
2/17/12
You should know I'm man enough by now! Seriously gorgeous one, we need to be more careful. I can't have M find

out. 3 o'clock, don't wear any more than necessary. I need easy access!! xxxx

I hate RiskiWager already; I hate his stupid, self-regarding e-mail address and I hate the way he thinks of himself as some kind of macho sex god. And who is M? It can't be Madeline, surely?

From: MissAtkins@bmail.com
To: Riskiwager@hotmail.com
3/19/12
Daddy Bear's back from London, won't let me out of the house. Cannot fucking STAND IT when I can't see you, I'm climbing the walls. Please text me, I need to hear your voice, even if it's only in my head. Can't eat anything for thinking about you. He just made a "spag bol" and I had to sit on my hands so I didn't throw it at him. H came round today, look in her satchel if you dare! Love, love, love baby cakes xxxxxxxxxxxxxx

From: Riskiwager@hotmail.com
To: MissAtkins@bmail.com
3/19/12
Sorry I had to cancel last night, I wanted to see you just as much as you did. Gorgeous girl, you can't text a bunch of times like that. M was staring me out all through dinner. I'm starting to think that turns you on, but it doesn't me. And the note . . . you mustn't. OK? If we get caught, it'll ruin everything. Looking after H tonight, will try and call at 10:30 if you can sneak out. Until then xx

I can almost taste her desperation and so can he. H must be his child, surely. The gaps between the e-mails are frustrating, other messages surely deleted. I can't shake the feeling that she's laid it all out—*For You*. Perhaps the You is William after all. Perhaps she intended him to find all this after she was gone.

> **From:** MissAtkins@bmail.com
> **To:** Riskiwager@hotmail.com
> 3/25/12
> I want to tell you something. I want to shout it out really loud, and it's killing me I can't. I love you. I want to tell you every time I see you, but something stops me. Weekend with King William was almost bearable cos I had you to think about. I thought about you all the time, and I mean ALL the time!! Cannot WAIT to see you tomorrow, have another surprise. Meeting up's gonna get a whole lot easier xxxxxxx

Poor, dear William. That must be that Catskills weekend he talked about, the one time they'd slept together in months. It makes me hate her, I can't help it. If her insidious cruelty really has destroyed his ability to love, then that crash took not one life, but two.

> **From:** Riskiwager@hotmail.com
> **To:** MissAtkins@bmail.com
> 3/25/12
> Thank you sexy girl. Reckon you didn't tell me cos school gates aren't best place!!! C u later xxxxxx

School gates? Suddenly it dawns on me who Riski Wager might be. Richie to Riski only involves changing a few letters, and God knows, his behavior was risky enough to merit it. I put the phone down, feeling like I've been punched in the stomach. I can't bear for William's betrayal to be so total. How could they have inflicted such humiliation on him? Maybe I shouldn't have done this, kept pushing for information that might have stayed buried. Am I an unwitting part of his torture?

I read his last e-mail again, struck by how shifty it is. Far more kisses than Richie normally awards her, which I'm sure is an attempt to distract her from his lack of response, and a subtle slide into text-speak like it's no more than a teenage snog. She wouldn't have been stupid enough to miss it though: that's why she's kept it. It's an evidence log. The question is, who did she lay it for? There are only two e-mails left, and I quickly scan them.

From: MissAtkins@bmail.com
To: Riskiwager@hotmail.com
4/17/12

Please, please call me, I'm begging you. You KNOW how I get!! I'm so, so sorry about last week, I've told you how sorry I am. What else can I say?? I know I mustn't text when you're with her, but I just get to missing you so much and I can't help myself. I mean it, I literally can't help it. There's some stuff I need to tell you when I see you which will help you to understand, stuff I haven't told anyone. I'm lying in our bed right now wishing you were here, and my head was on your chest, and I could tell you all the things that are inside it. That's all I want, to tell you everything, and for you to tell me everything. Soon we can do that, can't we?! Brought Madeline here today and told her we might be coming for a secret holiday, and she's really excited. Haven't told her the holiday's forever yet. It's gonna be SOOO good. Feel like you've saved me from my boring, stupid existence, like I would have died. I really think I would've you know. Do you feel like that too? I know you do, even if you don't say it. You are such a boy!! Love you, love you, love you, S xxxxxxx

So she really was going to leave him. And yet—when he asked if she wanted a divorce she was distraught. I would ask myself why she didn't simply take a well-timed get-out clause, but I know her well enough to answer the question myself. She wouldn't have wanted to hand over the control, would have wanted to make a dramatic exit entirely of her own making. Or maybe—maybe she only wanted to leave him some of the time? Maybe the gaps between these e-mails tell a different story?

I read this last one again. There's something so juvenile about it, more teenage than I ever remember her being when she was only just past being one—all those exclamation marks and capitals. It's such a one-sided conversation too, like she's making up a version of the relationship that matches her fantasy. Something tells me his side of the story was very different.

From: Riskiwager@hotmail.com
To: MissAtkins@bmail.com
5/18/12
Did u get my text? Sorry I couldn't call. Would be great if you came out to LA, but it is way too obvious! You know that, don't you? Will call you once I'm back. Stay well. x

And that's where they end. She's left enough though. At least I know who to call.

CHAPTER TWENTY-THREE

I STARE OUT OF THE LIVING ROOM WINDOW INTO the night, wondering what to do. I've let too much time elapse: it's past seven o'clock now, pitch black, which means it's past midnight at home. Right now I want to speak to Jules more than anything in the world; it's not just because I'm so desperate for her advice, it's also a primal need for my big sister to know exactly where I am. Even if she's thousands of miles away, it will make me feel safe.

I know that soon I'll have to call William, but now I've come so far, I want to get hold of the last few pieces. I hope he won't hate me for what I've done. I don't know anymore—not here, not now, sitting in this dingy room, the slice of desiccated lemon from Sally's vodka and tonic sitting in the glass. Did she think she was coming back? Would be here to wash it out, to empty the ashtray, to start a new life? Or was it all a game? Was she like a little girl with a playhouse in the garden, enjoying the fun of let's pretend, safe in the knowledge she'll be tucked up in her own big bed come nightfall?

There's only one person who can answer the question. I force my shaking hands to page through the numbers in her phone, dial Richie's number, but then, as I hear the first ring, I bottle it and hang up.

I'm not quite strong enough yet. Then I get out my own phone, and call the one person I know will most likely be still awake.

"I'm just this second walking through the door," says James, picking up on the first ring. Just the sound of his voice suddenly makes everything less twisted.

"I'm so glad you're there," I say, a sob rising up in my throat.

"I'm glad you're there too. Well I'm not actually, I wish you were here. It's shit when you're not. How's it going?"

"Don't ask," I say, but then I tell him absolutely everything. He tries to interrupt a couple of times, but I need to just vomit it all out. Holding it all in has felt so utterly toxic.

"Lithium," he says, when I eventually stop. "It makes total fucking sense."

"I'm not looking at my e-mails, so I couldn't Google it."

"You know what lithium is! It's for bipolar."

"But that's like, a proper mental illness."

"There's different types, it's come up in a couple of cases at work. Some types of it you can function with."

"But then, if she was medicated . . ."

"She wouldn't have been before. Back then. And anyway, it can be really hard to get the treatment right. It can even make it worse."

All those jagged fragments of our friendship start to swirl past me like they're trapped in a kaleidoscope, recolored by the idea of her illness.

"Poor Sally," I say, starting to cry. "I wonder why she didn't just tell William, they could have shared it then."

"Maybe she did."

I think about the conversations we've had; the look on his face when he said "a few sessions of therapy," his utter dismissal of the idea that Madeline might need professional help, the oppressive control of his family. Perhaps she thought it would give them another reason to think she wasn't worthy of being a Harrington.

"I just don't think he knows. And the prescription's made out to Atkins." Was this the secret she was so frightened and relieved that she was going to have the chance to share? I hope Richie's noticed a missed call from that familiar number, is suffering a little of the anguish that she went through. "I'll get it out of Richie."

"Don't you even think about ringing him."

"I've got to, I've got no choice!"

"Don't be so fucking ridiculous. He could be dangerous."

"Now you're being ridiculous. He's some middle-aged dad who was looking for a cheap thrill."

"Livvy, don't. You don't even know for absolute sure it's him." I stay silent, reading the frustration in his breathing. "Seriously—I'll come out there."

"You can't just come out."

"Then you can't do it. I won't let you."

There's a break in his voice as he says it.

"Thank you. I'm really glad you care . . ."

"I do care," he says, voice low. "I really care. I hate you not being here, and not just because you do all the cooking, or because I secretly like the Carpenters and I can't admit to myself. Fuck! I think I do. Like the Carpenters."

"Which one do you like best?" I say, grasping onto the silliness, the familiarity of our well-worn routine.

"*Close to Yo-ou*," he sings, turning his voice into a warbly falsetto.

"That was really lovely, James," I say, giggling.

"They kind of do, you know."

"What do?"

"The birds. The whole suddenly appearing thing."

I can hear something in his voice—something spilling out of him that I never dared to believe could come back, not after that day in the pub all those years ago. I think of the relief in his eyes, and even now, it scorches.

"That's birds for you."

I can hear his breathing, searching for the right words. James never bothers to choose his words, they just tumble out in a confident jumble.

"You were right about Charlotte, by the way. I felt like shit for a bit, and then it was like it had never even happened. Like I'd just wanted to feel like that about someone, and she'd happened to walk past. But it wasn't her I wanted to fall in love with."

"Obviously," I say, trying to banish the wobble from my voice, "she's a robot." Since when did the world go so weird on me? I look out of the window, trying to steady myself, but the sight of the New York skyline makes everything feel even more alien.

"Do you get what I'm trying to tell you?" he says.

"Sort of," I say, twisting one of the buttons on the horrible velour sofa.

"Obviously I love you, and I probably don't say it enough, but . . . I love you, love you, Livvy. You're not my mate anymore, I don't ever want you to be just my mate again."

"Oh." I wish I could establish some kind of mental order, but the shock of all of it is too great. If I were James I'd be slowed by my lukewarm response, but I'm not James—he's got a mission, and he won't be deterred.

"I know you're going to think this is insane, but hear me out. I think we should just get married. We know each other backward, we know we love each other, we've both been through those shitty breakups . . . Why waste any more time?"

"I think that might be the most romantic proposal ever recorded," I say, then realize from his sharp intake of breath that the time for joking has passed.

"Look, Livvy, I know it's a shock and you're right in the middle of something massive, but please just think about it. No one knows you like I do, or the other way around. I've never trusted anyone like I trust you. There's no one I'd rather be with, anytime, ever. And I know as much as I've ever known anything that I'm going to feel exactly the same when I've got no teeth and you're wiping my bum."

I laugh, I can't help it. I do love him—how could you not—but I can't find the surge of unbridled joy that I always thought this moment would bring. That sense of completion.

"Only you would do this," I say, starting to get frustrated.

"What?"

"Try and go straight to the finish line, do not pass go. We haven't even . . ." I'm too embarrassed to say it, a tide of shame rising up at the thought of that fumbled attempt in my cramped single bed.

"That? That'll be fine," he says, a warm, dirty laugh escaping out of him. "And I don't agree with you about the other bit. You're my best friend. Who doesn't want to live their life with their best friend?"

I want to swaddle myself in the comfort blanket of his certainty, but I can't do it. All I keep thinking about is William, wondering how he would feel if he knew that someone else was proposing to me. Perhaps he'd be relieved, his rampant guilt soothed by me becoming someone else's responsibility. The thought winds me. Do I really want to carry on alone?

"Okay, I'll think about it," I say, my voice small, but then a rush of anger almost knocks me to the ground. It's the thought of the years I've spent staring through the bars of my love for him, waiting for him to notice. "Did you know?" I say, my voice shaking. "All that time, did you know how much I loved you? If you know me so bloody well, surely you smell it on me?"

He pauses, and I hear a clicking sound. I know exactly what he's doing, he's playing with one of those ink pens he always uses, stamping the nib in and out. He'll be biting his bottom lip as he tries to formulate a response, struggling between his knee-jerk tendency to tell a woman what she wants to hear and the fact that it's me, and whatever he says, I'm still Livvy.

"I didn't want to engage with it, I wasn't ready. I was being a twat, basically, but Livvy . . . don't let pride ruin this for us. It's all about timing, isn't it?"

"Timing? Are you not worried that I've just had my heart mashed to a pulp?"

James gives a dismissive snort, too certain of himself to self-censor.

"He's not right for you, Livvy, he'd bore you rigid, trust me. You're like . . . you're the kindest person I've ever known, and it's got mixed up in your head with something else. All you need to do now is come home. Just come home to me."

I sink my hot cheek against the velour. So much of what he says makes sense, and yet . . . I can't say yes. But is this just another one of my romantic get-out clauses? Here I am, with a man I love, have loved for a lifetime, promising himself to me, and all I can think about is a man I've known for less than six months who's in love with a ghost?

"I'll think about it."

"Don't overthink it, Livvy, that's all I'm saying."

Love conquers all is such a stupid generalization—as far as I can see, we need a thousand different words for love, like the thousand-odd words that eskimos have to tell each other about snow. And this love—it needs a different word now. I've changed, and so has it.

"James? I love you too. I don't say it enough either."

"I know you do."

"But I can't marry you."

"Livvy . . ."

"Please, James, just listen to me. It was what I wanted for so long, and I don't love you any less, but now . . . it's not right anymore. It's not our time, not for me. My heart's not mine to give." A sob escapes me. "But I don't want to lose you. Please don't let me lose you."

And suddenly I realize that James is crying too, real tears that convince me absolutely that this is more than just a symptom of his need to feel like he's winning at the game of life. Why am I so contrary? Am I just like Sally, but with the sharp edges blunted?

"I'm so sorry," I say, hiccupping from the tears.

"Thanks for telling the truth."

"I couldn't lie to you."

And eventually, once we've sat there for half an hour or so more, not saying all that much, we put the phone down on a chapter of our friendship that will always be more precious than I can put into words.

Once I've put the phone down I give way to the tears—proper racking sobs, curled up in a fetal ball on that horrible sofa. Somehow I manage to fall asleep, waking up in the middle of the night with my neck aching and my clothes clammy on my body. I want to leave, but I don't think I'll be easily able to hail a cab, and I've no idea how to ring one. I could probably somehow work it out, but I'm too exhausted, every drop of strength used up by the day I've just had, any remnants desperately needed for what's to come.

Instead I gingerly crawl into Sally's bed, the irony not lost on me. I've done this metaphorically so many times over the last couple of months, looking over my shoulder, the guilt almost too great to bear. The sheets seem newly laundered, although I can smell a whiff of Chanel No. 19 clinging to the pillow case. And suddenly it's not scary. Suddenly it almost feels like a surreal kind of comfort.

I know that it's stupid and egotistical of me to think that those carefully curated messages are a trail of breadcrumbs intended for me, but doesn't any kind of love require a healthy dose of magical thinking, even a love that's as corroded and battered as ours? I look at the half-empty pill bottle that I abandoned on the bedside table, then shake a lone white tablet onto the pinky expanse of my palm, where it lies, small and innocuous. I'm sure she never had them when we were friends: what kind of lonely journey did she go on to get to that place?

I sleep fitfully, waking time and time again, shaken by nightmares I can no longer grasp hold of once my eyes are open. At seven-thirty I give up on the illusion of rest, desperate now to leave this fetid hiding place of hers. The sky is gray and oppressive, the river a thick streak of brown. It's such a relief to be safely ensconced in a cab, heading back into Manhattan, but the knowledge of what it is that I have to do means the relief is short-lived.

I take my unwashed, unbrushed body via reception for my key, earning myself a knowing look from the bright-eyed girl behind the desk.

"Good morning, Miss Berrington, you've got messages," she says, looking down at her screen. "A Mary Reynolds has called twice today."

I give her a weak smile and take the elevator upstairs, treating myself to a long, hot shower. "I'm doing this," I declaim into the stream of water, not sure exactly who it is that I'm promising. Then I get dressed, putting on a smart black dress that I packed to make Flynn feel that I was authoritative. I mustn't stumble.

The phone rings a few times before it's picked up.

"What is this?" says a low voice that I immediately know for absolute sure is Richie's. "Who is it calling me?"

"It's Livvy," I say, a tremor running through my body. "You met me at the funeral. William sent that e-mail saying I was coming out for work."

He tries to cover.

"Sure, Livvy. Got it. But why are you calling me from Sally's phone?"

"I've been going back through her last months, trying to find out what really happened. I know everything, Richie, almost everything. I need you to meet me and tell me the rest."

"Why are you doing this?" he says, his voice red and angry. "You must know I can't talk to you."

"You've got no choice. I can tell from those e-mails what a selfish bastard you are, but you must surely realize that William needs to know the truth? He can't go into that hearing without it."

He laughs a nasty, mirthless laugh.

"No he doesn't. Trust me, I'm protecting him."

"No you're not," I say, fury flaring up inside me. Despite his political savvy, that innocence of William's is always so obvious to me. It's one of the things that made me fall in love with him. I hate the fact that he has this viper buried in his nest. "You're protecting your perfect life."

I hear a door opening in the background.

"Me and Hannah and Mara and Daddy are going to the Museum of Natural History. It will be very interesting. Are you going to come too?"

"Hang on, sweetheart, I'll be right there."

"You're joking, right? He's already here, staying with you?" I feel sick, poleaxed by the reality of William's proximity. Why can't life be simple? Why can't we be two stupid, innocent people falling in love under the benevolent shadow of the New York skyline, rather than two bleeding victims, too injured to remember what happiness is meant to feel like? "You need to come meet me right now, or I'll ring Mara and tell her everything."

CHAPTER TWENTY-FOUR

RICHIE DEMANDS WE MEET BY THE BOATING LAKE IN Central Park, no doubt hoping that the biting cold will keep our assignation brief. All I can think of is the multiple *Sex and the City* episodes when the girls would trawl around the edge, discussing their tangled love lives, and how much I would envy their imaginary friendships, stubbornly refusing to admit how much of a nerve it hit. I watch the young families who are out for a Saturday stroll, excitable toddlers muffled up in layers of wool, a dog or two adding the icing on the cake. I want that, I really do. I think of James, feeling a stab of guilt at the hurt I'm causing him. It's not my head that's stopping me—there's a million logical reasons for signing up to his plan—it's my heart. My heart will not play ball.

Richie keeps me waiting a good fifteen minutes, so by the time he does arrive, hunched over in a stylish moss-green pea coat, I am as freezing as he no doubt hoped. He's every bit as technically handsome as I remember, but he exudes an air of shifty weakness that cuts it off at the knees. He doesn't even bother with any pleasantries.

"Why are you doing this?" he says, slamming to an abrupt halt. "Tell the truth."

"How can you, of all people, question my honesty?"

"That's just sanctimonious bullshit," he says, flecks of spittle spraying from his mouth. "You're no better than me. Scrub that, you're way worse. Lola and Mara were on the phone for hours last week, talking about the stunt you pulled, throwing yourself at a grieving man. You're just playing the long game. Trust me, you lost."

I can't look at him, frightened of what he'll see in my eyes; the agony I feel at losing William, a pain so deep that I could sink to my knees and howl. The contempt in his voice makes me terrified of what William would have said, takes me back to how he dismissed me in front of everyone at the funeral. I'm so doggedly convinced of his truthfulness, but perhaps the heartfelt things he said to me in private are no different from the lines James spins hapless girls to get them into bed?

"I'm not," I say, forcing my voice to stay steady. "It's too late for me and William, I know that. But I"—the word "love" nearly tumbles, carelessly, from my lips, but I don't allow it to spill out into the chilly air—"care about him. He's torturing himself, thinking he could have saved her."

"Jesus, it was nothing, Livvy! I was totally honest with her about that, she just wanted to hear what she wanted to hear."

The way he spits out "she," it's like Sally's there in front of him, taunting him, demanding something he won't give.

"Whatever you think it was, you can't let him go into the hearing without all the facts. What if the insurance people know more about it than he does?"

I think of him, standing there, all alone, not even a lawyer to flank him. It makes me think of that little boy, straining out of the school picture, trying his hardest to get it right.

"And you think *I* know what happened?" says Richie, with an angry shrug.

"I think you know more about . . ." I gather myself, trying to stay strong. James was right, I'm too ill-equipped for this fight. "About the end than anyone else does." He looks at me, contempt in his eyes—but beneath the contempt there's something else, and I'm pretty sure it's fear. Months spent trawling William's controlled features for the smallest cues has made me a master. "And I'm not going away until you tell me."

He jerks his head toward a nearby bench and veers toward it, not bothering to look back.

"You've never been married, right?"

"No," I say. How can he tell? Is it a lucky guess, or do I just exude it?

"It's a marathon not a sprint," he says, looking out to the lake, across the vista of higgledy-piggledy families, all doing their best to make it work. It's funny how that tableau means one thing to me, and one thing to him. "Heard of compassion fatigue? Fidelity fatigue's not so different."

I can just imagine him, swilling coffee and preening himself in a marketing meeting for some stupid band: he's the kind of person who thinks in sound bites, authentic feelings sacrificed on the altar of a good quote. Watching how little his cold, well-turned features register I realize how different it is from William's kind of impassivity. There's an emptiness about Richie that I can imagine Sally mistaking for depth. It was always the ones she couldn't have who triggered that desperate need of hers. That frustrating distance William can have is, I think, the opposite; it's as if he was told when he was tiny that feelings were bad, that they must be rounded up and penned in like an unruly flock of sheep. It doesn't mean that they're not there, just that they need to be lured out.

"How did it start?"

"She just used to look at me," he says, and I know exactly what he means. When you got caught in the full beam of Sally's headlights it was hard to not be blinded. "We'd go away in a foursome, or we'd have dinner, and she'd just give me enough that I couldn't turn away." I nearly tell him that I get it, but then I decide he doesn't deserve even the smallest drop of my sympathy. Is it even sympathy I'm feeling, or is it relief at hearing the Sally of recent years described in a way that I recognize? He turns to me, almost pleading. "But she wasn't like I expected."

"What *did* you expect? You liked that she felt dangerous. It was hardly going to all wrap up neatly when you'd had your fix."

"She said that Mara was her best friend, but Jesus—it was like she wanted to get caught. She'd call all the time, I even found her outside the apartment one night. She was waiting for me to come back from a business dinner, she wanted to . . ." he looks away, then swivels back toward me, "she wanted to fuck in the car, Livvy. What kind of crazy idea was that? My kids were upstairs."

Oh God, how I used to envy that easy sensuality, that lack of self-doubt. You could see it in their eyes after she'd slept with them, a punch-drunk look they got that made me feel like such a wallflower. It was why it hurt so very, very much when she crossed that invisible line and tried to take what was most precious to me.

I take out the phone, trying to gather my thoughts, noticing how hungrily Richie is looking at it. I was an idiot not to forward the messages to myself.

"Looking at these, it sounds like you were both going to leave."

"No!" he says, residual frustration spilling out. He's been here before. "I never said that."

"But she thought you were."

"Sally liked . . ." he balls his hands up into fists, "she liked the big story. I would never leave my family. I love my kids." He says it like he deserves a gigantic pat on the back for his nobility. "And William loves her."

That present tense, it hits me in the guts like a wrecking ball. There really is no hope, I know that.

"Did she love him?"

"I guess," he says, unconvincingly. Poor William. "Jesus, it's not like I don't care about him. It would destroy him if he found out." He looks at me, sensing my inner turmoil, twisting the knife. "Livvy, I seriously doubt I was the first. That jewelry in the boxes that he called Mara about. I didn't give her that stuff."

A feeling of sickness spreads through me. I wish I didn't believe him, but I do. Perhaps it is better that the inquest goes ahead, reaches its half-baked conclusion, and William starts down the long road toward acceptance without all this painful, lurid detail. But I do still believe there's power in truth, however uncomfortable that truth is—at least the picture is in focus, the details clear and stark. How can he ever stop grieving when he knows in his heart there's more to discover, more left out there in the ether, floating free, unclaimed? And he does know, I can tell by the way he's shut me down, time and time again; it's a door that's slammed shut in fear, not one that he swings closed, secure in his certainties. Richie's watching me carefully, waiting for my next move.

"I don't want to hurt William any more than you do. At least if I know everything . . . I don't want to get things wrong, make it sound worse than it was. You packed up the apartment, yes?" He gives a guilty shrug of assent. "There's some papers, an appointments diary."

He nods.

"If you let me have it, I'll have everything. And I'll tell him what you said, that you weren't going to steal her from him. If he just has these e-mails that's what he'll think."

And that's when I see him flinch, haunted by the knowledge of what the worst actually is. I remember him at the funeral, how marooned he looked, staring into the middle distance, unable to make it back to dry land.

"What was it, Richie? What sent her over the edge? She told you about the bipolar, didn't she?" He nods, mute. "Did she stop taking her medication?"

"She was always coming on and off them, saying she didn't need them. That's why she never wanted him to know. She wouldn't believe she was ill."

We sit there in silence for a minute or so, his gaze trained out on the lake, that same sense of painful dislocation he had at the funeral. I can see a titanic struggle going on between self-preservation and a need to offload the crushing weight of his secret.

"Tell me."

"She pushed me too far."

"What do you mean?"

THE LAST TIME I SAW YOU

"She was crazy. She had this whole plan, she'd got that apartment, turned out she'd been moving stuff into some storage place from like, week three. She'd even put my name on the paperwork . . . I wasn't signed up for any of it."

"And you told her?"

"I had to spell it out to her. She went absolutely nuts."

I've never known anyone who hated being thwarted the way Sally did.

"Was that when she drove off?"

"No," he says, slowly shaking his head, his voice heavy with it. "She took my phone, she said she was gonna call Mara and tell her everything. I grabbed her, and I shoved her against the wall. I said some godawful things to her, Livvy—and then she just ran out of the place. That was the last time I ever saw her. Do you think if I hadn't . . ."

I look at his pale, haunted face that seems to have aged ten years in the time we've been talking, and find I can't help but feel sorry for him now. He's a vain, weak man who sleepwalked into quicksand right up to his neck.

"I'm not excusing you. It's unforgivable what you've done to William, but it wasn't you driving that car. It wasn't your fault."

"Don't tell him. Please don't . . ." He breaks down. "I don't want to lose my family, not that too. They're all I've got."

And as he sits there, his shoulders shaking beneath that expensive pea coat, I can see again exactly what Sally would have fallen for. She would have loved that effortlessly stylish exterior, so different from William's tweedy rigidity. But that's all it is—a thin, shiny exterior as fragile as a robin's egg—whereas William has a deep well of strength right at his core. The tragedy is that he could have held her, kept her safe, if only she'd let him.

"Look, just let me have the diary. I'm not going to tell your wife. It's up to William whether he does or not."

He's as good as his word: a porter delivers the diary to my hotel room a couple of hours later. In the meantime I've just lain here, flat on my back, utterly spent. Now I grieve her, now the picture's starting to come into focus for me. You didn't have to leave. You didn't have to push away the people who loved you most. If you'd let us keep hold of you, you'd have had everything. I think of Madeline, that fierce bravery of hers. She needs to be able to let go of her secrets too.

Eventually I call Jules, pouring everything out, with all the extra pieces that today has thrown up. She too offers to fly out, baby in tow, and I realize that between her and James I feel ridiculously loved.

And now I'm here, holding the purple cloth diary between my hands, steeling myself to open it. I slip it into my hand-bag and set off into Manhattan, looking for somewhere where I can be less alone when I finally open its pages.

CHAPTER
TWENTY-FIVE

I ASK MY FRIENDLY CONCIERGE WHERE I SHOULD GO, then jump in a cab and direct it to the West Village, where I find a French bistro that's perched on a corner just down from the Magnolia Bakery. The little I'm seeing of New York makes me know that, like Sally, I could absolutely love it, but there is no time to start the affair.

The diary sits there in front of me, waiting for me to pick it up. It's not a diary diary, it's scribbles and fragments written opposite the appointments side. The sight of her loopy, excitable writing still fills me with sadness. I take another swig of my Fleurie, a wine I didn't even know existed before William educated my adolescent palate, and start to read.

12/5—R messaged. Knew he would. Couldn't help himself, he said. Love knowing I can still do that to someone. Course it's wrong, but we can't help it. We need it. We're animals basically, aren't we? We just forget it sometimes. Got to school really late, too distracted, made M promise not to tell W. Cost me in cake!

1/20—Hamptons was AMAZING. Can't believe they didn't notice. Thought W would smell him on me when I came upstairs from the garden but he had his nose buried in a book, as per. Wish I could tell someone. Wish I had someone I could trust (not Mara!), it's bubbling up inside me. Nearly told Dr. Henry but I know he'd think it means I'm "acting out."

2/4—William said how lovely last few weeks had been. It's better this way, better for all of us. Looked at him stirring some stupid soup he'd made and thought, I do love him, just not like that. When I'm happy, he's happy, so what's the harm?

3/20—Me and Mara had lunch at The Spotted Pig and she said I had a glow! Should've felt bad, but it made me giggle instead. I'm a bad person.

4/25—M's school concert. She looked so sweet on the stage, all togged up in the white frock I bought her (burned the receipt in an ashtray, W would go mad, but she needs to do her mama proud). Couldn't stop crying, had to hide my face in my handbag. I love her so much. Wish I was better at being a mommy mommy. He's better than me, really. Hope she won't miss him too much.

5/4—No calls, not one. Nearly booked myself flight out to LA to surprise him, but don't want to get it wrong. Got so angry I didn't know what to do with myself. HATE this. Was going to Dr. H for emergency appointment but he makes it worse, makes me feel like a proper nut job. Keep telling myself it'll all be OK when we're properly together.

5/27—W and me. Took Maddy for burgers and we all sang in the car coming home. If only it could always be like this. Today I never want it to end. I wish that I could trust tomorrow.

There's more entries than these few, but I simply flick past them, rather than tracking right through them like an amateur detective. I can see now that I've gone far enough, that it's for William to take the final journey with her and decide what the truth of her state of mind really was. The scribbled appointments are almost as sad as the diary entries—*Maddy, dentist, Josh, cut and color*—little fragments of normality that she somehow couldn't squeeze the juice out of. And no wonder Madeline was so clear about what her name was, Maddy was obviously her mom's special privilege.

I'm looking increasingly incongruous, the Saturday night crowd starting to trickle in. There are couples of all ages—uber-cool twenty-somethings, trendy glasses banging against each other as they kiss, harassed thirtysomething parents snatching a much needed date night, even a white-haired couple at the head of a big table, looking like they're waiting for their unpunctual family to come help them celebrate an anniversary. I look to my waiter, trying to ascertain if he's wishing me gone, but he gives me a warm smile and a gesture that tells me the table's mine as long as I need it. Every single stitch in the tapestry goes straight to my heart. I'm so glad I'm here, I think, able to watch all of life going by. I take my phone out and make the call I've both dreaded and longed for.

"William, I'm sorry to call you out of the blue. I'm in New York."

I tell him that I need to talk to him, and he doesn't question me too closely, simply tells me, in a rather business-like way, to meet him in a hotel nearby called the Venice. I'm waiting for him in its low-lit lobby, my hands shaking as they clutch the diary. I went back via my hotel, got the rental agreement, the phone and the tag. It's time to hand everything over.

It takes twenty-eight interminable minutes for him to arrive, but then finally he appears. He strides through the doors, impeccably dressed in a navy coat, still exuding that almost pathological confidence, that poise, that never wavers. And yet, as he gets closer, I start to see the cracks. His eyes look even more hooded than normal, with bluish circles so dark that they look like bruising. His skin is dull, and there's more stubble on his jawline than I've known him to permit. That's when love surges right back through me, when I spot the shadow self that's trapped beneath the exterior, utterly vulnerable and utterly alone. I'm not sure how long I'll be able to stay.

"I'm so sorry," he says, as I stand up. He leans in and awkwardly kisses my cheek. "I hope you haven't been waiting too long."

"No, it's fine," I say, trying not to feel devastated by the formality of it. All I want to do is put my arms around him, tell him how much I miss him, but tonight is not about the two of us. No night ever will be.

"Can I get you a drink?" he says, standing aside to let me pass.

I can't quite speak, so I just give him a mute nod, and we head to a tiny little bar concealed behind a velvet door in the far side of the lobby.

"This bar's a bit of an inside secret," says William, attempting a smile. Once we're sitting down, drinks in front of us, he starts to apologize again.

"William, please, don't. There's nothing left to say." An expression of hurt crosses his face, and I think about qualifying what I said, but I know that if I don't tell him, right now, everything that I know, I will lose the strength. I hope it won't make him hate me. "I've found out some things about Sally . . ."

As the words land, his face pales, the bluish shadows beneath his eyes rendered even darker. I hope he can see in my face how much I still care—that even if I cannot walk alongside him, the part of my heart that he's colonized forever will be there with him in spirit. The part of me that has been shaped and molded and indelibly changed by the time that we've spent together, its intensity more relevant than its brevity. And there it will stay, a solid monument within my internal landscape, even when I'm someone else's, and he's just a portly married man that I say a quick, heartfelt hello to when I collect my adolescent goddaughter for the annual date she probably wishes I'd forget to keep.

"Do go on."

"There's something I should have told you a long time ago, but I didn't know if it mattered, and I didn't want to give you anything extra to worry about . . ."

I bring out the tag, and I lay it on the polished rosewood table, sliding it toward him as I tell him how I came upon it. Then I tell him about the storage unit and the apartment, all in a rush, then falter when I come to what it is that I found there.

"I'm sorry. I need some water."

"Of course," he says, summoning the barman. Once he arrives, I can see him suddenly unable to speak, and it's me who asks for it, in little more than a whisper. When he's gone, William smiles at me, a smile that is obviously so hard for him to muster that tears spring to my eyes at the sight of it.

"Livvy, you should have told me," he says, voice hoarse. "You shouldn't have gone off like that."

"I don't blame you if you hate me for it—"

"I don't! I could never hate you. But you shouldn't have had to do all this alone."

"I did try and tell you that I had suspicions. Madeline's secret place?"

He looks away, swallows. I think he's still numb from the shock of it all. And yet, the worst is still to come.

"You did, it's true. And believe me, despite what you think, nothing you can tell me would be worse than what my imagination has conjured up over the last few months."

I take the diary out, put it on the table, then put the phone on top.

"She can tell you," I say.

"You found her diary?"

"Richie took it." William's face drops, white-hot anger springing up in those hooded eyes. My hand moves almost unconsciously toward his, but then I pull it back. I think of what Richie said, what Lola said: I don't want the slightest sense of the two things becoming confused. "I'm so sorry. I thought about not telling you, but you don't deserve any more lies or half-truths."

"How . . ."

"She was ill, William. She was bipolar. I've been reading about it. When it's type two you can manage it, live what looks like a normal life, but it's a constant struggle. I really don't think she set out to hurt you."

He sits there, that vein that always gives way pulsing in his forehead, his hands clenched into tight fists.

"Did you always know that?"

"No! Of course not. I found her medication, at the apartment. It's all in her maiden name."

He slumps into a profound silence, and I sit there, waiting for him to come back.

"She should have told me," he says, vehement. "What on earth did I do that made it so impossible to tell me?"

I look at his helpless face, searching for something that will help.

"That was Sally all over. She hated showing weakness. And . . ." I sit there, trying to form my thoughts. "I don't know . . . but I think for all that bravado, there was maybe a part of her that hated herself. It would explain why some of the time she hated the people who loved her. When we loved her it contradicted what she felt, secretly somewhere inside." I shrug. "I might be wrong about that."

"It makes a sort of sense to me." He looks away. "Nothing could ever stay the same with her. She couldn't appreciate peace."

"The ordinary bits."

He shrugs, shaking his head. Then he turns to look at me, his eyes burning.

"Why did you do this? The truth of it, Livvy, I need to know."

His gaze almost frightens me. It pinions me, demands an answer I don't know that I even know myself.

"I didn't set out to do it. I just wanted to try and be around for you, and then I found I . . ." I can feel myself blushing. I didn't want to cross the line, but the crossing of it is part of the story, "wanted to be around you. And I just kept feeling like things didn't add up. I did it for you, William, because I thought you'd be trapped by the not knowing, but if I'm honest I also did it for me. I didn't know it until she died, but I've been trapped by her for years."

"Thank you," he says, then stands up, dropping forty dollars on the bar. "I don't mean to be rude, but I've got some things that I need to deal with. Would you mind if I leave you?"

CHAPTER TWENTY-SIX

Three Weeks Later

IT'S NINE O'CLOCK WHEN THE CAB FINALLY PULLS UP outside: I run down the three flights of smelly stairs and burst my way out of the steel front door. There she is, my sister, looking up the noisy Chinatown street, trying to take it all in. Christmas lights are strung up and down it, twinkling over the crowds of people spilling out of the restaurants and grocery stores that line both sides. I've loved the bustle of it these last few weeks, the way it's allowed me to be alone without feeling too alone, but now I've got my favorite person in the world right here in front of me, I'm overjoyed that the solitude is at an end.

"Look at you with your New York pad!"

"Trust me, it's not fancy," I say, grabbing her bag and leading the way.

It really isn't. It was cheap as chips on Craigslist, the cramped hovel of an NYU professor who's left town for Christmas, but it's perfect for a newly unemployed homeless hobo such as myself. The moment of truth with Mary came on the Monday, the day after I'd walked and walked around Central Park, thinking about every single dusty corner of my life and deciding that I couldn't face coming home quite yet.

"I'm astounded by your lack of professionalism," she started, "but maybe that's my own naivety. It seems to me that all I've done over the years is make allowances for you. I would never have sent you on that assignment if my back hadn't been against the wall, and it turns out my instincts were right. I'm not sure you've got a future here after this."

"No, me neither."

"I'm sorry?"

"I *was* really unprofessional," I said, with none of that cringing fear that always takes hold when she transforms herself into the hissing dragon of my nightmares. "I just don't think my heart's in it anymore. That's why I'm resigning."

"Resigning?" she said, a tremor of amusement in her voice. "There's my Livvy, the eager to please girl I know so well. I reckon we need a probation period, a change of title. If we give it a year you'll be back to where you were."

"I'm not resigning for you, I'm resigning for me. I don't want to do the job anymore. In fact, I hate it."

"You hate it?" She gave a patronizing laugh. "Trust me, Livvy, there are people queuing round the block for a job like yours."

"You're right, scrub that. It's not the job I hate, it's doing the job for you." I heard her sharp intake of breath, and started to feel a little remorseful (as well as conscious that at some point I'd be needing a reference). "I've learned so much from you, Mary, and I'll always be grateful for that, but it's time to grow up. I never know where I stand, and I can't live like that anymore."

"You're being ridiculous. What will you do?"

"I'll temp if I have to, and I want to see if I can write. The truth is, my life doesn't fit me anymore."

And suddenly, standing there in the middle of Central Park, I realized that I was free.

"It's cozy," says Jules, looking around the tiny kitchen-dining-sitting room that is the heart of the apartment. It's funny, it's even smaller than that dingy box in New Jersey, but it doesn't matter because it feels like someone's real home. We sit on either end of the corduroy sofa with our knees pulled up to our chins, glasses of cheap red wine clutched in our hands.

"Is it okay not having Nathaniel?"

She looks pained for a second, and then she gives me a smile.

"It's three days. It'll be great for the two of them. And it'll be great for us." She shakes out her shoulders. "I'm just me for a bit."

"I love him to bits, but I'm so excited we're doing this."

"Me too." She grabs my hand. "It's not like I don't miss it too, you know."

"Really?"

"Course."

I've already told her everything, but we talk about it all over again, my tears coming as I describe that last meeting.

"I just miss him so much," I say. The downside of having this time to myself is that I've had all the time in the world to feel his absence. I didn't know it at the time, but through all of that searching for answers, I was still somehow alongside him: his life was there in sharp relief, as well as the knowledge that I would have to take it all to him once I'd assembled the pieces. Now there's simply the loss, the long road to walk until I start to believe I could love someone else like I love him.

"His e-mail *was* lovely," says Jules.

"I know."

The problem is, that its loveliness makes the fact it's over even harder to bear. He sent it to me the Wednesday after we met, and I printed it off in an Internet café, tears streaming down my face. I've kept it with me ever since.

Dear Olivia,

Bizarre and inappropriate though this may sound, it was a great pleasure to see you last week. I had spent the weeks before fretting constantly about the pain I caused you, and berating myself for the cowardice I displayed at Madeline's christening. The kindness you have shown to both of us in recent months is something that I will never forget. She will never forget it either, even if her means of remembering it are not conscious ones. You have helped us both with a transition that has been almost unbearable, and indeed continues to be so.

And that is why I could not continue to bleed you dry, while offering so little in recompense. You of all people—so vital, so loving, so effortlessly funny (having had the chance to laugh these last few weeks has been the best medicine I could ever have asked for)—deserve much more than that. And I feel sure that you will find it. How could you not? How could any man not meet you and avoid feeling utterly unmanned? Please don't allow any residual hurt around me to hold you back, and please do not interpret my behavior as a rejection: it is quite the reverse. And that is why it was right and proper that you released yourself—that insidious cowardice of mine might have prevented me from doing so indefinitely, and yet I couldn't have lived a life with you knowing that my contribution to the relationship was inadequate, that I was keeping you from the kind of full-blooded connection that you deserve.

Despite what you might think to the contrary, I am also very grateful to you for finding out what really happened. Your clear-sighted knowledge of Sally's character allowed you to cut through the lies and secrecy that clouded her death. After months of foggy confusion, I took a long walk through the city and made a couple of clear decisions. Firstly I texted our friend Richie, asked him to meet me, and punched him soundly on the jaw. It was intensely satisfying and I like to think you would have been proud of me! He had to tell Mara that he'd been mugged, but I think that their relationship can survive one more lie. I'm certainly not going to involve myself any further: one thing I've learned from these last few months, or maybe years, is that every relationship has a unique infrastructure that no one beyond those two participants can truly judge or understand.

Talking of which, the next thing I did was to call off the hearing. I read everything, read it time and time again, and I feel even more sure that she didn't want to die, but equally, that I didn't want to drag her fragile mental process through a public forum. In fact, I question why I allowed it to go as far as I did: perhaps it provided a distorted reflection of the questions that tortured me. Thank you for liberating me from them: however painful the truth is, it is at least the truth. Now the insurance company has called off the dogs, I'm more than hopeful that the police will feel happy to stand firm with their original verdict of accidental death.

I dearly hope that in time we will be able to be a part of each other's lives. My decision to make you Madeline's godmother was not one I took lightly, or from some misplaced sentiment about your complicated relationship with Sally. I cannot imagine a finer person for her to aspire to.

With much love and infinite gratitude,

William

I'm scrunching it up again, tears rolling down my cheeks, sinking into Jules's so welcome embrace.

"It will get easier, Livvy."

"I don't regret it."

"Don't you?"

"How can you regret love? It's like finding a unicorn. It hardly ever comes along."

"And definitely not James?"

I point at my snotty, tear-stained face.

"Look at me. Everything William said about me and him is how I feel about giving James this. He deserves someone who can't imagine being with anyone else. And even if I wanted to fool him, he knows me too well."

"So what if William had never come along?"

"But there's no such thing, is there? He did. And if he hadn't, I'm not sure James would ever have started thinking of me like that. I know him, I'm sure there was an element of competition. And I got less sappy too, stopped following him around like I had a head injury."

Jules laughs, and hugs me again.

"So you definitely can't move back in?"

"No way. We need to redefine things. To be honest, we needed to do that anyway."

"Mom's really excited, you know."

I cannot believe I'm pushing thirty-six, and I'm moving back in with my mother.

"I was worried Dad'd be hurt I'd chosen her house, but it seems like he's Mr. Sunshine now he's got a girlfriend. I couldn't believe how jolly he was when I Skyped him."

"You know he rang Phil and asked him to come around and teach him how to Skip? He didn't want to tell you that he didn't know what you were talking about." She grabs my arm. "Oh, and Mom's said they can come for Christmas!"

"Him and Margery? And he's said yes? We're all spending Christmas together?"

"I think she's secretly quite pleased she doesn't have to feel like she's ruined his life anymore."

There's something rather perfect about the imperfection of that. While some of me agrees with William—knows that I couldn't go back into the place of clinging desperately to a tiny little piece of him—I also know now that there's a million different ways for happiness to look. I hope he doesn't end up as lonely I was, waiting, fruitlessly, for all the cracks and joins inside himself to knit together and release him to start again. But does that ever happen to men? No doubt Trixie will slyly introduce him to some halfway decent blonde at the precise moment he's become too exhausted to keep manning the barricades. I feel myself starting to wobble, and I push the thought away as hard as I can. I hate the idea that on some level we were too close to perfect to make it.

"But think about it," I say, "she won't want to look too spinstery in front of Margery. God knows who she'll shake out of the tree to pull her cracker."

Jules laughs, tops me up.

"You're going to be all right. More than all right. You're going to be amazing."

I hurt, every piece of me hurts, and yet the next three days are still heaven. It's one of the things I've learned about grief, how it sharpens everything: the colors are particularly bright right now.

Those thousand words for love I'm coming up with? One of them would express the kind of love you feel for a sibling—the way it's both boundless and complicated, lightly dusted with those stupid spats you've been having since birth, and underpinned with the knowledge that you'd lie under a bus or wrestle a tiger if that was what you had to do to protect them. I've got absolutely no spare cash for shopping, and Jules is far from flush, but we still trawl around the Park Avenue stores and marvel at the five-figure gowns, even trying a couple on just to annoy the snooty saleswomen. We buy makeup in Bergdorf's, try on high heels in Saks, and drink coffee on the roof of Barneys. Of course it all makes me think of Sally, makes me imagine her sweeping through these swing doors and flexing her plastic until it reached melting point, or sipping champagne on this same roof. I hope she was happy some of the time, properly happy rather than simply high, waiting for the sky to go dark again.

It's amazing how little money you need when you're with someone you want to spend every waking moment with. And I do, I really do, despite the odd flare up about how long to keep the bedroom light on ("Stop reading, Livvy!").

I say that to her on the last day, as we walk around the spiraled interior of the Guggenheim Museum.

"Me too," she says, threading her arm through mine. "We should try and do something like this every year. Even if it's just the Travelodge in Reading." She giggles. "You know what I mean. Sometimes that's just us."

"I'm sorry if I've been crap the last few months."

"You haven't!"

"I have a bit. I've been so wrapped up in . . . in everything"—I'm nervous of saying William's name out loud, I know how it echoes inside of me—"and meanwhile you've been going through loads of your own stuff."

Jules went back to work a little while ago, and on the face of it is doing absolutely brilliantly. She did call me from the loos a couple of times in tears—the emergency toilet call seems to be a bit of a sisterly specialty—and I made sure I was always on the end of the phone, but I know I would have had more to give if I hadn't been so consumed by my own traumas.

"You have been there, you just don't notice. Just seeing you is enough. Makes everything feel normal."

"Do you feel like you again?" I ask her.

"I think me's a bit different now, but still me, if you know what I mean. I don't feel like I'm having to get to know a whole new person."

"I know exactly what you mean."

I do, I really do. I wonder how long my confidence in the new version of me will last when I'm back on home soil.

I thought Jules would want a big New York night out for her final evening, but she insists that all she wants to do is stay in. I'm a little bit disappointed, truth be told, but her wish is my command, so we load up with goodies from a deli on the Upper West Side and take our places either end of the tiny sofa. I don't want it to be over, not yet.

"You are going to come home, aren't you?" she says, squeezing my toes. They're clad in thick wool bed socks due to the lack of warmth from anything other than the feeble blow heater that's wheezing out occasional puffs of hot air like an ailing baby dragon.

"Yeah, course. I can't afford not to, apart from anything."

"But you do want to?"

"Ye-es," I say, trying not to sound as reluctant as I feel. "I'm in a bubble right now, but I have pretty much blown my life to bits."

She starts developing that worried-big-sister look.

"There's a million things you could do with the writing. You could train as a journalist, maybe."

"I'm thinking about it. Mary paid me last month, incredibly, but after Christmas I'm going to have to make some serious decisions."

We're laying into the mozzarella balls and bagel chips when the doorbell rings. I look at Jules, baffled.

"Shall I ignore it?"

"No, you need to answer it."

"But I don't know anyone except you, and there's three flights of stairs."

"Could be important." I get up, sighing grumpily. She wiggles a finger at my feet. "And you need to lose those socks."

"Don't be so bossy."

"Seriously. You might slip."

I toil down the three flights of smelly stairs, shivering.

"Hello . . ." I say, through the reinforced door.

"Hello," replies a familiar voice.

My heart pounds in my chest, my legs shaking like a baby colt's.

"Are you going to open the door? It's perishing out here."

"Yes," I say, without actually making a move to open it. Tears are streaming down my face, my heart too open, too undefended, for this. I can't bear another perfectly constructed conversation about why we can't be together. If he's here to tie up the loose ends, I'd rather leave them trailing.

"I can absolutely see why you'd want to leave me outside a walk-up in Chinatown. I would probably feel exactly the same way. But I would very much like to talk to you. When I told you I'd miss you infinitely more than you would know, I had no idea how infinite infinite might prove to be."

"I can't be your friend."

"I don't want you to be my friend, Livvy. I want you to be beautiful Livvy. Adorable Livvy. Love of my life Livvy who happened to come along at the worst moment possible."

Then I do open the door, tears streaming down my face. I grab the lapels of his perfect cashmere coat and shove him.

"Don't say things like that if you don't mean them."

"I do mean it," he says, wrapping me up in his arms and holding me against his chest. For a moment I relax into it, but then I pull myself out of the circle they make.

"I meant everything I said. And so did you. I don't want some half relationship. It will hurt even more . . ." I'm crying in earnest now, "even more than this."

"I'm not going to sell you a pup, Livvy, and I'm not saying that it's going to be plain sailing. But I won't abandon you again. And if you'll let me, I'm going to try my damnedest to overcome the truly atrocious timing and concentrate on the fact that when you meet the person you want to spend the rest of your life with, then you owe it to the universe to do everything that you can to make it happen."

He looks down at me, his gaze intense, and I look back up into his face. Something there has shifted, there's an animation and a presence that I've never detected before—it's only now, seeing it, that I realize how much of him was permanently out of reach.

"Can we at least go somewhere and talk about it?" he says, giving me that kind smile that always destroys me.

"Yes, but I'm paying. And we're not going anywhere fancy. Let me grab some shoes. I'm guessing Jules won't be surprised."

She's not. I turned my cell off a week ago, and apparently William was determined to actually speak to me, rather than send any more e-mails. He contacted Jules the second day she was here, Jules told him how heartbroken I was, and he decided it was time for a grand gesture. The problem is, I'm not sure I believe in grand gestures. Not now—not after all those conversations about how ordinary is overrated. I say as much to him once we're ensconced in the tiny Chinese restaurant a few doors down. The aged couple who own it are one of the few constants of the last few weeks, and they greet me with a sweet enthusiasm.

"You're not thinking of staying, are you?" says William, taking in the row of ducks, hanging from their feet, which dangle perilously outside the kitchen. The man slaps down a pair of handleless cups of hot, peculiar-tasting tea and I smile up at him.

"I might," I say, then watch his face slide downward into an expression of abject misery. I grab his hand, unable to keep it up. "No, of course not. I'm coming back in a few days."

His face lights up with pleasure, and a lump rises in my throat. It's so lovely to watch his emotions run free.

"Just tell me how it would be different. Because everything in your letter made total sense. That was almost the worst thing about it. I couldn't argue any of it, and I couldn't hate you."

My voice rises as I say it.

"Did you *want* to hate me?" he says, hurt in his eyes.

"No, but hating you would have been a load easier than loving you and knowing I could never be with you."

I look at him, stricken. Why did I let that escape? All those months of picking my words with such care, and here I am, throwing open the doors and switching on the lights.

"Do you?" he says, but I don't answer. "Because I wouldn't be here if I didn't love you."

"Can you even say that?" I ask.

"Yes. In these extraordinary circumstances I think I can. In fact I think I cannot not. It's not necessarily comfortable or appropriate, but absolutely nothing about this situation is."

"But how can it have changed so much in a few weeks? How do you expect me to believe in it?"

"I know it must seem abrupt, but . . ." He looks away, gathering his thoughts. "Of course it's all still a tremendous shock, but the thing that's surprising is, that it also isn't. We half know things, don't we? We deny them to ourselves. The truth is, it wasn't a happy marriage. We were trapped in it, we both loved our daughter, but we . . . this might sound callous, but I hadn't been in love with her for a long time. I knew what my role was, and I didn't deviate from it. I wish with all my heart that she'd told me about her illness, that she'd let me help, and I know that's one of the things that will prove hardest. But the truth is, you were right when you said that sometimes it's better to admit that a marriage is fatally flawed. To not soldier on."

"What, you think you should have divorced her?"

He shrugs.

"I wouldn't have wanted to leave Madeline. I would have worried about her being in sole charge. She could be tremendous fun, and then she could suddenly seem almost indifferent to her." It makes sense of those lines she scribbled in the diary. "But us as a couple—we talked about half relationships, but I've shared more with you in these last months than we had in years. I loved the idea of it, the memory of it, more than the reality."

"Really?"

"Yes, and I buried myself in my work. I'm utterly disgusted by the thought of her and Richie, but in a way I was more involved with my work than I was with her, the two of us communicating via Madeline. It's a lot of pressure for a little girl."

"What a dreadful situation."

"Don't feel too sorry for me. I do feel intensely guilty for ignoring the signs. I should have realized that her moods were more than just a tendency toward depression and a quick temper, but it was easier to simply feel grateful when the sun shone." He smiles a crumpled sort of smile. "As you may have noticed I'm not always terribly good at talking about feelings."

I think of the first time I saw Sally in full meltdown, that night the Nutty Professor had dumped her. I can still remember how helpless and terrified I felt in the face of her desolation. I'm not surprised he backed away from its force.

"You're doing pretty well now," I say, tracing his knuckles with the very tips of my fingers.

"Don't get too used to it. It might very well be a one-off." I roll my eyes at him, and he smiles again. "I don't remember her being like that when we met," he continues. "It got much worse after we married."

"She was the same when we moved in together. Once she knew that she had you, she needed to see how much you could take."

"There's so much to try and work out. You were right, incidentally, about the counseling, we both need it. In fact Madeline's already begun. Play therapy, it's called. Apparently she makes the most tremendous crashes happen between her dinosaurs."

"I'm glad."

"But knowing that I didn't drive her to her death—the relief of that. Whatever I might have said, it was always my fear. And I do truly believe it was an accident. The diary entries, they're so up and down. She might have been devastated about Richie, but she might as well have decided he was beneath her notice a few days later. She just shouldn't have been driving in that terrible weather in such awful distress."

"But walking away from the hearing—it's so brave. Have you been left with the most horrendous debts?"

"What's the phrase? I'm going to downsize. That apartment's got about as much character as a fridge, and there's no earthly reason why Madeline needs to be privately educated. My parents are appalled, of course, but I'm too old to subject myself to living off pocket money." He looks at me, sheepish. "I'm sorry he was so rude to you at the christening. And most of all that I didn't stand up for you."

"There are going to be a lot of people who are horrified by this," I say, holding his gaze. "And I'm not prepared to sneak around like we're the ones having an affair."

"I know. But I've wasted so much of my life worrying about what's socially acceptable. I'm ashamed to say it was probably a big factor in me not admitting that my marriage was a sham. And I don't care anymore. I've been amazed in recent weeks by how long the list of things I don't care about has turned out to be. And the other list, the things I do care about . . ."

He looks at me and smiles.

"We can take it gradually. Baby steps."

"You mustn't treat me with kid gloves. I'll get terribly spoiled."

"I won't," I say, and he reaches across the table and kisses me.

"Shall we eat?" he says. "I've heard the duck's outstanding."

Once dinner's finished we wander out onto the street. William puts his arms around me again.

"I suppose I should ignore my internal howls of protest and let you get back to Jules?"

"No," I say, reaching up to touch his face. "I've got a request."

I do. I want to go dancing, somewhere silly and uncool and ridiculous. I want it to be so loud that we can't hear each other, and we can't carry on talking about the vagaries of life and death. William does some Googling and finds somewhere suitably awful back in midtown. It's bloody freezing, but I ask him if we can walk: I love having him there beside me, pointing out landmarks and telling me stories of his own New York life. It's so utterly different from the time I've spent getting to know the city on my own, the loneliness of not having a person to share the wonder of it with.

When I tell him that I'm moving out of my apartment-share, he stops in his tracks and spins me toward him.

"Gosh, I'm so relieved to hear you say that. I did sense . . ."

"Sense what?"

"You and James. That I was something of an intruder."

"Really?"

"Yes. It wasn't just about you feeling that *my* heart was out of bounds."

I squeeze his hand, glad in a way that he cared enough to notice. I had my own ghosts. James and I have agreed not to speak for a little while, but I'll get in touch when I'm back. I truly believe that in time we'll find a healthier version of him and me. I don't want to lose him too.

We walk through SoHo and NoHo, past the boutiques and cool bars, my love affair with New York well and truly in the ascendancy.

"Will you miss it?"

"No," he says simply. "When a chapter of your life is over there's no point lingering over the last page."

And then, finally, we're there. And it's terrible, a cheesy bar full of overdressed blondes and smart-casual-clad men, who William identifies as the very definition of Bridge and Tunnel. It's perfect.

"Come on then," I say, dragging him onto the center of the disco-ball-lit dance floor where they're playing some dodgy hip-hop. And follow me he does, swiftly proving that he's every bit as left-footed as he claimed all those months ago. I couldn't care less, because at least he tries. We stumble around, we laugh, we kiss and, just for tonight, neither of us care about anything else at all.

CHAPTER
TWENTY-SEVEN

Two Years Later

"Livvy . . ." says Madeline, poking her head around the door of the kitchen. Right at this second I'm trying to get a cake out of the steaming oven, so it's hard to look around, particularly as I'm the size of a couple of bungalows.

"Yes, darling?"

"You do know I'd like it much, much better if I had a sister?"

"Absolutely. But it's not something we can choose. You'd love a little brother too, once he was here."

A look of petulance crosses her face, a look I know from a time long before she was so much as a twinkle in the sky, but then it passes, as it tends to these days. She's a much happier little girl than the one I met, and I don't think that's just my own wishful thinking.

"Okay. I'm going to the beach with Sophie and her mom."

"Home by six, please."

She nods, and I smile at her, wanting to know for sure she's okay. It's not an easy day.

"Bye, Livvy."

She's as good as her word, and as soon as she's arrived, I call William in for supper. Our Brighton house isn't grand, but it has a lovely big garden, and William proudly drops a muddy heap of potatoes onto the table, newly yanked out of the ground. It was only me who quit my job—I think he likes the taxing, exciting, secretive world he works in more than he thought he did in the aftermath—but he does love having a proper space to play at being a horny-handed man of the soil. He says it's meditative, not a word I'd have heard from him back in the day, and I do think it's helped him get some trust back in the rhythms of the world. The counseling made him feel worse before it made him feel better; he had to rip off a bandage that I think he'd worn his whole life, and for a while the world seemed to him like a very scary place. He would worry that something terrible would happen to Madeline or me, or that I would leave him.

It's true, it wasn't easy, but I never would have left. I loved him too much. I didn't move in with them immediately, and we're still engaged, not married, but our commitment was total from the moment we found each other again. His family has come to accept me, as much as they accept anyone, and Lola and I at least exchange Christmas cards. I did try talking to her, but I think that Sally's bewitching power is still too great for her to hear me. I don't waste too much time worrying about it. We've made new friends down here, and some of the old ones have stuck around too.

James lives with a girl he met at work, a sweet thing who's five years younger than him and thinks that the sun shines out of his behind. He loves her, I don't doubt it, but I'm not sure what kind of name I'd give to that particular brand of love. I do feel sometimes, when we see them, that she's like an exotic pet—a beautiful Siamese cat that he likes to show off—rather than an equal. It's not in my interests to overanalyze it, even though I know that, for me, the fact that William is my best friend, as well as everything else, means the world. And James and I are proper friends again too, although I don't think he's ever entirely got over me choosing a balding stuffed shirt, as he sees it, over him.

"Sorry," says William, taking my hand. "I should have given you more help, rather than playing around in the mud." I smile at him, hoping that he can see in my eyes that I know that he was doing more than that—he needs time away from me, thinking time, on a day like this. "Did you get your pages finished?"

I still do some freelance copywriting here and there, but I'm trying to finish a book of short stories, encouraged by the writing group I joined when we moved down here. My friend Susie's from there, the best friend I've made in a long time. She's the one who made the coq au vin that I'm ladling out.

Then we all sit down together, raising our glasses. William's is a crisp Chablis (only two small ones these days), while Madeline and I have cloudy apple juice.

"To Sally," we say.

"To Mommy," she says.

William has put a couple of candles around that lovely picture of them together, Madeline in her pristine uniform, that sits in pride of place above our fireplace.

"Happy birthday," says Madeline, her bottom lip starting to wobble. William springs from his seat, and gives her a hug.

The cake is a tradition that Madeline came up with during the therapy, a way of remembering how old Sally would be, and not leaving her stranded at the age she died, getting further and further away from us. I light the candles, and she blows them out, though it takes her a couple of goes. Sally would have been thirty-eight: I think, briefly and vainly, how old I'm getting, and then chide myself. She lost so much. I look at William. "To Sally," I whisper again, raising my glass a fraction, and he smiles.

"Excellent blowing," says William, smiling a complicated sort of smile at me.

"Definitely," I agree, watching her, wondering what's going round in that clever, willful head of hers.

"You do know that I would much, much rather have a sister, don't you?" she says, looking between us. "Boys are not at all my best thing. Though Nathaniel is nice for a boy. He will only be a cousin though, I will be a sister."

That's the only thing I don't like about being down here—being separated from Jules. We manage to see each other every couple of weeks, nevertheless. She loves William and Madeline almost as much as I do, so she never minds packing Nathaniel into the back of the car and driving down.

"We do," we say in unison, then look to each other, our eyes meeting in a way that makes it all feel okay.

"Have I ever told you about the day your mom threw me a surprise party?" I start, knowing that this story, like many of my stories, will demand some pretty big omissions. Nevertheless, Madeline pulls her chair closer to mine, her eyes rapt. I'm glad, so glad, that now we can remember the good bits without being blindsided by the bad.

To Sally.

ACKNOWLEDGMENTS

THANK YOU TO MY UNPARALLELED AGENT, SHEILA
Crowley at Curtis Brown, who has been such a support and
a champion for the last few years as well as being a great
person to have a gossipy lunch with. Thanks too to the rest
of the Curtis Brown team, particularly Alice Lutyens and
Becky Ritchie.

Equal thanks to my wonderful and patient editor, Jo
Dickinson, whose brilliant notes made all the difference.
And also to the wider Quercus team.

Thank you also to Lucinda Prain at Casarotto, for being
both an excellent mate and an excellent film and TV agent.

A lot of people read this book when it was a work in progress. Particular thanks to my mother, Stephanie—I'm sorry
I instantly regressed to a sulky thirteen-year-old when you
tried to give me your excellent notes on chapter two.

Huge thanks to Anne Mensah, for being the most over-
qualified script editor in the world, and taking time out

from her insanely busy job to read it twice right at the end. David Cameron may be an expert chillaxer, but you are not.

Thanks also to Sophia Morphew and Caroline Henry for early reads.

Much of this book was written in the LA sunshine, and I'd like to thank my dear friends there for making it so much fun. Stefanie Leder, Mabel Tannenbaum, and also Hilary, CJ Fahey, Carter and Sean, Sally Robinson, Tonje Kristiansen. And the staff of GTA and the Rose Café for all the coffee and sympathy. It seems a long way away now on a rainy London Sunday.

And a big thank-you to Claudia, Don, Leyla, and Toby for letting me a feverish chunk of it in snowy Ottowa. It was a very lovely time.

Huge love and thanks to Damian Barr. Go the 50ps!

And to Carol Biss. I couldn't ask for a better Mother Superior.

And to Polly, Shaun, and Barclay for all the Tilton House love. It's still my favorite place in the world to write.

With so much gratitude to my parliament of wise owls, Kitty, Diana, and Charisse. And also to Francesca and Jodie.

And lastly, with so much love to Kate Martin, Kate Evans, Sophia, Clova, and Kay for all round greatness. Special thanks to Kate E for my latest goddaughter, Martha. And also to Matthew and Karen for Madeleine.

ABOUT THE AUTHOR

ELEANOR MORAN is the author of three previous novels: *Stick or Twist, Mr. Almost Right,* and *Breakfast in Bed,* which is currently being adapted for television. Eleanor also works as a television drama executive and her TV credits include *Spooks, Being Human,* and a biopic of Enid Blyton, *Enid,* starring Helena Bonham Carter, which she conceived as a result of a childhood obsession with the author. Eleanor grew up in north London, where she still lives.